CHELSEA REACH

THE PERFORMERS

CLAIRE RAYNER

CHELSEA REACH

Book 9
THE PERFORMERS

WEIDENFELD AND NICOLSON
London

For Graham Tarrant
Another word lover

THE LACKLANDS

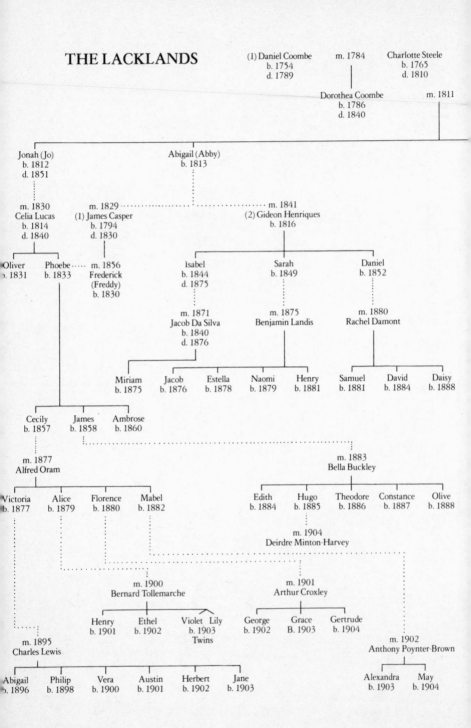

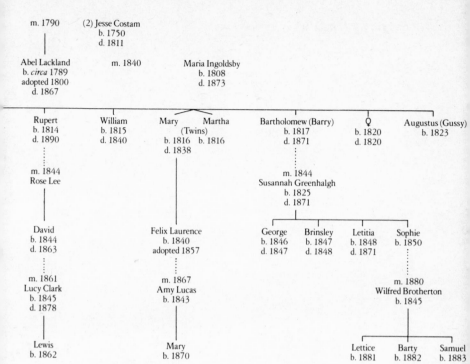

m. 1790   (2) Jesse Costam
b. 1750
d. 1811

Abel Lackland   m. 1840   Maria Ingoldsby
b. *circa* 1789   b. 1808
adopted 1800   d. 1873
d. 1867

Rupert	William	Mary	Martha	Bartholomew (Barry)	♀	Augustus (Gussy)
b. 1814	b. 1815	(Twins)		b. 1817	b. 1820	b. 1823
d. 1890	d. 1840	b. 1816	b. 1816	d. 1871	d. 1820	
		d. 1838				

m. 1844
Rose Lee

m. 1844
Susannah Greenhalgh
b. 1825
d. 1871

David	Felix Laurence	George	Brinsley	Letitia	Sophie
b. 1844	b. 1840	b. 1846	b. 1847	b. 1848	b. 1850
d. 1863	adopted 1857	d. 1847	d. 1848	d. 1871	

m. 1861
Lucy Clark
b. 1845
d. 1878

m. 1867
Amy Lucas
b. 1843

m. 1880
Wilfred Brotherton
b. 1845

Lewis
b. 1862

Mary
b. 1870

Lettice	Barty	Samuel
b. 1881	b. 1882	b. 1883

THE LUCASES

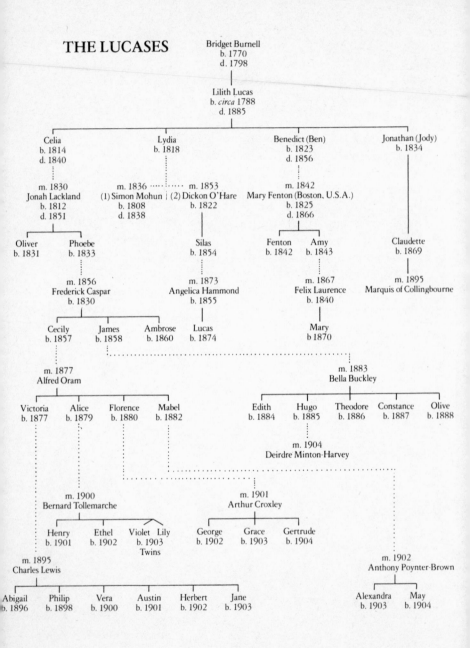

Bridget Burnell
b. 1770
d. 1798

Lilith Lucas
b. *circa* 1788
d. 1885

Celia
b. 1814
d. 1840

Lydia
b. 1818

Benedict (Ben)
b. 1823
d. 1856

Jonathan (Jody)
b. 1834

m. 1830
Jonah Lackland
b. 1812
d. 1851

m. 1836 ········ m. 1853
(1) Simon Mohun | (2) Dickon O'Hare
b. 1808   b. 1822
d. 1838

m. 1842
Mary Fenton (Boston, U.S.A.)
b. 1825
d. 1866

Oliver
b. 1831

Phoebe
b. 1833

Silas
b. 1854

Fenton
b. 1842

Amy
b. 1843

Claudette
b. 1869

m. 1856
Frederick Caspar
b. 1830

m. 1873
Angelica Hammond
b. 1855

m. 1867
Felix Laurence
b. 1840

m. 1895
Marquis of Collingbourne

Cecily
b. 1857

James
b. 1858

Ambrose
b. 1860

Lucas
b. 1874

Mary
b 1870

m. 1877
Alfred Oram

m. 1883
Bella Buckley

Victoria
b. 1877

Alice
b. 1879

Florence
b. 1880

Mabel
b. 1882

Edith
b. 1884

Hugo
b. 1885

Theodore
b. 1886

Constance
b. 1887

Olive
b. 1888

m. 1904
Deirdre Minton-Harvey

m. 1900
Bernard Tollemarche

m. 1901
Arthur Croxley

Henry
b. 1901

Ethel
b. 1902

Violet Lily
b. 1903
Twins

George
b. 1902

Grace
b. 1903

Gertrude
b. 1904

m. 1902
Anthony Poynter-Brown

m. 1895
Charles Lewis

Abigail
b. 1896

Philip
b. 1898

Vera
b. 1900

Austin
b. 1901

Herbert
b. 1902

Jane
b. 1903

Alexandra
b. 1903

May
b. 1904

ACKNOWLEDGEMENTS

The author is grateful for the assistance given with research by the Library of the Royal Society of Medicine, London; Macarthy's Ltd, Surgical Instrument Manufacturers; the London Library; the Royal Borough of Chelsea Libraries; the London Museum; the Victoria and Albert Museum; Leichner Stage Make-up Ltd; Raymond Mander and Jo Mitcheson, theatrical historians; Miss Geraldine Stephenson, choreographer and dance historian; Mr Brian Coe, Curator of the Kodak Museum, Harrow; Rachael Low, film historian; the General Post Office Archives; the Public Records Office; the Archivist, British Rail; and other sources too numerous to mention.

For the third time in half an hour the wind sent a spatter of rain hissing along the sparse grass of the churchyard and round Luke's already cold wet ankles and this time he almost cursed aloud; but then, remembering where he was, bit back the words and tried to look as solemn as befitted the occasion.

Not that the others looked all that solemn, he thought, staring round at them all; complacent lot! You'd think they were at a picnic rather than a funeral, to see the animated way in which they murmured to each other, and the jauntiness of the men's steps and the elegance of the women's clothes which, though black, looked exceedingly handsome and well-fitting. Their furs and heavily-feathered hats positively gleamed with money, and the sweep along the church path of the half-trains on their rich cloth skirts showed a contemptuous disregard for the dirt that other hands would have to clean away.

'Spoiled madams!' he told himself with all the disdain he felt for such social parasites. 'Spoiled selfish madams,' and for a moment considered turning on his heel there and then and going off and leaving them, instead of behaving as was proper and returning to the family house to complete the obsequies.

But they were forming up now into the return procession, looking like a row of glossy black crows and seeming even more cheerful now that Miss Martha Lackland was safely tucked into her corner of the churchyard here in Smith Square; and, as they began to walk towards the gate underneath the dripping trees, their heads bent against the wind beneath shining silk umbrellas, he fell into step behind them almost automatically. The moment had passed for heel-turning, obviously; if he marched off now no one would notice so there would be little point in doing so, and at the house there would be, surely, a drink and a little something to eat which would, he could not deny, come very welcome to a person as hard-pressed as he was for the price of both.

Not that he was starving, of course. Dear old Edwin would never let anyone go hungry, any more than he would see a fellow with nowhere to live, but all the same, it would be agreeable to drink someone else's liquor and eat someone else's victuals for a change. And these opulent crows were connections of a sort after all; why should they not provide a needy young man with a little sustenance?

So, stifling the consideration that in so thinking he was displaying not a little social parasitism in his own right, Luke climbed into the last of the waiting carriages (for this funeral was a well-organized affair and would not use new-fangled motor-cars as some less stylish ones did; for this family it had to be proper carriages with four sleek black horses apiece, each with nodding plumes on their black harness) to drive through the blustery busy March morning back to Tavistock Square.

Getting out of the carriage again proved to be a lengthy affair, for each mourner had to be decanted and admitted to the house in strict order of precedence.

First, Lady Lackland Caspar, the niece (both directly and by marriage) of the dead Martha they were all here to mourn, went with a sprightly gait up the shallow flight of steps that led to the front door of the house, ostensibly leaning on the arm of her stout widowed daughter Cecily who huffed and puffed a good deal as her very straight-backed mother urged her along – Cecily looking for all the world as though she had been upholstered into her black satin gown by one of the costlier furniture emporia in the Tottenham Court Road.

They were followed by Sir Frederick, his spare frame neat in its mourning-suit and with a fringe of sandy hair showing under his top hat. He, Luke allowed, as he watched him go up the steps the requisite three paces behind his wife, was not a social parasite; a hard-working man at his hospital, Nellie's in Covent Garden, from seven in the morning till seven at night, six days every week, but still time to talk to impecunious young connections from the Colonies when they appeared, uninvited, on his doorstep, unlike his haughty Phoebe who showed very clearly her opinion of those who lacked this world's goods. He looked much younger than his seventy-five years, Luke thought with some affection as the pair disappeared through their doorway, and then had to admit that Phoebe too looked young for a woman who must herself be past seventy.

That they should be the progenitors of the vast brood of people who were now surging up the steps behind them seemed almost absurd; first their daughter Cecily's four handsome daughters with their four prosperous husbands and their numerous children and then their son James with his wife Bella, followed by their five offspring and their various spouses and children, all looking as much like the elder Caspars' own children as their grandchildren and great-grandchildren. But then they were a fecund family altogether, these people, for now going up the steps was the Landis family, the nieces and nephews of the senior Caspars, with their cousins the Henriques, and they were a goodly number, heaven knew; such a collection of handsome youths and pretty girls as well as splendidly set-up adults Luke could not remember seeing in one place at one time before. And for a moment he felt a little bleak at the thought that he was not really one of them. He was at most a remote connection and it was kind of them – well, of Sir Frederick – to regard him as enough of a relative to be bidden to a family funeral at all.

But then, as he watched the next surge of well-dressed people go up the steps, at last allowing the stragglers and the less important mourners like himself to leave their carriages, he hardened his heart; he would not feel kindly disposed towards them all, he would *not*. They were social parasites and that was that; he must remember that fact, and not be seduced by their good looks and their riches into admiring them in the least.

'Good morning, m'boy,' someone said wheezily behind him and he turned his head and, almost without volition, smiled.

'Good morning, sir!' he said and took off his borrowed top hat with a small and slightly flourishing bow. 'I trust you are well?'

'Hmmph – well, you ask? Well? How can a man be well on

3

such a bitter blowy day with the rain driving him to a consumption, I swear, and every joint in his body aching? Well, you ask! Indeed, I'm not, my dear boy, indeed I'm not. But it's good in you to ask me. Good in you.'

'Well, sir, your looks don't pity you, as they say,' Luke said heartily and smiled a little more widely as he looked down on the shining bald head and pudgy face above the exceedingly round paunch, all of which showed the obvious good health of their owner. 'You look a deal better than I feel on this cold morning, I do assure you.'

'We need a little inner warming, that's what we need,' the old man said and bumbled busily up the steps as Luke stood courteously aside for him. 'Some of my brother-in-law's good brandy, that's what you need, and me too, only I daren't touch it for fear of the indigestion it'll be sure to give me, sure to give me. Good morning to you, Jeffcoate,' and he let the elderly butler divest him of his topcoat and stood there rubbing his hands together as the butler did the same for Luke.

'A melancholy occasion, Mr Oliver, sir,' Jeffcoate said, and Luke, looking at him, was startled to see that his eyes were moist and rather reddened. 'To see Miss Martha buried, a melancholy day.'

'Well, yes, yes, Jeffcoate, melancholy of course, but she's had a fair innings you know, a fair innings. Another four months, that's all, another four months and she'd have had her ninetieth birthday, you know –'

'Yes, sir, Mr Oliver, I know. That's what makes me so sad, sir. I knew her so long, you see sir. Like my father did before me. I never thought of her as being old –'

'We're all getting on now, Jeffcoate, my dear chap,' Oliver said, and his voice was less bumbly now, and gentler. 'You and me – well, that's the way life is, that's the way life is. We're still here for a while yet, so we'll soldier on, hey, soldier on? Yes –' And he moved on into the big tessellated hallway with the handsome mahogany furniture to take a glass of brandy from the tray held ready by the footman standing stiffly waiting, and took himself across to the fireplace in the far wall to drink it, in spite of, Luke thought with a small grin, the risk of indigestion.

Luke himself took a glass of the brandy and then, moving with apparent casualness but some dispatch, climbed the thickly-carpeted stairs to the drawing-room above where he was sure there would be more footmen – this time with trays bearing food. He was not disappointed, for there was a goodly supply of madeira cake and macaroons and maids of honour and other assorted comestibles and he managed to swallow a considerable quantity without being too obviously greedy as he stood leaning against the wall and staring about him.

The room irritated him just as much as its owner, Lady Caspar, for it was as perfectly fashionable as she was, with a great deal of marble and marquetry about and Ambrose Heal furniture elegantly disposed amidst pink and green curtains and wall-hangings and carpets. He stood there chewing her cake and drinking her brandy and despising her pretty drawing-room, and altogether feeling very superior to his company and his surroundings.

Such money-minded creatures as they all were, he told himself scornfully, as snippets of conversation about gilt-edgeds and bond issues and dividends, and the dividends and the profits made by the drugs manufactory and the returns of chemists' shops that the Henriques owned came drifting through the scented warm air towards him. Such philistines! Not an artistic bone in any one of their bodies. And he pushed down the intrusive awareness that the room in which he was standing and at which he had sneered for its fashionable looks was in fact rather beautiful and as artistic and artful as the most discriminating eye could want. He was determined this morning to see nothing but ill in these connections of his, even if doing so meant deluding himself to a certain extent.

Because he knew perfectly well that, although some of these Lacklands and Caspars and their many relations were indeed business men, dedicated to making money with great enthusiasm and not a little skill, there were others who worked just as hard at their chosen profession which was far removed from commerce – that of the surgeon. This was a family of doctors, as he was well aware. In addition to Sir Frederick, now standing on the other side of the room in close conversation with his son James, there was Mr Lewis Lackland, the well-known surgeon for women's complaints, who was now leaning against the fireplace with his head bent as he listened to the chatter of his singularly beautiful wife, Miriam.

'But even he went and married an heiress!' Luke thought and felt better. What else could he do, aware as he was of his own lack of success in his chosen field of endeavour and his own poverty? And then with a moment of honesty he thought bleakly, 'I'm jealous of them all. That's what it is. I'm damned jealous –'

And that was so disagreeable a thought that he could not handle it at all, and he turned with a sharp movement and set his empty glass down on the nearest occasional table with a small clatter and moved away towards the door. He would go, and the sooner the better. To stand here alone and lonely and hating himself was no way to spend time. Ill-mannered though it would be, he was going to go without a word to any one of them. Immediately.

His movement was so sharp as he turned that he blundered into the person standing nearest to him, a tall sturdy figure in close-fitting black serge, with dark hair pinned thickly on top of her head to reveal a long and rather pretty neck.

She stumbled a little at his impact and turned to show a pleasant face with a wide mouth and narrow green eyes which became even more narrow as she smiled and murmured an acknowledgement of his apology, stepping to his left. He apologized again and this time stepped to the right as she, trying to accommodate him, stepped to the left; at which point they both laughed aloud and stood contemplating each other.

'It's so silly when that happens, isn't it?' she said, and he noted that her voice was rather deep for a girl's and liked it; so many modern girls trilled like canaries, and set his teeth on edge. 'But it's almost inevitable! I'll stand still this time and let you walk round me.'

'Thank you,' he said, but made no move to go. 'Er – I'm Lucas O'Hare. How d'you do?'

'And I am Lettice Brotherton Lackland and how do *you* do?' And she put out her hand and after a moment he took it and they shook formally.

'Brotherton?' he said then, more because he needed

6

something to say to continue the conversation than for any other reason; he felt suddenly much less anxious to leave this nest of social parasites than he had been. 'I thought I knew all the family connections, but I've never heard that name before.'

'Haven't you?' She smiled again a little sardonically. 'I'm not a bit surprised! It was supposed to have been changed altogether. But I chose to keep it.'

'That sounds very – interesting. Will you explain?'

She shrugged and then made a little face. 'Oh, it's not important really. It's just that – well, my mother – she's a niece of Aunt Martha – oh, dear, I suppose I ought to say was – my mother Sophie inherited her grandfather's fortune on the condition that she became a surgeon called Lackland. So, when she married, you see, my father had to change his name. He was Wilfred Brotherton. And after he died I thought – well, I decided to put Brotherton back in my name. That's all.'

'Your mother is a surgeon? How extraordinary! I never heard anyone speak of her –'

'I don't supppose you have. She works in Yorkshire, you see. In Haworth. She's rather poor and –'

'In spite of her grandfather's fortune?'

'Oh, she spent all that on her clinic. In Haworth. Went through it in no time, organizing medicines and a water supply to some cottages and milk for babies and – oh, all sorts of things like that. She spent most of the mill's money too, after Papa died, but Samuel, he's my younger brother – he looks set to put the mill on its wheels again, so that's all right. Marvellous with wool, our Samuel! Anyway, she's still beavering away there, working incredibly hard, but people in London don't know much about her – it's all so far away, isn't it?'

'Well, yes, far enough – and you? Are you here to enjoy the elegant society of the metropolis? I imagine life for a young lady is less than exciting in – where did you say? Haworth?'

She seemed to bristle a little. 'If you think I'm just a silly girl come to London to do a bit of husband-hunting, then you must think again! I am a student, Mr O'Hare! I am not one of these silly empty-headed misses you –'

He put out one hand towards her, and then drew it back,

sharply, uncharacteristically embarrassed. 'I'm so sorry. I meant no insult, I do promise you! It's just that – well, most girls are just – I mean, not many of the girls here are precisely one of the New Women, are they? Just look at them. You can understand why I –'

She laughed then and looked over her shoulder at the rest of the room, still humming with people, and at the groups of her girl cousins clustered in elegant groups with their heads together and clearly, by the actions of their hands, discussing fashion, and at the slightly older married women who were equally clearly deeply absorbed in discussion of babies and servants as well as fashion, and she nodded.

'Well, yes, I suppose I see what you mean. They're dear good girls, of course, but a bit – well –' and she slid her eyes sideways at him and gave a wicked little grin and he felt suddenly that he too was behaving more as though he were at a picnic than a funeral and tried to look serious.

'A student, you say? And what do you study? Would music be a good guess?'

'A very bad one,' she said coolly. 'I'm a medical student. At Nellie's, you know,' and she lifted her chin and looked at him very directly, watching to see his reaction.

Aware now of walking on thin ice, he schooled his face and showed no surprise at all, nodding back at her equally coolly.

'Indeed! Then you plan to practise with your mother, I take it?'

She relaxed at once, and smiled at him, once more the cheerful easy-to-talk-to person he had first thought her.

'Oh, as to that, I can't say! I'm barely past my first year, you know, and there is so much still to learn I feel positively exhausted just thinking about it. I can't imagine myself ever actually practising though I know I will of course. As to Haworth – well, to tell the truth, you were right about one point. Haworth is really awfully dull. No theatre to speak of, no concerts, no –'

He lifted his chin sharply. 'Theatre? You care for the theatre?'

Her face seemed to light up and she nodded, full of energy and eagerness.

'Oh, yes, passionately! I sneak off to the play at every chance! Barty – he's my other brother, and he is here in London studying at Nellie's too – there he is, over there in the corner talking to Cousin Phoebe – he gets very waxy with me about it! Whenever I ought to be swotting over the bones of the skull or whatever, there I am yearning over Granville Barker or Gerald du Maurier – poor Barty! He thinks a bluestocking like me should be above such interests as play-acting, but you see, I'm not quite as blue about the legs as might be thought! And I dearly love a play.'

He kept his face as straight as ever as he listened and then said casually, 'That is most interesting. I am an actor, you know.'

She was all attention at once. 'You're an – oh, really, this is too bad of me! Here I've been chattering on and on about myself and not a word about – Now, tell me everything! You said you are Lucas O'Hare? That is a name I don't know – so you can't be a connection. I'm sure if there were any actor in the family other than dear old Uncle Oliver, who is not precisely an uncle of course, more a cousin, but still – well, I'm sure I should have known. So do tell me! Who are you, how do you come to be at dear old Aunt Martha's funeral and above all, do tell me all about your acting.'

Now he did smile and stopped putting on his little performance of being very detached and insouciant.

'I *am* a sort of connection, actually. All very difficult to explain, and I'm bored by genealogies – you know the way all the old biddies go on and on about who married who and how people are related to each other – but I can tell you that my grandmother was Lydia Mohun and my great-grandmother was Lilith Lucas. It's from her I have my given name – though all my friends call me Luke – and I'm much indebted to her for it! It proves, doesn't it, that I come from a long line of distinguished performers! And they were in some way linked with the Lackland family by marriage, I'm told. Uncle Oliver's and Lady Caspar's mother and my grandmother – Lydia Mohun – were sisters. It's all a bit confused, I dare say, but when I left South Africa to come to London, my father told me to make contact with them, and so I did. Sir Frederick has been very kind, though I must confess that sometimes I find some of the others a little – well –'

She nodded. 'I know – those Oram girls can be very tiresome! And Cousin Phoebe – well – let's just say I know what you mean. So you have famous actresses in your ancestry! I can't pretend I know their names, but then I don't suppose you know my famous ancestor, do you? Abel Lackland?'

'Abel – I can't say I –'

'There, you see! We are as distinguished as each other when you consider ancestors and neither is the least impressed. I dare say the said distinguished forebears are spinning in their graves with disapproval of our flippant ways – though from all I've been told of old Abel Lackland, he might perhaps have been less – oh well! I'm sure that what really matters is what one does oneself and not what others have done, though I sometimes have trouble convincing my dear Mamma of that!' She made a little face and grinned.

'Proses on at you, does she?'

She looked a little embarrassed. 'I really mustn't complain of her, for she is the dearest Mamma, but you see, she is so very –well, *remarkable*. She became a doctor at a time when no lady could ever consider such a thing – the amount of perseverance she showed really shames me sometimes – but it is such a lot to live up to –'

She looked a little solemn for a moment and then, as she caught his eyes on her, reddened a little, and said hastily, 'But there, I'm doing it again – prattling only of my own affairs. Now tell me, where do you act? What sort of acting do you do? And where may I come and see you perform?'

'As to that, I must tell you that the answer is nowhere at all! At present, I'm without a part. Times are, as always in the theatre, a little hard. But I have one or two things in view, you know, one or two things –'

'I'm sure you have!' she said warmly. 'What sort of acting do you most enjoy? The new drawing-room comedies at which Mr du Maurier is so gifted? Or do you prefer the old school – Granville Barker, and so forth? Or perhaps you offer the sort of entertainment that Uncle Oliver gives in his supper rooms?

now those I *do* so much enjoy! I know it's more music-hall than theatre, but it's really such fun –'

'Yes, it is, and no, I don't. I'm your all purpose run-of-the-mill-try-anything sort of man, but I don't dance or sing, so the Celia Supper Rooms can't offer me any sort of employment, I'm afraid. I only wish they could! Sir Frederick did suggest it when I first arrived in London, because he knew I'd been working with my father in a travelling theatre around Durban, but I had such high-flown notions then! If I'd had the sense I have now, I'd have tried my hand and perhaps learned how to do it – music-hall, that is – for I was young enough then – just twenty-one – to be still teachable. I'm not saying I can't still learn, you know, but the time really is past for kicking my heels up and burbling comic songs, so there it is – I shall have to do without the help of the Lacklands –'

'You don't like them – us?' she said after a moment, and he had the grace to turn a little pink.

'That sounds very disagreeable of me,' he said. 'And I must apologize to you. It's just that sometimes, when I look at them all, I think – well, they really are so very *rich*. They can spend an evening at the theatre and never count the cost, and hardly ever do, because they care more for money than for educating their souls, and there are people in this town who care desperately about the plays they can't find the money to see, and it all seems so *wasteful*. So I suppose I sound a little sour sometimes. I'm sorry.'

'There's no need to be sorry. I know what you mean. When you want to do something very badly and other people seem not to care about it, it makes you boil, doesn't it? I always wanted to act, you see, and no one else ever did anything but laugh at me – oh dear.' And for a moment she looked as bothered as a child caught out telling falsehoods. 'That sounds so disloyal and I don't mean it to, when I have such splendid opportunities that other girls don't have, but – well, I don't know many actors. Indeed, I never met one to talk to ever before, so I suppose my tongue ran away with me –'

He laughed, and again felt that sense of relaxation she was able to create in him. 'You're really rather a surprising person to meet at a funeral. A woman medical student is strange enough, but one who's as stage-struck as I am – really, you amaze me! Perhaps this famly has more to it than I thought, if it can produce people like you!'

'You don't have to mock my family or me,' she said, stung. 'I was being perfectly serious.'

'And so was I, I promise you. I wasn't mocking in the least. You *are* surprising. I was hating this morning – I mean, quite apart from it being old Aunt Martha's funeral, but then, she was very old, and I hardly knew her – but you've cheered me greatly. I do thank you for allowing me to almost knock you over.'

She was silent for a moment, and then nodded, seriously. 'Then I will apologize for being so prickly. Let's stop talking about me, then, and talk about you and the theatre. If you could choose what you'd like to do, what would it be?'

'Do you really want to know?'

'I wouldn't have asked if I didn't.'

'I'm sorry. Again, that was ill-mannered of me. Well, then, I'd like to run my own theatre. Not a big fashionable one, you understand, but a special one. A –' He stopped and shrugged. 'Well, an ordinary one, really, but cheap. Good work, but cheap seats.'

'For the people who can't afford to buy the better ones? The people who are *not* like my family,' she said and he reddened.

'Oh, please, do forget that! I've already said I –'

'It's forgotten,' she said at once. 'All forgotten. It's a splendid idea, that. Where would you have your theatre?'

'Wherever I could. It won't matter where it is, you see, as long as it isn't in the smart streets – the West End. It's got to be where ordinary people live and work, and heaven knows – there are enough parts of London like that!'

'Why don't you do it then, instead of just waiting till a part you like turns up?'

'Money,' he said and lifted his eyebrows comically at her. 'I'm just a man on his own – no income other than that I earn for myself. My father used up all his mother – Lydia Mohun, you'll remember – left him, running his theatre in Durban. So it all ran out by the time he died, so I just don't have the sort of cash my own theatre would need. I'm successful in my work, of course, make enough for my own needs, but to start a theatre of my own –' He shook his head. 'That would cost a vast sum.'

'I see. Well, can't you persuade other people to join you? Other actors and so forth? You must know them all – couldn't you ask people like – well, du Maurier, say and –'

He looked uncomfortable then and she glanced away politely, not wanting to embarrass him. Clearly he did not know such people, not being quite as successful as he'd like her to think – and she had to admit she had never heard of him, interested in theatre matters though she was, and an eager reader of all the newspaper reports of actors' doings – and she would not have hurt his feelings for the world. He was much too interesting for that.

'I doubt that people like that would be interested,' he was saying gruffly. 'These matinee idols, they care more for their own pockets and the silly giggling girls who swoon after them than they do about the real art of their work. I've no use for them –'

'I'm sure you're right.' she murmured, and still didn't look at him, all too aware of the way she had herself been used to do a fair imitation of swooning at the plays of the handsome Gerald du Maurier when she had first come to London, although now, of course, at almost twenty-five she had long outgrown such nonsense. 'Well, I can only –'

'Lettice, I've been looking for you, my dear!'

A stocky young man tapped her on the shoulder and Luke frowned slightly. He was thoroughly enjoying this girl's company and was far from willing to have outsiders pushing in and he opened his mouth to say something sharp, but Lettice smiled at the newcomer and said, 'Oh, Barty! Here is a new cousin I'm sure you didn't know we had! Lucas O'Hare, my brother Bartholomew Lackland.'

'How do you do?' The stocky young man looked briefly at Luke and then back at his sister. 'We really must be on our way, Letty. I've a lot of work I want to do, and so should you – there's a viva next week, remember, materia medica, and I'm sure you will want to settle to your work. Good afternoon, Mr – er –'

She held out her hand and smiled, and Luke after one cool stare at the rather pompous Barty smiled back at her and took it.

'I hope we'll meet again at some other family affair,' she said. 'A happier one, of course – goodbye –' And she was gone, Barty's hand on her shoulder in a proprietorial way, weaving their way through the hubbub of departing relatives and leaving him standing there feeling not a little surprised at how sorry he was to see her go.

He watched her from the window as she and Barty went down the steps into the street and set off at a brisk walk across the gusty daffodilly gardens in the centre of Tavistock Square, and thought, 'I'd like to talk to her again sometime –' and then swore softly as he realized he had no idea where she lived.

But that, he told himself as he said goodbye to Sir Frederick with further murmured condolences for the loss of his elderly aunt, was remediable. One day, when the time was more suitable, he would call on Sir Frederick, braving the condescending stare of his wife, and casually enquire as to his young kinswoman's whereabouts. And then –

'And then what?' he thought gloomily, as he walked across the square himself, on his way back to Chelsea. 'With no money to spend and no work to do to get any, how can I possibly pay any attention to a young woman of such obvious standing? Emancipated New Woman she may be, but that didn't mean she wouldn't expect the sort of courteous attention from a young man to which she was entitled – and that takes money. Damn it!'

Lucas O'Hare was both an elated and depressed young man as he went striding back to his friend Edwin Zander's house that March morning in 1905. Life was really treating him damnably at present, offering lollipops with one hand and snatching them back with the other. He really would have to try to find some way to improve his affairs and that quickly. At his age – and no one could pretend that thirty was exactly the first flush of youth, he told himself grimly – it was high time he was set properly on his way to success. High time. He would have to see to it.

And Lettice for her part went home to her lodgings in

14

Gilbert Place in Bloomsbury in a similar state of mixed elation and depression. To have met so interesting a man – an actor!, and one who had such an amusing face with its quirky narrow-lipped mouth and those very dark eyes beneath such thick dark hair – only to be snatched away from conversation with him by the demands of her materia medica textbooks, was maddening. Of course, she told herself loyally, as the hack which Barty had hailed went bowling noisily along the Tottenham Court Road, of *course* her studies were of the first importance. She was a medical student, a privileged young woman who had to carry the banner which her mother had first hoisted thirty years before, had she not? Not an ordinary girl who could indulge herself in friendships with interesting actors with ambitions to run their own theatres.

'Damn it,' she thought, and took a perverse pride in thinking a swear word that, emancipated woman though she was, she could not actually say aloud. '*Damn* it!'

2

Luke spent the rest of the day on a more than usually determined search for work. His last part had been in a rather dull Christmas pantomime in the suburbs in which he had played an indifferent Robber in *Babes in the Wood*; it had offered him a bare half-dozen rhyming couplets to learn, but they had been so dismal as to be almost impossible to remember, so he had been glad when the last curtain had come down at the end of January, even though that had meant an end to the slender salary the part had provided. He had then spent several days in February desultorily seeking another berth but it had been a bad time of year, as everyone said; the more successful pantomimes were still running and occupying the theatres and the summer tours were not yet being put together, so he had allowed his depression to overcome him and had spent the past few days in doing little but sitting at home with Edwin and his friends, thinking more and more about his fantasy of his own theatre and not trying to find work at all.

But today's meeting with Letty Lackland had spurred him. He had set out for the funeral, to which he had been bidden by Sir Frederick, in his now customary state of lowness and would have expected, had he thought about it at all, to be even lower by the time he went back to Chelsea. But now he was invigorated and he put it down to the breath of spring that was at last in the air; rainy and blowy though the day was, he felt that winter was at last behind them and the year promised to be a good one after all.

That was why he felt so energetic, he told himself, as he wheeled away from Tottenham Court Road to plunge into the narrow streets of Seven Dials on his way to Shaftesbury Avenue instead of to Chelsea Reach as he had first intended.

That was why he suddenly felt that presenting himself at the theatre managers' doors could lead to something useful. It was nothing to do with Miss Lackland at all. Nothing. It had been interesting to meet so lively a lady of course, and he had enjoyed their conversation, but that was all. Now, out in the open air, he was ready to do something more positive about his workless state; it was no more than that.

So he told himself firmly as he began the familiar trek from management to management: first to the Palace Theatre at Cambridge Circus to see what was doing there (the answer was nothing for Luke O'Hare or any other straight actor since they had another of their variety bills in hand); then to the Garrick to see what Mr Arthur Bourchier might have to offer (another blank – he was already in rehearsal for a play due to open in a week's time); then on to the New Theatre for a word with Charles Wyndham's people (who had no time to talk to anyone today, sorry, try again next month, sorry, not today); and then the Beerbohm Tree office (sorry, he's in Stratford, getting ready for the Shakespeare Birthday Luncheon and the Festival, you know, try again in May); and so on and on and on.

His improved spirits were short-lived, and he felt the depression creeping back over him like rolling waves of London fog. There'd be no point in going over to the Royal Court at Sloane Square; the Vedrenne Barker management, everyone knew, had their favourite people, and rarely cast outside those fortunate ranks for new actors, even as supers. The new George Bernard Shaw play *Major Barbara* at the Court, under the Stage Society's management was another that was already fully cast, and anyway, Luke had no desire to work with that fiery Irishman, after the stories he'd heard about his scorn for actors from some of the other people who had ventured into his pieces. And Granville Barker and du Maurier and the other damned matinee idols all had their regular companies in full strength. Which left, for the London theatres, only the Guv'nor at the Gaiety. And everyone knew that old George Edwardes was only concerned with girls and comedians and had no interest at all in legitimate actors of the likes of Luke O'Hare. It would be a waste of time even trying, not worth the shoe-leather he'd use walking to the top of the Strand.

It was getting late now. The lamp-lighters had been on their rounds for some time as the short afternoon dwindled into a blue velvet dusk, making the streets glow with the soft radiance of the incandescent gas-mantles, and the chestnut-sellers were on every street corner offering passers-by their smoky bagsful with shrill cries of 'Penny a bag, they're luverly, penny a bag, they're luverly!' Shop windows were now spilling their lights cheerfully on to the paving-stones to illuminate the clerks and lady typewriters and milliners hurrying home to firesides and kipper teas in the suburbs of Kilburn and Holloway and Shepherd's Bush; and everywhere couples went arm-in-arm, talking busily, happy to be together on so damp and windy an evening.

Luke stood on the corner of Coventry Street, his hands thrust into his trouser-pockets and his chin tucked into his high starched collar and watched them gloomily, full of his own misfortunes. All so busy, all so much better off than he was, even though their jobs were hard and dull and deeply boring. At least they had jobs, at least they had somewhere to go, a purpose in life. What did he have, apart from his ridiculous ambitions? Nothing at all, not even a home to call his own, sponging on his friends, meeting magnificent young ladies and being totally unable to do anything to further the acquaintanceship – life was altogether ghastly.

At which point his native good humour at last took over and he laughed at himself, lifting his chin from his collar-points, and straightening his shoulders. This was absurd; to behave in such a miserable fashion over the inevitable fluctuations of his trade! This was what being an actor was all about; he'd learned that from his father, Silas, in those long years of trekking around the Durban area with their 'Shakespeare on Wheels' company, and from Dickon O'Hare, his grandfather, who had told him from his earliest infancy of the difficulties as well as the delights of the stage life. To stand now on a London corner glooming like King Lear just because he was in a temporary bad patch was lunacy. The scene would change, a new backdrop would fall into place, a whole new act would start; it had always been so in the past – he'd spent half his life on the boards, so he should know – and it undoubtedly would again. What he had to do now was cheer himself up and stop acting such a Cheltenham tragedy inside his own head.

A little entertainment, that was the answer – but not one he could afford, damn it all. Even the price of a pit seat at a music-hall would strain his exceedingly slender purse to breaking-point. It would have to be home to Edwin's and with luck, some good company among his lot of friends. It was an odd night when someone didn't drop into 47 Cheyne Walk and liven things up.

But he needed something more than that, because it was only seven o'clock, and the Chelsea droppers-in didn't start their dropping in until close to midnight. What could he possibly do for the next four or five hours to keep the glooms at bay?

A cheeful boy went by on a bicycle, his neck wrapped in a huge striped muffler and a cap of ferocious green tweed pulled over his ears, whistling 'Bedelia' from the new George Grossmith success at the Gaiety, and Luke lifted his chin from his collar and thought, 'Uncle Oliver! I'll go and see Uncle Oliver –' and felt his spirits rise again. That was one person he knew would always welcome him, and at the Celia Supper Rooms there was always warmth and songs and dancing and fun. He'd go there.

And he turned on his heel and made his way back towards Covent Garden, pushing through the crowds of Leicester Square with a jaunty step and whistling 'Bedelia' loudly and tunefully as he went.

The Gilbert Place lodgings were, as always, snug and comfortable when they reached them. Mrs Partridge had lit their living-room fire early that day, and kept it asiduously fed ever since, so by the time they had climbed their pair of stairs, rather pink about the nose and rosy about the cheeks, to reach the red plush and mahogany interior of their sitting-room (for Mrs Partridge was one of the old school, and liked the good old solid furniture of her mother's day, not this nasty boxy Tottenham Court Road stuff everyone was making such a fuss of, rubbishy sticks *they* all were) the room was like a hot-house.

Letty peeled off her black mantle with a sigh of relief and unpinned her straw hat with its black feathers and threw them both on her bed in the small room that adjoined the sitting-room, while Barty tidily hung his in the wardrobe in the rather larger bedroom to which he had laid claim the day they had first come to London.

'For I am, Letty, the man of this establishment, and it's only right I should have the bigger room,' he had told her loftily, and she, excited enough about being in London at all, had cared too little to argue with him.

Now, as she stood in the tiny space between her bed and her dressing-table and massaged her tired neck, she was irritated, not for the first time, at the thought of Barty in the masculine splendour of the larger room and then grinned at her own reflection in the mirror. 'Silly!' she murmured aloud, 'Silly!'

For what did it matter if Barty needed to put on his great show of superiority? It hadn't been easy for him, growing up in his older sister's shadow, even though the gap between them was only a year; he had always felt it keenly, especially so after their father died and it became even more clear to him that his life was under the control of women, his masterful Mamma mostly, but to a lesser extent, his tall and handsome sister. Letty knew how it irritated Barty that she was the same height as he was – perhaps even a smidgeon taller – and that he felt his lack of inches sorely. She also knew how he yearned to be the masterful male and, maddening though his resulting pomposity sometimes was, her affection for him made her try to let him have his own way when she could. If it made him feel better and did her no mischief, why should she not indulge him? As long as he did not interfere much in her ways and ideas, she could bear with him, dear old Barty.

But today he was being extra tiresome. All the way home from Tavistock Square he had scolded and nagged at her for not circulating more during the morning, for not making the most of her opportunities.

'For', he had said, looking more than usually solemn, 'we do need all the family closeness we may obtain. We have been out of the family swim for a very long time, with Mamma so foolishly determined to waste all her energies there in Yorkshire and if we are to obtain the best practices for ourselves once we qualify, it is essential we are well established here in London. So you should have talked to Mr Lewis Lackland and his wife and to Sir Frederick, instead of leaving it all to me. And I saw that wretched pushy Henry Landis and the other one – David Henriques, the one who looks like a dago – both of them being very attentive to Sir Frederick, while all you could do was stand and gossip with some wretched hanger-on and –'

'He is not a hanger-on,' she had said as mildly as she could. 'He's a cousin, and most interesting. I saw no reason to crawl like Henry Landis, rather than talk to Luke – and if the only way to get on and establish ourselves in London is to suck up to people, then I for one will gladly go back to Mamma's clinic and spend all my time with her wretched runny-nosed babies, so there!'

'You know you loathe Mamma's clinic and babies as much as I do,' Barty had said shortly. 'You can't tell me you have any notion of working in Yorkshire after we qualify, for I know better. And if you've any sense you'll listen to me and do as I say, for I understand the world much better than you do, and have the sense of a man. You may regard yourself as a New Woman with all your fancy notions about votes, but for all that, you're just a girl, after all. You're lucky enough to be in at Nellie's – don't ruin it all for yourself, and for me, by being so foolish –'

At which point she had shut her ears, letting him rattle on in the same old grooves. She had heard all this before from her ambitious brother, about the need for good connections and a circle of important friends in building a lucrative practice, and about his anxiety regarding her headstrong ways. She would listen no more; she had other things to think about.

Like Luke O'Hare. What an interesting young man he had been – so courteous and yet so definite in his opinions. He didn't talk to her as Barty and most of the other medical students she knew talked to her, as though she were a mentally retarded child with a few clever ways. She knew that all men

21

spoke to girls like that; indeed this man Luke had started to talk so, but had realized very quickly that she was not like her Oram and Landis cousins (who were, truth to tell, exceedingly stupid, even more stupid than most girls, and that was saying a great deal) and had at once mended his ways.

That had been a most interesting facet of him, and she had sat in the hansom and thought of all he had said, of the honest way in which he had explained his ambitions for his own theatre, and she said to herself, against the droning of Barty's words, 'I do wish I could meet him again. *So interesting –*' and then sighed, knowing full well that the chances of doing so were slim, unless he put himself out to arrange it. And he had shown no sign of wanting to meet her again.

'So, I had better forget him,' she told herself firmly now and went out into the sitting-room to ring for Mrs Partridge to bring up their lunch so that they might eat and then settle to the afternoon's boring session with their materia medica textbooks. Wretched textbooks; the work at the hospital was well enough, if sometimes disagreeable, but at least it wasn't too boring. The facts about pharmacy were desperately so, and she looked forward to the hours that stretched ahead to bedtime with no pleasure at all.

Mrs Partridge came struggling up her linoleum-covered staircase with a great deal of puffing and muttering, weighed down with a vast tray on which she had loaded all their lunch dishes, and set about spreading the white cloth over the red plush one on the central table and arranging the china and glass and cutlery, and then the bread-and-butter and soup (for people ate their dinners early in Mrs Partridge's world, so a light lunch was all a body needed) chattering all the while of the doings of the other tenants of the house, and of Gilbert Place in general. Letty stood beside the fire staring at the flames and trying not to think of either Luke O'Hare or materia medica, and Barty settled himself at the table, ready to serve the soup and cut the bread as the master of a household should.

'There, and if I didn't nearly go and forget your letter, miss!' Mrs Partridge said and pulled a thick square envelope from her apron pocket. 'Lose my silly head, I would, if it wasn't nailed on with golden nails by the Good Lord Hisself. Here it is, my dear, and you enjoy the reading of it. Comes from your mother in Haworth it does, and you'll be eager to read her good words, I do know,' and she went off busily leaving Letty to make a furious face at her departing back, irritated as she usually was by their landlady's open inquisitiveness.

'What does she say, Letty?' Barty asked, ladling soup into the bowls. 'Is there any news of Samuel and that foolish Skipton girl he's got himself involved with? Wretched female's trying to snare him and so I told him last time I wrote, but he won't –'

'Since I haven't read the letter, I can't say yet,' Letty said and sat down in the armchair to open it. 'And if that soup is for me, you may put it back in the tureen, for I don't want any. I ate too much cake at Tavistock Square.'

'Then you are foolish, for it is not healthy to eat sweetmeats and to miss your meals as a result,' Barty said promptly. 'And furthermore –'

'Oh, pish!' she said and turned her back on him. 'I want to read my letter. So be quiet!'

And Barty, looking daggers at her, settled to his lunch at last and left her to read her letter from her mother in peace.

Not that it was a peace that lasted long. She felt her ire rising as she read the closely-written lines, in that strong sloping hand, and wanted to have her mother there beside her, to explain, to argue it out, to stop her from saying such foolish things –

'My dearest Letty,' Sophie had written. 'I trust that you and Barty remain well, and are seeing to it that Mrs Partridge takes adequate care of you. See to it that all your underclothing and bedding is well aired after laundering, for it is still very early in the year, and the cold can be treacherous. Your health, as you well know, is a precious store that must not be diminished heedlessly.

'Now, my dear Letty, I must write most strongly about the terms of your last letter to me. I searched it carefully for signs of your involvement with your studies, for discussion of the problems of clinical judgement you may have come across, of the sort that Barty writes me often in his letters, and I was sorely disappointed. It is a matter of great pride to me that you have followed me to Nellie's and will go on into the practice of medicine, and I know you know of my pride, my dearest girl, but it is not enough that you have qualified yourself to be there. You must go on working with all the energy you have to complete your studies and reach qualification! To be a medical student is not enough; you must be a *diligent* student, working harder than the men, for whom life is always easier, and showing them in every way you can that you are their equal. Indeed, I know you to be their superior, Letty, but they do not! And the only way they will realize this is if you work, work, and work even more as, I am forced to remind you, I had to in my student days. It was never easy, for I had to earn my keep at the same time, running a girls' hostel, as you will recall. But I do not wish to make a disagreeable exhibition of my own experiences, only to impress on you, my dearest daughter, that it is *application* that you must show. And when I receive from you letters that talk mostly of attendance at meetings about obtaining votes for women – a no doubt laudable idea, but impractical in the extreme as I well know, for there are not many women who are capable of thinking about such matters usefully – I am incensed, for it really is a nonsense at the moment. You cannot fritter away your precious time at Nellie's on such affairs.

'I do not often forbid you anything, Letty, if I can help it, but I must now tell you firmly that I cannot allow you to attend any more of these meetings with hysterical women who meddle in affairs they do not understand, and must instruct you to work harder at your books. I know Barty does all he can to encourage you, and he does show in his letters a most lively awareness of the need for work. I hope you will pay attention to his example.

'And may I also say that while I know it is necessary for a young person to have some entertainment, I do feel you harp too much on these plays you attend. Of course go to a theatre *occasionally* – I used to greatly enjoy such entertainment myself – but not every week, Letty! You cannot indulge yourself so when there is so much study to be done!

'Enough of my prosing on – I can imagine just how you are looking, mulish and as cross as two sticks, as dear old Bessie would say. She sends you her dearest love, by the bye, and has baked a parcel of parkin for you, which is being sent down by the railway and should be collected, together with the length of new tweed and the books I promised you. Ask Barty to see to it that they are fetched from King's Cross Station as soon as maybe – they will have arrived there at the same time as this letter reaches you.

'Now, my dear Letty, I am sure you have taken my little lecture to heart, and do realize how foolish you have been in becoming involved with these absurd vote-hunting women. I am the first, you must agree, to say women should do as is best for their talents – I fought a great battle myself to reach my own qualification – and I encourage you in your efforts most warmly. Your dear brothers are exceedingly precious to me, as you know, but you are *special*, Letty, and that is why I speak as I do. These foolish women are not going to help any of us, they will merely antagonize men to no purpose, for I have yet to meet any sensible woman who has any real political interest at all – it is just not part of a woman's mind, as is caring for the sick. Give women the vote, I am certain, and the result will be chaos. They are not all as wise as you believe, my dear!

'So, enough – I will try to say no more, unless you write me letters like your last! I trust that those of the family to whom you speak are well. I am sad indeed I could not come to London to pay my last respects to Aunt Martha for whom I had a very deep regard and felt much gratitude – her kindness to me in my own student days was great and I will never forget it – but we have had a whooping cough epidemic here, and I was not able to leave. Sadly, two of the Pickles babies from Stanbury died. Bessie was most distressed, for they were great-nephews of her husband's, she says. My dearest love to you, Letty, and to Barty, and tell him my next letter will be to him. Samuel is well and busy and sends his best love. Your own mother, Sophie Brotherton Lackland.'

'Well, what does she say?' Barty said loudly and she realized as she folded the sheets that he had repeated the question several times already.

'It is a private letter to me,' she said shortly. 'But she sends her love and you are to collect a parcel for us both at King's

Cross. She'll write to you next week –'

Barty nodded, looking pleased with himself. 'Then she has told you about the time you waste at those stupid political meetings. I am glad. It really is most –'

'Did you complain to her of me?' Letty said wrathfullly. 'Is that why she has lectured me so? Not just because of my letter to her? Barty, if you do not stop this meddling in my life, I swear I will –'

'Meddling? Pooh!' Barty said, uncomfortably, and put his napkin on the table and got to his feet. 'It is not meddling to be concerned about you. And –'

'It is meddling of the most disagreeable and – and sneaky sort!' Letty said furiously. 'And I tell you now that unless you behave a great deal less like a schoolboy who's been made a monitor and regards himself as God Almighty in consequence, you and I are going to have great problems! So bite your tongue, Barty Lackland, and mind your manners!'

And she thrust the letter into the bodice of her black serge gown and swept into her small bedroom to skewer her brightest, reddest and most frivolous hat onto her head, and to put on the matching red mantle that both her mother and Barty had been dubious about when she had first bought them (and about which her brother Samuel had been unexpectedly complimentary, telling her it made her look like a most delightful gipsy) and swept back into the living-room with her head high, pulling on her gloves as she went.

'Where are you going?' Barty said, staring at her with almost as ferocious a scowl as she was staring at him.

'That is none of your concern!' she said loftily. 'I will tell you only *out*. Good afternoon! Work hard at your books, young man!' And she seized her reticule on its long silver chain and went clattering down the stairs and out into the street, revelling in the huge exhilaration of having thoroughly lost her temper.

It lasted well into the afternoon, time she spent indulging herself by wandering around the big shops in Regent Street, from Swan and Edgar's up to Dickins and Jones and all the smaller establishments in between, admiring hats and shawls and feathers and ribbons and all the latest fashionable fripperies that were offered here in the heart of the most important and undoubtedly richest city in the world.

But as the day wore on, even tea at Fuller's could not make her feel as uplifted as she had been; she had to admit, rather gloomily, that a whole afternoon spent looking at fashion was more than a little boring; that she had seen enough of clothes and hats and scents and jewellery to last her a month, and that she wanted something interesting to do. *Really* interesting. She had no intention of returning to Gilbert Place until the latest possible moment – she could catch an omnibus at any time up to midnight – in order to give Barty the thoroughly frightening lesson he needed. But it was now only seven o'clock, and the shops were closing. How could she possibly just wander around the streets for so long?

Theatre, she thought. A play? That would be agreeable but it was still three days to the start of the month and the arrival of her allowance, and truth to tell her funds would not stretch to any but the cheapest seats in the gods, and that would mean sitting alone among people who were less thoughtful of the well-being of a girl out on her own than they might be. Emancipated was one thing, she told herself ruefully, foolhardy quite another.

That was the point at which she realized she had the perfect answer to her dilemma, for a boy on a bicycle went by, whistling a familiar tune of a lively sort, and she found herself thinking, 'Uncle Oliver! Of course – I shall go to see Uncle Oliver!' And she set off, walking quickly through the bustling streets towards Covent Garden and the Celia Supper Rooms.

3

Oliver sat at his corner-table, watching the stage with his face set in a frown that made his usually cheerful round cheeks look almost comical. This was the fourth Harry Lauder imitator he'd seen this month; if he heard another chorus of 'I Love a Lassie' sung by a man in a skimpy kilt, he'd throw his dinner at the wall, he told himself, if not at the damned kilt itself. Of course the song was going to be an enormous success, and of course it was necessary to have it sung at the Celia Supper Rooms if it was to keep its reputation as being a bang-up-to-the-minute place for the toffs, but did he have to suffer the awful tedium of listening to so many mediocre versions?

'I'll let you know,' he said as, at last, 'Mary, my Scots bluebell!' brought the song to its close. 'Let you know, my dear chap, just leave your address will you, with my Miss Enoch there, and we'll be in touch. Free are you, if we need you, free for Monday, hey? Good, good – be in touch –'

He got to his feet and pulled his old-fashioned turnip-watch from his waistcoat-pocket and peered at it, muttering under his breath, and then went bustling about the rooms, staring closely at each table, tweaking the silver into position and rearranging the little red shades over the individual electric lights of which he was so proud, and then putting his head through the red velvet curtains that shrouded the stage to make sure his scene-shifter had everything ready for the first performance of the evening, due to start in less than half an hour. The man looked at him over his shoulder as he pulled a marble pedestal with an arrangement of ferns and parma violets on it into the centre of the stage and grunted, 'She ain't in yet, Mr Oliver –'

'She'll be here, she'll be here, never lets anyone down, no

28

need to worry about Marie – make sure there's a weight behind that pedestal, it's got a nasty wobbly look about it to me, and I want no trouble tonight, not tonight, she doesn't get here that often – be about it now.'

Oliver bustled on his way, checking the dressing-rooms, to be sure his artistes were in, and then hurrying to the kitchens to peer into the barrels of oysters and the great trays of devilled bones and the meat-pies and the custards and jellies, much to the irritation of his chief cook, a large woman with very red arms and an even redder nose who watched him with her lower lip thrust out like a shelf. But he went before she could explode at him – as usual, for this was a ritual they went through every evening at the Celia – and at last made for the main doors to unlock them ready for the evening's business.

As he arranged the red curtain that covered the entry to keep out the evening chill, and fastened back the great mahogany street doors, hansoms were already wheeling into King Street to stop outside his establishment. The horses steamed a little in the chill March air as men in the long ulsters and curly-brimmed toppers which were currently so fashionable handed down girls in the richly-frilled and pleated gowns and the long fur tippets which were all the rage, and the big feathered and fruited hats which were perched so cheerfully on their piles of tightly-curled hair bobbed a little as they hurried across the cobbles to the pavement.

Oliver rubbed his hands together and smiled and becked his head and uttered little cries of welcome and cheerfulness as the Celia Supper Rooms filled up and the waiters began their long nightly stint of rushing from table to table bearing great trays laden with food and drink above their heads. Seven o'clock – and they would not stop now until well past midnight, not easy on the feet of ageing men who had already worked the four hours from eleven to three filling Covent Garden business men with luncheons. But tonight even the most tired of them looked cheerful, for they had a special performer, one who delighted the experienced and highly cynical staff as much as she did the customers. Tonight was to be a good one at the Celia, and within half an hour of the doors opening the place rang with chatter and the clink of glasses and silverware and

29

laughter, almost drowning out the sprightly tunes that came from the three frantic musicians in the minute orchestra pit, scraping and banging away at their instruments as the sweat trickled down their shining red faces.

But still Oliver scowled, sitting at his own special corner table, watching his establishment make money as it always did, and wishing quite heartily that it did not. For she had started again that very afternoon as soon as the rest of the family had gone, leaving just himself and Cecily to share luncheon with the chief mourners. He had told her that he did not wish to discuss the matter, that it was his own affair, but that made no difference to his determined sister. Phoebe just went on and on, until even Freddy had murmured remonstrances at her.

'My dear,' he had said, as he leaned forwards to light a cigarillo for his brother-in-law – for Phoebe was not unduly punctilious, as were some hostesses, about smoking at her luncheon-table – 'please, let us not discuss such matters now! It's sad enough we lost our Martha today – must we talk of death for ourselves?'

'Oh, Freddy, you are absurd!' Phoebe said and trilled a practised little laugh. 'I am not talking about *dying*. Only about business. It is quite ridiculous, you must agree, for darling Oliver to be so rich and successful a man and yet to have made no sensible organization of his money – nor plans for its future.'

'I am here to organize my own affairs, Phoebe, organize my own. Don't see what difference it'd make to the business, don't you know, if I do as you ask. I mean, dammit all, begging your presence, my dear,' and he sketched a bow at Cecily, 'but I must say it, what difference will it make? I dare say I'll arrange matters well enough soon enough. Soon enough, yes. Just don't have time to think of it at present, what with the Celia bein' so busy and all, very busy you know, fully booked three weeks in advance. Helps of course having topliners like dear old Marie, but even without 'em we do well – so why should I – I meantersay, Phoebe, it's not as though your children are hard pressed in any way or –'

'Indeed they are not,' Freddy said sharply and pushed back his chair as Cecily reddened slightly. 'I must go to Nellie's now, my dear, and leave you, but I do beg you, no more of this. Oliver will make his will when he's ready, and I'd take it kindly if we left the subject alone. Goodbye, Cecily, my dear. Keep yourself well. And goodbye old man – no doubt you'll be dining as usual on Sunday? Splendid, splendid. My dear –' And he kissed Phoebe's cheek and left them, shaking his head slightly at his wife as he did so.

'You men are all the same,' Phoebe said irritably, after he'd gone. 'I try to be sensible, as women usually are, are they not, Cecily?' and the silent Cecily as usual just bobbed her head at her mother. 'And what do I get but silliness from both of you! It is absurd, and I *will* say it, for a man as warm as you to be so – so *personal* about his dealings with his money. You should have a man of business to sort it all out and arrangements made for the Celia to be kept in the family when you and I are – have gone our ways and –'

'Let someone else run my affairs and I'll have fewer affairs to run,' Oliver had grunted and kissed his sister and then his niece, and gone on his way with relief. It was bad enough they had buried poor old Martha today, without this starting again.

But now, sitting at his usual corner-table, he had to admit Phoebe was right. He could not go on as he was. He had been seventy-four last birthday. Seventy-four. He sat and contemplated the long stretch of years that lay behind him, and sighed a little gustily. Seventy-four, and still running all his business affairs himself. Not even the banks knew what he was worth, or where all his assets were, for he had, with some confused notion of keeping his success quiet, opened accounts in several of the establishments in Lombard Street over the years, and to tell the truth couldn't be sure himself where all his fortune was, or even how much he had.

'It must be close on £25,000,' he thought now, and sighed again, plunged into gloom by the mere idea of such wealth. Success was a burden, really; back in the days when he had been forced to take over the Celia from his poor dead father, and had to scrimp and save and struggle to rebuild it after the fire that had nearly destroyed the Rooms as it had destroyed its owner, making money had been what it was all about. He had worked, heavens knew he had worked to make it. He thought now of the many years of desperately long nights of slog and the all-too-short mornings of sleep and wondered bleakly what it had all been for. Where was the satisfaction now?

For fun, he told himself then, trying to believe it, almost saying the word aloud. It's all for *fun*, for the joy of seeing a damned good show on that little stage, for the delight of taking unknown performers and providing the start that would lead them to the top, and then seeing them going there to become great stars. Lottie Collins, he remembered, and the Great Vance and Gus Elan and Charles Coborn who first sang his great success, 'The Man Who Broke the Bank at Monte Carlo', right here on the Celia's tiny stage – happy days. Fun days –

And now all it had led to was too much money and a sister nagging him to make a will to give it to her grandchildren. Oh, she talked sense enough in her terms. There she was with that great crew of them, and it was natural she should look out for them and where better could a man leave his money but to his own flesh and blood, his own nieces and nephews? It would be no pain to do it really, for he liked their father well – a good cove, old Freddy, one of the best, indeed rather more so than his wife was – and to leave his money to Freddy's children and their children would be reasonable enough.

But no fun. That was the trouble. No *fun*. Seventy-four I might be, he thought, watching the curtain-raising act going into his patter song, dressed in pearly-buttoned suit and billycock hat, seventy-four I might be, but I'm not dead yet, by a long chalk. Lots of life in me yet. I want to do better than just sit here and go on making more money and being nagged about making a will for it all –

The patter song went on, the man hooking his thumbs into his highly regrettable waistcoat as he capered about the stage, and the diners laughed and cheered him, putting on a happy show of being working-class music-hall patrons, while enjoying the very comfortable middle-class comforts of the Celia's superb champagne and food, and Oliver sank into an even deeper reverie.

Seventy-four, and what had he done with his life? Never married, though he had cared for girls enough. Oh, yes, he'd cared. He let an image of the young Amy come floating up into his mind's eye and sighed gently. Still pretty today was Amy, old as she was getting. She'd looked really delightful at the funeral. Must be – why, dammit, she must be gone sixty. It doesn't bear thinking of, that. And there had been one or two other pretty girls who had passed through the Celia's doors, but none of them had come to anything, and now all he had was Phoebe's family. Nice enough people, those Oram youngsters, and James's crew weren't bad, but really, they were no part of him. He needed more, now he was older. Someone of his own. Someone who would matter to *him* and only him –

The waiter who usually looked after him was standing beside the table bending solicitously. 'Sir? Mr Oliver, sir? Sorry to disturb your concentration, sir, like, but there's this young lady and gentleman, like, said as 'ow they was told by you they could come any time an' there they is, sir, and me with not a table to offer, on account the word's gone round as our Marie's on tonight and –'

'Eh? What?'

'Well, sir, I thought as 'ow, sir, maybe they could share this 'ere table, seein' as 'ow you'll be around an' about a bit, like –'

Oliver looked over the waiter's shoulder, peering into the crowded rosily-lit room and then smiled, a wide and cherubic smile, looking for the first time that evening, the waiter noticed with relief, his usual self.

'Why bless me, it's you again, is it, young man? And – well, well, well, if it isn't my dear Sophie's girl!'

'Letty, dear Uncle Oliver, it's Letty. Don't call me Sophie's girl! I mean, I am, but it's so dispiriting to be labelled by one's connections, you know!'

'Indeed, I do!' Oliver said heartily. 'Indeed I do and apologize for it. Shan't do it again. I'd not be pleased if anyone called me Jonah's boy, at that, so I should know better! It's a delight to see you, a delight – come and sit down, and we'll have a little champagne and generally blow away our blue devils!'

'Feeling the sadness of the day, sir?' Luke said and looked a little bothered. 'I'd not wish you to think I – we – were insensible of the fact that the family is in mourning, but we

33

both thought independently of coming here and so we –'

'Isn't it absurd?' Letty said, as she allowed the waiter to take her red mantle and hat. 'We both had the same idea at the same moment! I felt as low as it was possible to be and *so* in need of a little cheering and thought of you, and as I walked in the door, who should I bump into, literally, but Cousin O'Hare here.' She smiled up at her tall escort and Oliver thought suddenly, 'She's a lot handsomer than I thought, a lot handsomer –' and waved the waiter on his way with a demand for champagne and a platter of oysters and brown bread and red pepper sauce as Luke O'Hare settled Letty and then sat down himself.

'Indeed, it really is a strange coincidence,' he was saying, as Oliver took his own seat again. 'There I was, as miserable as only a man who has been hunting a job all day can be, and thinking gloomy thoughts about the profession and why I'm in it and, lo and behold, along comes someone to blow the miseries away. I sometimes have a definite feeling that I do have a guardian angel after all, though I've long realized that he must be a lazy devil for all I've seen of him this past few years.'

'Times bad, m'boy, times bad?' Oliver tapped Luke on the arm a little awkwardly. 'I've told you, if you can learn to sing, work up a nice little act –'

'It's good of you, sir, but no. It's not my line of country at all. And I don't want favours, you know. I'm not exactly a tyro, and if I can't get work by my own efforts after all these years, I've no right to be in the business –'

'Indeed, indeed,' Oliver said. 'But there's no need to be too independent! I'll keep my ears open, see what's about, let you know if I hear of anything useful. Now, champagne and – ah! Hush – there she is – our Marie!'

The red curtain had swished closed on the coster singer in his billycock hat to a fair spattering of applause, and now the little pit orchestra began to play again, this time a rather plaintive little melody and at once the audience seemed to become still for a moment, tense with expectation, and then began to clap as the red curtains swished and opened again and a buxom woman, past the first flush of youth but with a great deal of spring and energy in her steps, came on to the stage to howls of delight from the diners, many of whom banged their spoons on their glasses to ring their welcome.

'All right, all right –' she bawled as the orchestra strove to overcome the competing noise, and the listeners settled at last as the tune started once more, and the woman, in a frilled muslin dress and with a large hat very heavily trimmed with lace and birds' wings and fruit and ribbons, began to sing:

> The boy I love sits up in the gallery,
> The boy I love sits smiling down at me –
> Can't you see, a'waving of 'is hankerchee –

A plaintive tender little tune, and she gave it all the pathos and charm it could carry, her rather large protruding teeth glinting in the footlights, and Letty, watching her, was enchanted. And then almost without seeming to move she changed, became a cheeky, winking outrageous street-urchin capering and bouncing with an impudence that was totally disarming as she roared into her next song:

> I always 'old with 'avin' it if you fancy it,
> If you fancy it, that's understood –
> And what if it makes you fat,
> I don't worry over that.
> For a little of what you fancy does you good–

'Cheeky stuff,' Luke shouted in Letty's ear as the audience became even more hysterical with joy, and she shouted back, 'I know – but it's splendid for all that –' and he grinned at her, delighted to find her so sensible. Too many girls of her class turned up their well-bred noses at performers like Marie Lloyd, with their earthy reality and street wisdom, regarding them as 'vulgar'. It was a joy to meet a girl who knew how to respond to such honesty, and he found himself once more thanking whatever lucky star it was that had sent them tumbling into each other in Oliver's doorway this cold night.

It was more than half an hour before they'd let their Marie go, making her sing one after another of her most popular songs and bringing her back for chorus after chorus; but, at length, she threw one last toothy grin at them and was gone, on her way to top the bill at the Holborn Empire before going on to do the same at the Metropole in Edgware Road, and the

Celia's customers had to settle for each other and the still sweating orchestra to entertain them.

'Now we can talk,' Luke said, and smiled at her. 'At least until Oliver comes back,' for Oliver had gone to see his top-of-the-bill attraction safely into her cab and on her way. 'It really is a most fortuitous happening that we should both choose to come here tonight!'

'Isn't it?' she said and smiled widely. 'But I have to tell you the truth about why I'm here. I had the most frightful dust-up with my brother. I was so waxy, I thought I'd best be out of the way. So, I went shopping – well, looking at the shops you know – and then –'

'And then', he said as she hesitated, 'decided it was much too soon to go back and that he should be left to stew in his own juice for a while?'

She laughed delightedly. 'Yes! How did you guess that?'

'Because it is precisely what I should have done, in your shoes.'

'And why are you here? Because *you* were miserable and needed to be cheered a little?'

'Now it's your turn to know precisely how I feel. What made you think that?'

'Because this morning when we talked I thought – well, it seemed to me that you were – well – being brave, but that you weren't precisely happy at present. That you're finding your work a problem and –'

'Finding work at all is the problem,' he said and grinned at her a little crookedly.

'I thought that was the case. I'm sorry, I really am. I know how miserable it is to spend all your time doing what you don't wish to do, and how much you long to be doing something else –'

'But how can you know that? You are doing something exceedingly interesting – you can't possible be bored by *your* work. Can you?'

She reddened a little and then bent her head to watch her fingers kneading a piece of bread into pellets. 'Oh, no, not bored, precisely. It's just that – well, it's hard to explain. It's just that, well, it wasn't precisely my choice to be a medical student, you see. As long as I can remember, Mamma has told me that was what I was to be, and so I am. And it always sounded so – well, so dramatic, you know, and used to make the old ladies around Haworth open their eyes so wide when I told them my ambitions. That I enjoyed. Saying it, you know. So I just did. But now, I often think that – oh, never mind. Tell me what you did this afternoon to make you even more miserable than this morning, for you were when we met at the door, weren't you?'

'I had been looking for work and finding only leisure,' he said. 'And I don't want to talk of it. Tell me what you would rather do if you were given your choice.'

She looked at him with her head on one side, consideringly. Around them the roar of noise that well-bred people can make when they are enjoying themselves went on and on, but she could have been alone with him in a wilderness for all she was aware of them. She nodded after a long moment as though she had asked herself a question and obtained the answer she wanted, and said, 'I would like above all things to be an actress. There! I've said it. Do you think me quite absurd? Because I know I am no beauty, and lack any of the qualities actresses need –'

He shook his head almost impatiently, staring at her very closely. 'If you think an actress needs only beauty then you're quite adrift. I've met many women who call themselves actresses who are little more than faces, and no talent at all. You need to be more to be really successful in this business that I'm not actually earning my living in at the moment. Like talent, and energy – and experience. Have you ever tried?'

'At school. I was in many of our plays and poetry-readings. I've a tolerable voice you know, and my teachers said I understood Shakespeare well and –'

'Teachers!' He dismissed them all with a wave of his hand. 'They know nothing. It's what's inside you that matters! Like the *need* to make people feel and understand and cry and laugh and – it's difficult to explain. If you've got it, you know. It's the only thing that keeps me plodding on, because I know I've got it. I was born to be an actor, but the trouble is I'm still too young to play the sort of parts I'm best at. I'm a character

37

actor, you see, not just a pretty youth. I could easily play Lear, now, at thirty, and I know it. But these managements – they look at me and say, 'Hmm, not exactly a lead juvenile, are you? Come back in a few years, my boy, when you've matured into the parts! Then we'll cast you.' Pah! Such idiots. And here I am eating my heart out, knowing what I've got and none of them will let me give it. Well, I'll get there eventually – the thing is, are you sure in the same way? If you want to be an actress then you've got to be very sure –'

She stared at him, her forehead puckered. 'No one's ever taken me seriously before when I've said anything about acting. School people, I mean. I wouldn't dare to tell Mamma, of course, but I did tell teachers. And they talked only of – of propriety and the difficulty of young well-brought-up girls being in such an occupation and so forth and said I should forget it, and be happy doing drawing-room theatricals when I married and had my own establishment. So, that was that. And now you're saying –'

'I'm saying nothing. I'm just asking you how much you *need* to act. For if you don't have a great need burning your belly, then you'll never get anywhere.'

He was quite different now, no longer the polite and charming young man she had met that morning, but a bigger person, sitting here with his eyes wide and dark with the intensity of what he was saying; his shoulders outlined squarely and heavily against the smoky glow of the big dining-room made him seem older and yet stronger, a greater presence altogether and she felt her chest tighten with a lift of excitement and said tentatively, 'I don't know. I've never dared to think about it, you see. How could I, with Mamma so heaven bent on making a doctor of me? It matters more to her than anything. It is all she's thought of for me since I was born, I swear it. She had a sister once, you see. She was called Lettice too, but she died when there was a typhoid epidemic in the village, and Mamma has never really forgotten her, I think. And when she named me for her, she's told me, she swore I'd make it real for her sister Letty. That I'd do for her all the things she couldn't do for herself because she'd died when she was only twenty-three. So that's how it's always been – I'm to be a doctor, like Mamma. How can I know about acting, when – when I've never dared to think properly about it?'

'But you have thought about it, haven't you?' He still had that special look, still seemed older and stronger, and she felt the comfort of being with him spread further and further into her.

'Yes. Often. But not properly, you understand. Just dreaming. Never planning. Only wishing –'

'Do you know many actors? Know what the life is like?'

She laughed aloud at that. 'How could I possibly? I only know doctors and mill-owners and – and landladies and patients and people like that. You're the first actor I've ever talked to properly.'

'Would you like to meet more?'

'Indeed I would!'

'There'll be some people at Chelsea Reach tonight. There always are. Will you come?'

'Now? To Chelsea? With you?'

He looked impatient suddenly. 'Yes! I'm asking you – come and meet some other actors, find out what it is you might be missing. Or escaping, as the case might be.'

'Barty –' she murmured and looked down at the little fob-watch pinned to her bodice. It was almost eleven o'clock. 'Barty. And tomorrow – I must be at the hospital at nine –'

He said nothing, just looking at her, waiting a little impatiently, and she said after a moment, 'Yes – I think I will. Why not? I'm a grown woman, after all –'

He laughed then. 'Indeed you are, indeed you are!' He looked round for Oliver and some of the extra presence he had seemed to dwindle and he was the charming young man again, agreeable and friendly but without that extra excitement, and for a moment she regretted agreeing to go with him. But then she caught his eye and he smiled and she decided she was not sorry at all, and she *would* go. And she pushed away the image of Barty's disapproving face which rose to her mind's eye.

'Uncle Oliver!' Luke was saying. 'You've been so kind. Thank you immensely for your hospitality. And for that splendid show. She is quite magnificent, is she not?'

'An old friend, a very old friend of mine,' Oliver said

puffing himself up a little and smiling happily. 'Glad you came tonight. Will you both come again? It's so delightful to see such cheerful members of the family about the place – delightful. And one day, when there's more time, we can talk of the theatre and the work you'd like to do, m'boy. Shan't offer you work, promise you that, but I know people, you see, know 'em all. Might be able to help you along the way, find you a berth that suits you – come again soon.'

He watched them go to the doorway together, Luke holding Letty's arm in a protective grip, and gave another of his little sighs. Now, if only he had a pair of young ones like *that* to call his own; how agreeable that would be, how comforting. And wouldn't that stop Phoebe nagging, wouldn't it just.

After a moment, his lips curved into a little smile, as the curtain by the doorway billowed and settled again behind the departing figures. Now, there was an interesting thought. Wasn't it?

4

She could smell the river as soon as they got out of the hansom, and when Luke had paid the man, and the horse had gone clattering away down Cheyne Walk towards Albert Bridge and its warm stable in Lambeth, she stood for a moment in the dank air with her head up, letting the scent of rotting wood and green water and mud fill her nostrils.

'You like the river?' Luke said, and his voice sounded loud in the dimness.

'I hardly ever see it,' Letty said. 'I remember once, just after I first came to London in the summer, going to Hampton Court. But that was different –'

He laughed. 'Very different. There it's all picnics and swans and prettiness. Here it's shrieking gulls and boats full of rubbish and heaven knows what villains lurking below the Embankment!' And he tucked one hand into the crook of her elbow to lead her along the pavement to number 47. 'But it's more than that, for nearly all of the people who live hereabouts are artists and sculptors and so forth, though there are writers, and some ordinary people too. A splendid mixture – for me that's one of the charms of the place. I couldn't abide to live somewhere like that house in Tavistock Square, where everyone is so – well, I musn't be insulting to your family again, must I?'

'No,' she said a little primly, but smiled in the darkness. 'Who does this house belong to, then? A painter or a sculptor or a writer or an *ordinary* person?'

'That is not kind in you!' He pushed open the gate and led the way up the brick path, and she could just see the cut privet hedge dripping sadly on each side of it as they passed. 'I did not mean to sound as though I was insulting people who are not artists, of course! I just meant –'

'I was teasing. I knew what you meant,' she said. 'And of course artists *are* very extraordinary, aren't they? I never met one, of course, not a real one, only people who play a little with water-colours, not people who actually work all the time at it, and I am sure they're remarkable. So, is this house that of a writer or an artist?'

But he had rung the bell and the door had been opened by a neat parlourmaid before he could answer her, and he stood back to let her go in before him, and she did, feeling suddenly shy and gauche. There was a good deal of noise coming down the stairs from the direction of the drawing-room, loud voices and laughter and a piano playing a ragtime tune in a sketchy but sprightly manner, and anxiety lifted in her chest. She really shouldn't be here, so late at night, with a comparative stranger, although of course he *was* a family connection, and Barty would be very nasty about it all and – and she turned her head to say as much to Luke, but he was already struggling out of his coat, and the parlourmaid was standing waiting expectantly for hers, so she bit her tongue and took off her mantle and hat and allowed herself to be led up the stairs.

The house was decorated in the same very modern style that Phoebe had used for her Tavistock Square drawing-room, except that here the colours were yellow and mauve and much more lavishly used, there being not an inch on any surface that was not painted or covered in fabric, and the sinuous curves of the furniture and carpet design were much more luscious and twisting. It was like walking through a Bond Street art gallery and she thought of the last time she had gone to the theatre, to see the D'Oyly Carte company in *Patience*; '– a greenery yallery Grosvenor Gallery foot-in-the-grave young man!'

But the young man who was now standing by the balustrade on the upper landing was anything but 'a haggard and lank young man' like the one in Gilbert's song; he seemed to be square in every way, with a square solid jaw and square solid shoulders and hands and trunk – even his eyes, it seemed to Letty, looking up at him, were square and solid.

But then he smiled, and his face changed, losing its slightly solemn look and becoming all cheerfulness as he cried, 'Luke, you wretch, where *have* you been? There's Jessica been nagging this past hour, and Philip asking and Johanna and dear old Septimus Scott and all totally *bouleversé* because you're not here to amuse them. And who might this charmer be? Welcome, ma'am, to the Zander Collection, and *why* have we not met before? I thought I knew every interesting woman in all London, and here you are, all –'

'Pay no attention to him whatsoever, Letty,' Luke said and grinned at her. 'May I present my good friend Edwin Zander, who talks far more than any man should but can't help it, poor chap, because he's just an ignorant American and –'

'And he is an even more ignorant South African and a sly one to boot, hiding you. *Where* did he find you?'

'At a funeral,' Letty said and smiled and held out her hand. 'I am Lettice Brotherton Lackland, Mr Zander, and I am happy to meet you.'

He took her hand in both of his and beamed up at her – for now she had reached the first-floor landing she discovered she was taller than Edwin by half a head. 'Not nearly as happy as I am to meet you. At a funeral, you say? How very stylish! Or does it just mean that you're a relative of this wretched creature here? Well! You look mighty fit on such a connection, ma'am, mighty fit!' And he let go her hand to slap Luke on the back and then to lead them amiably into his drawing-room.

Letty felt she had never seen so many extraordinary people at one time in all her life. She was not unused to crowded social occasions; from her earliest youth her Mamma had taken her to as many such gatherings as presented themselves, believing it necessary to her education. Balls and receptions in Bradford and Keighley, private parties in the rich mill-owners' houses around Haworth and Skipton, had been regular experiences in her younger years, and since coming to London she had spent long hours with the medical students at Nellie's all crushed together in the lecture-room. But all that had been no preparation for this crowd, who were, she decided after one startled glance, as exotic as a cage full of parakeets.

The men were the ones she noticed first; such lavish whiskers on chins and cheeks, such flowing locks on noble heads, such ferocious eyes and gleaming teeth – everywhere she looked there seemed to be such men until she blinked and looked again and saw that there were others who were, comfortingly, more commonplace: older men with balding heads and sparse white hair and younger ones with neat moustaches and far from noble heads, indeed, quite ordinary people, but even they had an air of strangeness about them. They wore soft collared shirts and velvet jackets and flowing silken cravats which quite belied their mature years and ordinary faces and she felt her lips curve as she looked at them.

And then the smile faded as she looked at the women, and felt at once exceedingly dowdy in her neat black serge. Many of them, too, wore their hair dramatically loose, often bound with a fillet of silver or gold cord round the forehead, with matching tassels at the back which hung down to blend artlessly with their curling locks. They too affected the Bohemian style, many of them being dressed in loose robes or richly painted silk with their arms emerging, pale and interesting, from drooping fabric-heavy sleeves.

She touched her own gown nervously, all too aware of its shortcomings and then relaxed a little as Luke murmured in her ear, 'Oh, no – such a collection! Most of the most dismal hangers-on. Not the people I hoped you would meet. Don't be put out by them, please. You'll find some of them are quite tolerable. Ignore the silly ones, that's all!'

'Dearest!' A voice fluted beside them and Luke turned and smiled at the girl who was standing there, her hair, a light reddish gold which was dressed in a mode that was half-way between the currently high-on-the-head look, that most of the girls Letty knew used, and the loose Bohemian style of the other women in the room, lit to a gleaming richness by the electric chandelier overhead. Her gown was a very fetching soft green, well-fitted and only a little *outré*, compared with the other women around her. Letty felt more frumpish than ever as she looked at her, for the girl had, in addition, an exceedingly pretty face with big round blue eyes and a skin that was flushed a soft rose.

'Jessica!' Luke said, and sounded genuinely pleased. 'How good to see you! I thought you were playing the North somewhere with Irving?'

'My dear, hadn't you heard? Ill, poor man – quite ill! They've cut the tour and what could I do but come to London to see what was happening? Not much, I can tell you – I swear I've been to every management there is, and not one of them with more than a civil good morning to offer, and expecting me to be grateful for that.'

'Don't I know it!' Luke said with great feeling. 'I spent the afternoon the same way – oh!' Suddenly he remembered Letty standing beside him. 'Letty may I present Miss Jessica Kemp – Jess, my cousin Letty Lackland.'

'Oh – howdedo?' Jessica flashed a glance at Letty, and a swift but clearly not very interested smile, and turned back at once to Luke, tucking her hand into his elbow and managing to draw him into the crowded room, leaving Letty standing at the door. 'Now, do tell me, dearest, to whom did you go, and what did they say and –'

'Oh good!' Edwin Zander said on her other side and drew her, in her turn, further into the room. 'Now I have you all to myself to show off. Now, come and meet everyone. Such *lovely* people, everyone of them. Philip Steer, may I present Miss Lackland – Miss Walker, Mrs Bryans, Wenlock Rollins, Miss Lackland, Septimus Scott, Miss Lackland –'

He shot from group to group, dragging her with him, introducing her at such a rate that she hardly had a moment to acknowledge them all, let alone speak to them. But at last he reached the centre of the room and the press of people made it inevitable that he slow down, and she could respond to his presentations.

And could be responded to, which was more to the point. A tall and painfully thin middle-aged man looked at her and said hopefully, 'D'you work in stone, by any chance, Miss Lackland? We've a place going, you know, at the Great Cheyne Studios and if we don't find an agreeable tenant for ourselves Palmer and I may well find ourselves saddled with some oaf like Septimus Scott over there – don't say I said that, of course, but I'm sure you'll understand how we feel. Unless you're an admirer of said egregious Scott and his hideous productions of course, in which case forget I spoke. But you look too intelligent to be anything so foolish. Tell me, Miss

Lackland, what *do* you work in?'

She blinked a little, surprised at the intensity of his words, for his face was lugubrious in the extreme and showed no change in expression however venomous his speech. 'In a hospital, actually,' she ventured and the man stared at her, and then at Zander and said blankly, 'What?'

'Oh, how, exactly? Are you one of Miss Nightingale's young ladies?' A plump woman in a particularly shapeless and very old William Morris print gown who was standing beside the tall man peered up at her. 'I have a cousin who has a daughter who wishes to be a nurse – very laudable, indeed. I have such admiration for you, a most disagreeable task, so unaesthetic, yet so full of soul –'

'No, I am not a nurse,' Letty said, a little nettled. She was so often asked this that sometimes she wanted to snap her answer back. 'I am a medical student at Nellie's – Queen Eleanor's hospital, in Covent Garden. I have been –'

'Glory be!' the tall man said. 'Palmer – come over here! Here's a remarkable thing, now, a New Woman who really *is* new – one who does something about getting her place in a man's world and not just talks about it –'

'What is it, Gillick?' The man called Palmer was as short and heavy as his friend was tall and thin. 'Have you found us a tenant for the back studio? There's Scott over there swearing he'll –'

'No such luck – but interesting for all that. A lady doctor, no less! Or will be. Miss – Lackland, I think you said?'

'Lackland?' The dumpy little woman said thoughtfully. 'I know that name – Sir Frederick Lackland Caspar, is he a connection?'

'My mother's cousin,' Letty said, and looked over her shoulder, a little alarmed as other people came towards her, attracted by the vivacity of the group around her. 'She was a medical student at Nellie's herself for a while, before she went to the Royal Free, that is – well, not precisely a medical student. She worked there as a nurse at first, but one with special opportunities and – well, I'm sure that is not very interesting and –'

'My dear, it's *riveting*,' Zander said. 'You're the first lady

46

doctor I've ever seen, let alone met, though I'm told I once knew one at home in Baltimore. But that was another *world*. Do tell us now –'

'I'm not a doctor yet, you know,' Letty said almost desperately. 'Just a student in my first year in London, and much to learn yet. I doubt sometimes I shall ever complete my training, to tell the truth, because –'

'Because she has a fancy for our profession, Edwin my old friend,' Luke said, and pushed through the people to stand beside her, and the relief must have shown on her face for he looked reassuringly at her and smiled. 'So we'll have none of you trotting out your symptons for the poor girl –'

'Too bad, too bad,' Edwin said with a mock grumbling note in his voice. 'And here was I all ready and eager to display my most *fascinating* disorders for her, and you come along and spoil it all.'

'Stage-struck, Miss Lackland, was it?' Jessica was there now, too, and was leaning against Zander in a proprietorial fashion that happened also to display her very pretty figure to great advantage. 'So many people who know nothing at all of the profession fall in love with it, don't they, Luke? Ah, well, they get over it, I dare say, when they discover how difficult it all is. The trouble is we make it look so easy, do we not? The art that disguises art –'

'Not at all,' Luke said roughly. 'It's not that difficult a profession if you get the feeling right. *Live* the part, read the lines as though you thought of them for yourself in a moment of emotional experience – and then it's easy. It's natural, not forced, and comes out the way it should. That's the real art of acting, not mere gloss and artifice –'

'Now, Luke, I've told you before, that's all very well, but in practice it doesn't work for your average bread-and-butter performer –'

A man in a green velvet jacket with a neatly-pointed beard and the darkest eyes Letty had even seen spoke up from the far side of the group. 'It's making sure the wretches can learn the lines written for them and know their way about the stage, that's what matters – I've suffered too many productions with country characters who ache for the boards marching about like ducks on a pond and driving every competent actor around them to perdition and back not to think otherwise. I've told you before –'

'No, no, no!' A tall girl in a strange crimson gown that looked to Letty as much like a sack as a woman's garment, spoke with great intensity. 'You couldn't be more wrong, Stanforth! In my opinion –'

'They're off, they're off!' Edwin cried and threw his hands in the air in mock despair. 'Come, Miss Lackland, we shall have a little supper and leave these thespians to talk their heads off. I have all *sorts* of delicious comestibles set ready in the dining-room, and we are to eat alfresco, for it's much more fun that way. Now, do tell me, Miss Lackland –'

'Please, call me Letty,' she said, as she allowed him to lead her towards the door. 'And really you know, it is getting late, and perhaps I should be –'

'Letty, such a delightful name! My Mamma had a friend called Letty and I loved her dearly, and I'm sure I shall love you dearly too, as I love all my friends. Now, we have some excellent Bradenham ham and a heap of the most delectable *pâté de foie* you ever saw, besides the most wicked ices and cakes, wicked because I insist always that my chef puts twice as much cream in as he should and I'm sure that is why I become ever rounder with each day that passes –' And he patted his undoubtedly well-modelled belly and looked back over his shoulder at her with such a comical expression on his face that she could not help but laugh as she followed him down the stairs.

The dining-room was as pretty and as elegant as the drawing-room, but coloured in a more restful green and cream and she looked around with appreciation as he loaded a plate for her and then led her to one of the small tables against the wall as numbers of his guests followed them into the room and fell on the laden table as though they had not been fed for a week. Clearly Edwin Zander was a generous host, and his guests made the most of his offerings.

They were joined very swiftly by several others, and she sat there crushed against the comfortable bulk of Edwin and listened as they chattered on and on about acting, about music, about books she had never read, and people she had never heard of, and pretended to be interested and to eat the food in front of her even though she really was not hungry at all. She was feeling tired now and a little dispirited, although she told herself firmly that had nothing to do with the fact that she could see Luke on the other side of the big room listening attentively as the red head of Miss Jessica Kemp bobbed busily with the vivacity of her conversation. She was no child, she did not need wet-nursing at a party, even though it was one at which she knew no one; she did not depend entirely on the goodwill of the person who had brought her, and if he chose to spend his time with people with ridiculous red-gold hair, that was his affair. She cared not a whit. It was just that she was getting a little tired.

'My dear man, let them vote and at once we have anarchy!' the man Gillick was saying in response to something Zander had said about an event he had heard of in Manchester. 'You know that as well as I do, and to suggest that women are as fit to vote as men is to bring anarchy into the world. Look at your servant girls. Look at the models who drape themselves all over our studios so badly because they are so stupid. Look at –'

'And what about the hansom cab drivers who care for nothing but rooking us of tuppences? And what about the street beggars and the muffin men who are stupid as any servant girl, and –'

'And what about Septimus Scott?' Palmer said, and everyone laughed, for at once Gillick snorted with disgust. 'Well, be reasonable, man! There are as many stupid men unfit to vote as there are women and –'

'There are more stupid women, however. Look how grateful one is to meet a female who has some wit and ambition, instead of one who is a crushing bore –'

'Nonsense!' Letty blinked, startled to hear her own voice. 'That really is nonsense, Mr Gillick. I have more often been bored to tears by a man's prosing on and on about matters he barely understands than you have suffered women doing the same thing. We, poor creatures, are taught from our infancy how great a sin it is to bore a man, and are most carefully educated to recognize the signs of tedium and to stop at once if the man we are with seems at all put out. But no man ever thinks himself bound to consider the sufferings of his female companions as he goes droning on and on in his ignorance – I assure you, Mr Gillick, women are as intelligent as men, as fit to vote as men, and in many ways more fit!'

'I knew it,' Gillick said lugubriously. 'A New Woman of the painful sort. I withdraw my invitation to be a tenant in our studio, even if you do decide to leave your hospital to the men and become a sculptress, which heaven forfend –'

'You must forgive him, Miss Lackland,' Palmer said as the others round the table laughed. 'My colleague here always behaves badly when he is worsted in an argument. And you worsted him. I agree with you wholly – there is no reason at all why women shouldn't have the vote once they are of an age to show wisdom and –'

'The same age as the men, surely!' Letty said swiftly. 'Why should they have to wait till they are thirty when the men vote at twenty-one?'

'Because most women are so ill-educated that they need more time to equip themselves for the rigours of the ballot-box, Miss Lackland. You must surely agree that it is an awesome responsibility –'

'So awesome that shopkeepers and cab-drivers and firemen who can barely write their names regularly worry themselves into their graves every time an election comes around to alarm them,' Letty retorted. 'I do see the power of your argument, indeed I do!'

A crack of laughter went up and she reddened, aware of holding the centre of the group, and she subsided as Luke appeared on the far side of the table and raised his brows at her.

'I see you've taken to us here, Letty,' he said. 'Arguing already! – it's the life-blood of this house, you know. There's nothing Edwin enjoys better than verbal fireworks, unless it's a few fisticuffs. Now, that he *really* enjoys, hmm, Edwin?'

'Not as much as handsome interesting ladies,' Zander said promptly, and leaned over to pat Letty on the arm. 'I couldn't be more delighted that Luke brought you to us, Letty. You must come to us often and cure our foolishness. We shall start a committee at once to fight for votes for women, if you like. How will that be?'

'Exceedingly dull, I should think,' Jessica's voice drawled over Letty's shoulder and she looked up, and reddened even more for as she did so Jessica caught Luke's eye across the group and gave him a conspiratorial smile that made Letty feel she had been caught eavesdropping. 'I met some of these women in Manchester, and I can't tell you, my dears – so dreary I nearly fell asleep whenever they uttered a word. There are so many more exciting things to do that I can't see any need for fussing about politics –'

'It will be the vote that will give us the chance to get all we want from the world –' Letty said hotly and then wished she hadn't, for Jessica produced a smile of pure delight and said silkily, 'But my dear, it is the easiest thing you can imagine to get what you want in this world! Just ask a man for it! I never have any difficulty at all, I do assure you!'

Another crack of laughter and then Edwin stood up and clapped his hands and cried, 'My dears, all of you, there's to be music now! I've asked the most charming lady – Maria Colleano – to join us as soon as the Opera is over – she sings only in the chorus at present, but she will one day be a great diva, I'm quite sure, and I believe I heard her at the door, so upstairs, all of you, and settle yourselves beside the piano. Peter, I *know* you will play for her. We can have some more of your precious ragtime later on – and dear old Ernest, stop looking so glum and come and help me arrange chairs and so forth –'

There was a surge of movement towards the door, and Letty was grateful for she felt a lift of fury in her at Jessica's mocking glance, even more than at what she had said, and she knew her own hot temper too well, especially at the end of so extraordinary and exhausting a day, to trust it.

'Luke,' she said quietly as the others moved away. 'I trust it won't be regarded as discourteous if I leave quietly now? I have the most nasty of headaches, and it's very late and –'

'Of course,' Luke said. 'I dare say you do feel the fatigue of the day. And I didn't bargain for one of Edwin's protégées from the Opera myself! I must be honest and say that I'm not in the mood for one of the divas of the future – or the present, come to that, and I'll be glad to escape too. I'll say your farewells to Edwin, shall I? And tell him you will visit again? He truly wants you to, you know. He isn't a total poseur!'

Letty smiled briefly and tried to look pleased. 'How kind,' she said. 'Very kind. I do have my studies, of course, and –'

'– And you still want to meet more actors, don't you?' He spoke as though she had said nothing. 'Tonight he had a top-heavy pile of his sculptors and painters – that man Gillick is really tiresome – but another time it will be better. You'll see.'

'Well –' she began dubiously and then bit her lip as Jessica Kemp appeared at the dining-room again.

'Luke,' she cried and made a small moue. 'Here you are! Edwin sent me to find you. Do come upstairs, my love. This Colleano creature is about to pour forth her all and they need you –'

'I must see Miss Lackland home, Jessica,' Luke said. 'Please tell Edwin, will you? I'll see him when I get back –'

'And I shall be here too –' Jessica said at the same moment that Letty, mortified with embarrassment, said, 'But I can go home alone, Luke, there is no need to escort me –'

Jessica smiled sweetly at her. 'There, you see, Miss Lackland? We don't need any votes do we, when the men are so caring of our welfare? Very well, Luke, I shall tell Edwin, and we shall see you when you return. Goodbye, Miss Lackland, and Luke, do be quick, for there's so much I still want to tell you –'

And she was gone, leaving Letty to follow Luke to the front door and to be helped into her mantle, that handsome red mantle she'd put on with such high spirits so short a time ago though it seemed like an eternity now, feeling like a tired child rather than the New Woman she had set herself up to be.

5

The students were collecting at the top end of the ward as usual, their voices kept low as they gossiped, watching carefully for Sister Sycamore, who was, of all the hospital's terrifying sisters, the most terrifying.

All down the long room with its serried ranks of beds the frilled-capped nurses bustled, their print dresses and vast starched white aprons swishing busily as they went from bed to bed straightening the counterpanes, arranging each turned-down sheet at its precise eighteen-inch level, plumping pillows and generally making each patient look as much like the others as possible. Sister Sycamore admired neatness above all things; Sister Sycamore liked highly-polished brass fittings; Sister Sycamore had a taste for tidily-aligned heads on pillows, and such was the power of Sister Sycamore's personality that her tastes were as law in her domain. Woe betide any patient and above all nurse who dared to do anything to mar the perfection of her view of Sycamore Ward.

Of all Nellie's sisters she was the one who least objected to the loss of her personal name (for it was a long tradition here that all sisters bore the names of their wards rather than their own; Sister Elm and Sister Spruce as well as Sister Sycamore looking after the men, Sister Buttercup and Snowdrop and Primrose taking care of the children, and Marigold and Violet and Woodbine the women) for as far as she was concerned it was right and proper it should be so. The only way a ward at Nellie's could be well run, she would tell her nurses over and over again, was with total selflessness and total devotion to the tasks involved. Sister Sycamore, who, when she was not working, slept and ate in a tiny room that ran off one side of her ward and who had never been seen out of her uniform with its high sugar-icing starched cap and floating ribbons, embodied all that a ward sister should be, and it was natural that she should. Had she not been taught by the great Abel Lackland himself, the founder of Nellie's, when she had been a raw young girl? ('Sister Sycamore a *girl*?' ribald students had been known to mutter. 'Never! She was born at the age of fifty!') And had she not been a friend of Miss Martha Lackland who had known Miss Nightingale in her prime? And had she not been a close intimate of old Nancy, the first of Nellie's sisters, who had lived to be gone eighty and who had made the nursing tradition at Nellie's all it should be? Indeed she had, and she never forgot all that, and never allowed anyone else to do so either.

Especially students. Sister Sycamore despised and loathed students as the lowest form of hospital life, even lower than the junior probationer nurses whom she harried so mercilessly. Students, in Sister Sycamore's opinion, were useless hulks who cluttered up her ward to small purpose and needed constant vigilance if they were to be prevented from committing some fearful act of mayhem on her patients – a view that changed miraculously the day they qualified and became doctors, after which she treated them with the proper respect and amity due to their status. It took a brave and remarkable student to emerge from his three years walking the wards at Nellie's without scars from Sister Sycamore's bitter tongue.

But for all the scorn she poured on the men students, she had ample left for Letty, whom she regarded as so low a form of life as to be virtually invisible. When Letty had first enrolled and been taken round the hospital by her cousin, Sir Frederick, Sister Sycamore had looked at her, tipping her chin high in the air – for she was a diminutive lady – and said nothing. She had just looked at Letty, and then at Sir Frederick and sighed very softly. And that was all. And today she was as distant with Letty as she had been on every other occasion she had met her since.

Not that Letty minded all that much today. She stood with her back to the big main doors, as they all waited for Sir Frederick to come and start his teaching round, and let Sister Sycamore share out the day's cases to the other students, leaving her out as she usually did, and made no shift at all to insist – again as she usually did – that she should be assigned one. It just didn't matter; not when she had so much to think about.

She stood there staring down the long ward, at the slanting bars of sunlight that patterned the polished wooden floor beneath the high windows, and saw nothing of it. She heard the rattle of trolleys and the faint hiss of weary breathing from the nearest patients and the crackle of flames from the fireplace in the great central stack, and listened to none of it; she smelled the odours of wax polish and carbolic and illness and spring flowers from the vases set on the central stack and registered none of it.

All she could see was herself, walking along the pavement towards Mrs Partridge's front door in Gilbert Place with Luke by her side, little more than a shape in the darkness, for the side street lights had long since gone out leaving lighting only in the main thoroughfares. All she could hear was the echoing rhythm of their footsteps on the stones as they moved through the midnight chill. And all she could feel was the faint touch of his lips on her cheek and his hands on her shoulders as he bade her goodnight.

It had been so startling, all of it. She had left Chelsea Reach in a seething temper, so put about by Jessica Kemp's behaviour that she could have burst out into a torrent of words, and so filled with irritation at Luke for finding the horrid creature agreeable that she wanted to shout at him, too. But he had spoken so cheerfully in the hansom he had found to take her home to Bloomsbury, had been so warm and amusing that she had been quite convinced long before they reached Knightsbridge, only half-way home, that she was the silly captious one, that to be offended by a person like Jessica Kemp was to be sillier than the girl herself and that to be irritated with Luke was childish nonsense. It was not his fault the girl was a flibberty idiot!

So it had been a delightful ride through the almost deserted streets, occupied only by a few late roisterers going home and the occasional policemen in their shining black capes and helmets stumping heavily from shop doorway to shop doorway, talking to him, laughing with him, just feeling comfortable with him. And then, as he delivered her to her doorway, had set her key in the lock for her, had kissed her in that cheerful almost casual fashion, she had been left speechless. Of course it was just a cousinly salute, no more than that. A mere brushing of her cheek with his lips, a mere clasping of her shoulders, but all the same –

The students swayed, rustled and came to a sort of ragged attention as the big double-doors whispered open and Sir Frederick came in, his spare shoulders neat and straight under his morning coat and his thin hair, almost white now but with a sandy rustiness about it that remembered the strength of its original colour, arranged neatly over the balding crown.

'Good morning, gentlemen, ma'am,' he said and Letty blinked and returned to the here and now at the sound of the greeting he had devised to include her always; other surgeons and physicians who taught Nellie's students addressed the group always as 'gentlemen' making no shift at all to recognize that one of their number was anything but, but never Sir Frederick, punctilious, kindly and always rather worried-looking Sir Frederick. She really must try to pay attention to him this morning, however abstracted she felt, for he deserved it; and she caught a glance from Barty at the other side of the group, his tiresome pompous 'now-you-behave-yourself' admonitory look and she bit her lip and refused to look at him.

She had had enough of Barty, who had nagged all through breakfast, and all the way on the walk to the hospital, and she would not, she would *not* pay an atom more attention to him. However justified he was in his complaints. She had to admit that last night she had behaved badly. He had been almost out of his mind with anxiety for her, poor Barty, when she walked into their sitting-room, swinging her red hat by its ribbons and with a half-smile still on her lips, and she should not have laughed at him so saucily and gone sailing off to bed and slammed the door in his face the way she had. She would have been just as anxious had their situations been reversed, quite terrified for his welfare, and she had treated his concern with no respect at all. But all the same, she had suffered for her sauciness, listening to him go on and on this morning, and saying not a word in her own defence, so she had paid her shot. Enough was enough – she'd ignore him from now on; and just think about that journey home last night and the way Luke had held her shoulders and kissed her cheek to say goodnight –

'Miss Lackland!' She started and her gaze, which had glazed over, sharpened and she looked round to find them all staring at her, Barty with a look of hopeless disapproval on his face, Sister Sycamore with that wooden glare that behoved ill for everyone and Sir Frederick a little pained, while the other students barely concealed their grins.

'Miss Lackland, I fear you slept ill last night? I do not usually have to address you three times before you reply,' Sir Frederick said reprovingly and Letty blushed to the roots of her hair.

'I'm sorry, sir,' she mumbled. 'So sorry, just thinking – didn't mean to –'

'I wished to know, Miss Lackland, whether you intend to make this morning's round with us or whether you would prefer to leave us before we commence?'

'Sir?'

He sighed softly. 'Clearly you have not been listening for some time, Miss Lackland. I have already explained that today we are to discuss the role played in urinary disorders of the male by enlargements of the prostate gland. This will involve some investigations of parts of the male anatomy you may prefer to avoid sharing with us. It will be possible for you to make the studies necessary for your examinations in text books, and you can study the relevant anatomical structure in the anatomy room. I merely wish to know if you prefer to leave the study of the living patient to us –'

She tilted her chin, and was glad she had already blushed at his rebuke, for at least that meant she could not blush again.

'Of course I remain with the round, sir,' she said. 'You will remember it was agreed when I joined the school that I would receive no special concern due to my sex, and I am not, after all, the first female student that has been at Queen Eleanor's –'

'No,' he said, and turned to begin his walk, 'but I wished to give you the opportunity to withdraw should you feel some delicacy about the morning's subject. Very well, gentlemen, ma'am, we shall discuss. Who is our first patient, Sister?'

'Mr Cranmer, sir, if you please.' Sister Sycamore rustled the papers in her hand. 'He was admitted last night with acute retention. Mr Fenton-Smith passed a catheter with some difficulty, and drew off thirty-seven ounces of urine, which when tested showed pus and blood to be present in some quantity. The catheter was left *in situ*, and drained a further twenty-two ounces this morning and he seems a little more comfortable now. However, he has some fever, and complains of pains in the loins and has a furred tongue and foul breath –'

She jerked her head, and at once a junior nurse came with screens and the first bed was surrounded by them as the students shuffled alongside to stare solemnly at the man in it over Sir Frederick's shoulder.

She tried very hard to pay attention as the sheets were pulled back, and the man's belly and genitals were exposed, tried hard to listen to what Sir Frederick was saying about the effects of occlusion of the urinary tract by enlargement of the prostate gland and tried hard to be interested in the facts he gave regarding the hazards of surgery and the problems of infection and bladder-drainage in such cases, but it was no use.

All she could think of was the night before, in Chelsea Reach. Of the glitter of the people she had seen there, of the talk and the sound of ragtime piano music and the laughter and the gossip – all so far away and so different from this vast room with its quiet bedfast patients filling the air with the scent of their anxiety and disease, its crackling fire that did so little to bring real comfort to the chill of the place, and the drone of Sir Frederick's voice going on and on about kidneys and bladders.

The patient was examined and the talk went on and on, students offering their answers to Sir Frederick's careful questions, and again she tried to listen, admiring Barty for his quick grasp of the principles of the case, and the others too for their abilities, and saying nothing herself, grateful to Sir Frederick for not questioning her. The procession moved on to the next bed, and then the next and she trailed behind as the morning ground on its long way, thinking her own thoughts, caressing her agreeable memories of the previous day and listening less and less to what was going on around her.

Until they reached their last case and Sir Frederick sent the students scattering about their tasks with individual patients, this one to pass a catheter under Sister Sycamore's gorgon eye, that one to dress a suppurating wound, the other one to test the rows of malodorous flasks that stood ready in the urine-testing annexe by the sluice and she breathed deeply at last, looking forward to slipping away quietly, grateful to Sister Sycamore for not giving her a task to do and so working for her benefit, rather than the reverse. But Sir Frederick's voice pulled her back.

'Miss Lackland!'

'Sir Frederick?' She paused with her hands on the big double-doors, and lifted her brows at him.

'I would appreciate a word with you. In ten minutes, please. In my office. And – er – Miss Lackland. You may remove your gown if you are leaving the ward.'

Again she reddened, and looked down at the calico gown that covered her neat blue worsted working-dress, and bobbed her head and began to untie the strings that held it in place behind. It had long been a rule at Nellie's that students making rounds in the surgical wards should wear washable coverings to their own clothes, and to have forgotten she was doing so was very clear index of how abstracted she was, and how uninterested she had been in the morning's activities. It had been bad enough that one of the junior nurses had had to hiss a reminder to her to put a gown on when she had first come into the ward; to have to be reminded again to take it off was almost the outside of enough.

She went on her way soberly, walking down the polished wooden stairs that led from the second floor where the surgical wards were to the great hall below, with its black-and-white tiles underfoot and the sombre statue of the founder, Abel Lackland, glowering down from its corner, feeling exceedingly low. It was all wrong to feel like this; to be so withdrawn from her work, to find it all so burdensome.

'Burdensome,' she whispered beneath her breath as she reached the door that led to Sir Frederick's private office on the far side of the little lodge where Nellie's head porter, resplendent in blue serge and brass buttons and silver-gilt medals held sway over all the visitors and outpatients who dared to cross his hallowed portals. 'Burdensome. It shouldn't be like that – burdensome.'

But it had been so for weeks now, and was getting worse. Opening a book to study was a chore, not the solid if quiet pleasure it had been in her schooldays when learning languages and history and philosophy. Thinking about patients and their ills was distasteful, if not downright disagreeable sometimes, instead of interesting, and she would watch her fellow students sit and talk to their patients and make their examinations, obviously fascinated and concerned in spite of their usual posture of ribaldry, and wonder why she could not find the same involvement they did. She would listen to the physicians and surgeons discussing knotty points of medical practice and find boredom struggling in her, and feel guilty about it. This was what she had worked for all those long years at school. This was what she had planned for and dreamed of, ever since she had been a child – to be a medical student at Nellie's.

'This is what *Mamma* planned for and dreamed of,' she whispered to herself, standing there in front of Sir Frederick's tall window and staring out at the street beneath full of bustling busy people, and shuffling sick people, and hopeful people, and fearful people, all coming to and from Nellie's, the core of their well-being here in their noisy slum. 'It isn't what *I* dreamed of, is it? That's what's wrong. I dreamed of something so different –'

And last night she had been given a glimpse, however distant, of what that dream was. Those people last night at Chelsea Reach were her sort of people. Silly, some of them. Poseurs too, she'd no doubt, and hangers-on to the real artists. Like that man Gillick hanging on to Septimus Scott and pretending to despise his work (which of course is very good, for hadn't Letty seen examples of it before?) But never mind if they were poseurs and hangers-on. They were part of the world that she wanted to be in. Not aseptic medical creatures, smelling of carbolic and dealing always in sickness and death and disease. Not people who stood beside beds in which tired sick men lay and had to display their pathetic nakedness to staring students who cared only for their disease and nothing for the art that lay in their souls.

'This is ridiculous,' she said aloud then and turned to stand with her back to the window and stare at the fire instead of the sad people outside. 'I'm a medical student. I'm not an artist. Or an actress. I can't be. A *medical* student –'

The door opened softly and he came in and stood there for a moment and then smiled at her, putting both his hands to each side of his neck and pulling against the muscles to relieve his tension and she smiled back, comforted by his presence. Such a friendly nice man, her cousin Sir Frederick. 'I could tell him,' she thought suddenly. 'I could explain to him how I feel about being here. That I feel all wrong –'

But then he moved across the room to sit down at his desk and the atmosphere changed subtly; no longer relaxed and easy as when he had come in, but proper and correct again, a senior lecturer facing an unsatisfactory student, and she felt her shoulders stiffen as he looked up at her.

'Miss Lackland,' he said and now she knew he was to be serious, for usually when they were outside the lecture rooms of the hospital, away from the wards and the operating theatres, he was cheerful and relaxed and addressed her as his dear Letty.

'I am concerned about you, and I must speak to you of my concern. I have been talking to your brother – no, you must not be wrathful! I approached him about you because I was concerned. He did not speak to me willingly, nor would he I am sure, although he has your best welfare at heart. I understand from him that you are not working happily at your studies?'

'Really, Sir Frederick,' was all she could say.

He sighed. 'And I can see for myself that you are not working well at your clinical classes. I had hoped you would make this easy for me, my dear. That we could discuss whatever problem it is that comes between you and your work and remove it.'

She was silent, and he looked at her for a long moment, his eyes, those faded tired eyes a little narrowed, and then he nodded, and became even more serious.

61

'Very well. You choose not to make it easy. So I will do as I assured you from the start that I would do – treat you exactly as I do the men, and I will speak to you now as though you were a young man who has been lazy and tiresome and making poor use of his opportunities in the way you have been doing this past three months. I shall also tell you of the letter I have received from your mother –'

'My mother!' Letty burst out and this time she felt her jaw tighten as well as her shoulders. 'I find that insupportable, sir! I am twenty-five years of age, and an independent person, and not beholden to my mother for any care. I am sure I respect her wishes, and understand her concern, but she surely should not meddle in my affairs by writing to you, whatever she may write to me –'

He shook his head. 'You forget yourself, Miss Lackland. Your mother and I were friends, as well as cousins, long before you were born. We have every right to correspond –'

And for a moment his attention seemed to waver and lose its strength as she stared at him; he seemed to soften as his eyes glazed and he looked back down the avenues of the years to a distant past when he had been a younger man and her mother had been an eager girl with ambitions bigger than she was, and she had needed him – but the moment shivered and broke into shards which melted into the morning sunlight that lay across the floor, and he was his stiff and serious self again.

'She is concerned that you should be using your time here to its best advantage. I am asked to let her know that you are happy, and can deal with all that is required of you here at Nellie's. And I must ask you now, how do I reply to this letter?'

She felt it lift in her then, felt the anger spread warmly from the pit of her belly up and into her throat, to burst out into the luxury of words. She made no effort to stem them, just stood there with her head tilted up and her face red with the intensity of her feelings and let it all roll out.

'You may tell her, Sir Frederick, what you please! You may tell her the time of day, or the state of roads in the city or the price of local eggs. I don't care tuppence for what you tell her, now or in the future! I am twenty-five years old, I have my

62

own income, I am free to decide for myself what I will do. And I will not be tormented in this fashion about what I do by anyone – by anyone, do you hear me? You may complain to me if you choose about your own observations of my activities. If you see me work badly, if you see me ill-mannered then you may tell me so. But you have no right to treat me as a child and tell tales to my mother about me, nor to listen to her complaints. Nor have you any right to quiz my brother about my affairs or activities! I do as I choose, not as others bid me choose. And I choose, now, to leave this hateful hospital and refuse to say another word. And that is precisely what I am going to do. Good morning!'

And she marched out of the room, glancing back over her shoulder just once as she did so to see Sir Frederick's almost ludicrously startled face staring back at her over his mahogany desk. And that almost made her laugh. Or cry. She wasn't quite sure which.

6

'I can't say I like it,' Oliver said fretfully, and wriggled a little in his chair. 'I never have. Seen any amount of course. After all, it ain't all that new, is it? They've been showing this stuff the past ten years or more, to my knowledge –'

'But this is better,' the man in the curly bowler and the much too lavishly-checked ulster coat said and shifted his cigarette from one side of his mouth to the other, rolling it between his teeth. 'You can't compare the other stuff to this, Mr Lackland, now can you? This is class, this is; this is quality; this is the real entertainment of the twentieth century, this is. I tell you, the millions'll be flocking to see it long after the likes of this –' And he swept his yellow-gloved hand round in a comprehensive and definitely dismissive manner. '– Long after the likes of this is just a tired old joke what no one laughs at no more. It's no skin off my nose, Mr Lackland, if you says no, I tell you, there's plenty more got all the foresight this business needs who'll jump at it, jump at it! I ain't selling, you understand, so much as offering an opportunity –'

'Yes, yes,' Oliver said testily. 'You can spare me the sales talk. I've been in this business far too long to be bamboozled by that sort of chat. I'm a downy bird, and it's what I'm buying I look at, not the face of the chap who's selling,' and he flicked a glance at the man's over-red visage and waxed moustache with its finely-twisted points and looked as sneeringly as the man had looked at his Supper Rooms.

Which made him feel a little better, for it was true he had been cast into gloom by the whole wretched business. More and more music-halls that he knew of were adding a few minutes of this damned device to the end of their programmes, and as a result more and more of his customers had been asking him where the Celia's version was. Some of them had been complimentary admittedly, glad not to have their eyesight ruined by the nasty thing, but others, and they were in the majority, actually complained, seeming to feel a little cheated.

'I still believe it's just a flash in the pan,' he growled now. 'Once we've all bought the equipment, spent a fortune making you lot rich, then what? The bottom'll fall out of it as the people get bored, because you can't compare this with a live act like Marie Lloyd, can you? And then where'll we all be? Poorer and wiser, I've no doubt –'

'Miss Lloyd 'as made one of these for herself,' the man in the checked ulster said in an elaborately offhand way, and began to rewind his machine. 'She knows the good of it, you see. *She* knows that this'll be around long after we're all dead and gone. Wants to leave a bit of 'erself behind, does our Marie. Got foresight, she has –'

'Humph,' Oliver said, more uneasy than ever. 'I suppose I could have another look. Got anything apart from that damned fire-engine and baby that's obviously a bundle of old clothes? Sick of seeing that chucked out of the window, that I am. Boring –'

'Try this,' the man said promptly, and busied himself about his machine, cranking it carefully and then, waving one hand at the waiter by the door to switch off the light again, setting it in motion.

Oliver stared gloomily at the square white screen that the man had rigged in front of his handsome red plush curtain, where it looked as incongruous as a boil on a bald man's head, and the images began to flicker across it. A man with moustaches as ferocious as those adorning the face of the ulster-coated character cranking the machine beside him stood and ranted silently at a cringing girl in white muslin and with her hair curling wildly on her head – though not as wildly as her eyes rolled in terror – while behind them an old man, so bent and twisted that he looked like her great-grandfather threw his hands up in the air and appeared to weep noisily. All, however, happened to the accompaniment only of the machine's buzzing, and went on getting more and more frantic, and somehow more and more silent as the melodrama unrolled itself. Villain seizes girl, old man weeps, heroic soldier arrives too late as girl is taken off by moustached villain –

Oliver watched it and sighed again. How could anyone offer such a melodrama without a sound to make it exciting? How could anyone really believe that this nonsense would topple such performers as Marie from their pinnacle?

Almost as though he had spoken aloud the man in the ulster coat said, 'They goes mad for this one, you know. Booin' the villain, aahing over the girl, shouting them on – you can't always hear the piano, I tell you, when they get going, and you've got a proper orchestra you can use, of course, and make it even better. There – happy ending, all right and tight –' as the last shadows hiccupped and then faded leaving the white screen blank again. 'And I've got a good seven or eight more you can see. Show you the catalogue, glad to. None of 'em more than a few minutes long, you understand, so you can be flexible, you know, flexible. One day put on just one, next day when the soubrette gets drunk or the comic gets a fit of the vapours, you can drop in half a dozen. Makes you less dependent, see, on the vagaries of the bleedin' performers. And we all know how vague they are.'

Oliver, who only the night before had had to send an urgent message to the Holborn Empire to get the bottom of the bill to come over to fill in for him because his clog-dancer had slipped on a bit of rotten fruit on his way across Covent Garden and twisted his ankle, sniffed and then sighed. It was often one of the most difficult problems he faced as a proprietor, he couldn't deny – maybe the damned machine could come in handy at that –

'Good shows, aren't they?' the man said. 'Get the best we do, from France you know. Got some really magical stuff with disappearing virgins, wizards, the whole thing. More expensive though, mind you.'

Oliver tilted his head sharply. 'France? Aren't any of them made here?'

'Oh a few, a few. Up in Yorkshire like, and in Brighton. And there's Paul, of course, over at Muswell Hill. But we don't have many people around what really understands how to do it, you see. Takes a bit of money to get it right, and business men, they don't fancy trying their cash. Take it now when they can see it easy, that's their motto, instead of what it ought to be, which is invest in tomorrow. But it's all the same with money men, ain't it? It takes artists, ones that understands the entertainment business to see best what's got to be done. That's what these coves in France – Gaumont and that – that's what they've done, you see. Dare say one of these days we'll find some as'll take enough interest to invest a bit of both money and artistry and make really good pictures here. Now that'd beat the French, eh? And the Americans. They're doing it more and more, they are –'

'How much?' Oliver said abruptly.

'How much are the Americans doin'?' the man said and pursed his lips. 'Well –'

'No! How much money does it take to make picture-shows like these? And then when they're made, how much to get them to the places that need 'em? I mean, you make copies, I imagine?'

The man stared and then, slowly, nodded. 'That's right. Then you rent 'em, see. I let you have this one this week, see, then I comes and takes it away and gives you the one Joe Doakes over at Canning Town's had, an' give him the one you've had – and that's how it works. Got to make sure you get lots of variety, see? Can't show the same ones too near each other in case the people go to better houses. Is that what's worrying you? It needn't. I can make a special deal with you, you pays a little more, gets the new ones first off, before anyone else, see? Then –'

'You didn't say how much it costs to make the pictures in the first place. What sort of money would it take to do what you said business men don't do – look at tomorrow?'

The man grinned. 'How long's a piece of string, Mr Lackland? I dunno, and that's a fact! I'm just what you might call a distributor. My job's selling the machines to show the pictures, see, and then getting the reels sent out and collected and the rent paid properly. How could I know about more'n that? They won't tell me, will they, what their costs is! Might give me too much ambition to get some of their profits, eh? I mean, in their shoes, I wouldn't tell me either –' And he laughed fatly at the quality of his joke.

Oliver was silent for a moment and then he said abruptly, 'I'll take it. A machine and regular changes of picture every week, right? But I want some more information about the business as well. See to it I get it, and get it soon, and you've got a steady customer. If you don't get the information I need, I'm as likely to lose interest as not. So it's in your *own* interest, isn't it, to find out? We'll have a drink on it, then? Good. Brandy and soda – fine. Will! B and S for my friend here and a glass of Vichy water for me –'

And he settled down to listen to the man in the ulster brag and chatter about himself, quietly thinking his own thoughts all the while. And if they included consideration of Phoebe's response when she heard what he was planning, and a certain amount of malicious pleasure at how angry she would be, that was no one's business but his own.

And he thought with even more pleasure of telling his young cousin about it all, and how *he* would respond and almost hugged himself. He'd started the morning very miserably, bearded as he had been by this pushy salesman, but now he knew that his sometimes somnolent guardian angel had been wide awake this morning after all. Everything was going to turn out very nicely, very nicely indeed.

'My dear man,' Edwin said roundly. 'You must stop such thinking immediately. It's not at all healthy, I'm sure of that. Why, let a man go against his true nature and almost *anything* could happen! And it's your true nature to be an artist of the stage. To see life and drama come to reality beneath your expert touch, to build a world of fantasy and culture for the audience which will improve their souls, to –'

'All very well, my friend, all very well,' Luke said and grinned at him as cheerfully as he could, difficult though it was considering how low he was feeling. 'But what good does it do a man's true nature if his true body is starving for want of the victuals he can't earn? How much life and drama come to reality under dead hands? Because I tell you that's the way of it, and it's no good dodging it. I've been trying to get work with all the strength I have, and the hard truth is no one wants me. So, I have to look at reality for my own sake rather than an audience, and find some other occupation –'

'Now, Luke, we've been through all this before! As long as I'm here you don't have to fret yourself about starving and –'

'And I've told you, Edwin. I value your friendship. I appreciate your care of me, but it is not possible to go on as we are any longer. I have lived on you long enough. It's got to stop.' And his tone was so final that Edwin, even though he had opened his mouth to protest, closed it again, and began to busy himself pouring tea and handing round crumpets.

'Well, at least take a crumpet before you go and starve on the street,' he said with some acerbity, after a moment, and the others laughed and the awkward pause slid past them as Luke accepted the crumpet and chewed it with as good an imitation of enjoyment as he could.

Not easy, though, not easy at all. For the past week now he had been thinking harder and harder about the future. There was no management in all London he had not approached for work, no touring company office he had not visited, toiling up dismal cat-scented staircases galore, sitting in umpteen chilly dingy rooms containing just a table and a couple of chairs and a telephone with other eager workless actors as desperate as himself; there was no day on which he had not had to bite back his anger when lordly well-fed managers were offhand with him, or traipsed the pavements until his back ached and his legs dragged and his irritating cough was almost unbearable, making his chest tighter and cutting his breath short.

And he had become more and more tired as the week had gone on, especially as he was not sleeping well. He lay each night in the comfortable bed that Edwin provided for him on the top floor of his pretty house and felt as though he were lying in a furnace, for all that Edwin's windows were kept open to the air and it was a wet and cold March still. He slept fitfully, waking often in a flood of sweat, and dreaming vividly when he did manage to doze off. No wonder each day started so heavily, no wonder his store of resilience was rapidly dwindling.

He had decided this very morning, as the bells from Chelsea

Old Church had woken him with their agreeable cacophony, lying in bed and staring up at the clouds scudding greyly across an even greyer sky. He had to make changes in his life. He had to find some sort of occupation that would pay a living wage, find his own lodgings somewhere and set out on real life, maybe even find a girl to share that real life with – not to be considered, he told himself and wrenched his thoughts back to the present. It was a damned shame after so many years in the business, but there it was; he was clearly not cut out to be a success as an actor, deeply as he cared for the profession and long as he had been in it. Maybe, one day in the future, he would find some sort of interest that would hold him to the fringe of the past when he had graced stages in South Africa as well as London, and would remember the young days when he had been hopeful and happy; but now the time had come.

And tears had pricked his eyelids and he had hurled himself out of bed so violently that his cough started up again and almost made him throw up, it was so persistent.

Now catching Jessica's eye on him across Edwin's tea-table he felt his chest tighten again. He would not have had her party to his discussion with Edwin for the world, but what could he do? She had come into the drawing-room, hurrying up the stairs ahead of the parlourmaid who waited to announce her, bursting in just as he was embarked on his explanations, and Edwin, dear man though he was, was so lacking in tact that he had insisted on going on with their conversation even though they had an audience, quite unaware of the embarrassment it caused Luke. And Luke, weary as he was, had accepted the fact and let it all be blurted out.

Now she looked at him with her eyes wide and melting, and said in deep thrilling tones, 'It will be a tragedy!'

'Now, don't you start, Jessica!' he said sharply. 'It's my own affair, after all –'

'Not entirely,' Gillick said, and reached for another crumpet. He had followed Jessica into the room, at which point Luke had finally had to accept that his affairs were to be a matter for public comment, as everything usually was in Edwin's house. 'All artists are part of each other. When one allows his artist's soul to die we are all diminished.'

'Hardly an original thought,' Luke said tartly. 'Donne, however, was speaking of all men and not just artists.'

'Oh, Donne,' said Gillick and waved his hand airily. 'It doesn't matter what the dead said – it's what the living do that matters. And anyway, you always speak of all men as though you were part of them. Like the way you went on and on about having a special theatre for the poor. Such stuff – as if ordinary men mattered as much as artists! It is the privilege of the clay-souled to provide sustenance for the true creators. Is it not, Edwin? Don't you find it a privilege to care for our Luke here? I'm sure you do –'

'Gillick, shut up,' Edwin said good-naturedly and then stared at him as he put down his tea-cup. 'What was that you said about a theatre for the poor?'

'Oh, you remember, Edwin! Or weren't you there that day? May I have another crumpet? Too delicious – Luke went on and on about it one night when I wanted to talk only about my sculpture – so boring he was. About running this theatre for poor people where they could watch improving plays and eat a meal and drink and probably copulate as well, he's so concerned for their comfort, all for a few pence –'

'There is no need to be excessively offensive,' Edwin said, and made a little grimace at Jessica. 'Such a man, my dear, but what *can* you do?'

'I ignore him as any intelligent person would,' Jessica said with great dignity. 'He's too stupid to worry about. But he's right, you know, Luke. You did say you wanted to run your own theatre, don't you remember? We were all here and Edwin was at the opera, and you said –'

'I said more than any sensible person should,' Luke said loudly and got to his feet. 'It was just a daydream. Now, I really must be –'

'A theatre for the poor,' Edwin said slowly and then smiled widely and clapped his hands together. 'Do you know, I think that's a capital notion. Let's do it, shall we? We'll build a theatre somewhere and –'

'Not just somewhere,' Luke said shortly, unable to resist putting Edwin right on what he had long regarded as his own private fantasy. 'It has to be in the middle of a poor area.

Where people who need it can reach it, you see. Not where the rich people's theatres are, in the West End, but where people can walk – they haven't the money to spend on travelling in cabs and buses for their pleasure. And not just an ordinary theatre, either. It's got to be a place that people can use comfortably. Where there can be tables as well as rows of seats and –'

'Well, then, let's find the place and do it!' Edwin said, and poured himself yet another cup of tea. 'It sounds a splendid notion and –'

'And it costs money, a great deal of money,' Luke said savagely. 'It's not like buying a bag of apples, you know!'

'Well?' Edwin said and smiled sweetly up at him over his cup. 'You know perfectly well that I have any *number* of bags of apples at my disposal! Don't make me remind you, my dear boy, that my poor dear old Pa was a great deal richer than was good for him. There's no shortage of money for such projects as interest me and –'

'Oh, Edwin, do stop being so – so – Look, I don't want any more charity! I don't want to throw your kindness or your hospitality in your face, but you know I'm right. I can't go on sponging on you this way, and to say you'll now buy me a theatre just because –'

Edwin raised his brows at that. 'Did I say I'd buy him a theatre for himself?' He looked round appealingly. 'Did I? I just said, let's *do* it! I remember perfectly well. My exact words were "Let's find a place and do it." Weren't they, Jessica? Yes. So, let's! *My* theatre of course. I'll own it. I'll pocket any profit – bless my soul, but my dear old Papa there in his Wall Street heaven must be beaming down on me – I'll take the money and *you* earn it for me! I'm offering you a berth, you stupid creature! It's clear to me that a popular theatre where people can eat and drink and enjoy themselves could be a source of much money – and I want to make some. How's that? You go ahead and do the work and make it for me! Will that soothe your wretched Puritan conscience? If I didn't know better, I'd say you had Boston ancestors, so help me I would.'

Luke stood uncertainly for a moment, poised to turn on his heel and go, but held by the calmness of Edwin's tone. There was nothing at all histrionic about it, as there was when he was making one of his jests or was being wildly ridiculous; he sounded perfectly serious and that confused Luke considerably.

'I mean it, Luke,' Edwin said gently, and again produced that wide and cheerful smile. 'I'm not being merely generous, you know. The fact that I enjoy being so is beside the point. This time I'm being my poor old Pa's son. I truly believe that such a project could, in time, make money. And I'm asking you to make it for me. Of course, if you'd rather hold on to the idea for your own profit, maybe you can borrow money from a bank or wherever and do so. I'm just saying I'll gladly take the idea from you, employ you –'

'I never saw it as the source of any great fortune,' Luke said slowly. 'All I ever wanted to do is the work I care about, in the way I want to do it, and to keep myself modestly on the proceeds. I want it to be cheap and cheerful entertainment for people who wouldn't get it otherwise. If there's profit to be made – well, fair enough. Let it. But it was never my prime goal.'

'Then make it one of them! Not the first, you know, not a matter of *primus inter pares*, but a matter of some significance when all others have been dealt with. Get the quality right and the organization right and the prices right – for even the most poor must value most that which they pay for rather than that which is free – and what is left is for me, for my investment! What do you say, Luke?'

'Oh, Luke, *please* do!' Jessica leaned forwards and breathed the word with great intensity. 'And promise me you'll cast me in the best roles and –'

'Only if you're good enough,' Luke said absently, never taking his eyes from Edwin's face. 'Everything has to be of the best. It can be cheap, but it's got to be good –'

'Then that's settled!' Edwin said with huge relief. 'Now press that bell, dear old Gillick, and demand quantities of fresh crumpets from whomsoever comes toiling up from the noisome depths to answer it. And tomorrow as ever is, Luke, you shall go and find your place and start our theatre. Such fun, my dears, such fun!' And then, as he caught Luke's dubious eye, he added hastily, 'And so lucrative. Eh, Luke? So lucrative!'

7

She sat in an end seat well to the back and kept her chin tucked forwards, not wanting to be seen and not sure why. She was, after all, a free agent. Why should she not attend a public meeting if she wanted to? No one could say her nay. She had to keep telling herself that; that she was as free as air, her own person, entitled to do what she wanted to do when she wanted to do it.

She shivered a little then for it was a chilling thought, making her feel bleak and lonelier than she had been all week, if that were possible. And the big sparsely-populated hall, with the rows of mute chairs and its soiled cream-painted walls and its smell of dust and disinfectant and cats was gloomy and cold too, adding to her deepening sense of melancholy.

The last speaker banged her fist on the lectern and repeated her theme phrase once more, this time in even louder tones. 'Taxation without representation is tyranny – and I for one refuse to be the victim of the tyrant any longer than I need be. And I beg you all to share my resolve. To vow as I do and refuse to bear this yoke any longer. To agree, as I do, that the fight must go on. And on. And on. Until we win –'

The applause that followed as she sat down was scattered and thin because there were so few people there, but it was fervent for all that as individual women clapped their hands together with all the passion they had and then, one by one, slipped out of their seats and moved towards the platform to stand and talk to the three women who had been sitting on it.

Letty contemplated them a little sadly. She too would have liked to be there beside them, joining in the chatter, being as eager and as angry as their faces showed they were; there were just a dozen women, mostly wearing rather dowdy clothes (a fact she suddenly despised herself for noticing, for surely it shouldn't matter that much what a woman wore?) with their heads close together. One of the speakers had disappeared now, but still the people there looked as though they were worth talking to; yet somehow she could not bring herself to join them, and she sighed softly, and began to collect her gloves and scarf ready to go.

She had come in on an impulse because it had looked somewhere different to be, and after all, she *was* interested in the question of votes for women. The torn poster flapping forlornly in front of the Methodist Meeting Hall in Pimlico had offered, she had thought confusedly, some encouragement of her decision and perhaps moral support in her present situation, but now she knew it had been a false promise. Had there been more people there it might have been different. As it was, the thinnesss of the audience of which she was a part underlined her present loneliness, as well as the loneliness of the past week.

Day after day she had spent wandering the streets of London, sometimes looking in shops but more often seeking libraries and museums for comfort, for there, she felt, she could linger without seeming conspicuous or spending money, and though she was not in any way short of cash (for she had her allowance for the month barely untouched) it seemed prudent to be thrifty. After all, she had to be alone now. She had never had cause to worry about money, but if she had, then Barty would have been there to help. But now Barty was not there, and she could not lean on him for anything. And for a moment she felt her eyes start with tears.

'Oh, must you go at once?' It was a rather deep voice and she looked up, startled, to see the rather dumpy figure of the middle-aged woman who had given the last speech from the platform.

'I'm sorry – did I make you jump? I'm Dora Montefiore. I noticed you, and wondered who you were. We get used to seeing the same faces, usually, you see.'

'Oh, yes – I'm sorry. I saw the notice outside as I was passing and I thought –'

'Please, don't apologize! We want people to come in.

Millions of people! The trouble is they usually don't. It's going to take time to convince them we're right to argue as we do. Are you a member of the Union?'

'The Union?'

'The WSPU – Women's Social and Political Union, you know! The Pankhurst family's affair – you know them? From Manchester – and Miss Kenny and the Pethwick-Lawrences and – no, I see you're not. Perhaps you were at the meeting at Westminster last month? When there was such a fuss at the House of Commons?'

'I wish I had been,' Letty said and under this woman's basilisk stare felt ashamed that she had not, for she was a powerful personality and somewhat overwhelming, though clearly kindly disposed towards her. 'I wished to, when I heard about it, but my brother was tiresome and –' She reddened and then said hurriedly, 'and I had my studies to worry about as well, of course. But I shall go to the next, I assure you –'

'Good. It will be on 12 May. Don't forget – what studies?'

'I beg your pardon?'

'You said you were busy about your studies. What studies?'

'Oh, at Nellie's. Queen Eleanor's hospital, that is. I am – I was – a medical student.'

The powerful woman looked fierce for a moment. 'Was? Why was? Have your family – this brother – have they prevented you? Women should aspire to the best of occupations. Medicine is indeed one that –'

Letty stood up at last and bent her head to smooth her mantle in order to hide the redness that covered her face. 'No,' she said shortly. 'I – I have other ideas, other ambitions. I chose to end my studies myself.'

'Other ambitions? What can possibly be more ambitious for a gel than the study of medicine?'

Letty looked up at her now, beginning to feel the same rise of irritation that Frederick had caused. 'Other ambitions,' she said stonily and stared coolly back, and after a moment the dumpy woman with the very dark eyes that had been staring at her so hard laughed, a short bark of laughter that had real mirth in it.

'Quite right!' she said. 'I should indeed mind my own business, and mind it I shall. Come and have some tea with the others. Perhaps we can add ourselves and our work to your ambitions. We're always looking for new recruits to the movement, and you seem a likely enough lass to be of use to us. Will you come?'

'I'm not sure – I mean I'm not sure I want to be a recruit, or –'

'But you approve of the notion of votes for women?'

'Oh, of course! It's just that –'

'Well enough. No one will force you. Come and have some tea anyway. It won't be a case of selling your soul for it, I promise you.'

Letty laughed then and the dumpy woman twinkled back at her and then tucked her hand into the crook of Letty's elbow and led her up the now empty hall towards the little room at the back where the remainder of the women had gone.

The tea was hot and sweet and comforting and there were crumbly shortcake biscuits and gingernuts and Letty suddenly realized how long it had been since breakfast, and how little she had eaten then, and took them gratefully, and began to relax. The women sitting around in the little room accepted her calmly, making room for her as one of themselves with an easy camaraderie that made her relax even more, suddenly aware of how different the atmosphere had been at Nellie's where she had been so much the outsider, so much the lonely one.

She said as much, impulsively, to Dora Montefiore who was sitting beside her and Dora cocked a knowing eye at her and said with unexpected gentleness, 'I thought you looked lonely.'

'Yes –' Letty said, and drank some more tea, suddenly confused and shy.

'Is that why you left your studies? Because of the loneliness?'

'No – yes – perhaps. No – I can't say it was that. It was –' Letty stopped and shrugged, feeling again irritation at being quizzed, and Dora said easily, 'Oh, very well. If you want to go on being lonely, keep it to yourself –'

'No, I don't. It's just that – oh, I get so *cross* with the way other people keep trying to run my life for me. It's as though there are other people inside my head all the time saying do this, do that –'

'Maddening, isn't it? But it's always like that. Always people who imagine that because you're a woman you can't possibly know what you want. I've been fighting that all my life – the wicked injustice of it, the way men will waste our brains and spoil our opportunities –'

'Oh, it's not that – I mean, I never think about it as *men* meddling. It's more my mother actually. And my brother agrees with her, and gets his ideas from her, so I can't blame him –'

And then she was telling her new acquaintance all about it. About her mother's lifelong intention to make a doctor of her daughter. About her own secret desire to follow a career in the theatre. About her furious anger at Frederick and the way she had stormed out of the hospital and gone to her lodgings and packed her clothes, much to Mrs Partridge's horror, and marched out of there too, still in a white hot rage, taking a hansom cab to Victoria, where there were so many hotels, and choosing the first that looked clean and respectable, and moving in. How for the past week she had been struggling to decide what to do next; about the letters she had written to her mother, to her cousin Frederick, to her brother, telling them she was now her own woman, and would be living her life in the way she thought best, and would be following her own desires –

'– And now,' she finished bleakly, 'I don't know what to do next. It's all very well to say I want to be an actress, but I've no real experience, no understanding of the way actresses obtain parts. I'm just – I feel so *stupid*. As far as I can see, I'm going to have to go back to Nellie's and tell them I'm sorry and try again. I mean, I can't just sit in a hotel for the rest of my life, can I? I've no friends in London, really, and the people who come and go through the hotel – well, they're not there long enough to get to know them, and even if they were, I'd be worried. I mean, talking to people you don't know can be risky, can't it, for a girl on her own? Or do I just go back to Haworth and work with Mamma and feel her being disappointed at me all the time? It doesn't bear thinking of. None of it bears thinking of –'

'Where did you get this notion of being an actress? Was it because you're pretty? Did your friends at school tell you you should because you were pretty?' And there was a hint of steel in Dora's gruff voice.

'No!' Letty said furiously. 'It isn't mere vanity, and I won't have anyone say it is! It's – it's because it matters. It's the way Luke said – it's having a great need burning in you –'

'Luke?' Dora said, and sighed and shook her head. 'That's always the way of it. Some sensible likely lass who has the possibility of shaping up to be worth something, and what does she do? She finds a man who gets in her eyes and blurrs her vision and ruins everything! I imagine it's really his fault you left your studies, hmm? Not your Mamma at all –'

And because talking to this fierce but caring as well as invigorating woman was so comforting, Letty did not feel anger at her words but sat and thought for a long moment and then smiled a little shyly and said, 'Well, I can't deny he did set me on my ears somewhat. I hardly know him, of course. He just turned up at Aunt Martha's funeral and we began to talk, and found we were cousins – well, sort of cousins – and then he took me to a party at his friend's house – they're all very Bohemian, in Chelsea Reach, you know, and it all seemed –'

'And your own life seemed insupportable. I know. I remember feeling the same way a long time ago –' And Dora's eyes glazed a little and she stared at Letty with an expression so lugubrious that she wanted to laugh, but also to cry a little.

'Listen, my child, take some advice from one much older than you. No, I'm not trying to live inside your head for you. I'm not telling you what to do, I know how infuriating that is. I'm just offering advice – take it or leave it. Go and see this young man, tell him what you've done and see if he –'

Letty was scarlet. 'I can't! How could I? It would look as though I were throwing myself at his head, and I couldn't do that!'

'Why not?' Dora said calmly. 'Why ever not? What does a man do when he meets a girl he likes the look of and wishes to know better? Why, he courts her! He goes to visit her. He

sends her gifts and pays attention to her. Now, why in the
name of all that is common sense should a girl not do the same?
Why should a girl have to sit and wait with her hands folded till
a young man comes to *her*? The only way you'll get what you
want in this life, my girl, is to go and get it. It's because women
have always been so biddable and patient that we must now
fight so hard for what is our natural right – the chance to make
decisions about our country and our own lives. And not only
through the ballot-box. I keep telling everyone that there is
more to politics than speeches and meetings and sending
demands to Parliament! It's the way women *think* that has to
be changed, and the way they behave – when you do that with
every individual, then you have a power of women who are at
last as self-reliant and as strong as the men! And then we'll
show ourselves fit to have the vote, fit to be the mothers of the
next generation –'

'But –' Letty began, but she could not stem the flood of
Dora's oratory.

'– and if what you want is a chance to feed that burning need
you say you've got, then you must go where the food to satisfy
it may be found! Go to this Luke, tell him you've decided to
follow your bent, and use his knowledge to set you on your
way!'

'There was an actress at that party,' Letty said abruptly after
a moment. 'A very pretty girl. We were speaking of votes for
women, and *she* said that it was easy for a woman to get what
she wanted. She just had to ask a man for it – I thought that
was –'

'Pah!' Dora said with great disgust. 'Such are the enemies we
have in our ranks, such are the women who have to be
educated out of their stupidity! I am not telling you to go and
ask your Luke for the chance to do as you choose! It's not a
donation from a – from a master to a servant! I am saying you
should use him as you would use any friend to guide you on
your way. Would you hesitate to ask a *woman* friend to aid
you in this way?'

'A woman?' Letty said and frowned slightly. 'Well, I don't
suppose –'

'Of course you wouldn't,' Dora said roundly. 'You know

81

you wouldn't! Then why be so squeamish about asking a man? Because you regard yourself as his inferior?'

'No!' Letty said hotly and then, 'Well, yes, perhaps. It's easy for a man, isn't it? They can do as they wish, when they wish. They don't have people fussing over their well-being or saying they're silly to want the difficult things – because they're men –'

'That doesn't make *you* inferior, my dear child! It makes the world we live in inferior! You see how right I am? It's because there is such injustice that the WSPU is needed. Will you join us? Help us change the inferior aspects?'

And Letty stared at her and bit her lip and then felt her face soften into an involuntary smile. 'Do you know, I think perhaps I might – I just might.'

'And will you do as I suggest regarding furthering your ambitions to act?'

But this time Letty shook her head. 'I don't know. I – that's something I must think about more.'

'Well, don't think too long,' Dora said tartly. 'Because in my experience, too much thinking halts action. I keep telling them all that –' And she waved her hand at the other women sitting gossiping over their tea-cups. 'It's action we're going to need, not talk and good manners. Women's behaviour, you see – we have to prevent women from thinking that their behaviour is governed by their sex –'

She had raised her voice a little, and one of the others turned towards her and said cheerfully, 'Dora on her hobby-horse again? What action are you proposing we take now, Dora? Shall we march on the House of Commons? Or should we –'

'I know what I'm going to do!' Dora said, 'and it's what I said I would.' She got to her feet, collecting her scattered belongings. 'I'm going to refuse to pay the rate demand that reached me this morning. It's a final demand and I shall send it back to the Town Hall just as I did last time and mark it in red ink, "No taxation without representation" and then sit back and see what happens. Last time they sent the bailiffs in to take my furniture. This time, I shall barricade myself, in, right and tight, and they'll have to lay siege to me before I shall leave and certainly before I shall pay. Direct action, you see, that's the answer, direct action!'

She had surged towards the door now, and she stopped and looked back over her shoulder at Letty and nodded at her, her expression once again fierce. 'And you do the same, young woman. It's the only way, you know, the only way!' And she was gone, leaving Letty thoughtfully staring at the door as it slammed behind her.

8

They had taken the tram to the foot of Highgate Hill, and then an omnibus which creaked and swayed its way through the eternity of suburban streets and miles of privet hedge and acres of tiny front gardens with their few early daffodils, to the top of Muswell Hill. And Luke asked himself wonderingly why on earth he was going on this wild-goose chase. He knew what he wanted to do; he had the time and, at last, the finance to do it, and yet he was allowing himself to be embroiled in this mad scheme of Oliver's. And wasn't it ironical, he told himself, as he stared gloomily out of the omnibus window at the grey pavements creeping past, that after all those long weeks of desperation when there was no work to be found anywhere that two interesting matters should come up at the same time?

Not that Oliver had seen any problems about Luke's commitment to his new plan with Edwin when he had explained what it was he wanted to discuss with Luke. The old man had come panting up the stairs from his cellar to where Luke was waiting and greeted him with much fuss and a conspiratorial air that was rather funny, Luke had thought, until he became irritated at Oliver's exaggerated concern that no one – not even his own waiters who had been in his employ for thirty years or more – should overhear them.

'I received your message, sir,' Luke had said in his ordinary tones. 'Though I was most surprised that you knew where I might be found and –'

Oliver had shaken his head at him, pursing his lips to enjoin hush and then said loudly for his waiter's benefit, 'Oh, as for finding you, my boy, nothing easier. I just asked about, you know, asked about. I know so many people in London, you see, and they all know me, and sooner or later they tell me what I need to know! It was one of the managements gave me your address. Glad you could drop in, good to see you! Will, you've left the brandy and seltzer on my table? Good, good – now you – er – you just pop into the cellar now and doublecheck the six dozen of claret that came in yesterday, that's a good chap. Yes. Tell them I'm not to be disturbed as you pass the kitchen, will you – yes, that's right. Six dozen of claret –'

And then there had been much play with brandy bottle and siphon and glasses and Luke, who had much to do now that he had at last found his premises, with all the work to be set in hand, became more and more impatient; but at last Oliver leaned forwards and explained what it was he wanted Luke to do.

Luke had listened open-mouthed and then shook his head in amusement.

'My dear sir, you can't mean it! I know the things – seen any number of 'em and thought some of them particularly good. I remember the pictures they sent back from South Africa during the war – it was remarkable how much like ordinary men those Boers looked, was it not? – but I said then and I say now, you can't expect these silly little films to take over from real artistes! We work with an audience, you see! That's the difference, and it's the audience that makes it all happen. I know myself as a performer what the difference is between a good house that cares for your work and a lackadaisical one that does not. I'm twice as good for a good audience, half as good for a bad one – I can't imagine working in front of one of these contraptions, and I'm out of work! Or was – The point is, sir, even if I were still in want of a job, I'd find it painful to work in such a way. So why should the established stars take the trouble? That's the question –'

'You tell 'em Marie's done one, and they will! You mark my words. She's a big lady in every way, our Marie, and she carries the profession with her. Now, I've seen the film she's already made with this Yorkshire firm, and I tell you, it's not a patch on what it could be. All they did was put her on a bad stage, with a bad set, and light it like a – like a circus and the result –well, you'll see for yourself when we get there –'

'Get where?'

'Muswell Hill, dear boy. Muswell Hill! There's a man there, got a studio, all the equipment, we can get the information we need and see how to set up our own. I've been into it, got all the costs. I reckon my investment can be – well, never mind that. That's my side of it. Enough, shall we say, enough to be interesting. Then, with you running it, d'you see, and making the films, and me seeing to the distribution and so on, we can –'

'Now, just a minute, sir, just a minute! Me doing what?'

Oliver sighed gustily. 'But I told you, my dear chap! I want to film all the great stars of the music-hall, every one of them. Harry Tate and Charles Coborn and *all* of them, and show them in the places where they can't work because there aren't any theatres for them, and then, use them in special big shows. I can see really long films – an hour or more – with a proper bill but a top-of-the-bill artiste in every position, all done like a show here or at the Holborn or Collins's; but it takes an artiste to make sure it's done right, though, that's the thing. The ones I've seen, they're made by *photographers* –' and the scorn in his voice was blistering, '– not by stage people, who under-stand about lights and sightliness and getting the – the *presentation* right! I grant you there are one or two who make some clever stuff – I saw some those Gaumont people did, very clever, witty, you know? Like fairy transformations with all sorts going on – but it's still not real *theatre*. That's what we're going to do. Lackland and O'Hare, we'll be, film producers! Now don't you think it's a capital scheme? And you can perform on the films yourself, don't you see, and spread your own name. Once we've got the music-hall films done and the great performers saved for ever – and they can't live always can they? – then we can do plays and all sorts of things, even Shakespeare maybe, with actors behind the screen to say the words for them and –'

Luke had to interrupt the flow of excitement and he did so with some desperation in his voice. 'Mr Lackland, I do understand what a kindness you're trying to do. I do see what you mean about keeping people alive by putting their performances on a screen but you've just explained the major

86

problem yourself; having to have actors to say lines! What sort of performance can you get out of Marie Lloyd when you can't *hear* her? It's the way she sounds as well as the way she looks – and the same's true of all the others. Imagine 'The Man Who Broke The Bank At Monte Carlo' in dumb-show! It just won't mean anything. I can't see it, sir, I really can't.'

'You will when you've actually looked,' Oliver said confidently and then guffawed at his own joke. 'Now my boy, we really must be on our way! I told them I'd be there this afternoon, and I've got to be back in here to open tonight at six, for the early doors are bringing in more and more trade and I really must be here by five to check everything, so on we go. We can take a hansom to the tram-line and then –'

And now here he sat in a swaying omnibus going through remote corners of North London while the old man at his side puffed cheerfully at a small and odiously strong-smelling cigarillo and stared contentedly out of the window, clearly very pleased with his scheme. How could he disabuse him? How could he make the poor chap see what a mad notion it all was? He was rich enough, Luke knew, to pour a lot of money into an abortive plan and still not be unduly hurt in his pocket, but it would be better to prevent him if he could –

And anyway, he had his own work to be getting on with. He had found the ideal site for his new theatre, only a mile or so down the road from Edwin's elegant little house. There on the river bank staring glumly across the mud to the Battersea side stood a dilapidated warehouse, reeking of the soap and washing-soda it had once stored (which could have been worse; imagine if it had been a tannery!) and sadly in need of nails and hammers and new timbers and paint. But its position was perfect, there on the corner of Luna Street, and easily reached from the Battersea side of the Thames where lived his potential audience, the poorly-off people he most wanted to serve, by means of the bridge that debouched just a few hundred yards along the Embankment.

He had already signed a lease with Edwin for the premises (to the amazement of the landlord who had thought no one would ever want such a derelict heap and had therefore charged the lowest rent possible, and to the delight of Luke, who was as careful as ever of Edwin's purse) and today had planned to set about finding carpenters and painters to put the interior to rights. And there was furniture to be bought and the stage to be equipped and the flats to be painted and – so much to do, and here he sat on a Muswell Hill omnibus on a cold early April afternoon trundling out to look at some mad film for this old man. It was crazy, quite, quite, crazy, and he turned to say as much to Oliver, regretting the generosity of nature that had first made him obey the old man's slightly incoherent letter of summons, and then agree to travel this far with him.

But even as he turned his head the bus stopped and Oliver said gleefully, 'Here we are!' and went hurrying off the bus as eagerly as a child going on a picnic.

'Well, sir, I've come this far, so I might as well finish,' Luke said as he followed. 'But I must warn you that I'm not enthusiastic about this scheme at all. I can't see that it is right for you to invest in it – though of course that must be your own affair – and I'm quite sure that with my own affairs in the state they now are, I cannot tear myself in two to help you. Even if I believed it to be a good thing to do so –'

'Oh, you will see, Luke my boy, you will see!' Oliver said jovially, and hurried him along the tree-lined road so fast that Luke, young as he was, almost had to puff to keep up with him.

The building they finally reached seemed ordinary enough from the outside; a large erection suitable for an office. But once they had gone inside and announced themselves to the neat young woman at the enquiry window, and were shown the rest of the establishment, Luke realized that he had walked into a whole new world.

They were met by the proprietor, a thin-faced man, black of beard and of eyes, who was taciturn but friendly enough.

'Afternoon, Mr Paul, good of you to see us,' Oliver said fussily. 'My young friend Luke O'Hare – colleague, you know, colleague. We need not take too much of your time, we hope, but we'd be glad of your guidance. Good of you to offer it, seeing as how I intend to be a competitor!'

'I doubt that need worry either of us unduly,' Paul said

drily. 'There's enough work for all of us. Business is barely started, barely begun. And anyway, science, you know, science –'

'Mr Paul is a scientific instrument-maker by trade, Luke,' Oliver explained busily as their host led the way through long ill-lit corridors to the rear of his building. 'Always was most interested in the scientific aspects of the film, you know. Right, Mr Paul?'

'Right,' Paul said, and threw open a door. 'Here's the studio.'

Luke stood very still and his eyes widened. They were in a big iron-clad area with vast wall-high sliding-doors, now open to the air, and with an even vaster glass skylight let into the roof. At one side was a small but elegant stage, backed by a frame which held a backcloth depicting a scene of unlikely bucolic peace complete with cows and sheep and remarkable numbers of flowers. He could see, even from this vantage-point the outlines of traps on the stage, and above it there was a hanging bridge from which were dangling a number of pieces of assorted scenery. In front of the stage there was a form of railway, and on it a camera – big, square and of highly-polished wood – was mounted, with a man with his head bent over it cranking madly. On the stage itself were a very large number of people, all leaping about very busily, enacting, as far as Luke could tell, a comedy involving a very obviously pantomime cow and a couple of actors in cat-skins. There was a great deal of noise and laughter and shouting and running to and fro altogether, and anything less like the usual disciplined activity on a stage Luke couldn't imagine.

'It's a new one this, new idea, you know,' Paul said, and leaned easily against the door watching his people in their frantic activity and chewing on a cigar he had just taken from his pocket. 'Thought we'd try the funnies, you know. The customers like 'em. For my part, I prefer my actuality stuff. Much better. I shan't do more of this. It's good for making money no doubt, but there's more to work than money.' He turned his head and spat some of the chewed tobacco from his cigar to the floor. 'Anyway, it means employing actors. And they're more trouble than they're worth –'

89

'Ah, that's because you're a scientist, my dear Paul!' Oliver said, more jovial than ever. 'That's what I've been telling my young friend here. You scientists have given us this superb instrument – and the cameras are superb, they really are – but you don't have the real understanding of the art form, that's the trouble. Putting on a show, that takes someone who knows about *acting*, like my friend Luke here. He'll give us some comedies and some plays that will really set 'em on their ears. Then with your actuality films and our entertainment films – why, we'll soon change the face of people's lives!' And he winked heavily at Luke to warn him to say nothing of his other plan to screen all the great music-hall stars.

This time Luke didn't feel inclined to be amused or to scoff. There was something in this film business after all, he decided, as they made their way to another part of the building where Paul, now much more animated, began to show them some of the best of his actuality films; pieces of no more than eighty or ninety feet brought back from the Boer War, longer pieces taken in the Swiss Alps, and a very long one indeed, fully 240 feet, of the Delhi Durbar a couple of years previously, all moved silently across the screen; it was all somehow much more enthralling than the many jerky and rather silly films he had seen at music-halls and in special lantern shows in the past few years and he had to admire it; all, that is except for the film of Marie Lloyd which was as poor as any he had ever seen, and showed none of that great artiste's magnetic effect on an audience.

Of course, it's better when there's a musician about,' Paul said, as he rewound his film carefully and stowed it back in its cans. 'Trouble is, most of the exhibitors try to economize. I think you need a proper orchestra. Three pieces at least, more if you can – and someone reading too, where it's a story you're telling. If you try that, you'll be all right. But keep an eye on your exhibitors, that's my advice. They're the ones who spoil the work. They're the ones you have to watch out for –'

Before they left, Oliver, with a briskness and a firmness that Luke would not have expected in him, had discussed the purchase of a good deal of equipment, had the information he needed about purchasing more, and had arranged dispatch of some of it to his own premises, together with an order for the basic film material they would need to start on the new project. And Luke, riding back through the dwindling afternoon to the bright cheerfulness of Covent Garden found himself agreeing, with reservations, to do as Oliver wanted.

'But you must understand, sir, that my task at the Gaff comes first –'

'The Gaff?'

Luke reddened a little, with some pleasure and pride. 'It's my new venture, sir, with Edwin Zander, which I mentioned to you. We've taken a large warehouse on the Reach, and we're calling it the Chelsea Gaff, to attract the customers from over the river. There'll be beer, you know, and food, and good shows, all for sixpence the night's entertainment. The place has to be gutted, and rebuilt from the stage up. Now, once we're set up there may be more time to do as you want. I could use some of the daytime to make your films as it will be evenings when the Gaff is open. But not till we're set up, you see –'

Oliver almost rubbed his hands together in delight. 'See how it all works out?' he crowed. 'Here's you with your stage still to build and here's me needing a studio and –'

'Now, just a moment, sir!' Luke said, alarmed, following him off the bus as they made their way back to the tram-line at the foot of Highgate Hill. 'I'm building a theatre with Edwin, not an establishment like the one we've just left and –'

'But my dear boy, why not both? Eh? Why not *both*? I've got some other studio information too, you see. There's one behind the Tivoli, in the Strand, you know, that has a stage set on a huge cup and ball. There's a cup in the centre of the stage underside, and a ball cemented into the ground beneath, and there's wheels on each corner, and a steel plate for them to run on and there are sliding-doors all round the three sides of it; then, when there's a film being made, why, you turn the stage the way the light's best, open the doors and there you are!' And he beamed breathlessly at Luke over his shoulder.

'But theatres don't have stages like that!' Luke said, and then stopped and said slowly. 'But that doesn't mean they can't, does it? I take it this revolving stage can be fixed to face front in the usual way?'

'Of course!' Oliver cried. 'Of course – you use flats and curtains and ground-rows and all the rest of it for a normal presentation at night, but in the daytime when the sun's up and the light's good, you stow it all, turn the stage and lo and behold, you've got a studio! If I were your friend Zander I'd be most taken with the notion. Excellent way to get the best return for his money, using a building that way, I'd have thought, wouldn't you?' And he peered shrewdly at Luke and at last fell silent as the tram clanged on its way down the Camden Road past the stalls selling fruit and vegetables and fish and sheeps' heads to the busy citizens of Holloway, and left the ideas to work like yeast in his young companion's head.

Which they did. The thought of finding a way to repay Edwin more quickly for his help in starting his theatre was not the only attraction of the idea that Oliver had set before him. It was the work that he had glimpsed so very briefly on that Muswell Hill stage that had grasped him. He had seen the way the camera moved back and forth along its track, seen the way it was possible to focus the audience's attention on just one performer and so saw, albeit dimly, the great possibilities there were in the method. The possibility of telling stories in a theatrical way, but with changes of emphasis of the sort that usually had to be obtained by clever manipulation of the stage lights, had great excitement in it, and he felt his pulses quicken as the ideas fermented in him.

'Give me time, sir,' he said at length. 'I need to think more and to talk to Edwin. But I begin to take your points, indeed I do –'

'I need a young partner,' Oliver said with an air of great casualness, but looking sharply at Luke under his brows. 'I can't hide from you the fact that I've got mighty bored of recent years. The Celia is the heart of my fortune of course, and it is also of prime importance to me that it should continue to be all it was when – that I – as my poor father would have wished. He was – I wish you could have known him, Luke. He was such a – well, it's a long time ago now, a long time. And with no son of my own to pass the place on to, there's – well, it's seemed there's little excitement in life for me just recently. Just had to sit and listen to m'sister talk about her boys and girls, which is right and proper, you see, right and proper, but I need someone of my own –'

They had reached the doors of the Celia now, and Oliver halted and looked up earnestly at Luke. 'Do you understand what I'm saying, Luke? You're a cousin and –'

Luke, beginning to feel uncomfortable and yet deeply touched by the old man's obvious sincerity, said awkwardly. 'Not exactly, sir. My grandmother –'

'Was my mother's sister. Indeed she was. I've been through all the family papers, and I know how we're connected. And where we get our taste for theatre from.' He looked wicked for a moment and gave a malicious little giggle. 'Ancient history, my boy, ancient history, but my grandmother – your great-grandmother – she was a great performer, she was! The superb Lilith Lucas. Such an actress – the town will never see another like her. And my other grandparent – Abel, from whom I take my Lackland name, you know – he hated her most heartily! It amuses me greatly, I cannot deny, to think of you and me being together so amiably, as we would be in a business we shared. And if you were my partner, it would have been what my father wanted, you know, for it always saddened him that his father hated his wife so – my mother, you understand, the Celia who gave her name to my Rooms.' And he peered up, in the now almost indigo twilight, at the buildings stretching above him and at the lights beginning to shine through its tall elegant windows and sighed, 'Dear me, I must be getting old. All this mumbling over ancient history! But there, you'll understand, I dare say –'

'Yes,' Luke said and after a moment bent and put his hand on the old man's shoulder and said simply, 'Thank you. I'm grateful to you for putting this work my way, and I shall speak of it to Edwin in as positive a way as I can. I think I can say it is very likely he will agree to our plan. And as for our becoming partners – well, sir, may I take some more time on that? It isn't that I lack concern for you, that I do not recognize the goodness of heart that prompts you, but I – I need time. I can't –'

'Dear me,' Oliver said mildly and blinked up at him in the dimness. 'Dear me, of course I understand! But don't take too long m'boy. I'm seventy-four, you know, seventy-four. It's high time I arranged my affairs. M'sister Phoebe keeps telling me so!' And he cackled suddenly and shook Luke firmly by the hand and disappeared inside the Celia Rooms.

9

Sir Frederick's lecture had been going smoothly for half an hour, and he had been feeling quite pleased with himself, believing he was imparting to his students a genuinely useful grasp of the problems of phthisis, when he suddenly noticed her sitting quietly at the back of the lecture room and faltered. One or two of the students looked up from their busy scribbling of notes to stare at him in some puzzlement, but he recovered quickly and went smoothly on his way, outlining the effects of pulmonary cavitation, the risk of systemic spread to become miliary disease and the discussion of the methods of diagnosis, including Röntgen Rays and the various medications that were of any value – few as they were. But all the time his words came out in their measured and careful sentences his mind was in a confusion. To see her again after so long should have been only interesting, and perhaps a little agreeable; to find his pulses thickening in his ears and his belly lurching the way it had had amazed him. So many years ago, it had been, so many years; how could he still feel that surge of excitement and despair that he used to find in her company? And then his lips quirked a little as he thought of just how long it had been; almost thirty years ago, when he had been a man in his prime, a stripling of forty-five or so. To have found a woman exciting then was reasonable; to find her exciting now was a great compliment to his health and strength.

At last the clock crept round to eleven and as the students stretched and packed up their notebooks and pens and went clattering away to their next lecture in the wards with the other consultants, he stood there staring up at the back row where she remained seated, silent and very still, looking back at him.

'Well, Sophie,' he said, and was embarrassed at the

huskiness in his voice. 'Are you well?'

'Tolerably, Freddy,' she said. 'Tolerably,' and at last got to her feet and came walking down the steep aisle towards him. He could not help but notice how handsome she still was. Her hair, once so dark and curly, was white now but as rich and springing as ever; and her figure, while undeniably thicker than it had been, was still shapely and firm. Her clothes were sober and respectable, if lacking that gloss of town fashion his wife always displayed, being of neat well-cut dark green serge, and her posture was erect and proud without being stiff. He felt his lips curve with pleasure at the sight of her as she reached him.

'It is good to see you, my dear! After so many years – you look splendid! As charming as ever –'

'Freddy, I am fifty-five years old, and no longer need compliments, if I ever did, which I take leave to doubt. You know why I'm here, of course.'

'It isn't difficult to surmise,' he said drily. 'Will you come to my office and take a cup of coffee with me? We can talk there.'

'No time,' she said briskly and he looked at her face, unsmiling and a little creased between the brows, and nodded a little heavily.

'I can understand your anxiety, my dear,' he said gently. 'But nothing will be gained by driving yourself too hard. I dare say you haven't breakfasted if you've come down on the morning train?'

She brushed that aside with an impatient gesture. 'Freddy, for heaven's sake, we can't waste time fussing over breakfast and such nonsense. Where is she? What efforts have you made to find her?'

He turned away and began to straighten his lecture notes on the small desk, packing them into a neat parcel which he tucked under his arm.

'None,' he said at length and looked up at her and then as her brows snapped together added calmly, 'No, Sophie, don't rail at me. That is too easy. Instead, use the same sort of diagnostic skill you would apply to a patient. Imagine your Letty is not your daughter, behaving in a manner which you find not to your taste, but see her as a patient displaying symptoms. She is a young woman who is aged almost twenty-five – she reached her majority four years ago. She has an adequate if not princely personal income which is hers entirely to control. She is intelligent, has been well-reared and educated, and above all has been taught by a woman who is of strong mind, great determination and great will. You. The result of all this is to produce a person who is clearly well able to think for herself, to act for herself and who can, I believe, be trusted to behave sensibly in most matters.

'Now, what is she in fact doing? What are her symptoms, in other words? She is thinking for herself and rejecting a course of action that had been chosen for her, by others, from her earliest youth. She is taking steps to make her own decisions, and also to ensure that she will be free to do so. She is refusing to allow any persons who might deflect her from her intentions to find her, in order that they may not put on her any pressure that she would find it difficult to resist. Those are the symptoms, are they not?'

'You are being quite absurd, Freddy,' Sophie said, and her voice was clipped and her eyes narrowed as she stared at him. 'My daughter is alone in London after having been brought up carefully in a small town where all knew her; she has chosen wilfully to detach herself from her brother's protection, and from my guidance as well as from your teaching, to go and racket about the town like some hoyden, and all you can do is talk of symptoms and –'

'Oh, I doubt she's racketing around town like a hoyden or any other such dubious character,' Freddy said mildly. 'The Letty I had come to know these past months was a young lady of good sense and excellent manners. I cannot imagine that she will have changed so radically so soon! I do not see her with her face painted and her gowns cut too low simply because she has chosen to leave Nellie's.'

Sophie looked a little uncomfortable at that. 'Well, no, I was perhaps a little – but you must agree, Freddy, that her behaviour is unsupportable! I have been in a state of the most painful anxiety ever since her letter came, and have been sleepless with worry over what she may be doing and where she is!'

97

'Yet it has been a week or more since she went, Sophie, has it not? When did you receive her letter?'

She reddened painfully at that. 'Oh, I know, I know! It was a week ago I heard from Barty, and her letter came shortly after, but I had a clinic full and no locum to deal with my surgeries. I had to wait until Dr Bernard could come over from Heptonstall before I could leave, and then did so, at once. It is no lack of concern on my part that I did not come as soon as I heard – I have a duty to my patients and –'

'Of course you have, Sophie! You are a physician, are you not! You worked as hard as any person I ever knew to become so, and have ever since you qualified been providing the best of care to the people of your town – because you put your vocation over and above all personal considerations. That is right and proper, is it not?'

'Well, of course – but – you seemed to feel my concern to see the locum settled before I left indicated lack of concern for Letty, so –'

He shook his head, and smiled at her. 'No, my dear, I simply wanted you to realize that Letty is her mother's daughter! She has put her vocation before her personal considerations, before her duty to you and her undoubted love for you and her brother. She has chosen to live her own life in her own way; just as you did, and, as I recall, in the teeth of considerable opposition.'

'I had no parents to guide me or to care about what I did!' Sophie said, her head up. 'They were dead when my opportunity arose, and my brothers and sisters too – I was alone. It was different for me –'

He shook his head again and put out a hand towards her, but she ignored it and he drew back, but still spoke in the same reasonable and affectionate tone of voice.

'My dear, you cannot convince me nor, I think, yourself, that any parental opposition, had they been alive, would have made an atom of difference to you. The young Sophie I recall so well was a woman of iron soul and fiery temper, who would do what she could and cared nothing – or remarkably little – for what she should. And she has reared a daughter worthy of her. A girl who will do what she needs to do. She wrote me a

98

letter which made me feel far less anxious about her than I might have done, for it was so eminently sensible, so like the sort of letter her mother would have written if she had been in the same situation.'

For a moment he thought she would weep, for her eyes glistened and her mouth drooped, and he put his hand out again; but at once the soft look on her face changed, and the glistening in her eyes became a hard glitter and her mouth lost its softness and became tight.

'I begin to think you positively encouraged her in this lunatic behaviour!' she said harshly. 'You seem singularly unconcerned for her welfare or her safety! Would you be so casual were she *your* daughter?'

'I am not being casual,' he said, his own face tightening at the sting. 'I am trying only to help you regard your daughter with affection instead of anger. No daughter of mine would have had the strength of purpose to act as decisively as Letty has, more's the pity. But I swear to you that had I had a girl with even half of Letty's good sense, I would react to her behaviour – whatever it was – precisely as I have to Letty's. When she wrote to me as she did, expressing her feelings so clearly and so wisely, I knew I had done her an injustice in regarding her as a merely lazy and inattentive student. She made it as clear as it could be made that she needed to live her own life in her own way, and I am happy for her that she feels able to make such decisions. I can't believe she wrote to you in any less honest terms. And as a woman of strength and determination yourself I am amazed that you can't see that you are wrong to come here to seek her out as though she were a stupid child of the ordinary sort, in need of protection from herself.'

'What sort of mother would I be if I were not concerned?' Sophie burst out. 'How can you imagine I would be anything but eaten with distress at –'

'Concerned, of course,' Freddy said gently, 'anxious and distressed naturally. But to be so punitive as to come and try to seek her out and, I imagine, reprimand her – it is that that I find sadly out of kilter in you.'

'I don't care what you think!' Sophie said furiously and turned and marched to the door of the lecture-room, pulling her green mantle over her shoulders as she went. 'I believe it to be my duty to find her and bring her back to her studies and that is precisely what I shall do, whatever you say! And –'

'Sophie, please – don't let us part bad friends! I had hoped – we enjoyed a special friendship once, and I had hoped we could perhaps renew it even after so long a time. Please, don't go in a rage. Where can you go, anyway? This is London, my dear – you can't just walk the streets and hope to see her somewhere!'

She stopped and looked back at him but he could not see her expression, for her eyes were shadowed. 'It was because we were once so – such friends that I had hoped you would be in sympathy with me. It is why I sat and waited through your lecture to speak to you. It was an excellent lecture –'

He gave a little crack of laughter at that. 'Thank you. It is a subject in which I have taken a close interest this past few years. Please, Sophie, what are you going to do?'

'I am indeed going to search for her,' Sophie said after a moment. 'And I shall find her –'

'My dear, how?' he said, reasonably, and this time it was she who gave a little laugh.

'I shall think as she did, that is all! As you have pointed out so carefully, she *is* my daughter. I know her mind as well as most, I imagine. And she is logical and practical. She will have chosen to go to an hotel while she collects her ideas and plans and will know that she must avoid the sort of establishment the family would use and where she might be seen. She would know that on the rare occasions I have come to London this past few years, I have stayed at the Domus Medicus of the Royal Society of Medicine in Wimpole Street, and will therefore avoid that district. She will also avoid any district where you might be likely to meet her out and about, so that means the hotels in the Euston and King's Cross district are unsuitable, living as you do at Tavistock Square.

'However, she will know that districts within close reach of the other railway stations are well-provided with hotels of a reasonable quality, and she will seek one of those. Not Waterloo, I suspect – a shade too near Covent Garden, for all it is the other side of the river. Which leaves either Paddington or

Victoria. I shall start by visiting hotels in Paddington, of which there are rather fewer than there are in the Victoria area, as I recall, and if I'm systematic, should do well enough. You see, Freddy? I am determined to find her, and find her I shall!'

He shook his head and sighed. 'I dare say you will. But whether you will be happy when you succeed is another matter. Sophie, come back and see me, when – whatever happens? Please? When you are – when you feel a little less distressed, perhaps we can talk as we used to and – it would be agreeable, wouldn't it?'

She stood very still by the door, and then after a moment said quietly, 'And how is Phoebe?'

He was silent for a moment and then said in a colourless voice, 'Well enough. Busy with the grandchildren and great-grandchildren. I – it gets a little lonely, sometimes, Sophie.'

She said nothing, staring at him with those shadowed eyes and then, sharply, shook her head and went, leaving him standing beside the desk in the deserted lecture-room feeling rather older and more tired than he had for a very long time.

She did it precisely as she said she would. Barty had wanted to come with her, but she had refused briskly, pointing out to him that it was of great importance that he keep on with his own studies.

'It is bad enough Letty is wasting so much time,' she said. 'She will have much to catch up with, both in lecture notes and in practical work. It would be wasteful in the extreme to put you in the same situation, so you continue your work as though I were not in London at all, and I will bring her back here as soon as I find her. Mrs Partridge will see to it her room is ready, I'm sure.'

And Barty, obedient as ever, returned to his books, and she put on her most comfortable boots and went out to look for her daughter, starting in Paddington to which district she took a hansom cab, and argued sturdily and successfully with the cabby when he took her for an out-of-town flat and tried to overcharge her.

She stood for a moment outside the first hotel in Sussex Gardens, a tall terraced house with a neat notice offering

'Respectable Rooms, All Services, Every Consideration Given', and stared down the long grey street at the multiplicity of signs that adorned it, and for a moment quailed, for it seemed that almost every other building was a similar sort of hotel; but then she took a deep breath and began marching up the front steps to the small entry of this first hotel, demanding imperiously to speak to the manager at once since she had an enquiry to make.

She had thought carefully about how to make her search and knew that there was a considerable risk of being refused the information she required, for hotel managers were experienced and wily creatures who knew better than to become involved in any matter that might cause talk and bring ill-repute to their establishments; so she had planned her approach accordingly.

It worked well. The manager of the first hotel listened to her tale of a sick patient who had been in her care – and she had brought careful evidence of her own status as a physician – and who now needed to be found forthwith if she was not to become more severely ill. Sophie did not say the girl was disturbed in her mind but managed to convey the possibility with great delicacy, and at once the man was all eagerness to aid her. They searched the register for names and Sophie scrutinized handwritings as carefully as she could; and went on her way certain that her quarry had not stayed at any time at the Tyburnia, leaving behind her a manager deeply relieved to know that he had escaped the dreadful danger of harbouring some sort of lunatic.

It worked with the same efficacy at each hotel she visited, especially as she became more and more adept at her tale, and she read register after register, seeking ever more desperately for some evidence of her daughter's presence, and finding none.

By the end of the day she was exhausted to the point of tears, a rare experience for Sophie for, over the long years of struggle to run her clinic in Haworth and the long years of her lonely widowhood, she had learned to become the self-sufficient and determined person she was. Not for Sophie Brotherton Lackland the luxury of hot tears. Not for her the weakness other women used as part of their stock in trade. She had been softer, once, perhaps, had known what it was to allow herself the freedom to be weak, but not now. Now she was all steel and whipcord, a strong woman with powerful ideas and a matching will. And she had willed it that she would find her erring daughter, and find her she would, weary though she was.

Part of her fatigue was due to the effort she had to make to keep Freddy's words at the back of her mind. Somewhere deep inside herself she feared he might be right; that Letty had behaved as Sophie herself would have done, that she was a young woman of sense and ability who could cope well enough with her own life and who had – a painful thought indeed – only run away as she had because she had told herself her mother would be so opposed to any attempt on her part to lead her own life in her own way. That was not to be thought of, the possibility that Letty had fled into hiding for fear of her own mother, the mother who loved her so very dearly. So Sophie put her head down and went on, doggedly, marching along the grey pavements in the cold April sunshine, covering miles of the Paddington streets.

And then, after forcing herself to stop for supper in an ABC tea-room, where she ate a poached egg and drank some over-brewed tea (for her physician's mind told her that she must eat or be ill) she took a cab to Victoria and started again.

It was at seven o'clock, when the streets had leapt to evening life in the gaslight, when shop windows poured their cheerful beams along the paving-stones under the blue velvet of the spring sky, she found what she had been searching for for so many hours – Letty's signature, clear and unambiguous, in a register in a small hotel in Ebury Street.

But she was too late.

'Miss Lackland, madam?' the manager said. 'A very nice quiet young lady. I'd never have thought she was ill in any way, that I wouldn't! She left this afternoon, madam. Seemed very happy, she did – told me she was off to be an actress, madam, and was to be staying with her friends. No, she didn't say where. Just that she was to stay with friends and be an actress.'

10

Letty sat on the dimity counterpane of the bed and stared out of the dormer-window at the cluster of sooty chimney-pots and the sparrows squabbling noisily in the gutters of the steeply-sloping roofs and wanted to giggle. It seemed too absurd to be sitting here, surrounded by her own possessions so neatly and agreeably arranged that the room looked as though she had inhabited it for ever, and to be part of the household. Somewhere far below her she could hear the tinkle of a piano; someone was playing the Barcarole from *The Tales of Hoffman* and then there was a little burst of laughter as someone else started the gramophone and the shrill notes of Nellie Melba's voice rang out. There were footsteps clattering on the stairs and people singing and altogether the house seemed to hum with activity and life and above all youth. And she hugged herself delightedly and curled her feet under her and went on staring dreamily at her pretty new lilac-and-white bedroom, trying to get her thoughts in order.

It had all happened so neatly that it was almost as though it had been planned; but it hadn't been, or at least not the way it had turned out. Not that she hadn't intended to plan something like it; she had indeed taken Dora Montefiore's words very much to heart, and had virtually screwed up her courage to do as she had advised; but in the event it had not been necessary.

She had set out to do as Dora said; she had taken herself on the omnibus to Chelsea Reach, but had only got as far as Sloane Square, and then, frightened at her own temerity, had hurried down the steps and off, much to the indignation of the conductor who had been about to ring the bell and had felt so confused and shaky that she took herself to a tea shop for a restorative brew and time to think.

And as she had walked into the place, bustling as it was with people, for it was now early evening and the office-clerks and the shop-girls were seeking sustenance before rushing off to their suburban homes or to their evening's entertaintment, and stood for a moment looking round at the brightly-lit clutter of marble-topped tables and frilly-aproned waitresses, she was startled to hear her own name called. She looked round blankly, confused by the hubbub, for there was in addition to the clatter of china and glass and the gossiping voices a ladies' orchestra in the corner scraping away unevenly on ill-tuned fiddles. The total effect was bewildering; and then she heard her name again, louder, and this time he took her by the elbow.

She had stood and gaped at him, almost blankly, and he had laughed and said a little awkwardly, 'Oh, my dear, have you forgotten me already? Luke O'Hare –'

She had laughed too, a little breathlessly. 'No, of course not. I mean – I was just so startled to see you!'

'Not as startled as I was to see you! After all, this is my part of London rather than yours. I was having a little supper, in a hurry, before I go back to the Gaff to do some work, because I have to go on to Edwin's later – he's having another party and –'

'The Gaff?' she murmured and allowed him to lead her to his table, which was under a curling and rather yellowing palm and settle her facing him.

'Indeed, yes! So much has happened since we last talked – I must tell you all about it. But first tell me what you're doing here in Sloane Square of all places! It's a long way from the hospital surely! It's splendid indeed to see you here though, because I wanted to see you again, and was thinking about how to find the time – which sounds ungracious of me, but you'll understand when I explain – and there you are, just as though I'd conjured you up like a genie out of the lamp!'

She stared at him over the table as she peeled off her gloves, looking at him with pleasure but also with some surprise. He seemed quite different from the way he had been when they had last met; full of excitement and with his cheeks flaming red and his eyes glittering. 'But he's not well,' she thought suddenly, as the knowledge from the years spent beside her mother in her clinics as well as the hours spent as a Nellie's student sharpened her observation. 'He's thinner than he was, even after so short a time –'

'Now, first tell me what you will have, and then I will tell you all my news. Waitress! Ah! Tea, Letty? Toast or cakes or – No – you're sure – just tea, then, please miss, as soon as you like. Now, Letty, why are you here?'

'Oh,' she said lightly, 'just wandering, you know. I'll tell you my news when you've told me yours. You're clearly about to burst with it!'

He laughed at that, his eyes shining even more and then he leaned back in his seat and began to talk, and as the words came bursting out his hands, very eloquent long-fingered hands, made shapes and patterns in the air to illustrate what he was saying. He told her about the Gaff, and Edwin's determination that it should be Luke's affair to run as he thought best; he told her of Oliver's ideas about films, and how at first he had scoffed and then stopped to realize what a marvellous idea it was; he talked of carpenters and the cost of timber and paint, of the deviousness of builders' merchants and the stupidity of plumbers and plasterers and was altogether in a state of overpowering excitement. And she warmed to his happiness and stopped noticing that he didn't look well, indeed she quite forgot the idea had ever come to her.

And then, when her tea had arrived and he had returned to his neglected supper of an omelette, she began, haltingly at first, but gradually with greater fluency, to tell him of her own news. How she had finally crystallized her own ideas and decided that she had in her that special fire he had described that night at Edwin's house and how much she lacked the same fire when it came to the practice of medicine. How she had been staying at an hotel in Victoria –

He had put down his knife and fork with a clatter. 'You've actually left?' he said staring at her. 'You're living quite alone? What do your people say?'

'Yes, I have left. Yes, I'm living alone, and they don't know where I am so they can't offer me their opinions,' she said as calmly as she could, and after a moment he had laughed delightedly and leaned forwards and taken her hand between both of his and held it closely and said eagerly, 'Oh, well done! Well done indeed!'

'You don't think I'm a fool?' she said abruptly. 'Or – too – oh, you know. Pushy? Fast?'

'Not in the least,' he said and tightened his grasp on her hand. 'Not in the least. I think you're brave and tremendous! Not at all what I would have expected.'

She looked indignant at that. 'You mean you thought me cowardly and –'

'Oh pooh,' he said and let go her hand at last, leaving her feeling a little shaky about the wrists and knees. 'Don't be missish, like those silly Oram cousins! You know quite well what I mean. I think you were wise to do as you did, because we've all got to do what's right for us. It's not selfish – it just makes sense. If you're happy, then you make the people about you happy. If you're miserable, then however dutiful you are, you can't fail but make the people about you as miserable as you are. It's common sense.'

'I suppose so,' she had said, and then smiled into her tea-cup. Splendid Dora Montefiore! She had said something of the same and had been so right and Letty began to relax, feeling better than she had since the day she had gone storming out of Nellie's to live her own life in her own way.

'Now, my dear, we must make plans for you, must we not?' he was saying, signalling to the waitress for the bill at the same time. 'Later, we'll talk – but now I must hurry, because the wretched carpenter will be there, and I mustn't let him get the notion that I don't care about time-keeping, for indeed I do, a great deal. Come along now!'

'Come along? Where to!' she had said blankly as he pulled her chair back so that she had perforce to get to her feet.

'Why to the Gaff, of course,' he said impatiently, and she followed him out of the cheerfulness of the tea-shop to the busy dark street almost in a dream.

They had taken a hansom to the Gaff, and he had chattered all the way about the design of the stage he was to have, and the sliding-doors in the building which would enable it to be used as a film studio by daylight; and she sat and listened, happy just to be with him and no longer despondent or frightened as she had been. She was fast realizing, even though she hardly dared to put it into words, that she cared a great deal more for this young man than she had ever cared for anyone; that his face and his form and his presence beside her were all she needed to feel comfortable. She was going with him to something called a Gaff, she told herself dreamily in the swaying darkness as the clopping of the horses' hooves took them down the King's Road towards Luna Street, but she would as cheerfully have gone to hell if he'd told her he was taking her there.

He had plunged immediately into animated talk with the dour man in the dirty black coat and twine-fastened trousers who was waiting for them, leaving her free to peer about and she did so with a sinking heart, for she could not remember ever seeing a place so gloomy or so dirty. There were a couple of reeking oil-lamps hanging from filthy beams to provide the only fitful light there was, and on all sides she could see only piles of junk and dust and puddles of water where the roof had leaked on rainy nights. And she shivered as a rustle of sound told her that there were mice or worse around in large numbers, and the musty smell in the cold air reinforced that awareness.

She wrapped her mantle about her a little more closely and waited for him as stoically as she could, as he arranged with great detail the delivery of timber to renew the rotted ones that held the great doors in place and to build the new stage he required, and then saw his dour carpenter off the premises and came back to collect her.

'Well,' he said, eagerly. 'What do you think of my Gaff?'

'Why Gaff?' she asked, needing time.

'Oh, that's what the slum people used to call the cheap public-houses that used to give them a show – they were called penny gaffs, and they were dreadful! But my Gaff will be different! Not dreadful at all, but magnificent –'

'Tell me how it will be,' she said, not knowing what she could say that would be positive about this dismal wreck of a warehouse and he launched into his account at once and, as she stood there in the reeking ill-lit cold and listened, she saw it grow beneath his fingers. She saw the rows of painted benches with bright rag cushions on them to soften their impact, and the small round tables arranged between them, saw the gaily-painted walls, with the garish posters on them, and the broad polished oak bar at the back with its mirrors behind where beer and cider and hot sausages and little dishes of cockles and mussels and whelks would be sold to eager buyers. She saw the stage, neat and tidy with its swathe of red plush curtains – for no proper theatre tabs can ever be any colour other than the richest of crimson! – and the dressing-rooms to the side, with their running water '– for it is wrong and disgusting that actors should suffer such privations backstage as they do –' and the stores where scenery flats would be, and the workshops where the flats would be built, and the special locked rooms where the cameras would be stored, and she kindled as she let it all fill her mind and then, as naively as a child, clapped her cold hands together and cried, 'Oh, it's all so beautiful!' And he had caught her hands and swung her round in a sudden access of joy and laughed and laughed until he coughed and could hardly stop, and she had become quite alarmed for a moment as he had turned away with his shoulders bent. But then he had recovered and shaken away her earnest enquiries and they had walked back to 47 Cheyne Walk arm-in-arm, laughing and excited and chattering all the way. A magical time.

But then it had all changed, so much, and as she sat on the dimity counterpane and stared out at the chimney-pots she looked back on the evening – was it only last night? It seemed for ever ago – and tried to see herself as dispassionately as she could, tried to see how she had behaved, how it had been, how she had looked in others' eyes.

Jessica's eyes. She scowled a little at that thought and then dragged her mind back, making herself be a little creature sitting high in the corner of the drawing-room that night, watching the activity below, little Letty watching real Letty make a fool of herself.

Yet she hadn't. She couldn't have done, for otherwise how would she be here, now, knowing what lay in the future? It couldn't have been so!

It had all started harmlessly enough. There had been half a

dozen people sitting around the drawing-room, some on cushions on the floor, some lounging easily in Edwin's big chairs, and all looking as cheerful and eager as children at a party, and Luke had launched into an account of his progress at the Gaff, telling them delightedly that the next morning as ever was the real work would begin. Edwin had been delighted, too, and then, once he had all the information he wanted about the Gaff – for he became bored very quickly – had turned to her and demanded to know all that she had been doing for the past week, for '– I've missed you sorely, and told Luke over and over again to bring you here again, and he failed me *miserably*, the wretch that he is!'

Before she had been able to open her mouth to answer Luke had said, 'She's left the hospital! Isn't it capital? Such a splendid thing to have done, for she has decided to join us and become an actress – and I know she'll be splendid, won't you, Letty?'

And then Jessica had cut in, her voice light and easy, but with a bite beneath the surface that chilled Letty physically.

'My dear,' she had fluted. 'Such courage! And tell me, do, of your past experience! What shall you be able to tell the managers you have done when they sit down to decide in which new West End play to give you the lead?'

'I – I know I have not had a great deal of experience,' Letty had said, and lifted her chin to look at the other girl's mocking face, thinking at the same time how very beautiful a face it was, and feeling very aware of her own shortcomings in the beauty department. 'But at school, you know, I did all the best parts and we did a great many plays. I was Ophelia and Rosalind and –'

'Ophelia and Rosalind! Fancy that,' Jessica had drawled and looked sideways at Luke and sketched a wink at him and Letty had felt her face flame.

'I'll try, anyway,' she retorted. 'I know that school plays don't amount to much for professional actresses, but I do assure you that in Yorkshire we were considered very good indeed, and people came for many miles to see us and –'

'The ponies and traps must have burned up the roads,' Jessica said, even more drawling, and laughed and Letty took a deep breath to retort and then, as she caught an amused glance exchanged between Gillick (who was as usual sitting there drinking Edwin's wine and eating his food) and Jessica, subsided. Nothing she could say, she told herself miserably, would have any effect. Jessica was nasty and that was that. Letty had met enough such over the years to know that there were people who could not help but behave unkindly, and the only way to deal with them was with lofty contempt. She tried hard to be loftily contemptuous, but she knew she was not making much of a fist of it and began to be miserable again.

Luke had missed much of this exchange, busy as he was talking to Edwin about money, but now he turned and said, 'I've been thinking about our first production. We need something that is lively, and amusing, but not *too* light. We want to show people who might criticize our plans that we intend to bring good-quality plays to our Gaff. But we mustn't bore the customers, that's the thing, nor frighten them off, and much as I love Shakespeare, I think I might lose them before I start if I begin with him. So I wondered. Goldsmith perhaps –'

Letty had clapped her hands together at once and cried eagerly, '*She Stoops to Conquer* – of course! The funniest and most knockabout thing you can do, if you do it right. And it's a most tender romance too which audiences love and –'

He smiled at her swiftly, grateful for her immediate response. 'Indeed, yes. Just what I was thinking. Edwin?'

'Oh, for my part, dear boy, you must do as you think best! I am sure it will be splendid whatever it is –'

'And perhaps you can find a part for our shining new actress, Luke!' Jessica said and giggled, that little fluting sound that made Letty's face tighten. 'Though there are few small parts enough in the play as I recall.'

'I think you should try her for Kate, Luke,' Gillick said and grinned lazily at Jessica and, as though he had said it aloud, Letty felt his thought; that she would make a dreadful mess of any attempt at the part, and give them all great cause for mirth.

And Jessica smiled at Luke with great sweetness and said in a honeyed tone, 'A marvellous idea, is it not, Luke? Mind you, when I last played Kate, I remember the director told me that it had always been miscast before. That so often directors chose actresses who looked like the servant aspect of the role rather than those who looked clearly the lady, and that for his part he would always cast for the lady in the future, having seen me play it. It is an interesting idea, is it not?'

Luke looked at her, his face expressionless, and then at Letty, and after a moment said in a voice that showed no hint of any emotion other than interest, 'Would you care to try for Kate Hardcastle, Letty?'

'I have played it,' she said after a moment. 'Many times. We gave a dozen or more performances and –'

'Then we shall hear you now, shall we?' Edwin clapped his hands and jumped to his feet to start pushing furniture about, making a space in the middle of the drawing-room and harrying them all busily. 'We shall have the Gaff's first audition here and now, and it will be *so* exciting and wonderful – at once, now, Gillick, move the tea-tray and then this chair and –'

'Oh, no!' Letty jumped up and shook her head urgently at Luke. 'I can't – I really can't! I need time to –'

'There is often little time to spare in a busy theatre company,' Luke said. His voice sounded clipped, and suddenly she felt as though he had turned against her too. 'I think we must do as Edwin asks. He is, after all, the source of our good fortune.'

And then they were ready, and she stood there looking piteously at Luke, wanting to turn and run, but then, as she was about to do just that she again caught sight of that red-gold head and the enchanting face that was Jessica peeping over Gillick's shoulder and a germ of anger planted itself in her belly and began to grow. How dare that girl sit there looking at her so! How dare she be so certain that Letty Lackland would make a fool of herself! And somewhere up in the corner of the great drawing-room a little Letty peered down at her and huzzahed and egged her on, and she took a deep breath as Luke said, 'Well, what scene shall it be, Letty? Have you a favourite?'

'I – not particularly – Act Three perhaps. When Young Marlow first thinks Kate a servant –'

'I know the scene you mean. I'll cue you, then – ah – let me see – "As for Miss Hardcastle, she's too grave and sentimental for me." '

Letty took a deep breath and felt the years slip away. She felt herself eighteen years old again and standing there on the school stage with an audience waiting, alert and eager to be entertained, and the lines slid out of her memory on to the tip of her tongue and came out as they should. ' "Did your honour call?" ' she said.

' "No child. Besides, from the glimpse I had of her, I think she squints." '

' "I'm sure sir, I heard the bell ring." ' And now she felt more secure with the country accent, letting the burr enter it gently and adding movement too, bobbing a small curtsey as she said the line.

' "I have pleased my father, however, by coming down, and I'll tomorrow please myself by returning." '

Luke was now throwing himself into the part of Young Marlow with great satisfaction, marching about the room, his head down as he stared at his boots in the proper fashion.

' "Perhaps the other gentleman called, sir," ' Letty said, moving to follow Luke's moves, so that she put herself in his line of vision.

' "I tell you, no." '

' "I should be glad to know sir. We have such a parcel of servants." '

' "No, no I tell you –" ' Luke turned exactly on cue, looked Letty in the face and produced the slow dawning of admiration that the part demanded, saying in a new voice, ' "Yes, child, I think I did call. I wanted – I wanted – I vow, child, you are vastly handsome!" '

And Letty giggled and turned her head away and simpered in best Goldsmith style and said, ' "Oh, la, sir, you make me ashamed!" ' Across the room Edwin tittered and she got a glimpse of his delighted face, and over his shoulder Jessica's far-from-delighted one, and felt the strength move into her further and further; and swung on into the scene with great gusto.

' "Never was a more sprightly malicious eye! – yes, my dear, I did call. Have you any of your ah – what-do-you-call-it in the house?" '

' "No, sir, we have been out of that these ten days –" '

On and on they went, the scene becoming ever more rollicking as Young Marlow seized his Kate in his arms, as she struggled delightedly and Marlow made his exit with the famous, ' "My old luck – I never nicked seven that I did not throw ames-ace three times following –" ' and the room burst into applause, even Jessica having to make a pretence of putting her hands together.

'Oh, you were splendid, splendid, Letty!' Edwin surged to his feet and came bustling across to seize her by the hand and pump it up and down. 'Now, dear old Luke, tell me she *shall* play the part, will you? For I was quite enchanted! I don't know the play well, and I shan't pretend I do, but if it's all like that, then I shall love every moment of it and we shall make a fortune with it. Let's agree to give Letty her first part!'

'Oh, I would have thought Luke would want to hold real auditions for his first production,' Jessica said. 'Parlour-games are one thing, dear Edwin, but on a real stage, with a little voice projection needed, it's rather different. Poor Letty was having a little trouble, I thought, getting the vowels across the room, were you not, my dear? I did so feel for you – I know how difficult I found it until I worked and trained myself –'

Letty said nothing, for now the sheer enormity of what she had done had filled her. She had played a scene of Goldsmith in front of a group of experts, she the mere amateur, and the thought of it made her belly turn over and quite dissolved her voice.

Luke smiled then and touched her shoulder. 'I dare say we shall have to try again, on the stage, when it's built, but at present showing, Letty, I'd say you had an excellent chance of doing the part well, with training. You've got the essence in you though you've a lot to learn. I think I should let you try when we audition on the stage and we can see how you get on. I've few doubts you'll do well.'

'Better and better!' Edwin said. 'Then we shall see you every day, for after rehearsals we shall all sit here and be cosy together. I shall have a lovely time – where are you living, Letty my dear, now you've left your hospital? Have you far to travel to us?'

'I – I have a room in an hotel in Victoria,' Letty said, a little shakily, trying to control her voice and grateful to find she could speak at all. 'I shall look for lodgings a little nearer, I think, to make it easier – I mean, if you're sure you want me for the theatre, Luke –'

'I'm sure,' he said, almost casually. 'If not for Kate, in the event certainly for something. It will depend on how much time I have to teach. When it comes to the theatre, you see, friendship must come second to professionalism –'

'As you will soon discover, Letty, as you will soon discover!' Jessica said and laughed that maddening silvery laugh again, and kissed Edwin and went away in a shower of scented frills with Gillick fast on her heels.

'Lodgings?' Edwin turned back to Letty. 'I shan't hear of it! Not when I have this vast house to fill. I've been *bouleversé* since dear old Luke insisted he must sleep at his precious Gaff – he's using the office for his bedroom, and as cold as *charity* I swear it is, but he's as stubborn as charity is cold, so what can I do? So if you will come here then I shall be happy again to have my house full. I have a room decorated in the *sweetest* of lilac flowers – it will suit you to a T and you shall have it! Now, I shan't take no for an answer. Tomorrow morning, first thing, my dear Letty, put your possessions in a cab and come to number 47 and we shall hang out bunting to welcome you!'

And with her head in a whirl, and feeling in a curious way that, as Luke was no longer living at 47 Cheyne Walk it would be quite proper for her to do so, Letty assented. And now she sat on a dimity counterpane in a lilac room at the top of the house listening to the Barcarole and Nellie Melba fighting it out and staring out at London chimney-pots in a strange new world that was from henceforth to be all hers. And she didn't know whether to laugh with joy or shiver with apprehension, for both emotions were struggling in her and making her feel decidedly odd.

11

The family had not enjoyed themselves so well, nor had so much to talk about that was so enthralling for months, for most of the time the clan lived very proper quiet lives. Babies were born, grew up and contracted suitable marriages and more babies were born and that was about all. None of Phoebe's numerous grandchildren and great-grandchildren had ever been known to do anything at all interesting or discussable, according to the Henriques and Landis cousins, and none of the Orams and the Buckley-Lacklands had anything but contempt for the Henriques and Landises, who were of course so much richer than they and so much duller; but now all over London their drawing-rooms buzzed with chatter and surmise and not a little malicious laughter, certainly on the Henriques and Landis sides.

For Pheobe had lost her temper most spectacularly and had not minded one whit who knew it. When Freddy had brought his cousin Sophie Lackland to Tavistock Square to dinner she had been cool enough, not to say shrewish, but when he had insisted that he must accompany her back to Haworth because she was so distressed by her daughter's defection, Phoebe had been very put out indeed.

'Such a nonsense!' she had said at tea that afternoon at Alice Oram's to Cecily, loud enough for Rachel Damont to hear and enjoy, 'As though the woman wasn't perfectly capable of taking care of herself on a train! As for the daughter running away from Nellie's – what do you expect when you allow a girl to become a medical student? I thought it disgusting when this Sophie woman did it, and I think it just as disgusting now. The girl's clearly had an appalling hugger-mugger education and I for one am not all surprised she has taken to her heels. Freddy should know better than to involve himself with such matters, encroaching cat that the woman is. She set her cap at him once before, and I have no doubt she's doing it again. Widow, indeed! I'm not surprised her wretched husband died. It was his best policy I imagine –'

And then, as though that was not enough – for it was all over the family in a matter of hours that Phoebe was jealous of old Uncle Freddy and wasn't it too rich – Oliver came to dinner at Tavistock Square that very evening at the same time as Sarah Landis and her Estella – who was known by everyone to have the sharpest tongue of them all – and told Phoebe that he was to invest all his money in some newfangled film business and that he was to make Lucas O'Hare, a very dubious character indeed, as Phoebe was quite sure, his partner. And then he had added, 'And I think, a full partner, even though he has no investment, you know, for he is a cousin after all and most ill-provided for –' And Phoebe, never known for her self-control, had been most spectacularly angry and had scolded poor old Oliver quite shockingly while Sarah Landis and her Estella listened entranced, and had then developed a devastating migraine and taken to her bed for two days. Oh, it was all too delightful, according to the Henriqueses and Landises and too distressing according to the Orams and Buckley-Lacklands.

Not that any of it penetrated to the people who were the lynch-pins of the talk. Sophie picked up the strings of her life again in Haworth, running her clinic with her usual efficiency, if a little more grimly than she had been used to and, if she was distressed about her daughter, none but she knew it. Letters came from London but she said nothing of their contents to her younger son Samuel, nor did she refer to them or to Letty when she wrote her regular Sunday screed to Barty. It was as though nothing untoward had happened at all – until people looked more closely at Sophie's face and saw lines that had not been there before.

As for Letty in London, she was in a whirlwind of activity, and during each long working-day as happy as she could ever remember being. The Gaff was coming on apace and, as April melted into a glorious May, with day after day of sunshine in which the street-corner flower-stalls were alive with narcissus and primroses and violets and some early tulips, she became more and more expert at what she was doing.

Which was not acting, not yet; it was with hammer and nails and paint that she found she had skill, and under Luke's guidance and with the help of whoever happened to be staying at Edwin's house and was willing to join in, built and painted the store of scenery Luke felt they might need for future productions. She took great pride in her cottage exterior with round-the-door practical roses (made of paper twisted on to hempen branches) and in her cottage interior with slotted sections on the walls to take additional furniture and which was regarded by Luke as being very useful indeed not just for the stage productions, but also for the films when they started them. Her hands became roughened and a little scarred, and her hair seemed always to carry a faint hint of the smell of turpentine with it, but she did not mind at all.

For it was not just the joy of making things that filled her, considerable though that was. It was being with Luke in the companionship of labour that made her most happy. They would work side by side for long hours exchanging little more than monosyllables, and those mostly about the work they did. They would sit side by side over the lunch sent round by Benjamin Fickling, the landlord of the King's Head public house along the Embankment, eating cheese sandwiches and apple-pie with as much eager hunger as though they were oysters and lobster mayonnaise, and talking desultorily of the work or of nothing much at all. And all the time she felt the net of their relationship grow and tighten around her. It was not what he said or did; it was just being together that mattered.

And she knew, without his saying so, that he felt the same about her presence. He would whistle between his teeth softly as he worked, a tuneless little sound, and curse a little when he banged his fingers with the hammer, or a piece of wood misbehaved, and then grin at her and make a grimace, and there was a world of communication in their silence – a supremely happy time in many ways.

Now and again, at the end of the day, when they could do no more because they were waiting for a delivery of materials with which to make the rows of seating, or for the paint to dry so that they could get on to the next stage, they had time for other things, and Letty, on one evening when Luke had to be incarcerated with Edwin so that they could sort out their finances, went on an impulse to another meeting of the WSPU.

She had found a notice in *The Times* announcing a meeting at Chelsea Town Hall, and went along a little shyly, remembering how conspicuous she had felt at the first meeting; but this time there were more people there – obviously, she decided, because it was an evening and that made it possible for women who worked in shops and offices to take part – and altogether was much more lively than that very first meeting when she had met Dora Montefiore. There were two men speakers, Members of Parliament, and the audience shouted lively questions at them and barracked their answers if they didn't like them – mostly they did not – and generally behaved as women, in Letty's experience, did not normally behave at public meetings. She felt exhilaration lift in her at it all, and also felt her convictions, which had never been more than superficial on this score, harden and become more and more tinged with anger. It *was* all wrong that intelligent, sensible and capable people should be put regularly in second place simply because of the accident of their birth that made them women instead of men; it *was* all wrong that cruel men could treat wives as chattels, beating them, ill-treating them and their children, and generally making their lives a burden to them. And she sat at that meeting in Chelsea Town Hall, listening to the rolling phrases of the women who followed the now abashed Members of Parliament on to the stage, and thought confusedly of what she was doing and what she ought to be doing, for the burden of the speaker's message was that the lack of the vote limited women's ambitions, and was evil for that reason.

'While we are barred from the ballot-box', the last speaker declaimed, her purple, green and white sash fluttering around her with the intensity of her oratorical movements, 'we are effectively barred from the most essential professions to which we, as women as well as people, could bring great benefits. Women doctors and women lawyers are what women require, and how many are there? Pitifully few, sisters, pitifully few, for there is no power in womanhood, no strength apart from that which we must wield in secret, like puppet-masters, making our men dance to our piping.

'Where is the reward for a woman who passes through the long efforts required to make her a doctor if at the end of it all she cannot vote into Parliament the people who can improve the lot of her patients by improving their sanitation and their food and relieving the many injustices heaped upon the poor? Why should a woman suffer the pain of struggling through the studies that are required for her to be a lawyer if at the end she is not able to affect in any way, other than the devious man-controlling way, the law she is trained to practice? These injustices are what we fight, and not just the heart injustice of disbarment from the ballot-box –'

Letty applauded wildly, but even as she did she felt her thoughts milling around in her head: 'I should be at Nellie's, learning, looking after people, not just enjoying myself with Luke, painting silly scenery. I should be thinking of a future in which I will be of real value to the world, not just one in which I preen myself on a stage and do only what I enjoy. It's all wrong, but I'm so happy –' And she applauded even more loudly in order to drown out her own doubts. For she *was* exceedingly happy and she could not bear to do anything that would damage that fragile delight. She would close her mind, she decided, to such doubts and continue on the path she had chosen to follow.

But that evening had two results. First she wrote a little more about her feelings and thoughts in her next letter to her mother. She had written most punctiliously each week since leaving Bloomsbury, sending her letter from the main post office near Trafalgar Square at St Martins-in-the-Fields, so that there could be no risk of being discovered by study of the postmark, but the letters had been mere assurances that she was well and safe, and offered little that was personal apart from her firm intention to live her own life in her own way. But now she wrote at length, trying to explain to her mother just how she felt about her new life. About the excitements of the stage, even though she was not yet actually working for an audience; about the joy she found in the relaxed and unconventional company that frequented Edwin's house; about the sense of heady excitement she felt in being a genuine New Woman in the new twentieth century.

'For, dearest Mamma,' she wrote, 'it is a changing world, isn't it? In the few years I have been old enough to understand, I've seen so many changes that it seems the world is spinning faster on its axis in my lifetime than it did when you were a girl. Flying-machines and motor-cars and so many new inventions – where can the world be going, but on to greater and greater glories? What else can I do but fight for my place in that exciting new world? You had to fight for what you then gave me as a gift, but nothing that is given is worth as much as that which has to be worked for. That is another reason I'm determined to go on my own way.

'I so much wish you to understand, to realize that I did as I did, not because of lack of love or respect for you – indeed I love and miss you sadly, and respect you more than you can imagine – but because I had to do it. I wish I could help you to comprehend. I wish I could tell you where I am so that we could correspond, but I fear that if I did you would seek me out and be angry and try to force me to change and then we would quarrel and I would hate that. But if you wish to write to me, you could send a letter to the post office at St Martins-in-the-Fields, and I will collect it and then perhaps we can be friends again –'

But Sophie did not write and Letty wept half a night and then determinedly refused to think more about the situation, telling herself mulishly that if her mother wished to cast her off then that was how it had to be. It never entered her head that her mother's answering letter might not have arrived at Trafalgar Square, even though she knew lost letters were not uncommon, which in fact was what had happened. She just told herself her mother did not care and that was that, refusing to think of the long years of tender affection they had shared, of the pain she might be inflicting as well as experiencing.

Instead she turned her attention to the WSPU once more, which was the second outcome of her visit to the meeting at Chelsea Town Hall. She wrote a letter to Dora Montefiore, finding her address from the WSPU officials at the Town Hall, and offering her services to the Union, adding rather grandly, 'professional engagements permitting' and explaining that she was now part of a theatrical company and had limited time. But, she assured the formidable Mrs Montefiore in her strong sloping handwriting, she was available in any way that she cared to make use of her.

The day after sending that letter, the parlourmaid brought an answer for Letty to the breakfast-table, where she was sitting with Edwin and Luke and Peter Hast, an American actor currently visiting the house, and the Maleone sisters, another set of visitors, opera-singers on their way to Milan from Paris, and staying with their 'sweetest dearest Edween' *in transit*.

'The best thing you can do to help our cause at this stage', Mrs Montefiore had written in her very direct style, 'is to put on a play at once about votes for women. That will be of great interest to the audience, of course, for our support grows daily, and will make your company much talked of. Please arrange this and let me know and I will see to it that one is written –'

Letty tucked the letter into her pocket, wisely deciding not to mention it in this company. The combination of *naïveté* about the way plays were chosen for theatre production and the cool effrontery of Dora's demands would, she knew, cause great hilarity among them all, and she could not risk that, especially as at any moment now the front doorbell would peal and there would be Jessica on her usual morning visit on her way to the rehearsals in which she was involved for a new play to open at the Gaiety in a couple of weeks' time. She would laugh the loudest of any of them and be the most disagreeable about the letter, and there was nothing in the world that would make Letty ever give Jessica such cause for hilarity. It was bad enough that she was always about with her beautiful face and her red curls and her air of special intimacy with all the men, but most especially with Luke. The only way to treat Jessica, Letty had discovered, was with a stoical quietness, never rising to her taunts or appearing to notice her winks and asides; but it was not easy, and would be no easier if she knew that Letty had now chosen to become a committed and very determined champion of votes for women.

But she showed the letter to Luke, trusting him to behave well about it, and he read it with his lips pursed and then gave it back to her, and said, 'I think not, Letty. I have to entertain people who are poor, and who are much more concerned about where their next meal is coming from, than about the vote. They don't give a fig for such matters, so why give them such a play? But I'll come to a meeting if you like – will they allow me to be there?'

'I suppose so,' Letty said and folded the letter carefully before tucking it away in her bodice. 'They had men speakers last time – I suppose there could be men in the audience, but –'

'Well, next time there is a meeting, if there's no work to do, I'll attend. Then if there seems any material we can use on stage, well –' and Letty was content with that.

It was towards the end of May that the chance came to show Luke something of her new acquaintances. A short and very curt note came from Dora Montefiore announcing that she had refused to pay her rates to the Council and 'the bailiffs are due to come and collect goods in lieu of payment on 26 May next. I intend to barricade the house against them and have invited the Press to see the fun. Be so good as to be there and add your support.'

It was a sunny day, with a light breeze and birds chattering loudly in every tree with a faint blush of green to hide them, and the great doors of the Gaff had been left open to the morning light to allow the paint on the rows of seats to dry.

They stood in the doorway looking at it all, at the freshness everywhere and especially at the scrubbed boards on the handsome new stage and Letty gave a little skip of delight at the sight of it.

'There can't be much left to do, Luke,' she said, 'can there? I have just the dressing-room furniture to arrange when it comes tomorrow and the bar to organize with the glasses set out and the plates and all and then –'

'Very nearly,' he said and yawned suddenly and she looked at him sharply. In this bright sunlight he looked thinner than ever, she thought and although he was rosy-cheeked enough, somehow he had a peaky look and she felt her chest constrict a little at the vulnerability of him; he looked like a child somehow.

'We'll have the first full audition on Monday next week,' he went on. 'I'll see the announcement goes to the agents and the usual people. There'll be a considerable turn-out, I suspect. Times aren't all that wonderful at present, so there are plenty of good actors available. Then, with a little luck we can open in mid July, when we've had plenty of time for advertising –'

'Can we stop work for today, then, Luke?' she said. 'There's not a great deal more to do here and, if we're not to audition till Monday, surely we can give ourselves some leisure now? Let's go to Hammersmith and see Dora Montefiore's siege against her bailiffs. I'm sure it will be interesting –'

'And could be amusing too!' He looked a little brighter, less tired. 'You know, I think that's really a capital idea! We'll lock up here and have a little lunch and then make our way westwards. A capital notion – and we do need a break –'

It was a magical afternoon for Letty – or most of it was. They lunched at the King's Head and Eight Bells, in the snug little dining-room with the windows that overlooked the river, making great inroads into one of the landlord's best mutton pies – for Henry Smith, the publican, was famous for his baking – and then strolled along the riverside in the warm sunshine, past the rippling of the busy water and the fussy boats plying it, beyond Battersea Bridge to Fulham and further before deciding to ride the rest of the way to Hammersmith in a hansom cab. And all the time they talked and laughed and talked again and the silken network of friendship she had felt growing around them added many more filaments and tightened even more. He was becoming ever more important to her, and it would be foolish of her to deny it.

Not that she wanted to. She sat beside him in the hansom, her arm against his, feeling the warmth of him through the thin cotton sleeve of her gown and was deeply content. And when they reached their destination and found Upper Mall crowded with onlookers, most of them clustered outside Mrs Montefiore's house, she took his arm as a protection against the press of bodies in the most natural way possible.

There was a great deal of good-natured shouting going on, and several policemen were there watching, but not interfering too much. For a while Letty and Luke stood towards the back of the crowd listening and enjoying the fun, for that is what it indeed was.

Dora Montefiore's sturdy figure could be clearly seen at an upstairs window, waving to the crowd, and they waved and shouted back encouragingly and jeered when the bailiffs, three large and embarrassed-looking men, tried to push the door down below her and she leaned out and berated them loudly.

And then the fun increased, for Mrs Montefiore threw her window wide open and began to address the crowd at great length on the issue of votes for women and the injustice of having to pay rates while not being permitted to say how those rates should be used, and the crowd shouted back, jostling and laughing and making jokes.

So it was, by and large, a friendly affair until a few yards to the left of where Letty and Luke were standing a knot of loutish men in their thirties dressed in the heavy greasy clothes of the boatmen who plied the river from Putney to the city began to be less than funny with their comments. Their language became more and more lewd, and though Dora Montefiore ignored them and even outshouted them when she got enough breath, they began to collect some support among the crowd, from the less savoury-looking men scattered about.

'I think we'd better go,' Luke had just murmured in Letty's ear, for now the crowd was getting restless, taking sides for and against the louts, and Letty would have agreed and gone with him had not one of the men said something so revolting and so personal about Dora that Letty suddenly lost her temper. And to her own amazement she heard herself shout at the top of her voice, while staring directly at the man who had spoken so disgustingly, 'Be quiet at once! You should be ashamed of yourself!' and the man turned and stared back at her, and then pushed towards her, as the other people standing between them scattered before him.

'What did you say, lidy?'

'I told you to be quiet,' Letty's heart was hammering in her chest, for he was a very big man, with a scar on one side of his nose that made him look particularly ferocious. 'You're a lout and a coward to speak to a woman so –'

'Woman? She ain't no woman – she's a stinkin' lousy bitch as wants votes. No decent woman wants bleedin' votes – an' if you want them, then you're a stinkin' lousy bitch an' all. What do you say to that, whore?'

What happened next Letty was never quite sure. Behind her she felt Luke move, saw his fist come shooting over her shoulder and land on the scarred nose; saw the other men behind the big man come charging to his defence; heard other men shouting and joining in on Luke's side, and then there was a mêlée of fists and noise and shouting and, oddly, a blackness that seemed to drop over her head like a curtain that smothered her and completely blocked out the noise and the fists and the sunshine and everything else.

12

She seemed to be swimming in very deep blue water, heavy water which pressed on her head cruelly, but it could not hold her down, and the blueness thinned, became lighter in colour though still as heavy and then she was at the surface, opening her eyes and wincing at the brightness.

'Letty – Letty, are you all right?'

'No,' she said. 'It's heavy,' and was surprised to hear the huskiness that was her own voice and then another voice said, 'She'll be all right, sir. Just a bit of concussion, I reckon – most unfortunate –'

'I'd still like a doctor to see her – where is he? Can't you hurry him up? Oh, there he is! About time – look, she was hit by a –'

'Well, let's have a look then, nothing to fret over, I dare say –'

'But she was unconscious! It's going to be –'

The voices went on and on and she listened, detached but vaguely curious, wondering who these people were in her dream and then, as a hand was slipped under her neck and lifted her head, and a sharp pain shot across her left temple she realized she wasn't dreaming at all. This was all actually happening, and she cried out and the comforting voice which had worried about the arrival of a doctor was, she realized, Luke's, and she opened her eyes, gingerly, and tried to see him.

'Hmm. Bit of a contusion there, but nothing more, I don't think. Let me see your eyes, young lady – open them – that's it – no, don't squint, just let me see. Hmm. No problems there. Feeling a bit sick, are you? Probably – better have something handy, young man – bit of newspaper'll do if nothing else is available, yes – I thought as much – easy does it, easy –'

Bad as it was to be retching so horribly, to feel the way her stomach churned and rejected all its contents so summarily, it was much worse to know Luke was there and could see her discomfiture and then as she gasped a little and opened her eyes again she found that the person who was holding her head while she was sick was not the doctor at all but Luke and she felt tears of shame fill her eyes and sniffed dolorously and then wept and sniffed again.

'She'll do,' the doctor said cheerfully. 'More shock than any real damage. See she sleeps well the rest of the day and gets a good night and she'll be right as a trivet in the morning. Ah, is that the cab for her? Good – see to it you take that horse nice and easy, cabbie. Poor young lady's had a nasty experience and wants tender treatment. No, don't worry about a fee, sir. I was passing anyway and there was little enough for me to do. Good afternoon –'

Getting into the cab wasn't easy, for her legs felt singularly woolly, and she was painfully aware of people staring at her and murmuring sympathy as she was half-led, half-carried past the remnants of Dora's supporters, but at last she was in its stuffy leather-scented interior with Luke beside her holding her close in one encircling arm, and resting her now aching head on his shoulder seemed the most natural thing in the world to do.

At Edwin's there was more fuss and more exclamation, but Luke was very definite about her need to rest and, supporting her carefully, took her upstairs to her room and left her there, not too willingly, to allow the parlourmaid to help her get out of her now dusty and crumpled gown and into bed. She lay there with her cheek against the coolness of the pillow, grateful to be alone at last, and fell asleep, not with the memory of that horrid moment when she was hit reverberating in her mind, but with an awareness of Luke's arm around her in the cab.

She woke feeling remarkably refreshed. Her head ached only a little, and when she touched her scalp over the left temple, experimentally, it was sore, but not excessively so. She got out of bed carefully and stood on the bedside rug swaying for a moment, but then steadied and went over to the dressing-table to look at herself.

She looked pale, she decided, but not unduly ill, though rather crumpled, for her hair was tangled and curly over her shoulders, because the parlourmaid had unpinned it to allow her to sleep comfortably. She could see the faint bruising over her temple too, but it was not too obvious and, she told herself optimistically, by tomorrow it shouldn't look too bad.

Tomorrow. She made her way to the window to look out, trying to decide what time of day it was; it was dark, but the street-lights were still burning outside and they were usually doused well before morning, weren't they? It could be any time at all really, and she looked at her little fob-watch on the dressing-table, and frowned because it had stopped and she still didn't know the time.

Why it mattered she couldn't be sure, and then she realized that it could be because she was ravenously hungry. As the thought came into her mind she felt almost sick again, she was so hollow, and that made her decide that somehow, whatever the time, she had to find something to eat.

She put on her wrapper, shivering a little, for it was a pretty enough thing in white cotton trimmed with blue ribbons, but far from warm; suitable for wear on a May morning or a May evening, but not really adequate in the middle of the night, however warm the spring weather might be. 'It must be dreadfully late,' she told herself, as she very quietly opened her bedroom door and peeped out into the corridor beyond. There was not a sound to be heard anywhere; the window at the head of the staircase was a dim rectangle in the darkness, and she stood for a moment to accustom her eyes to the surroundings and then, creeping carefully and holding her wrapper close for fear its frills would disturb the ornaments on the many tables Edwin had scattered about the upstairs hallway, made her way to the staircase and down, holding her breath at the occasional creak as she moved over the carpeted treads.

Below, the hall was still and very cool, and her bare toes curled against the black-and-white tiles and she thought, almost surprised, 'I should have looked for my slippers –' But going back to fetch them was unthinkable, so she moved on, across the hall scented with the remains of the evening's cigars and brandy, and pushed open the green baize door that led to the servants' quarters.

Here it was even darker, and the smell was different; food and floor polish and soap and dust, and for a moment she quailed and wanted to go back to bed and forget her errand, until her belly rumbled and she knew she had to find something to eat, anything at all, and find it soon.

She moved on, the linoleum cold under her feet, running her hand along the wall to find her way and then saw at the end of the darkness a faint square of light. Thank goodness, the kitchen door, she thought, and the fire still burning – for the fine line of light flickered a little – so it can't be that late after all; and she moved on, more confidently now and fumbled for the handle and pushed the door open.

Luke had been sitting there in the cook's battered old rocker for a long time; how long he didn't really know. He had meant to go back to the Gaff to bed; but that had been impossible. Long after the others had gone up (Edwin thumping him on the back and assuring him he had no need to worry; Letty was a strong lady and anyway, he had added absurdly, 'She has all this medical knowledge you must remember, and that means she must be better able to be well than the rest of us poor mortals!') he had sat in the drawing-room alone, thinking and worrying. Then on an impulse he had gone upstairs and stood listening outside her door, but that didn't help for he could hear nothing at all and found himself wishing she snored, just so that he could hear her and be reassured. After that, bed at the Gaff seemed even less inviting though he was deeply weary, and he had gone downstairs again, to the kitchen this time because the drawing-room fire had long since faded into a heap of cooling grey ash, there to pile coals on the range and to sit and brood.

It was a comfortable place to be, and perhaps he had dozed just a little in spite of his anxiety. The fire had whispered and hissed in its shining black-leaded grate, crackling occasionally as the glowing coals fell inwards in a shower of sparks, and the old kitchen clock ticked loudly with a curiously comforting melancholy on the mantelshelf above it, while the big brindled cat who stalked the kitchen all day and slept there all night (ostensibly to keep the mice at bay but as far as he was concerned simply to be comfortable) snuffled and purred and even snored a little in his basket in the fender.

So when the door opened Luke jumped and sat bolt upright, sending the rocker moving madly, and stared across the room at the doorway and saw her standing there with her dark hair tumbled on her shoulders and with a frilled white wrapper held round her and her eyes huge in her pale face and thought, 'I'm asleep – must be asleep – dreaming – must be asleep –'

'Oh,' she said blankly and shrank back against the door and then he knew he was awake for the cat woke too and stirred in its basket and stretched and then curled up to go to sleep again and he jumped to his feet and came towards her and said, 'Letty?'

'I – I thought everyone was asleep, I'd no idea what the time is – and I'm so *hungry*.'

He laughed aloud at that and put out his hand and took her shoulder and drew her into the room. 'Then you're feeling better! You must be!'

'I'm feeling just starving!' she said and smiled at him. 'A bit of headache, but that could be hunger too. I feel like a child that's been caught out of school, now, creeping away here to rob the larder and being caught in the act.'

'I was so worried about you! I couldn't bear to go back to the Gaff because of it. I can't tell you how glad I am to see you looking so – well, come and sit down. My dear, no slippers? You must be frozen!'

She looked down at her feet, at the toes pink with chill, and laughed. 'I forgot them – until I left the carpet behind and found myself freezing on the hall floor. Oh, the fire is lovely –' And she sat down and extended her feet to the flames and rubbed them with both hands and looked up at him over her shoulder and laughed. He reddened suddenly and stood there staring at her and she felt her own face redden too and after a frozen pause turned back to the fire.

'Hungry,' he said after a moment. 'I'm sure you are. So long since lunch – and –'

'And I lost that! Shaming, wasn't it?'

'Not at all. If it's any comfort to you you were sick most neatly! I've seen people making a much greater exhibition of themselves, I promise you! Now, let's see what we can find. There was excellent mushroom soup at dinner, and some roast mutton and a side of beef –'

'Oh, no, I couldn't manage anything like that! Just something ordinary, truly – anything to fill the corners, that's all. A little bread or whatever there is. Do you think Edwin would mind us robbing his kitchen?'

'Edwin? Such stuff! He'd insist you ate the beef and all tomorrow's as well if he was here.' His voice became muffled for he was in the big larder and rattling about among the dishes. 'Look, there's all sorts of things here. Bread and sugar and butter and milk and –'

'That will do splendidly,' she called. 'Please don't worry about looking any further. Bread and butter and a glass of milk will do very well –'

'Poor fare on a cold night,' he said as he came out of the larder, the loaf of bread tucked under one arm, and the milk-jug and butter-dish and sugar-basin held precariously in his hands. 'Let me at least heat the milk and make toast for you –'

'Bread and milk,' she said suddenly, and her eyes creased with delight, 'I'm the greediest person in the world for bread and milk. Dear old Bessie used to make it for us when we were small and had chills, putting it in a big blue bowl with lots of sugar and bits of butter melted on the top – that would be heaven! But let me do it – please, you must be tired, if the clock's right. Is it really almost five in the morning?'

'Yes it is, and you must not do it yourself. You sit still, because I wouldn't dream of letting you do it. I'm a dab hand at bread and milk. They fed me on it when I was a child too, and I know the best way to make it, you see if I don't.'

He rattled around cheerfully, finding a pan hanging over the big stone sink and rinsing it in good housewifely fashion, which made her lips quirk, before putting the milk into it to heat over the fire and then cutting the bread into chunks on the big scrubbed wooden table. He spooned lots of sugar into the pan and added the bread and butter and then, after one more rummage in the larder, emerged triumphantly with a nutmeg and a grater and scraped it across the bread and milk to fill the big kitchen with the spicy scent. And then he stood watching it carefully as it hissed and bubbled round the edge of the pan as intent as though he were making the most complicated sauce.

'There's far too much there,' she said reprovingly, very aware of him there so close beside her, for she was still sitting with her feet on the fender feeling the grateful warmth unfreeze her toes. 'Greedy as I am, I can't manage all that – so wasteful of you to have made so much –'

'Not a bit of it,' he said cheerfully. 'I'm having some too, of course! Bread and milk is much too great a treat to miss –'

And when it was done and he'd found bowls – plain white rather than blue, but deep enough to hold all they needed – and long-handled spoons, he served the steaming fragrant mixture and then added a little more nutmeg with a flourish of his grater, at last setting her bowl in her hands before sitting down at her feet with the other, perching on the fender.

The food was ambrosial, and she sipped the hot milk and after a moment, laughing delightedly, followed his suit and blew on it to cool it; and they ate in companionable silence, as the clock ticked and the cat snuffled and the fire crackled at their feet. A peaceful yet exciting moment, and for the rest of her life it was to remain in her memory, a brightly-lit bubble of happiness. And Luke too was to hold the memory of it always, for he knew now for certain, if he hadn't before, that this girl was more to him than just a pretty girl. She was Letty. His Letty, whether she knew it or not, whether she cared for him or not. She, the essence of her, he knew, belonged to him and always would.

But he said nothing, eating his bread and milk and smiling at her over their bowls and then, when they'd finished, took the dishes away and set them in the sink and then came back to sit at her feet again on the fender and stare at the fire.

She too was doing that, leaning back in the old rocker, and swaying herself gently, keeping her eyes fixed on the flames that made their tiny leaps and spurts in the glowing embers, and he turned his head and looked at her, studying her face as carefully as though he had never seen it before. The darkness of her eyes, the way the lashes threw fine shadows on her lids, the hollowing at the temples above the soft curve of her cheeks, the faint dark down on her upper lip – all of it seemed to him to be inexpressibly sweet and important and he felt his own lips curl with pleasure as he looked at her and loved her.

And she could not help but be aware of his scrutiny and after a while let her gaze move away from the fire, slowly and almost langorously, and looked at him and she too smiled then and he moved, slipping to his knees from his crouching position on the fender so that he was immediately in front of her. He put his hands on her white frilled lap and she looked down at them and then moved her own hands so that they were set in his and he held them warmly and tightly and she raised her eyes and looked at him.

'You're very special, Letty,' he said after a moment and his voice seemed very loud in the quiet clock-ticking room and he said again, more softly this time, 'Very special.'

'Yes,' she said simply and leaned forwards so that she could put her face up to his, and as inevitably and naturally as if it were something they did all the time they kissed, and her lips were warm and soft on his. So they stayed for an eternity of a moment, but then, his need rose in him and he let go of her hands and put his arms about her and kissed her more fiercely, so that her lips opened beneath his and she put her arms round his neck so that they clung together for a long time.

But then he moved his head slightly and that seemed to affect her, for she gave an involuntary cry of pain and he was at once all solicitude.

'I'm sorry,' she said, and touched her temple in a gingerly fashion. 'That wretched graze – it hurt for a moment – it's all right now –'

'I'm wicked,' he said, at once all contrition. 'Here you are, barely over being concussed and I'm selfishly keeping you here! Dear Lettty, I do so want you to be happy and all I do is hurt you –'

'Oh, hush,' she said and touched his cheek with one finger. 'I'm not made of eggshells! To be with you like this is all I could ever want. Don't fuss, please. Not now or ever. Promise me.'

His eyes narrowed into a grin. 'I can't possibly make such a promise,' he said. 'I want to fuss over you for ever –'

'I'll teach you not to,' she said and kissed him again, putting up her face as trustfully as a child and he responded but made himself pull away and stand up.

'It's time you were resting,' he said. 'This won't do at all; it's almost six in the morning! The servants'll be bustling soon, and if they find us here in the kitchen in this compromising manner, even Edwin would be hard put to it not to be a little shocked. Come on, I'll take you upstairs.'

She went gladly enough, for now she was very weary again, though deeply happy, and she obediently went and they moved hand in hand along the dark passageway, through the green baize door to the hallway to where the light was lifting in the big window to an opaline dawn. They could hear the birds beginning a sleepy early chorus and could see the colour begin to creep into the monochrome shadows of the carpet and the furniture they passed as they tiptoed along the sleeping corridor.

At her doorway he kissed her again, tenderly, and she put her arms round him and he felt the warmth of her body through her wrapper and shivered with the excitement of it and with all the self-control he had gently pushed her away and opened her door.

Long after she had disappeared he stood there in the hallway outside her room looking out of the window at the brightening day and feeling as contented and as sure of himself as he could ever remember being in all his life. And as weary and in need of sleep as he could possibly be.

13

Persuading him she was fully recovered from her unfortunate experience was quite difficult, but at last he believed her, seeing her glowing face and obvious well-being; and anyway there was so much work to be done that it was impossible to spend much time arguing on the matter. The last detailed tasks needed to get the Gaff ready for its new life as a popular entertainment place took as much attention and time as had the major repairs, and together, with as much hindrance as help from Edwin and his friends, they set to to ensure all was ready for the most important next step – the auditions.

Faithful to his word Luke had sent out the notices of the play to be cast and according to the gossip reported back to Cheyne Walk from the actors' favourite haunts already many people had decided to seek parts with Luke's new management. He had not realized how well thought of he was by many of his colleagues, people with whom he had worked in the past, who now talked cheerfully of him to each other about how good he was. It comforted him to know that, for he was getting more and more nervous about his debut as a director. He felt wonderful about his new understanding with Letty, of course, but at the same time less than comfortable in general.

He thought a good deal about that as the next days passed in a flurry of business, wondering why he felt so low. He and Letty had agreed tacitly to say nothing to anyone of their new-found closeness; it was personal to them, their own affair, and the thought of Edwin and his other friends gossiping about and teasing them was insupportable. So they were circumspect in company, and seemed to continue as they had always been, as close-working colleagues but no more than that. But occasionally they shared the touch of hands or a speaking glance as they passed each other and so maintained the special warmth of the link they had fashioned that night before the kitchen fire in Cheyne Walk.

So he should feel better than he did, he told himself. At night, lying on his neat cot in the newly whitewashed cubby-hole which served as both his private room and office for the Gaff, he was restless and miserable, sleeping fitfully and waking in a heavy sweat over and over again, to throw off the bedcovers only to need to pull them up again as shivering overtook him. Day after day he felt more and more tired and also curiously irritable; once or twice he found Letty's startled gaze on him and realized that he had said something sharp and had to mutter an apology; and even Edwin remonstrated with him occasionally for his sharp temper.

But that perhaps was due to anxiety about the auditions, he told himself, and when the day arrived for them he felt a little better. At last they were on their way; at last real work could begin.

The day seemed interminable to him, though Edwin clearly was having a splendid time. He sat with a great ledger in front of him in which he entered the names of all the hopeful aspirants for parts and then watched with a studied frown as each went through his or her paces, first reading their own prepared audition pieces ('– and if I hear another *word* of that wretched Shaw stuff I shall scream!' he confided to Letty) and then a section of the text of *She Stoops to Conquer*.

Luke said nothing to any of them, just listening with a blank face and making notes, and at the end asking each actor and actress to leave a name and address where they might be reached, telling them that they could check here at the Gaff on Wednesday next, by which time the list of cast would be posted. And the would-be performers went away anxiously with no hint of whether or not they might have been successful in getting a role.

Even Letty shared that feeling, for when she went through her audition – and Luke had been punctilious in insisting that everyone should go through the process, no matter who they were, and that meant well-known performers as well as friends of the management – he sat and watched her quite unsmilingly.

She first offered the 'Mercy' speech of Portia from *The Merchant of Venice* for all it was so familiar and so many other actresses used it, because there had been no time to prepare anything else; she had just drawn on her memories of playing the part at school and done her best, rusty though she had known that would be. And when she played the same scene she had played in the drawing-room at Cheyne Walk all that time ago – so short a time in fact, though it felt an eternity – with one Donald Hyatt, a super Luke had employed to read cues for the performers, she felt Luke's blank response and shook inside. Could it be that she would not be cast at all? To hope to play Kate Hardcastle, the leading role, was too much; to consider the possibility that she would not be able to play any part was agony.

But that, she told herself, as she stepped down from the stage to the silence from the seats at the back where Edwin and Luke were making their notes, was not the way to be. 'If you are to be a good actress, you've got to be able to swallow the rejections as well as the successes. If there's nothing here for you, then there isn't. You'll just have to work backstage and learn and wait till you're ready to do more –'

When she watched Jessica go through her audition (for her play at the Gaiety had closed and she was seeking a new part) she felt even more dejected, for she was a most sparkling creature and floated about the stage like a sprite with her audition piece, an unfamiliar extract from a recent West End success that seemed to demand a great deal of silvery laughter and male knuckle-rapping with a fluttering rogueish fan, which Jessica wielded with great expertise. Seeing her being so entrancing, how could Luke possibly cast a novice like herself? Letty wondered and was deeply gloomy – until she watched Jessica do her scene from the Goldsmith play and felt her spirits rise a little, for it seemed to her that Jessica was playing in exactly the same manner as she had played the other piece, with fan and eyelashes and fluttering skirts much in evidence. And surely that was wrong for this part? But she stole a glance at Luke and he seemed to be interested, if not fascinated, by what Jessica was doing, and she felt even lower.

But she need not have done, for when the list was at last

pinned up Letty found herself cast as Kate Hardcastle, and Jessica as Miss Constance Neville, a decision which caused a great fuss and almost an argument that night at Cheyne Walk.

Letty was never quite sure what had happened or what had been said to start the argument, because she had remained behind at the Gaff that night to help young Donald – who was becoming something of a general factotum to the management – to prepare for the next morning's first rehearsal call, and when she reached Cheyne Walk the discussion was in full swing. She could hear voices raised as she gave her mantle to the parlourmaid and asked a little tiredly, 'What's going on?'

'Can't say, miss,' the parlourmaid said pertly, and then with her voice lowered added, 'though as far as I can tell Miss Jessica's in a rare old takin' over somethin' an' cryin' an' carryin' on alarmin'! But I can't say more'n that!' and she rustled away leaving Letty to go to the drawing-room on her own.

Edwin was sitting at his usual place beside the fire and looking, for him, quite distressed, with his round face puckered into a ludicrous expression of concern. Facing him was Luke who was standing by the window with his legs apart and his hands thrust belligerently into his trouser-pockets.

'Really, dear boy,' Edwin was saying as Letty reached the doorway. 'I can't see it would make so much difference! The dear child won't mind at all, I'm sure, and it would make everyone else happy and –'

'No, Edwin!' Luke almost growled it. 'If I am to be director for this management then I am. I know it is your money, but either you trust me to do what needs to be done or you don't. If you do, you must give me free rein to make my own decisions, with of course consultation from you when I need it. If you don't, then say so now, and I'll leave you to the project alone.'

Letty was standing by the door, hesitantly, for she felt certain that this was not a discussion she should hear, that it was private between Edwin and Luke; and she was about to draw back when she realized that Jessica was there, sitting in a heap of primrose flounces on the sofa on the far side of the fireplace.

'It doesn't matter,' Jessica said now in a muffled tone, and raised a very prettily tear-stained face to the two men. 'It really doesn't – I couldn't bear to see you two fall out because of me. Let it be, my dearest Edwin, and –'

Letty, moving with as firm a step as she could, came into the room and all three of them looked at her almost guiltily, even Luke, and she lifted her chin and said loudly, 'I have the impression that I should be taking part in this discussion.'

'Why, my dear Letty,' Edwin said and seemed to bluster a little. 'How good you look after so long a day at the Gaff! She does work so hard for us all, doesn't she? And look so wonderful? Luke? Jessica? Does not our Letty work –'

'Yes, I think you should be here,' Luke said in a harsh voice, and Edwin blinked and subsided and Jessica looked momentarily furious. 'The problem is, Letty, that Edwin would prefer Jessica to play Kate while I think she would be an excellent Constance. I think you should know of this, because –'

'Because after all, dear Letty, you will want everyone to be happy, won't you?' Edwin bleated a little. 'And you'll be the first to admit you lack experience and –'

'The last thing I want to do is upset anyone.' Letty was white now, and she stood very still in the doorway, carefully not looking at Luke. 'If it is better for the production that Jessica plays the part, then of course –'

'That is where we part company,' Luke said. 'I know Jessica to be an excellent performer. I bow to no one in my admiration of her as an entrancing girl who can make whole audiences adore her. However, I think for the production I have in mind she will be better as Constance, rather than as Kate who is, as I see her, an altogether more down-to-earth character than the one you play so well, Jessica. The real crux, of course, is who is in charge of this production –'

'Oh, you, of course,' Edwin said almost pettishly. 'I know perfectly well that no one can possibly do as well as you, and after spending so much as we have on the Gaff it is vital we start well and bring it to success rapidly. So if you're determined to cast as you will, there's little I can do although –' He brightened perceptibly. 'Have you given thought to understudies? It is essential that we have them, isn't it? Couldn't we arrange matters so that Jessica studies the part of Kate as well as Constance and then if –'

Jessica was sitting upright now, her eyes very bright. 'And then if Letty finds it a little beyond her grasp, why, then the play is not threatened!' she said. 'It's just that that concerns me, dear Luke! It's your first production. It's got to be right and to put it in the hands of someone so inexperienced, however good she may be –' and she flashed a sharp little smile at Letty, '– is asking for trouble. But if we all understudy each other, why then, as rehearsals go ahead we can see how we progress! I think you're very wise, Edwin darling, and very clever, and once Luke has done his first production, I think you should consider trying *your* hand, for you really do have a great deal of flair!'

'Luke,' Letty said quietly and looked directly at him for the first time. 'That seems to me an excellent idea. Why not try it? It makes good practical sense, and the decisions still remain with you.'

He stood there very still, not taking his hands from his pockets nor changing his belligerent stance, but she felt somehow that the energy had gone from him, that he was tired of the wrangle and even of the play, and after a moment he nodded heavily. 'Well, if that will please you all, let it be that way. But I tell you the decision must remain with me and only me –'

'Of *course*, dearest,' Jessica was across the room in a flurry of primrose flounces. 'No one would wish it to be otherwise! I'm sure we'll all get along splendidly now.' And she kissed his cheek and looked challengingly at Letty. 'And Letty, my dear, when we come to play our scenes together, I will do all I can to teach you, I do promise you! There's so much to be discovered about the character, you see, and I know I can help you do her tremendously well! Tomorrow then, my darlings! Splendid! Now I must run, for darling old Gillick is giving me dinner at the Trocadero tonight and I adore it there so!' And she was gone, leaving them all silent and weary behind her.

At first Letty thought it would be all right as rehearsals got under way. Jessica was so sweet, so helpful, and altogether charming that she began to feel she, Letty, had been the tiresome one, stupidly envious and unkind, and slowly she relaxed and felt safer and began to work better at her part. She knew the lines well, which was a great help as it meant she could concentrate on her moves, and she worked every spare moment she had, moving about the stage when everyone else had gone, familiarizing herself with it and repeating the lines over and over again.

The scenes with Lawrence Hearst, the rather quiet but very effective actor who had been cast as Young Marlow, she found a delight; those with Joseph Morris, a friendly old actor who was cast as her father, Mr Hardcastle, were comfortable and she felt that she got on well with those, and that Luke approved of her work. But somehow whenever she was on stage with Jessica or Mary Longton, who was playing Mrs Hardcastle, or Peter Hutchings, who was playing Hastings, she seemed to become inept and stupid. It was nothing any of them did, no lack of apparent co-operation or concern from them, but somehow she found that if she was going to stumble into a piece of furniture or forget a line or miss a cue it would be in those scenes; if she was going to be wooden and unresponsive, it would be in those scenes; and as the rehearsal weeks went on she became more and more anxious. Maybe she should have stayed at Nellie's and learned how to perform surgical operations, she told herself gloomily. It couldn't be harder work or more dispiritng than this.

The situation wasn't helped by the lack of opportunity to talk about it all to Luke. Had they had spare time together to talk, to relax, to be themselves, she was sure she could have learned how to be better in those difficult scenes, but he never had a moment to spare for her as he was now immersed as much in Oliver's filming project as in the play, and was working all the time.

Letty had remonstrated with both of them when Oliver came bustling into the Gaff on the Friday of the first rehearsal week, and she realized that the two projects were to go forward side by side.

'It's too much, Uncle Oliver!' she had said to the old man, while Luke was outside supervising the delivery from

Prestwick's, the manufacturers of their first precious cameras. 'He starts rehearsing us at eleven every morning and we work till well into the late afternoon. How can he film as well and –'

'That's not at all the problem, my dear,' Oliver said and looked at her owlishly over his round spectacles. 'These music-hall films have to be done first thing in the morning at this time of year, when the light's at its best, and anyway most of the performers are only available then, what with matinees and early doors. So it's perfectly all right, you'll see – Luke will still be able to start your rehearsals any time, without any trouble!'

Letty, though she tried to tell the old man it was Luke's health she was concerned about – for he really looked very tired indeed – rather than the convenience of the music-hall performers, had to give up as Luke came back ready to talk to Oliver about the work he wanted done. As they plunged into talk she could not interrupt without making a nuisance of herself.

Not that she didn't try, later on, to tell Luke that she feared he was overworking, but he brushed aside her anxiety, not unkindly, but making it very clear to her that he just did not want to be tormented about it. And though she loved him dearly, and was as sure as she could be that he loved her equally – for that magical hour in the midnight kitchen was enshrined in her memory, to be taken out often and contemplated with delight and then tucked away again – it had been only one fleeting time. They had not talked any more about themselves and their emotions, had not confirmed their feelings; though she felt secure in them, she did not now feel able to be persistent about the matter of the hours he worked. That would be too dominating altogether, she told herself. I couldn't bear to be that sort of female.

So, she bit her tongue and watched him and did all she could to lighten his load, making sure he ate lunch and dinner and had regular cups of tea or coffee – for he would have forgotten food entirely unless it had been put in front of him – and taking off his back as much of the work as she could.

But that was little enough compared with what he had to do. The setting-up of the camera, the skills of handling them – for

Oliver, determined his project should lack for nothing, had been exceedingly generous in his buying and had purchased two cameras, the most costly of Brockliss Motiograph projectors, new limelights and electric arc-lamps for the light source and a large number of cans of film – had to be solely Luke's responsibility. But she could and did deal with all the paperwork, making lists of shots as he used film to practise, and taking over the bookkeeping (and she was horrified to discover the price of film; fully one pound for every seventy-five feet, which gave just a minute and a quarter of picture time, and even then the costs were not finished, for extra sums had to be paid to have the film perforated so that it could be run through the camera and projector, and there were the added costs of developing and printing the film to be considered) and generally organized the office. With young Donald to fetch and carry and shift furniture and turn the special revolving stage and open the great doors to admit light, they managed well enough. But she could see Luke getting more and more tense before her eyes and worried about him.

He was worried about himself too, for he knew he was not well, yet could not decide just where his ill-health lay. Had he had a disease he could understand – a pain in his belly that meant indigestion, or trouble in his bowels or head or eyes – he would have sought medical help. But how could he see a doctor, he would ask himself, when all he had was this sense of illness, and the fatigue and the sweating?

And of course, the coughing, but he closed his eyes to that. It was just a dry cough, that was all. Nothing to fret about. Just a cough.

Until late one evening, the day before the dress rehearsal was due, and just a week before he was to start filming the first batch of music-hall artists who had been booked by Oliver to come to the Gaff.

That evening he could ignore the coughing no longer.

14

It had been a hectically busy afternoon which had continued long after the day's last rehearsal of *She Stoops to Conquer* had ended and the actors had scattered to their homes, for he had to prepare so much paperwork; there was the printing of the programmes and bill-posters to sort out – and that meant a new name had to be found for Letty, for she was most anxious that no one from her family should find her, and after a long discussion had settled on Bess Brothers, using her old nurse's first name, and a version of her father's surname – and also the matter of the Lord Chamberlain's licence. Not that there had been any doubt in anyone's mind that a licence to play at the Gaff would be granted, but there had been delays and tedious quarter-hours spent on the telephone and much explaining and nagging and persistence needed. That in its turn had been compounded by the requirement to obtain a licence to serve food and drink in the Gaff once they opened. But he had at last sorted all of it out and been free to turn his attention to the shot lists he had to prepare for the first of his music-hall films.

That had been at gone eight in the evening, and Letty had wanted to remain with him at the Gaff to make him some supper and help him, but she had been needed on the other side of the river at Lambeth, where the company's costumes were being made, for fittings and alterations to her first-act gown; she had lost considerable weight during these busy rehearsal weeks, and in consequence the gown looked far less charming than it should on her – though she herself looked very good indeed in her new slenderness – and go she had to. So, he was alone at his desk in the corner of his little office-cum-bedroom when it happened.

He had been sitting scribbling for a long time, it seemed,

very aware of the quiet emptiness stretching out beyond him, of the rows of blank seats waiting to be filled with eager audience, of the quiet stage with its set half erected waiting for the morning and the scene-shifters to finish their job ready for the dress rehearsal. The tiredness that had been so much a part of him for so long seemed heavier than ever, and pushing his pen over the sheets of paper took as much effort as climbing a hill; but he persisted, refusing to allow his body to dictate any terms to him.

A fly, buzzing around lazily, zoomed at his head and he waved a hand at it irritably and that small action seemed to affect his breathing, making it tighten, and he gave a little cough to clear it. But the relentless tickle started again, and once more he felt his breath catch in his chest and he coughed again, thinking, almost saying it aloud, 'I mustn't start coughing – I really mustn't or I'll go on and on and get even more tired –' but it was too late. A paroxysm was starting, one of those now hatefully-familiar episodes in which he could not control the need to cough and cough and cough –

He put down his pen and held on to the edges of the desk with both hands, for now, suddenly, he was giddy and the desk was swimming in front of his eyes and he coughed again and then again – and when he saw it he didn't really believe it; it was just the dizziness affecting his eyes, that was all. Those little red splatters on his sheets of paper were mere spots before his vision. They weren't real. They couldn't be.

They increased, became smudges, became small pools of viscous crimson and he knew it was true, for now he felt it in his throat and mouth and gagged involuntarily and still coughed; and now fear rose in him like a great bitter tide and somewhere at the back of his mind a tiny voice screamed, 'No! It isn't true – it isn't – not like this, not like this – no!'

It was the pressure of the edge of the desk on his forehead that told him he was all right, that he had just been overwhelmed by the dizziness caused by the coughing and that was all; shakily he lifted his head and then, with enormous effort, his shoulders and leaned back so that he was sitting upright at last and then with an involuntary movement, wiped the back of one hand across his mouth.

He saw it again then and knew it was true – dreadfully, terrifyingly true. The red smudge across his hand, the streaks on his papers, the metallic taste in his mouth; it was real. He hadn't imagined it – and he hadn't been destroyed by it. He had coughed blood, and was still here to know it.

Gingerly, experimentally, he took a shallow breath and then a rather deeper one and as the air moved coldly into his lungs felt the tickle start again and with an enormous effort of will did not cough; it took every atom of concentration he had to sit there and resist the desperate urge to clear that bubbling sensation, but he managed it and slowly the need subsided and he was sitting there safely, breathing and not coughing. And that was a huge achievement.

How long he sat there he was not sure, but after a while he knew he had to try to move and did so, delicately, and then with slowly increasing sureness. With neat fingers he removed the spattered sheets of paper from his desk and tore them into small pieces and dropped them in his waste-paper basket. He took his handkerchief from his pocket and scrupulously scrubbed away the stains on the wood where the blood had sprayed further. Then, with all the concentration he had in him, he moved carefully, pushed his chair back and stood up. Still no cough, still no more blood and he moved further, taking his coat from the back of his chair, sliding into it, and walking slowly, so very slowly, across the small office to the dark and silent auditorium beyond.

He was to look back on his actions with amazement. He was so methodical, so sure of what to do, and he did it; locking the office, walking across the Gaff and letting himself out and locking up again, and then, slowly and steadily, walking along the Embankment to the foot of Battersea Bridge there to hail the first hansom cab that came along.

Why he chose to go to Nellie's was another fact he was to marvel at, later on, when he thought about it at all. There were other hospitals nearer; why make the long journey from Chelsea to Covent Garden? 'Blood's thicker than water,' he had thought, sitting there in the swaying stuffy darkness behind the clopping hooves, 'blood's thicker than water.' And he had wanted to laugh aloud at the macabre pun but did not dare to, sitting there erect and as still as he could, totally refusing to think of what might happen to him if he started to cough again.

The cabbie looked at him curiously as he took his shilling fare and said hoarsely, 'You all right, squire? Look as queer as Dick's 'atband, that you do – white as a bleedin' sheet – d'yer need an 'and to get in there, like?'

'No,' Luke said and was surprised at how thin his voice sounded in his own ears. 'No thank you, I'll be all right now –'

'Oh, yers, you'll do all right 'ere,' the cabbie said. 'Good enough ol' place, Nellie's is. Takes good care of yer 'ere –' and he was gone, his horses' harness jingling as the wheels clattered over the macadam and disappeared into the darkness of the summer night.

Luke stood in the entrance hall, his hands in his pockets, willing himself to stand very straight, and looked around carefully, narrowing his eyes a little for the dizziness was there again, threatening to increase. Polished wood and squares of black and white on the floor and long wooden benches and flowers in a tall vase in front of the founder's statue and –

'Orspital's closed to visitors now, sir,' a voice said reprovingly, and a large personage in blue serge and a magnificence of brass buttons was standing there in front of him, and Luke blinked at him and said carefully, 'Sir Frederick Caspar, if you please. He is my cousin, and I must speak to him. Tell him Lucas O'Hare, his cousin – and God almighty, let me sit down, quickly –'

The blue serge arm came forwards out of the reeling dizziness that was climbing up from the black-and-white tiles of the floor and caught him, just in time. He knew it was just in time, for he was still standing upright when the dizziness turned into a total blackness and left him far behind.

'That's it, my boy – *that's* it. Just hold on, you're doing well, no need to panic. Just hold on. Breathe slowly – that's it – slo – owly – now, keep still. Yes, I know it's uncomfortable, but you must be still –'

He was lying on his back, and staring upwards at the lamp that was hanging just above his head and thinking lazily, 'That effect's good. It'd look wonderful on a stage – look wonderful on a film. Circles of light, lots of circles of light, look wonderful on a film.'

'Cold,' he said, and then contemplated the word with detached surprise. Why had he said it? He tried to move again and felt the constraints and said pettishly, 'I'm cold!'

'Of course you are,' the voice said calmly. 'You're packed in ice. Keep still.'

Luke turned his head slightly and gazed at him and then, suddenly, remembered.

'Thank God,' he said, 'Cousin Frederick.' And he frowned and stared up at the face above him as a hand was set gently but firmly over his mouth so that he couldn't speak.

'No talking,' Sir Frederick said. 'You are to be still and silent. I'll tell you what has happened and you can just use your eyes to tell me if I'm right. Close them in denial, hold them open in assent. Right?'

Luke opened his eyes wider.

'Good. If I remove my hand from your mouth, will you not attempt to talk?' Again Luke stared at him with his eyes wide.

'Splendid. You're a wise man. Now, you started to cough, and then you were coughing blood? Yes? Well, as soon as possible we'll give you a mouthwash to get rid of the taste of it. Nasty, isn't it? Yes. Right. We need now to find out precisely when and where the blood originated, do we not? Yes. In a little while we will remove the ice and allow you to be a little more comfortable. As far as I can tell the bleeding has staunched and the risk is diminishing. When we've done that, we shall take you to our special new department for a skiagraph. You know what a skiagraph is?'

Luke closed his eyes firmly.

'Ah. Then we must explain as we go along. But now, let's see what happens if we remove this ice. Nurse –'

Deft hands moved across him, and the weight of cold diminished and he closed his eyes gratefully – and must have forgotten to open them again, for he was asleep. Or more accurately knew he had been asleep, for now his eyes were open and the bed on which he was lying was now beneath a moving ceiling and he stared up at the lamps and the cornices as

149

they passed over his head, puzzled but not unduly worried by their movement; and then, as the cornices swooped and curved, he realized that it was his bed that was moving, not the ceiling, and that it had just turned a corner, and come into a big room.

'Skiagraph,' Sir Frederick said. 'We shall see if we can identify the source of your problems, my boy. It will take barely an hour or more of patience, and then we shall know what there is to be known. Nurse, see to it that Mr O'Hare is comfortable – Dr Dyke, we shall require several views, if we can obtain them without too much disturbance of our patient who is to be moved as little as possible. Luke, I shall explain to you what is happening. You have heard, no doubt of Röntgen Rays?'

Luke held his eyes open staring at Sir Frederick, and then after a moment frowned slightly and closed them and Sir Frederick chuckled.

'Most expressive. You've heard of them and yet know nothing about them – yes. Well, you are one of the many in that. These remarkable rays were discovered on the Continent some nine or ten years ago and have a most bizarre facility – they pass through soft tissue to show outlines of hard substances beneath the skin. They are used mostly to identify broken bones, for it is bones we see most clearly on the skiagraphs, the pictures that are developed of those parts we expose to the rays, but I have found that by using reduced doses of rays and less exposure it is possible to obtain some views of soft tissue and more importantly the *absence* of soft tissue. Cavities, my boy. And as you realize, of course, that is what we seek in your case.'

Luke snapped his eyes closed, and kept them so and after a moment Sir Frederick said gently. 'It can't be denied, my boy. I'm sorry. You have phthisis, of course. An haemoptysis – the coughing of blood – is a sure sign. There is obviously some cavitation in your lungs and we need to identify where. Some areas are – um – less alarming than others. Our pictures will, I hope, show us yours! Now, Dr Dyke here will set about the taking of the pictures. It is a painless procedure, I promise you, and you need not be alarmed by the apron and the heavy gloves

Dr Dyke wears. They are to protect him from the problems of dermatitis that afflict some people who use these rays a great deal. They are singularly powerful and we do not yet know all their effects. Hence the need for great care –'

Sir Frederick burbled on cheerfully, his voice relaxed and comforting, as the other doctor took over and now Luke again closed his eyes, not in denial this time but in fatigue, and let it all happen round him. He felt his body lifted slightly by careful hands and a hard flat object placed beneath his shoulders; he felt the movements above him as a big machine was wheeled close to his bed, and some part of it was arranged close over his chest; he felt other movement around him as the doctors retired and Sir Frederick's voice said, 'Take a deep breath and hold it until I tell you to let go – well done. Well done –' and a long, low buzzing sound filled his ears, and all the time he kept his eyes closed.

And then they moved him and did it again, and again, and he slid between dozing and waking, somehow not caring what was happening, until at last his bed was moving once more, and it was all over.

'Go to sleep, my boy,' Sir Frederick said. 'It shouldn't take above an hour or two to see the wet plates newly developed. Then we shall talk – sleep now – sleep now –'

He woke at the touch of a hand on his wrist and stared blankly at the face above him – a pretty girl's face framed in white and shining fresh in the morning sunlight – and he frowned, confused and suddenly angry, and tried to sit up, to swing his legs out of bed and get up, but she restrained him.

'Mr O'Hare, you're to stay very still, now!' she said reprovingly. 'Sir Frederick said to tell you he'll be back very shortly, but till he comes you're to lie as still as may be. But I'll give you a little wash and clean your mouth and all and you'll feel better able to be comfortable –'

'What –' he said thickly and again she shook her white capped head in reproof.

'No talking, Sir Frederick, said! You're on total bedrest, Mr O'Hare, and here at Nellies's I have to tell you that total bedrest means nothing at *all* but rest. Now, I dare say you'll be needing to deal with your bladder, won't you now? Here's a bottle and I'll – no! I told you, bedrest! I'll help you. You might as well get used to it, for that's the way it has to be from now on!'

He gave up fighting then, letting her do as she wanted, however undignified it was, as he tried to think. He remembered it all now, the fear, the blood on his papers, the ride to the hospital, the ice and the skiagraph, and his head swam as he tried to decide what to do.

'I must go –' he said suddenly, urgently, and again tried to sit up, but this time it was Sir Frederick's voice who reproved him.

'Now, don't make life difficult for my nurses, my boy! Well, you're looking better already. More comfortable? Good – we'll see about some breakfast soon –'

'Breakfast? What's the time?' Luke said and Sir Frederick sighed.

'I told you, no talking. It uses up too much energy and breath. It's six o'clock. I hadn't the heart to wake you last night to tell you the results of your skiagraph, and thought I would –'

'I have to go,' Luke said urgently, and then, as Sir Frederick opened his mouth again said loudly, 'I know what you said! But I have responsibilities. I have work to do –'

'You have pulmonary tuberculosis with considerable cavitation at the right apex,' Sir Frederick said equally loudly. 'You are infectious. Also, you have had one small haemorrhage, and there is a risk of another which may be less small. That, I would have thought, was enough responsibility for the time being, Mr O'Hare, wouldn't you?'

Luke lay back on the pillow and stared at Sir Frederick across the bed. The nurse was standing very still now and she looked at him with such an expression of sympathy on her round face that for a moment Luke wanted to weep, but flicked his gaze back to the older man standing there still and quiet in the morning sunshine that was pouring in through the small window beyond the screen that flanked the bed, and said hoarsely, 'You're sure?'

'Of course I am. I wouldn't tell you such a thing if I were

not. It isn't hopeless however, by any manner of means. We've learned a lot about these tuberculous lesions since we've had the Röntgen Rays. Look, here are your pictures –' and he held up to the light the metal frame he had been holding. It held a square of dark almost transparent film and as Luke stared at it he made out the image that the daylight picked out for him; the framework of his ribs, the large central smudge that he had to suppose was his heart (so large? so odd a shape? how very strange!) and he blinked, trying to relate that flat sheet of darkness to his own living, breathing body.

'You see?' Sir Frederick said, and poked one gnarled finger at a smudge high on one side. 'There is your disease – well-contained locally, I'm happy to say, and I have found that these high apex cavities respond well to treatment. You need not feel that you have been – that your life is unduly threatened.' And he gave the film in its frame to the nurse, who rustled away with it.

'Unduly threatened,' Luke said and closed his eyes for a moment. 'Unduly threatened. My father had phthisis. I know about the undue threat –'

'Nowadays it is better than it was,' Sir Frederick said calmly and Luke looked up at him, seeking signs of some sort of guile in his face, but he was as calm and casual as though they had been talking about a mere cold in the head. 'I have arrangements with my old friend Marcus Patterson who runs the new Brompton Sanatorium out at Frimley in Sussex, to take my patients – those of them that is, who might benefit from his regime – and –'

Luke was staring at him with his eyes narrowed. 'What regime?'

'After initial bedrest to ensure that any risk of haemoptysis is over, he provides a system of auto-inoculation and high feeding and modified rest. This allows the body to whip up its anti-toxins and thus increase its ability to resist disease. He has had excellent results in young and essentially strong patients like you. I suspect you've been neglecting yourself lately, for you look as though you have not been feeding well, but at bottom you're a fit enough young man. I believe we could benefit you greatly by sending you to Frimley.'

'I can't,' Luke said after a long pause. 'I appreciate your concern, sir, but I can't. I have a play to dress-rehearse today. I have work with Cousin Oliver to complete. I have responsibilities to many people – I can't –'

'Ah, yes, Oliver,' Sir Frederick murmured, and then suddenly smiled. 'Bless me, but you two have fluttered our dovecotes! My wife is most – well, that's beside the point at present. What matters is the fact that you are afflicted with a disease that needs care. If you refuse that care, the disease will increase. If you receive treatment now, you have every chance of getting well and returning to a full life. I can't force you to choose wisely. I can only advise you. And I advise you to go to Frimley. Or, if you prefer, I can send you to Switzerland where there are similar opportunities for care and where the weather is even more suitable for the open-air regime which can be added to the Patterson method. If you choose to accept that treatment, that is.'

'May I have some time?' Luke said after a moment. 'May I set the Gaff on its feet, see to it that Edwin knows how to cope, and then –'

'Time is yours, my boy,' Sir Frederick said and smiled thinly. 'All your life is yours. It's how you spend it that is up to you. You know that I'm right, don't you? That you should take treatment now?'

'Responsibilities,' Luke said, and sat up carefully, and swung his legs over the side of the bed, and this time Sir Frederick said nothing.

'I'll go back to the Gaff now,' Luke said, and lifted his head to stare at Sir Frederick. 'And then, as soon as all is straight, I'll come back and be grateful to you for your help. Is that a reasonable compromise?'

'It's your life,' Sir Frederick said again. 'Your time. Only you can decide what to do. I advise treatment forthwith. You decide –'

'I understand, damn it!' Luke said, with a flash of temper, and then bit his lip as Sir Frederick smiled again.

'That, you will discover, is a side effect of your disease,' he said in a conversational sort of tone. 'I find over and over again that young men with phthisis suffer marked unevenness of

154

temperament. As well as a considerable exacerbation of their – ah – carnal desires.'

Luke stared at him sharply then, and the sandy eyebrows lifted a little in response. 'And I must warn you that not only will you find that your body makes demands on you as a result of this infection, but that it is a highly transmittable infection. You can pass your disease to any other person with whom you have close contact. So take care who you kiss. And of course, how you cough. Cover your mouth whenever you do so. Don't spit in public. Stand well away from those with whom you converse, and generally keep your distance. If you do that and rest when it is possible, then you should cope well enough for a while. But come to see me often, and allow me to bully you into a better decision if your condition deteriorates. Does that sound a reasonable compromise to you?'

'Reasonable – yes. Reasonable,' Luke said wearily and very carefully stood up beside his bed. 'That's what I'll be. I promise you. Reasonable. But I must get back to the Gaff now. Please –'

15

What had started as puzzlement had now hardened into cold rigid anger. She would never have thought herself capable of such adamantine feelings, but now she was as controlled as it was possible for her to be.

At first it had been distress that had filled her. She had arrived at the Gaff particularly early, not only because it was the day of the dress rehearsal and she was excited and also badly needed time in which to talk to Luke about the problems she was still having in her scenes with Jessica and Mary Landon and Peter Hutchings, but also in order to talk to Luke about himself, for last night he had looked as drawn and miserable as she had ever seen him. It had upset her sadly to have to leave him to go to Lambeth. So, there she had been at seven o'clock, with her Act One gown in a large bandbox – for the costumier had worked late to complete it – eager and bright-faced in the morning sunshine, for it was a warm and caressing July this year, and bursting with energy and eagerness to see him.

Only to find the place shut up and silent. She had stood there at the big main doors, staring up at the newly-painted Chelsea Reach Gaff sign in great scarlet letters on the whitewashed front, and felt a lurch of fear. Was he ill? Was that why the doors were still locked? Was that why he did not answer the loud knocking she produced? She banged again, and this time called his name loudly, which was absurd for she knew quite well that he could not hear, not if he was in his office with the door closed.

She was still banging on the door when the hansom jingled to a stop beside the pavement and he got out and she whirled on her heel, her face alight with relief to see him, too glad that he was there to worry about where on earth he could have been at so early an hour. And, as the cabbie whipped up his horse and went rattling away she dropped the bandbox and ran across the pavement towards him to put her arms about him, not caring who might see them or gossip, for he was her Luke and the sight of his dear face was so comforting to her.

He turned as she reached him, her arms outstretched, and at once took a sharp step backwards, pulling his head back and away from her with an expression of cold rejection on it that made her stop short. 'Luke?' she said uncertainly. 'I – are you all right?'

'All right?' he said gruffly, and went past her, making what seemed to her an unnecessarily wide detour. 'Of course I am. Why are you here so ridiculously early?'

'I wanted to make you some breakfast,' she said and followed him over the pavement, picking up her bandbox as she went. 'I thought –'

'I've had breakfast,' he said curtly and unlocked the door and pushed it open. 'And I have a great deal of work to do. We won't be rehearsing until eleven so you might as well go away until then. Take a walk. It will do you good.' And he disappeared inside the Gaff leaving her on the pavement outside, her face white with anger and hurt and bewilderment.

What could have happened? He had been abstracted, heaven knew, these last weeks, busy and tired, but never as harsh as this, never as rejecting. She had stared at the blank emptiness that was the door of the Gaff and wanted to weep.

But she hadn't. She had instead pushed the bandbox inside the doorway and done precisely as he had told her to, turning on her heel and marching away down the Embankment with her head up and the skirts of her blue linen gown whipping about her booted ankles and her straw hat bouncing on her shoulders, for it had fallen off her head to be caught about her neck only by its ribbon and she was too angry to pin it on again. How dare he be so cool towards her? How dare he be so brusque? She would not tolerate it another moment; she would return, now, this instant, and tell him she hated him, his Gaff, his play and everything else about him and would return to Nellie's forthwith to –

To what? She had stopped on Albert Bridge, leaning over its

painted railings to stare down at the river, dimpling in the sunshine and busy with its fussy tug-boats and its great ponderous barges and officious police vessels and gazed at the glitter until her eyes filled with tears which were not entirely due to the light. To what? To tell Cousin Frederick that she was sorry, she'd meant no harm, she'd made a mistake, she'd come back now and be a good little student, and do as her Mamma bade her? Mamma, she thought then, and her eyes tingled even more for she suddenly missed her and wanted the sight of her handsome common-sensical face as badly as she had ever wanted anything in all her life.

But she had gathered her dignity and her own common sense about her and gone back to the Gaff, telling herself it was just fatigue in Luke that made him behave so, and he had a great deal to think about just now, and being a fussy child demanding attention was no way to ease his burdens. She would rehearse, and rehearse well, and would watch the others most carefully to see if she could identify just what went wrong in those tricky scenes, and she would play them better. That would show Luke how much he needed her, how silly he had been to be so cold and rejecting this morning.

That agreeable fantasy had lasted until the rehearsal began in a great pother over costumes that were not quite right and props that had gone missing and Jessica fussing interminably because her gown which was supposed to be a deep gold had come up a rather mustardy shade which she was sure ill suited her, at which point Letty could maintain it no longer, for Luke was even more distant with her when she tried to help than he had been earlier. He seemed hell-bent on keeping her literally at arms' length, turning his head away when she went to speak to him, saying hardly any word more than he absolutely had to in reply, and generally making her feel wretched as well as angry.

But she had gone on doggedly, getting into her costume with minimum aid (which greatly comforted old Ada Lee, the dresser who was taking care of all the women's parts, and who was being driven almost demented by Jessica) and even managing to apply her make-up without too much trouble, considering how inexperienced she was. And then the rehearsal had started at last, once the lights were set (and the technical rehearsal seemed to go on for hours) and she watched from the wings in every scene, determined that she would give the best performance of which she was capable, and needing to keep a close eye on all that happened in order to do so.

Perhaps it was the excitement of being in make-up and costume that did it; perhaps it was the fact that she caught Laurence Hearst's eyes on her, warm with approval and a sort of desire that she wasn't used to seeing but which she recognized immediately for what it was, or perhaps it was the edge of anger that caught her that was the cause. She did not know. All she knew was that whatever the trigger, she gave a sparkling performance and she knew it.

She moved about the stage with an assurance that gave her much greater presence than she had shown at any other point of rehearsal. She delivered her lines with a snap and a bite that made even the scene-shifters and Donald and old Ada, who knew the play to the point of boredom and back, laugh aloud and applaud. And she came off at the end of their big scene together to find Lawrence Hearst's arms about her and an over-eager kiss of congratulations on his lips which she dodged with skill and without offending him. She felt superb, and she rather thought she looked it, too.

And then when she looked at Luke, making notes at the back of the auditorium and saw Edwin blowing kisses at her while Luke sat with his head deliberately bent and refusing to look at her, her anger doubled, if that were possible. She would show him what she could do, she would show him what sort of a woman he was ignoring! Tomorrow night she would be twice what she had been in rehearsal, she promised herself; tomorrow night nothing would stand between her and a success that would bowl Luke sideways.

So she stood in the wings again and watched the scenes between Jessica and the others, her eyes a little narrowed now as she fixed her eyes on Jessica and on Jessica alone, rather than the scene as a whole to see what more she could learn, and this time saw, so clearly that she was amazed she had not noticed it before, just how selfish her technique was. She always managed to place herself on stage so that the lights caught her to her best advantage, and also just far enough above the level of her fellow artistes' view that they had to turn their heads to address their lines to her, thus setting themselves at a disadvantage from the audience's viewpoint. And she noticed something else, too; the way that, with an apparently casual touch or movement, she managed to change the positions, ever so slightly, of some items of furniture on the set. A table just marginally out of line, a sofa just a little further upstage than it had originally been set, and all the other actors somehow seemed less sure than she did. They brushed against the furniture, and had to move awkwardly to reach their destinations, and Jessica knew exactly what she was doing to them and revelled in it.

And Letty, acting so completely against her own character that she would not have thought it possible, took a leaf from her book. While the curtain was down and before it rose again on the scenes in which she had the most trouble she saw Jessica give the sofa a small push as she came off-stage, and slipped discreetly behind a flat to watch her go sweeping by, and said nothing. But while Jessica was touching up her make-up, and while the rest of the cast were distracted about their own affairs, Letty slipped on stage herself and rearranged the furniture again, in order to bring it back into a position that suited her better, giving her the extra space she needed. She was tempted to hide a prop, a piece of sewing that Miss Neville was ostensibly engaged upon at the start of the scene, but dismissed the idea almost as soon as it came into her head. She would not stoop as far as that, she told herself, and went off to stand on the opposite prompt side as quietly as she could in spite of her thumping pulses and uneven breath to wait for the scene.

And it worked. For the first time in all the rehearsals, it was Jessica who inadvertently sent a chair rocking, Jessica who missed a cue because she was uncertain where a move took her. And Letty seized on her unsureness to ride to her own triumph. The scene went like a dream as far as she was concerned and she came off at the end with her eyes shining and her head held so high she felt at least an inch taller.

And at the end of the long and exhausting day, when they

collected in a tense group to be given their director's notes, she sat and waited for some word of approval from Luke, some sign that he had seen how well she had done today and encouragement to do even better tomorrow, and was made angrier still, for he showed nothing. He went through his notes like an automaton, commenting on costume, or make-up, on entrances and exits, but saying nothing at all about the quality of anyone's performance. He merely thanked them all, told them to be in well before the half the following evening and then bade them all a curt goodnight before taking himself off to his office bedroom without a backward glance at any of them. And she had had to go back to Cheyne Walk with Edwin, wretched and feeling deeply lonely.

She had slept appallingly, the night seeming to unroll beneath her hot and crumpled pillow with the agonizing slowness of a nightmare; and tossed and turned, hearing Chelsea Old Church strike every quarter as well as every hour, and dozing only in a fitful fashion as the morning light lifted above the eastern chimney-pots.

But it did her no harm, for she sat at breakfast and listened to Edwin burbling on in great excitement about the great day that had arrived and the superb triumph that he was sure was to come tonight, and smiled politely and gave no indication of fatigue at all. She spent the morning helping the rest of the cast give the Gaff its last cleaning and sweeping so that it stood in perfect expectation of its birth, and the afternoon helping young Donald stock the shelves with stone bottles of ginger beer, lemonade and the barrels of bitter beer that would be needed, and still showed no sign of any feeling other than normal interest. But all the time her rage seethed beneath the surface and sustained her better than any food or drink or rest could have done.

The doors were to open at six and the curtain was to rise at seven; by half-past five in the warm afternoon, people were already streaming over the bridge from Battersea, for the word had gone round like a bush-fire that the new Gaff was to open at half-price seats. Threepence it would be for every seat in the house, and a proper play with costumes and scenery, and beer to be bought at the right tavern prices and no profiteering, not nohow. A night out for a tanner, no less. The crowd that gathered outside the big Gaff doors was noisy and pushy and smelled remarkably strongly of beer and moth-balls and sweat and a great deal worse, but it was a cheerful mob with no malice about it, and the noise it made penetrated to the dressing-rooms at the back where the cast were painting their faces and murmuring their lines over to themselves, and cheered them greatly. There was a world of difference between playing to an eager welcoming audience and a hostile challenging one, and this one sounded exactly what was wanted.

Letty in particular needed that sense of excitement and warmth and needed it badly. She had seen Luke only twice all day, for he had kept himself barricaded in his small office and busied himself about whatever it was he found there to do. Certainly he seemed not to care that other people wanted his company, that others needed his support on what was a difficult night for all of them. Even the rest of the cast muttered about the change in their director as they busied themselves with their preparations, and that comforted Letty a little for she had felt obscurely that it was a fault in her and her alone, that made Luke behave so unkindly. But if the others noticed it too, perhaps it was not she who was to blame –

And then she caught Jessica's eye as she leaned forwards to look in the big mirror with its frame of dozens of naked electric-bulbs. She was carefully painting her lovely curve of a mouth as Ada, busy with the goose-iron and a set of torn flounces at the back of the room muttered furiously about how Mr O'Hare hadn't got a civil tongue in his head when a person 'ad to ask a proper question and she for 'er part wasn't one to put up with it, no matter what, and Letty's heart twisted against the expression on Jessica's face and the look in her eyes as she flicked her gaze sideways to pick up Letty in the mirror.

'I wouldn't worry, Ada,' she said sweetly through stretched lips and then leaned back to admire her handiwork. 'He'll be all right later. I spoke to him about a party for us all after the performance but it's clear the poor darling's much too tired for such a thing, so I've booked a table at Romano's for just the two of us, and I promise you, my dear old friend, that by tomorrow's performance he'll be as sweet as pie. I understand how tense he is, you see – we've worked in plays together before, and I deeply understand the poor lamb's needs. He'll be splendid by tomorrow, you see if he isn't –'

And Letty dug her fingers savagely into her cold cream to clean the grease-paint off her hands and scrubbed them till they were red. It didn't make her feel any better but it gave her something to do to keep her eyes off the self-satisfied Jessica.

And so the anger grew and simmered and concentrated itself as the time for the first performance at the Chelsea Reach Gaff drew closer. Had she been a more experienced player she would perhaps have been grateful for it, welcoming the way it kept her mind off the ordeal that was to come and the responsibility she carried for the evening. After all, Kate was the lead part. If that went wrong, what could go right? But Letty did not think of that. She just stood in the wings and peered through the tiny peep-hole that Donald had rigged in the front tabs, at the bustling shouting orange-sucking beer-drinking and sausage-gobbling audience waiting for her, and nursed her anger to a white heat. She'd show them all, she would show them, and just who she would show what she didn't know, and didn't care. She was just primed for the performance of a lifetime.

And she gave it. The curtain went up to a great roar of welcome from the audience after Edwin had made his flowery speech about the sort of place the Gaff was to be and how its director, the famed and magnificent actor Mr Lucas O'Hare, was to run it entirely for their benefit, at the lowest possible prices, and after Luke had taken a brief bow to be introduced to his now and future patrons, and they settled down to rapt attention. The smell of their bodies and their ill-washed clothes and their food and their tobacco came wreathing up from the auditorium to create a sense of special closeness on stage, and Letty moved into it and absorbed it and gave to it and took from it to such a degree that it was as though she were a different person.

Luke, watching from the opposite prompt side in the shadows of a tall flat felt his belly wrenched with the pain of it.

He had seen the reaction in her face the moment he had pulled back so anxiously the previous morning, so afraid as he had been of passing on to her some part of his own hateful infection. He had seen the pain in her, the way her eyes had darkened first with distress and then with anger and had ached to go to her, to put his arms about her and tell her of the contagion that kept them apart. But how could he? She was a warm and generous creature, his Letty. She would not be held away from him for any fear of damage to herself, of that he was certain. Tell her he had tuberculosis and she would hurl herself into his care with all the energy and talent with which she was now hurling herself into the role of Kate. It couldn't be thought of.

And he stood there in the dark wings and watched that square of brilliant light centre stage, watched her run rings round Laurence and Joseph and all the rest of them, and wanted to feel the touch of her hand in his and the warmth of her breath on his cheek as desperately as he had ever wanted anything. He was here at the first performance of his own dreamed-of theatre; he was seeing the culmination of weeks of planning and hoping and enormous hard work, and all he could think of was Letty in a nightdress sitting barefooted and crumpled in front of a kitchen fire. It was misery.

He remained there in his secret place in the wings all through the play, not even emerging when the intervals came and the audience stampeded to the back of the Gaff to buy the bar dry of beer and eat every pasty and hot sausage in sight, trying not to think of the way his flesh was corrupt and evil, trying to tell himself he could be well, he would be well again, but not believing it. He was a sick and infectious and revolting creature, he told himself, almost wallowing in his self-loathing. And he had been fool enough to love a girl who loved him back, and that made him even more loathsome in his own eyes.

It was little wonder that at the end of the play, when the audience shrieked and stamped and roared its approval at the beaming sweating bowing cast, and most particularly at Letty for whom they had obviously developed a total adoration, that his feelings took over. It was little wonder that when Letty, trying to escape the crush on the prompt side which led to the dressing-rooms, chose in a moment of her own confused happiness and misery to run across to leave by the opposite prompt side, that he lost control.

She came out of the brilliance of the stage centre into the darkness of the flats and he stepped forwards to stand in her path and put out one hand to touch her.

'Letty,' he said, and his voice was thick and hoarse and tight with emotion. 'Letty, you were –'

She peered in the darkness, putting her hand up in a childish little gesture, to catch her thumb between her teeth.

'What – who?' she said uncertaintly and then, as he moved into the light her chin came up and she said, 'Luke,' without any expression in her voice at all.

'Letty, you were –'

'Good enough?' she said. 'Good enough for you?' And then she couldn't help it. Tears lifted in her eyes to make them glitter in the half-light and again she produced a childish gesture, as she rubbed the back of her hand across her nose and sniffed.

It was more than he could bear. He put his arms out and she seemed to fall into them and he was kissing her with a huge hunger, her cheeks, her throat, her forehead and then she turned her head seeking his lips with her own and as he felt her breath on his cheek the sense of what he was doing came back. He felt his own body as disgusting, as dangerous and revolting, and hers as all that was good and lovely; and the comparison, added to his fear of damaging her, combined into one single violent movement. He put both hands on her shoulders and pushed her so savagely that she stumbled back against the flat and it rocked ludicrously. And in a sort of mimicry of her own action he rubbed the back of his hand against his mouth, staring at her above it with his eyes wide with self-disgust and then turned and went plunging away in the darkness of the wings, leaving her there holding on to the swaying flat and still seeing, long after he had gone, that expression of sick loathing on his face.

16

'You seem rather given to running away, Letty,' he said, and though his voice was mild enough she felt the edge in him and reddened.

'That's not – I've come back here, haven't I? That isn't easy.'

'I wasn't referring to the fact that you left Nellie's. More to the fact that you left – wherever it is you've been this past three months.'

'I told you.' Her lips tightened into a mulish line. 'I explained as much as I can. I tried. It didn't – I was not able to cope. Now, I'm asking you to let me return to Nellie's.' She lifted her chin and looked at him very directly. 'I don't want to fail at everything, Cousin Frederick. I need to try again, however difficult it is, however much I –'

She stopped, abashed, and he smiled a little wearily. 'However much you may dislike it? Is that what you were going to say? No, don't try to deny it. I know you were. It's that that worries me, my dear. Medicine is a difficult life to say the least of it. You need to have strong feelings about it to be able to practise it well. Now, some people practise it for money and worldly success, and although that is not a motive I find attractive, I do not dismiss it. It has powered many excellent physicians and surgeons and gave them the energy to offer good care to their expensive patients. And even the rich are entitled to consideration! There are others who are driven by their religious beliefs, and wish only to serve their God in the shape of their fellow man, and we all know they are excellent for the poor and troubled. And there are some – and I hoped you would be one, for they are the ones I find most – well – like myself, I suppose – there are some who are driven by passion for the study of the human condition, mental and physical, and a desire to ease all, whoever they are. Those are the students I most yearn for, Letty, those are the ones who make the best practitioners. They don't merely *like* their studies and the life it leads to, they worship it. And you are now telling me that you dislike it, and are driven only by the need to avoid failure – personal failure –'

'It isn't like that,' she said and then shook her head. 'Oh, I don't know what it's like. All I know is that I want to come back to Nellie's. Does it matter what the motives are as long as the result is good? I can work, you know, and work hard. And I will, if you'll let me. And I'll qualify and be the best doctor that I –'

'No doubt.' Frederick got to his feet and walked over to his window to stand and stare out at the teeming street beneath and she sat there and watched him, her face still and tight. 'But is that a powerful enough motive to make you work well and happily? I think of your welfare as well as that of my patients, you know. To push a young person along a road that is not suited to them – it's not a loving thing to do.'

She took a deep breath and got to her feet, and began to pull on her gloves, keeping her head bent and grateful for the way the brim of her straw boater shaded her eyes. 'Then you're telling me I may not come back to resume my studies? Then – then I suppose I must think of some other activity. I dare say I'll find something –'

'If you would tell me more about what you have been doing and what went wrong, I could perhaps help you better.' Sir Frederick turned back from the window and looked at her with such an expression of concern on his tired, lined face that for a moment she wanted to weep, to throw herself on that spare old frame and tell him all about her pain, the way she would tell a father, and the shadow of her own much-loved and long dead father Wilfred, jostled in her mind with the shadows of the past few days and made her unable to say anything. She just folded her lips more tightly and shook her head and kept her eyes resolutely downcast as she smoothed her gloves over her fingers.

He sighed and came back to his desk. 'Well, I cannot force you to tell me, of course. And I can also not just turn you away. You may return, however uneasy I may feel at the moment about the request – but I do insist on one thing first.'

Now she could lift her head and she looked at him with her eyes a little narrowed and watchful.

'No, no need to be so anxious! It's reasonable enough, I'm sure you'll agree. My child, go home to Haworth for the rest of the summer. You look exhausted and need time to rest, and also of course, your Mamma is entitled to see you and to hear what has happened. You may not wish to tell me, but surely you'll wish to tell her?'

She stood and stared at him, trying to think of going to Haworth, seeing Mamma, sitting there beside her in their cosy sitting-room at Tansy Clough, the old grey house high on the moors, talking, telling her about Chelsea Reach, about Luke, about –

She shook her head. 'I cannot believe she will want me to,' she said bleakly. 'As you said, I have been rather given to running away, haven't I? To go to her after causing her so much distress and tell her of more distress – I can't.'

'You must,' he said calmly, 'mustn't you? You can't just refuse to speak to her. She may be a difficult and – shall we say – determined lady, but she loves you and has suffered much distress at your hands. Go to see her, and then you may return to Nellie's. Refuse to go and I must refuse to accept you in the next term's classes.'

'You said it is unloving to force a young person along a road that is not suited to them.'

He shook his head, smiling slightly. 'None of that, young lady! I'll not be manipulated that way, and never you think it! It is not being pushed to be sent to see your Mamma. You may not realize it, but you want to go. So, go and buy a ticket and be away with you. And I'll see you here at the start of the next term, in September. And Letty –'

She had reached the door and paused there, not looking back.

'– I shall be really glad to see you in September. I believe you could be an excellent doctor, whatever your motives, if you just talk to your Mamma and rid yourself of your pain. She can help you do that, if you'll let her. Goodbye, my dear. And let me assure you that pain does go away, eventually. Nothing lasts for ever.' And he smiled at her and she looked back at him for a long moment and then bobbed her head awkwardly and went away, leaving him sitting tired and yet curiously happy as he sat and stared at the closed door.

'Poor child,' he thought. 'Poor child. But Sophie will be happy again, to see her. I've done that much for my Sophie.' And he felt a little better, though still much more tired than he should have been.

The journey was a miserable business, for she felt sick with apprehension the whole way. And not just with apprehension at what her Mamma might say or do, but also about what was happening at the Gaff. When she had fled after the performance back to the house at Cheyne Walk, empty except for the servants, and packed her possessions in the pretty dimity lilac-and-white room, she had been too despairing with her own misery to care about anything or anybody but herself. The way Luke had hurled her away from him had said it all, and she could think of nothing else. Not of her responsibility to the company – and after all, Jessica could easily play her part of Kate – or to Edwin, who had been so cheerful a host, or what she would do in the future. She had just fled. And after another sleepless night in an hotel, she had first written a short letter to Edwin telling him that to her deep regret she had to leave him and his company forthwith, and apologizing for any difficulty this might cause him, and then gone to Nellie's, still acting solely and wholly on impulse, to see Sir Frederick and beg to be taken back. It had seemed to her that the only way she could live with what had happened in the dark wings by the side of the Chelsea Gaff stage was to expunge it from her life by expunging the Gaff from her memory, making it seem as though she had never met Luke, had never tried to be an actress, had never seen the Gaff or any of the people involved with it.

And when she bought her ticket at King's Cross for Keighley, after sending a laconic telegram to her mother telling her she was coming, and had settled herself on the train, she managed for the first few miles of the journey, as it rattled its way through the sooty crumbling North London suburbs out into Hertfordshire, to hold on to her intention to pretend none of it had ever happened. She sat there thinking only of how she would tell Mamma she was sorry for upsetting her, but would refuse to say what had occurred and how. Mamma would stop asking and at last all would be as it had been –

But then the apprehension moved in as she realized that she could not maintain that fantasy. There was no hope at all that Mamma would allow her to keep her own counsel, she told herself miserably, sitting there and watching the landscape flying past the windows, no hope that she would not be scolded mercilessly and made to reveal all her innermost feelings, no hope that she would not be forced to look again at that moment of utter rejection at Luke's hands, and she wanted to cry and was only able to control her feelings because the carriage was so full of the stout Yorkshire men and women and their noisy children who packed the train half-way to suffocation.

And so it went on as the train fled ever northwards through the long hot afternoon; Northampton, Leicester, Birmingham dwindled behind them and Trent and then Bingley and at last Keighley loomed up ahead, and all the way her thoughts twisted and turned in her head, repeating themselves constantly like animals on a treadmill and she slid ever deeper into her personal slough of despair. It was a relief to stand at last on Keighley station amid the grey stone buildings and the garish posters and hoardings advertising Nestle's Chocolate and Mazawattee Tea and Stephen's Inks in the cool of the early summer evening and instruct a porter to carry her bags to the Worth Valley train that would take her on the last leg of this tedious journey home.

She climbed the high twisting main street of Haworth from the station, leaving her bags to be sent up by the carter later, very aware of the duck-egg blue of the evening sky outlining those harsh slate roofs and lighting the cobbles to moments of irridescence, trying not to remember the high excitement she had felt when she had made the journey in reverse, last September. Then she had been bubbling with excitement, for she had been going to a new life, a wonderful life as a medical student. It had all seemed to be right and good then. Now it seemed only tedious and heavy and interminable – but that was a thought she must not entertain, for she was to return to Nellie's, to be a student again. After this visit, she must return –

The few lights that there were in the street glowed softly as the sky deepened to become a rich kingfisher blue and as she turned the corner by the Black Bull and took the familiar rest by the steps that led to the upper walk, and ultimately to the moor path that led up to Tansy Clough, she turned and looked down the hill towards the valley, back southwards to London and thought involuntarily, 'Luke, Luke, what are you doing now? Are you watching Jessica playing my part on your stage tonight? Did Jenny Drew take over well as Constance Neville? Do you miss me, Luke?' and then dragged her mind away and turned, ready to start the climb.

'Nay, 'tisn't, is it? 'Tis then – 'tis Miss Letty, or I miss my guess! 'Ow are yer, then? 'Ad enough o' they Londoners, 'ave yer? Coom oop to see t'family, 'ave yer, and get a bit o' Bessie's 'ome cookin'?'

'Oh,' Letty stopped and peered back through the dimness and then smiled. 'Josiah, is it? How nice to see you! Are you well?'

'Well enough,' the old man said, with his usual Yorkshire caution. 'I bain't complainin' – seen yer Ma then, 'ave yer?'

'I'm just going home now –'

'Then you'll not see 'er there, on account she's down the clinic, bain't she?' The old man sounded pleased to be the bearer of such tidings, and she smiled at him, remembering all too well that this was the way he had always been. It was comforting in a way to be back among her own kind again.

'At the clinic, so late?'

'Ah!' He said it with great relish. 'Got one o' they Ramsbottom bairns in again, always ailin' that lot, but with old Joe Ramsbottom for a granfer, what can you expect? You go down the clinic, Miss Letty, you'll see 'er there!' And he went on up the cobbled street leaving her to stare back down the hill towards the low narrow building that had once been a cowshed, but which her mother's money and efforts had converted into a neat dispensary and clinic for the poorer residents of the town.

She could see the lights burning there now, low and flickering in the long windows, and after a moment turned and went down the street towards them. It would be too easy to dodge the meeting, to go to the house and wait there – and also too difficult. To wait for Mamma would be infinitely worse than facing her now while her tension was so high, and anyway, there at the clinic they would in a sense be on neutral ground. At home at Tansy Clough there would be the long growing-up years she had spent there to cloud her feelings, the shadows of her childish self to come between them and diminish her adult status. She would see her mother here and now. It was the best way.

When she pushed the door open, her mother was sitting on a high stool beside an examination table in the middle of the big clinic room, leaning sideways over the child who was lying on it. The light was just a small oil-lamp that was set on a trolley beside the table, leaving the rest of the clinic in deep shadow and for a moment Letty stood in the doorway and looked at the scene; her mother, straight-backed and neat as ever with her thick hair pinned tightly on her head to keep it out of her way and her plain alpaca apron over her linen gown, the sterilizer that stood at the far side hissing gently and sending tendrils of steam curling up to warm the air, the cupboards of glass and chrome with their rows of bottles and dressings drums and instruments; it was all part of the fabric of her life, part of the very food she had eaten and the beds she had slept in as she grew up. To look after ill people in such surroundings was what she had been born for, what she had been reared for, and the past few months had been little more than a mad aberration, a nonsense, a crazy dream she had allowed herself to experience. She was home now with Mamma, where she belonged, and here she would stay. Never mind being a student, never mind acting, never mind anything. She would stay with Mamma and be her assistant, and live her life contentedly for ever doing it. And she took a deep breath, trying to convince herself her thoughts really reflected her feelings.

Sophie lifted her head after a moment and peered towards the doorway, frowning slightly.

'Is there someone there?'

'Yes, Mamma.' Letty moved forwards into the light and after a moment Sophie nodded, but her face was expressionless.

'I got your telegram,' she said and looked down at the child again.

'Mamma –' Letty's voice came thick in her own ears and she coughed to clear it. 'Mamma – I – I'm sorry. Sorry to have upset you. I did not wish to hurt you. Only to do what I –'

'Upset me?' Sophie looked up again, and smiled, a thin little curving of her lips, but a smile nonetheless. 'That doesn't matter. I've been upset more than once and recovered.'

'I – is it all right to talk now?' Letty moved closer to the table and looked down at the child lying there. She was pale, and her eyes were half closed and she was breathing shallowly and rather fast. 'Or are you –'

'I'm just waiting for the ambulance to come from the hospital at Keighley,' Sophie said never taking her eyes from the child's face. 'She needs a transfusion of whole blood. She has an anaemia that will kill her if she lacks it much longer. Her mother's up on the moors with the other children and anyway – well, I said, I'll keep her here till the ambulance got here. Poor little scrap –' And she put out one hand and brushed away a wisp of hair from the child's brow.

There was a little silence and then Letty said awkwardly, '– I have spoken to Cousin Frederick. He says I may go back.'

Sophie still didn't lift her eyes. 'Back to Nellie's? Why?'

'Because I want to. Because I – I was wrong to leave as I did, and I must try again. And he said I may. If –'

Sophie smiled then, her eyes still fixed on the child's face. 'If you came here first and spoke to me?'

'He told you?'

'No. I just know Freddy better than he thinks I do. He is –' And now she did look at Letty and her eyes seemed dark and shadowed. 'He is a very good man, Letty.'

'I know he is – but he doesn't – he did not press me too hard.'

'Are you telling me I must be the same?' Sophie said and still

173

her eyes were unreadable in the shadows.

'Yes,' Letty said baldly after a moment. 'Yes, Mamma. It is as I told you in my letters. I must – I must do what is best for me. At least, I must try. If it does not happen precisely as I would like – well, that is my problem. No one else's. But I must be free to do as I wish if I am to live any sort of useful life. I can't always be told what to do.'

'Is that what you have learned at those political meetings of yours?'

'No. Not precisely. But if I had it would be a good lesson. It is important that people think of themselves. But please, let us not go over old ground. I've come here to be friends again, Mamma. It made me very sad to be remote, indeed it did, but all the same, if the only way we can be friends is if I – if I am a child to you all my life, and do as *you* wish and *you* bid me and please *you* always, then it can't be. It wouldn't make you happy anyway –'

'I've discovered that.'

Letty, who had been about to go on on the same theme stopped short, and stared at her mother, leaning forward to peer in her face.

'What did you say?'

'That you're right. That I've discovered that I can't be happy trying to live your life for you. That you must be free to do as you think best, and that I musn't meddle. I've had time to think too, since you went to – wherever it was you went.'

The light glowed softly on Sophie's thick white hair and Letty wanted to put out a hand and stroke it, and then clenched her fist to control it, for the moment seemed to her to be a fragile one, all too easily damaged.

'I think you must explain more,' she said carefully.

'I've been too – I've loved you too much and not well at all,' Sophie said, and still she sat and contemplated the sleeping child who lay there between them. 'I felt always that I must care for you and protect you and push you more than the boys, for they are boys, you see. And that was wrong. If you're to be the woman I'd dreamed of you being, then only you can make her. I can't. So – I'm sorry, Letty, for being as I was. Too strong. I pushed you in the wrong way, and it's a great credit to you that you would not be pushed.'

She lifted her chin then and managed a smile. 'And perhaps a little credit to me that I reared you to be such a girl, don't you think? If I'd been as bad as Freddy made me think I was, then you'd have been ruined, wouldn't you? As it was, you're strengthened. Where were you, Letty? You can tell me, you know, for I shan't complain or meddle, I promise. I've learned, indeed I have – it's been a sad three months for me, my love.'

And Letty took a deep breath and leaned her elbows on the examination table, and as the small Ramsbottom child lay sleeping the shallow sleep of her illness between them told her mother all that had happened. Of how she had felt when Luke had first come into her life, and of the night in the kitchen when they had been so close – and the pain she had known when he had hurled her out of his life again.

'For he did, didn't he, Mamma?' she said and now tears were sliding down her cheeks. 'He must have hated me a great deal to treat me so –'

Sophie shook her head and put her hand on her daughter's arm. 'I don't know, my love. I can't pretend I fully understand the ways of men. I – I know what it is to be in love, as you are. I know what it's like to choose badly –' and Letty looked at her curiously in spite of her own misery, wanting to ask more, but Sophie shook her head and went on quickly, '– but I can't say why he behaved so. Only that –' She shrugged. 'Only that perhaps it isn't as you think. So often women misread men's behaviour. They're a strange crew, you know,' and the two of them looked at each other and felt the warmth and security of their shared femininity wrap itself round them like a comforting blanket.

There was the growl of an engine outside, lifting to a louder noise and then a vehicle stopped outside and the engine rattled to silence and Letty lifted her head. 'A *motor* ambulance, Mamma? Whatever happened to the old horses?'

'Oh, they went out to pasture,' Sophie said and got to her feet and began, very gently, to wrap the child in a blanket as she whimpered and turned in her sleep.

Letty chuckled. 'And what did Samuel say when you spent

175

the money on this one?' she said and Sophie looked at her and grinned her old familiar grin and they were pulled even closer, remembering the long years of wrangles between Sophie and her family as she determinedly spent all she could on provisions for the town's health services.

There was a nurse from the cottage hospital travelling with the ambulance and she took the Ramsbottom child and settled her inside; and then, together, Letty and Sophie watched the red tail-lights dwindle away as the noisy engine chugged back down the valley to Keighley, before turning to climb arm-in-arm back past the Black Bull to the moor and home.

They travelled in silence most of the way; indeed it wasn't until they got to the top of the moor and were standing beside the gate to the garden, feeling the soughing of the night breeze about their ears and smelling the faint heatheriness it carried, that Sophie said almost conversationally, 'You'll be going back to your theatre, then?'

'What?' Letty said, startled, trying to see her mother's face in the darkness. 'What did you say?'

'That you'll be going back? From all you say, it's the only place you really want to be, isn't it? The only place where you feel really happy?'

17

It was not until she was on the train again, going back to London that the full enormity of what she had done really came home to her. She had let everyone down appallingly, and most particularly Edwin, and all because she had not had the courage to deal with her own feelings. And for a while she wallowed a little in her own guilt and shame as the train sang and clattered its way over the rails through the lush August landscape, staring out mournfully at the ripening apples on the trees and the late poppies starring the cornfields as though they were symbols of decay and evil. And then, as the train rushed on through the industrial Midlands and black-plumed chimneys and coal-tips glowering heavily under the soft summer sky filled the view, her common sense – and some humour – took over and she shook herself a little and settled to reading the copy of the *Strand Magazine* that Samuel had given her for her journey, determined not to be so foolish. The resolve she had formulated this past fortnight would not be shaken so easily; she was going to be a new and more sensible Letty, and that was all about it. And even though she read the same page of the newest Sherlock Holmes story over and over again and took in none of it, she stuck to her resolve for a great many miles.

But then it became impossible to prevent herself from thinking about her own affairs any longer, and she put the magazine down on her lap and let her mind slide back over the past two weeks as her eyes stared out unseeingly at the flying landscape. At first, it had been as cosy as being a child again. She had felt much as she could remember she used to feel when she was small and had a chest cold, and had to be tucked up in bed and spoiled a little – wrapped and secure and peaceful in spite of the underlying hurt. She had slept well, long dreamless nights in her own familiar blue bedroom high under the eaves of the old house with the sounds and smells of the moor and the house waking her each morning, peewits and larks and the silly baaing of the mournful long-faced sheep and the scented heather and the coffee that Bessie was brewing with a great clatter in the kitchen far below; and she would stretch and then, moving lazily and with all the pleasure of knowing she had no reason to hurry, wash and dress and then come down to eat hot baps and honey in the small breakfast-parlour that overlooked the garden, alive now with roses and sweet-williams and mignonette and phlox, while Bessie bustled about her and chattered on and on about town doings, as spry and as busy as if she were a stripling of just seventy or so, instead of being past eighty. And then there would be long peaceful mornings pottering about the house and garden, or visiting Samuel at the mill – but never joining her mother at the clinic, for they had made a tacit agreement that this was not for Letty now; not the Letty who was to be an actress instead of a doctor.

For so it had been agreed, surprisingly painlessly for Letty. Her mother, she would have sworn, was an implacable sort of woman, one who knew her own mind and who would always see to it that others did, but she had misread the real power of her, Letty now realized. Sophie had the sort of strength that made is possible for her to admit she was wrong. Not for Sophie the weakness of bluster or stubbornness. She would think a situation through as clearly as she could and then act accordingly, even if doing so meant going directly against a previous decision or piece of behaviour. Had Letty stopped to think as clearly herself, she would have realized that, she told herself, walking high on the moors with the wind whipping her linen skirts about her ankles and snatching her boater from her head to dangle it down her back on its ribbon. There had been times, often, in her childhood when her mother had said to her, 'I'm sorry', apologizing perhaps for a patch of bad temper born of fatigue; but somehow Letty had just taken that for granted. She had noticed only her mother's determination to do what she believed was right, instead of being equally aware of her ability to know when she was wrong.

So the two weeks she spent there at home were tranquil and restorative ones. It hurt to think of Luke, of course, for there was no doubt now in her mind that she loved him as dearly as it was possible for her to love anyone. His rejection of her hurt abominably, but the pain did not diminish the strengh of that love. 'One day, perhaps,' she would tell herself as she lay on her back in the springing heather high above Stanbury and the smoke-curling chimneys of the valley cottages, staring up at the drifting patches of summer clouds, 'one day I'll be my own person again. One day I'll forget him. Perhaps. But until then I must just do as best I can to live a life that will please me and make me useful. For although it is no doubt delightful to love and be loved in return, there is more to life for an energetic and sensible woman than just love. I can and will be strong and useful, and forget all about beating hearts and trembling hands and breathlessness and –'

And then she would jump to her feet and run headlong down the rolling curves of the moor to Tansey Clough and tea with Bessie, burning up her distress in physical effort and thereby giving herself a huge appetite for Bessie's parkin and shortbread and wickedly rich fruit cake.

The evenings had been the best, in many ways. They would sit on each side of the fireplace with its slow-burning logs – for even in high summer the evenings were chill up here on the roof of England – and Sophie would read and Letty would sew, making herself a new gown in green silk she had bought from the best drapery shop in Keighley and sometimes they would talk and sometimes just sit, but always they would be comfortable together. And when Samuel was there it was agreeable to play cards or to sing to the tunes they could coax from the old cottage piano in the corner on which the three of them, when they had been small, had practised so laboriously under Bessie's proud and watchful eye, before rounding off the day with a cup of good hot chocolate and bed.

Now, sitting in the stuffy noisy train she ached for the peace of the old grey stone house in which she had been born, and the peace of the past fortnight that had so effectively bandaged the sore places deep in her mind, and then reminded herself yet again that from now on she was to be different. Energetic and different, that was the new Letty. And she sat up a little more erectly in her seat and stared out of the window at Trent Station, which was where they had now stopped, with such great purposefulness and severity that a passenger who had been about to open the door to enter her compartment thought better of it and moved down the train to find other accommodation.

Her determination held firm at King's Cross, where she marched to the front of the bustle for hansom cabs, secured one under the noses of several perspiring men and took herself off to the Royal Society of Medicine in Wimpole Street, where her mother had arranged she should stay for a few days.

'There is no need for you to pay vast sums for hotels, Letty,' she had said calmly when Letty had tried to protest. 'You must permit me to give you some advice, my dear, however determined you are to be your own mistress from now on. And you may use my Fellowship and its privileges as my daughter, and be safe and comfortable and give me peace of mind. Those hotels I visited did not fill me with any admiration, and I shall be happier knowing you are under a safe roof. Once you've organized your own lodgings of course it will be different, but indulge me until then.'

So she had, and now she settled herself in the Society's Domus Medicus, glad to be there, for it was conveniently located in the centre of the busiest part of the town, and from there she could most easily set about making her plans for her new future.

Her first task was to see Sir Frederick and tell him that she was not, after all, to return to Nellie's. She went to the hospital first, the morning after her arrival back in London, having dressed herself in the most serious clothes she could find that were fitting to the weather – and London was indeed sweltering in a particularly sultry August – decking herself in a severe navy-blue alpaca skirt and even more severely-tailored white blouse over which she wore a brief navy alpaca jacket and blue straw hat, and walking as straight-backed as she could in marked contrast to the curved-backed 'Grecian Bend' posture that all the fashionable girls were affecting this year.

She might be planning to be an actress, but that did not mean she was frivolous, and it was important that Sir Frederick should realize that.

But in the event, her efforts were wasted, for Sir Frederick was not there. He had been taken away by his masterful wife on a visit to Baden-Baden, so the hall porter told her (and he was the fount of all such information in the hospital and always had been, so she knew she could believe him), and would not be back until the last week of the month ready to start lectures again as the medical school reassembled in September for the winter. But he let her sit in Sir Frederick's quiet office to write him a short note, and she sat there for some time, trying to compose the right words, but she managed it at last, keeping it as simple as she could.

'Dear Cousin Frederick,' she wrote in her large flowing script, after a couple of false starts. 'I must tell you you were right to send me to Haworth and I am most grateful to you for the guidance that you offered. After much discussion with my Mamma and much thought on my own part, I have decided that I cannot after all be a successful medical student. It is the theatre that I most desired and I intend to seek a further career there. I thank you for your patience and for your excellent advice and look forward to seeing you again on some future occasion. Your obedient cousin –'

She went then to find Barty who had chosen to stay in London to work at Nellie's as a dresser during the summer months and so to advance his studies, instead of going home as so many of the other students did. After their first rather awkward meeting he agreed to share a luncheon at a tea-shop with her. They were polite and tense and after a while, feeling miserable at the coldness that lay between them, she tried to explain to him about her decision and why she had made it. But he shook his head at her.

'It is of no use making excuses, Letty –' he began and at once the old familiar irritation rose in her.

'I'm not making excuses! I have nothing to make excuses for. I want simply to explain why I –'

'There is no explanation you can give which a sensible person would understand,' he said stiffly. 'You caused me great embarrassment, not to say inconvenience. Time I should have spent about my own studies had to be wasted concerning myself with you and your silliness. How can you expect me to be other than angry?'

'How can I expect you to be –' She shook her head in disbelief, and then tried again. 'Doesn't it bother you at all, Barty, that I was so unhappy at Nellie's? That I felt only half a person while I was there? That my real interests were being stifled and –'

She stopped short for he was staring at her in blank surprise. 'Being stifled? How stifled? You talk such nonsense, Letty. How can you think I will take you seriously? No one was attempting –'

'Barty, I think there is no point in this discussion. You may be my brother but we are as far apart as any strangers and –'

'You really are absurd, Letty!' He addressed himself to his lunch again, cutting his meat methodically. 'How can a brother and sister be as strangers? Really, this is all such nonsense, and the sooner you come to your senses and return to Mrs Partridge's and settle down to some serious work again, the better.'

'I've tried to tell you I'm never coming back,' she said as patiently as she could. 'That I have other things to do. And that I'm going to do them!'

'Women!' Barty said and looked up at her briefly before returning his attention to his plate. 'Never any use for anything, obviously. I can't imagine how anyone could ever think there was any sense in making women into medical students. Mamma is different, of course, but there are not many like her. Yet you and your crew would have all such silly creatures as yourself voting – it doesn't bear thinking of.'

She got to her feet with a tight, controlled movement. 'Barty, I shall pay for my lunch as I leave. I see no point in staying here with you another moment. We shall only quarrel. Good afternoon, Barty. I doubt we shall see much of each other from now on. Family or not, we really have so little to talk about that there would be no point, would there?' And she went, weaving her way between the crowded marble-topped tables and the bustling waitresses, leaving him staring after her with his face a study in surprise.

She was more ruffled than she would have thought possible by this episode. She had long ago realized that she and Barty were far from similar, and that as the years carried them from squabbling infancy to young adulthood the chasm between them had increased, but she had never found him quite so impossible to comprehend as she had today; and that made her feel shaky inside again, less able to cope with the shiny new plan she had for her life – which was to find herself work in the theatre, somehow, and to build for herself a reputation as a performer that would carry her into an independent and busy future.

She had intended to find herself a job before going to see Edwin, which of course she knew she must, so that she would have the added strength of being settled in a part to shore up her resolve. It would be a way of showing him, she felt obscurely, that however badly she had behaved to his management, she could at least get a berth with another one. But she realized that she was being foolish to think so. It would be better, and much more honourable, to go to see Edwin first, to apologize for her abandonment of her part, and to make what amends she could.

Even though that might mean actually having to see Luke. That of course was the real anxiety that lay behind her present feelings of uncertainty. Not Barty's deliberate refusal to understand her and her needs, not anxiety about getting a part with another management (and she had heard enough about the vagaries of the actor's life to know that could be difficult) but sheer dread at seeing again the face that she so loved and seeing on it that expression of chill rejection.

But it was an anxiety that had to be contained, and a task that had to be dealt with. Edwin must be visited and that was that. And she washed her face and tidied her hair at the small mirror in her room at the Domus Medicus, to which she had returned after her unpleasant lunchtime meeting, and marched out into Wimpole Street to hail a hansom to take her to Chelsea Reach.

She became more and more tense as the cab pushed its way through the crowded streets, her cabbie cursing each and every other road-user with all the traditional fluency of his craft, and by the time it reached the King's Road was as anxious as it was possible for her to be, and after a moment leaned forwards and tapped on the roof. The cabbie lifted the flap and peered down at her and muttered a little as she told him to drop her at the top of Blantyre Street instead of going all the way to Chelsea Reach. But he pulled up his horse, and she got out and paid him, overtipping him by tuppence which cheered him a little, and then stood and watched him as he wheeled away eastwards again.

And then started to walk down towards Luna Street and the Gaff. The little houses she passed were drowsy in the heavy August heat, and the plants in the windows seemed to droop and pant just as much as the occasional dogs, sitting in what patches of shade they could find, and there was a thick smell of tar in the air from the melting road. Ahead of her the river glinted in the bright sunshine and there was a faint dazzle above it as the heat haze shimmered and moved the air.

'I must be mad,' she thought. 'Why did I come? Bad enough I behaved as I did – why make it worse by actually coming back? I should have written a letter to apologize, should have telephoned Edwin, even. Why did I have to actually come back?'

But she walked on, her eyes narrowed against the glare of the sun, until she reached the end of Luna Street and the mass of building that was the side of the Gaff loomed above her.

She made herself stop when she reached the corner; what she wanted to do was to turn sharply left and hurry along to 47 Cheyne Walk, or better still turn and hurry even faster back to King's Road to find another cab and go safely back to the West End and the search for a part with a new management. But this was the new Letty, the sensible practical independent Letty, she reminded herself, who did all she ought to; and she ought to turn and look up at the building.

The sign was still there, in its bright and cheerful crimson lettering. 'Chelsea Reach Gaff!' it bawled at the river, and its clutter of tugs and barges and motor-boats. 'Threepence a Seat. All Parts of the House!' 'Best Beer at Best Prices,' shouted another smaller sign and, 'Tonight at Seven' murmured a smaller one still. 'By Popular Demand. An Evening of Songs

184

and Recitations with Seymour Spurgeon, late of the Royal Theatre Leeds.'

Her heart sank as she stared at that. Had *She Stoops to Conquer* failed so abysmally so soon? It was only just three weeks ago that it had opened so hopefully. 'And I left it and didn't care who was to take my part,' she murmured to herself and, though there was no one there to see her discomfiture, she blushed with the shame of it.

She turned on her heel then and marched purposefully along the Reach towards number 47, past the bow-fronted houses with the trails of creeper clinging to their warm bricks and their little gardens dark green and shady and heavy with the fragrances of tea-roses and jasmine, forcing herself to put one foot in front of the other instead of doing what every fibre in her was yearning to do, which was to run as far away as quickly as she could. The river moved slowly on the far side of the road and the occasional van-horse went trudging by, head drooping in the heavy afternoon and sweat shining on wide flanks, paying her no attention at all. It seemed to her that in all the great city that was London she was the only person who was not sitting somewhere quiet and shady waiting for the afternoon to burn itself out.

There were butterflies moving among the privet hedges that lined the path to number 47 and she paused to watch them for a moment, seeing their vivid reds and blues dancing in the light so fast that they seemed blurred, and then taking a deep breath, she rang the door-bell. The front door had been left wide open, to allow in what cool air there was, and had been covered with a striped awning; after a moment the little parlourmaid appeared to peer in some surprise at Letty standing there on the doorstep.

'Well, I'll be – Miss Letty, is it? Well, I never did! An' here's me thinkin' we'd never see you ever again! I told Cook, I did, as 'ow I was sorry to know you'd gone and wonderin' why because I was sure I was that you was as 'appy as could be with your part in that there play –'

'Thank you, Edith,' Letty said trying not to sound too repressive. 'That's very kind of you – is Mr Zander at home?'

'Ooh, no, Miss! 'E's down at that there Gaff, ain't 'e? Got to

185

be, you see, on account there ain't no one else can do it all, and
'e's got to do it, poor gentleman and I tell you, in a right old
takin' 'e is about it, to be sure. Never one for workin' all that
'ard, our Mr Edwin, was 'e, Miss? No. And now 'e's got to be
there all day an' every day and worryin' 'isself sick all the time
about what to put on the shows because the people – they just
love the Gaff, you know. Don't seem to matter what show is
on, out they comes, full 'ouse every night, and so much to do,
and no one but our Mr Edwin to do it an' –'

'Please, Edith –' Letty put out a hand as though she could
stem the tide of words with it. 'I don't understand. Why is he
working alone? Doesn't – where is Mr O'Hare?' Even saying
his name was painful.

Edith stared at her and then shook her head in wonderment.
'Didn't you know, Miss? Well, there, I don't suppose you did
at that! I mean, 'ow could you? Seein' as 'ow you wasn't 'ere
yourself. Gorn, 'e is. Gorn and that's all about it, and there's
our poor Mr Edwin all of a takin' cos 'e's got to do it all on 'is
own!'

18

By the time Edwin returned she had recovered her composure. Edith had taken her to the garden room at the back of the house, where potted palms and aspidistras and grape ivies in vast pots made a green damp shade over the comfortable rattan furniture and brought her tea with lemon, and left her to sit there and stare out over the drowsy garden while she waited. And she drank her tea and tried very hard indeed not to think about Luke, and where he might be and why he should have gone.

She heard Edwin at the front door after about half an hour and jumped to her feet as his high petulant voice called Edith to bring him a large brandy and soda and to run his cool bath at once, and after a moment went to the door of the garden room and called, 'Edwin!'

He was standing in the hallway, taking off his straw hat and crumpled cream-coloured jacket, and she could see that his shirt beneath it was sweat-dampened and that twisted her throat a little, for he had always looked so bouncy and so neat and so comfortable. But now he was clearly dispirited as well as exhausted and she said again, 'Edwin!' but this time her voice was affectionate and a little sad.

He peered at her in the dim light of the hall and then his face lifted and he cried joyfully, 'Letty! My dear girl – you must be a veritable fairy queen, I swear, to appear out of nowhere like this! My dearest girl, how splendid to see you! You must permit me to kiss your hand, and indeed your cheek –'

He was bustling about her with every sign of being genuinely delighted to see her and she laughed and put up her face to be kissed, finding his attention not in the least threatening or improper although she undoubtedly would

187

have done had any other man, however good a friend, offered to be so familiar, feeling more comfortable and sisterly with him than she could ever remember feeling with Barty.

'You look hot and tired, Edwin. Do come and have some of my Russian tea which Edith so kindly brought me. There is plenty left and –'

'My dear, brandy for me, brandy! I need restorative care to my tissues, I do assure you and tea can never be as nourishing as good old brandy. Ah, Edith, splendid, splendid. Leave the decanter and the syphon and don't worry about my bath for a while – I must and shall talk to my dear Letty first. Now, sit you down, my dear, and we shall have a lovely cosy prose –'

'Edwin, why are you working at the Gaff?' She said it bluntly as he settled himself in a long cane chair and kicked off his shoes and relaxed into his brandy glass. 'Edith said –'

'Oh, dear me, is there *nothing* for me to tell you? Servants are as good – or as bad – as newspapers, indeed they are! Yes, indeed, I am working at the Gaff and I am very proud of myself, though I can't deny *exceeding* tired, for I have been running that wretched place for the past three weeks and do you know, it is actually making money! Hot as it is, they come pouring in every night and drink every drop of beer we have, however much extra I order for each night, and shout at the performers and eat all the food and generally have a most noisy and, save your presence, dear Letty, *sweaty* sort of evening and go off in high good humour leaving me feeling positively shattered. They tell me that Miss Bayliss – over the other side of Waterloo Bridge, you know – is sorely put out that we're doing so well when her Royal Victoria is struggling to get along, but there, as I told our barman what *does* she expect when she insists on making her establishment a coffee tavern? If there's one thing the people we cater for do *not* appreciate it is coffee taverns. Give 'em good ale, that's what they want! And whatever good show you can manage –'

'I saw that the play isn't running –' Letty said after a moment, and he nodded, not looking at her.

'No, my dear. We couldn't you see, for the cast seemed to – well, when we lost two of the leading parts and though we realized that we could understudy one and fill in we couldn't manage both – well – ' He shrugged. 'We've been using various performers for different nights. Like this man Spurgeon – sings songs about the sea, and so forth, you know, and they seem happy enough, as long as the beer's running, and next month I'm hoping to get them a good music-hall sort of bill and –'

'Lost two of the cast?' she said. 'Another as well as me? I came to say how sorry I was about that, Edwin, and to try to explain –'

'There is nothing to explain,' he said hastily. 'Nothing at all, I do assure you, I'd really rather not talk of it. We all have our reasons, my dear, and I'm sure yours were important to you –' and he buried his face in his brandy glass again and she stared at him, puzzled. Why should he be embarrassed, as he clearly was? If anyone had cause for embarrassment it was herself, not this man she had let down so sorely and she tried to say as much but he flatly refused to allow her to do so, burbling on and on in one of his great showers of chattering so that she had to stop and let him have his way.

But when at last his chatter about Seymour Spurgeon and his demands for money, and the barman and his peccadillos and the great difficulty of obtaining adequate supplies of fresh sausages in this hot weather had petered to an end, she said firmly, 'Well, if you will not let me talk about why I left the cast, perhaps you will tell me who else did so and –'

'Oh, as to that,' he said and now his face looked pinched and edgy, 'I have no objection, for I was most angry and still am. I had thought Jessica my good friend and when she – well, never mind. I will not talk of it after all – it makes me too angry. But she – well, there it is. She left and then Hearst did so, and what else could we do but disband and see what else we could offer? I spent hours, my dear, positively *hours* seeing the most ghastly people in the most dismal establishments, trying to find a filler and –'

'Edwin, where is Luke?'

'Eh, my dear?'

'I said, where is Luke? This is his affair, surely? He is the director of the Gaff. You are the owner and financial support of course, but it is Luke who should be doing all that work.

189

Why is he not?'

'Ah, well, as to that –' Edwin looked profoundly uncomfortable. 'As to that, it is difficult to –'

'Edith said he had gone. Gone where?'

'I really can't say, Letty and I would wish you not to keep on asking me and nagging me and –' He shook his head and now his voice became petulant again. 'It's too *bad* of everyone, it really is! All I wish to do is get this wretched Gaff running as it should now we have started it and put all that money in it, and all I get is complications! Now, my dearest Letty, I cannot, indeed I *cannot*, do another thing until I have taken my bath and changed my clothes. And then I shall tell you what we shall do – we shall go out to dine! Would you like that? I should, exceedingly. I should like to take you on my arm and escort you to a comfortable and elegant restaurant where we shall eat good food and talk and laugh a lot – now will you indulge me in that? I should like it above *all* things. *Please* say you will.'

She stared at him, confused a little by his mercurial changes of mood and then, at the sight of the small-child eagerness on his face laughed and said, 'But my dear Edwin – I am not dressed for fashionable dining! I am, as you see, merely in my daytime linen and –'

'Oh, as to that, there is no problem! Where are you staying at present?'

'At my Mamma's place – I mean, at the Royal Society of Medicine –'

'My dear, how very clever! Imagine being surrounded by all those clever doctors. One could have any number of megrims and nervous collapses and be *beautifully* looked after – where is this medical establishment?'

'In Wigmore Street, but –'

'No buts! I shall take my bath and dress while you rest here and read the *Strand Magazine* and then I shall take you to your doctors' den and wait while you change and then we shall have a lovely agreeable evening! It is all settled, and I shan't take no for an answer!'

Which was why she found herself seated at a crystal and

silver-laden table in the middle of Rules' restaurant in Maiden Lane in Covent Garden and drinking excellent champagne while Edwin talked with great seriousness with the waiter about lobster salad and *chaudfroid* of chicken and cucumber salad as though there were no other subjects of greater importance in all the world.

She looked around her, timidly at first and then with greater confidence as she realized that her new green silk gown was as fashionable as any other there, for she had always been deft with her needle, and she looked well tonight. She caught a glimpse of her own head in a distant mirror and almost primped, for her hair was looking particularly handsome, piled high in the latest mode and her long neck was elegantly framed by the low bodice of her gown.

Edwin caught her eye then and smiled at her and leaned forwards with his elbows on the table and said, 'My dear, you look as lovely as any lady here tonight – I am quite *bursting* with pride at being your escort! Even if the King comes in with his Mrs Keppel tonight, no one will look at them for you are so beautiful –'

'Oh, pooh Edwin, such stuff!' She laughed at him and drank some more champagne, but was pleased for all that. The new serious sensible Letty was of course above all such considerations as being regarded as beautiful, but that did not mean that tonight's Letty could not take pleasure in compliments.

'Now, while we wait for our dinner, may I ask you some questions? Or will you be angry?'

'I will be angry,' he said at once, trying to look severe. 'Because tonight I am not working at that wretched Gaff but leaving it to Donald Hyatt, for whom *heaven* be praised for he really is a most helpful young man and bids fair to be the best impresario London has ever known once he has grown up and fully learned the business, so I refuse to talk of work at *all*.'

'Well, I'll have to risk your anger,' she said after a moment, 'if I am to enjoy your expensive dinner when it arrives.' And she looked around again at the handsome well-disposed tables filled with handsome well-dressed people, at the cream-painted walls with their myriad pictures and the busy flying waiters with their napkin-swathed bottles and piled trays.

'And it would be a great pity not to enjoy it, wouldn't it? Please Edwin, you must tell me. What has happened to Luke? Why is it you are doing all his work and –'

'As for why I am doing all the work,' he said a little pettishly, 'I *told* you. It must be done by someone, and good as Donald is, he can't do it all alone. And I promised Luke I would – oh, there you see what you've made me do? Either you or the champagne has loosened my tongue shockingly –' and he stared down at his glass a shade owlishly.

'You promised Luke what?' she said remorselessly and he sighed heavily and made a face and shook his head at her.

'You really are so *persistent*, Letty! I did not think that of your character, truly I did not. Oh well, since I've gone so far – I promised him I would make sure the Gaff flourished; now it's started, you see. So, I must do the work, mustn't I?' and he drank more champagne and filled the glasses once more, and Letty sat and watched him and said nothing, knowing that now his verbal tap had been turned the words would flow well.

'You see, he cares about it so much, the foolish man! And if he can't deal with it himself, then I must, mustn't I?' And this time he sat silent so she had to ask him a question.

'Why cannot he do it himself?'

'Oh, as to that, I can't possibly say. He just had to go away, you see. And I promised him I wouldn't tell you and –'

'Promised you wouldn't tell me? Why me? Or do you mean you promised you wouldn't tell anyone?'

'Oh, no, just you. Well, mainly you. So I'm to tell no one. It's easier that way,' he said and drank some more. 'He was most *definite* that I was not to tell you, you see. So, I am not, for I am an honourable man, even when I'm tired and talking too much because the champagne has gone to my silly head. Don't take advantage of me, Letty, my dear. *Please* don't. I am Luke's friend, do you see, and I care for him most dearly. He bade me to tell you nothing, so I shall be a good friend, and I shan't. Now, here is our lobster, so we can be comfortable and say no more about it –'

He chattered all through the first course, cracking her lobster claws as well as his own with much hilarity and seeming not to notice how little she actually ate, nor how quiet she was, happy and bubbling in his usual fashion, and she was glad that he had had just that little too much champagne for it freed her to think her own thoughts.

And all she could think was that Luke had told his friend to make sure she, Letty, was kept well away from him. He wanted her to know nothing of him and his whereabouts. How much more definite could a man be than to act so? she asked herself miserably, pretending to eat her chicken salad when it was put in front of her. How much more obvious could he make it that he hated her?

Jessica's name came floating out of the tide of Edwin's talk then, and she lifted her head sharply and stared at him and he said, '– And there she was, making *such* a cake of Kate Hardcastle that I was glad, indeed I was, when I found she'd chosen to take herself off. I told Donald, I said, "My dear chap," I said, "We're better off *without* so bad a performer and –" but there, here I am, swearing I didn't want to talk of work, and chattering on and *on* about it. It's getting very boring to be this way. I really shall have to consider letting Donald do all the work, and hoping for the best. I really *cannot* go on wearing myself into a thread for the Gaff even if I did promise Luke –' And he stopped abruptly and stared at her, his face comical in its consternation.

'Please no, Edwin – don't leave it all to Donald to do!' she said. 'I know he is a very hardworking lad, and he does try, but really he can't manage all that alone! He needs help all the time. I know that from the work I did when I was there and –'

He stared at her then and after a moment nodded his head. 'You did do a lot, didn't you, Letty?' he said. 'I had forgotten that in all the fuss, you know. I had forgotten you did more than just play a part.'

'Yes,' she said. 'I did quite a lot,' and looked down at her plate again, remembering the long hours of painting and hammering and scrubbing. 'Quite a lot.'

He sighed, one of those gusty little sighs at which he was so gifted. 'It is a pity you are to be going back to your hospital,' he said with studied sadness and without thinking she said, 'I'm not. I've left Nellie's for good.'

He smiled then, a slow little smile that grew across his face and lifted it to a round self-satisfaction that made him look like a Cheshire cat and said softly, 'You know, I thought as much. You are *far* too good a performer to be happy off a stage, aren't you? Will you be coming back to us, Letty?'

She shook her head so firmly that one lock of her piled-up hair escaped and swung in a curl on her neck.

'Certainly not,' she said crisply. 'Of course not. The play is closed, anyway. No, I shall be looking for a part starting tomorrow. I've decided that I shall remain on the stage if I can – you're right about that, Edwin – but –'

He gave a little crow of laughter and put a hand on hers and said, 'I knew you were a fairy queen come to help me the moment I saw you this afternoon. I *knew* it! Dearest Letty, of *course* you shan't go trailing around the London managements looking for a part! There are no parts to be had, to speak of and anyway – please, my dear, come and help me with this wretched Gaff! I am positively *exhausted*, you know, and I'm worried about my money too –'

He smiled a little ruefully then. 'I know I make a great joke of the way I use up my poor old Papa's money but, you know, it isn't endless and I do need to watch some of my investments, and the Gaff is one of them – and I would be as glad as I have ever been glad of anything if you would come and look after it for me, with Donald to help you. Will you, Letty? I really can't go on much longer and I'd be so grateful to see it running well. We could start plays again, you see, if you wanted to, and I know that there are some splendid people about to advise on direction and so forth – will you, Letty? *Do* say yes!'

She sat and stared at him and then looked round again at the crowded restaurant, trying to collect her thoughts. Luke had rejected her, throwing her out of his life as hard as he could. He had gone to the lengths of leaving his precious Gaff too, and that meant he really was very determined to be rid of her. Had she any pride of the usual sort, she told herself, she would put herself as far away from him as he wanted her to be, and would not dream of working in his Gaff. But she was the new sensible Letty. She was to be the woman who cared for work and ability more than mere love. And to run the Gaff for Edwin would be a very satisfying thing to do as work, and would mortify Luke if he knew, and of course somehow Edwin would be sure to let him know for Edwin was hardly the soul of discretion and –

The thoughts tangled themselves in her head and she looked back at Edwin sitting there on the other side of the table, and his eager gaze and his undoubtedly tired face, for it looked lined and peaky for all his champagne-induced flush and thought confusedly, 'Damn it, I will. Why shouldn't I? And it really is a splendid opportunity – and won't it make Luke furious and won't it make his hateful Jessica furious too, when she finds out, which she will of course, just as soon as Edwin tells Luke wherever he is. For wherever he is, she's there too of course and –'

'Very well, Edwin,' she said and her voice was very composed. 'Very well. If you think I can do the work adequately, I will agree. But I wish for no payment. Not until I made a success of it. Then, if I show I can do it, we can speak of a salary –'

At once he leaned across the table and shook both her hands with great relief and considerable energy and beamed at her with such transparent pleasure that she had to laugh aloud. And the couple at the next table, looking across at her flushed face and glittering eyes, quite misread the situation and smiled indulgently at what they considered to be a pair of lovers. But Letty was filled more with anger than with any sort of love at the moment although she was quite unaware how handsome the emotion made her look.

19

It would have been easier, he told himself, if they'd left him inside, in the green-painted room with its cracked ceiling that made patterns that looked like maps of strange worlds and outlines of impossible animals. There he could lie and stare upwards and trace the lines with his eyes and forget about times and about where he was and why he was there. He could just be, could just count the breaths moving in and out of his body, just listen to his pulses muttering dully in his ears, just *be*. But out here where there were clouds and the leaves of the plane trees and eddying breezes and birds swooping and the sounds of traffic and voices coming up from the street far below it was not so easy to shut out the world and its busyness. Out here he could not push from his awareness his sickness, his helplessness and his aloneness. But they had insisted that this was where he had to be, and how could he resist? He had no power left to do anything but breathe and be and obey them.

Sir Frederick had been concise and clear about that, quite brutally so.

'My boy, this is the second haemoptysis you've had in a matter of days. I let you go back to your work against my better judgement the first time you coughed blood because you were so importunate and because it was a small bleed. Now, I don't care how much you beg and how much you demand, I will not permit you to leave this hospital. Not without warning you that you will die if you do, and that very soon, for the second haemorrhage was massive, and not without warning you that I will refuse to give you any further care if you go. You *can* live and you can get well again, I believe, but only if you give me *carte blanche* to live your life for you for the next few months. The decision is yours. But make it soon. You haven't a great deal of time to waste.'

That had been the punch that had sent him finally reeling into helpless dependence. It had been agony enough accepting the diagnosis in the first place, agony enough to be at the Gaff seeing Letty all the time and aching for her and being totally banned from being near her. If she knew he had this loathsome disease, nothing, he knew, would keep her away from him. But it had been agony piled on agony to have crumpled as he had and allowed himself to come so close to her that he might have passed on to her his contagion. To be told that prolonged hospital care now was the only way he could hope to live in the future had come as almost an irrelevancy after that.

He lay now in the high iron bed on the narrow balcony outside the green-painted room that ran off the side of the men's medical ward, his body wrapped in red blankets and his shoulders supported on piles of hard pillows and tried not to think of how it had been, of all that happened that dreadful night; but he could not stop memory from seeping into his mind, taking over every corner of it. In the green-painted room with the cracked ceiling there were mental rituals he could use to fill his mind and keep pain at bay; out here rituals did not operate so efficiently. And he closed his eyes and watched it all happen in the red glowing light there and knew the pain again.

Long after he had returned to the Gaff that night, a night that should have been full of excitement and happiness as the culmination of his months of dreaming, the awareness of what he had done to her had remained with him. The place had been empty, of course, all the actors having followed the audience out into the summer night and he had stood on the stage with its clutter of scenery and furniture, smelling the ghost of the evening in the air. There was beer and Leichner's grease-paint and the sour reek of the limelight and the gas and the glue-size that covered the flats, and human sweat and excitement and fear, all as tangible as though the place was filled with people. But there was only himself and the emptiness and his memory of Letty's stricken face with her eyes wide with amazement and fear and yet, somehow, love for him, and the way she had stood against that swaying flat when he had gone plunging away from her into the darkness of the street outside.

Had he infected her? The thought had gnawed at him over and over again, and his mind created visions of its own of ugly crawling disease moving from his own foul body into her smooth and sweet one, of hideous slithering germs creeping through those soft lips which had parted themselves under his own when he had kissed her, and he had actually made a groaning sound aloud, standing there on the empty stage of his Gaff.

And then he had stiffened as the sound reached him from the back of the auditorium, a rustling, a small flapping of footsteps, and he peered out into the shadow and said uncertainly, 'Who's there?'

'Now, who do you think it might be?' the voice had come as a whisper, unidentifiable in its breathiness, and for a mad moment he had thought wildly, 'Letty?' and had wanted it to be her and hated himself for such a want at the same moment.

'I don't know!' he had shouted, harshly, angry now. 'Who the hell –'

The rustling came nearer and now he saw her in the faint light of the single naked bulb that dangled over the stage as a working-light. She was wearing a thin white cotton wrapper and moved with a sinuousness that he had not seen her show quite so obviously before.

'Hello, my dear!' she had said and smiled up at him from below the footlights and then held out one hand to him so that he could help her climb on to the stage and automatically he had responded, so that she was standing beside him. 'I thought I heard you come back – I knew if I waited you'd come back. Why did you rush off like that, my dear old Luke? Did someone upset you?' And she moved closer to him so that he could feel her body's warmth and realized that she was wearing nothing under her wrapper.

'Jessica,' he said dully, and then, trying to behave normally, 'Hello. Why haven't you gone back to Edwin's to his party? I thought you'd all be there by now –'

'I waited for you. You've been a dreadfully long time –' And she moved even closer and put up one hand to touch his cheek.

It was hell. He would not have thought his own body could so betray him. It was Letty he loved; he knew that as sure as he knew the sun would rise tomorrow morning. It was Letty he needed and Letty he wanted, yet this girl had only to touch his cheek and the skin on the small of his back seemed to move and the muscles deep in his belly tightened. He tried to pull his head back from her touch and could not, for he needed that bodily sensation, needed that knowledge of the experience her body could give him and after a split second she ran her fingers down his cheek, so that one finger-tip brushed the corner of his mouth and at once the sensation increased, and became a loud shouting in his groins that made it impossible for him to think coherently at all. She was touching his neck now, slipping her fingers beneath the open shirt, for he had pulled off his collar when he had run out into the darkness and away from Letty, and the clamour of physical need grew louder in his ears, thumping and pulsing like a sea. He felt his own hands move then as though they were under someone else's control, and they reached for her, touching her shoulders, her arms, and then, slid forwards to reach inside the thin wrapper for her breasts.

He knew now, lying in that narrow iron bedstead on a balcony of Nellie's hospital in Tavistock Street, that she had known exactly what she was doing, and had understood how to make him react as surely as if he were a clockwork doll and she was winding the key, and he also knew the truth of Sir Frederick's warning to him that his disease caused an increase of sexual need; but he hadn't known any of that then. He had just been aware that she was rubbing her body against his hands, against his chest – for she had somehow managed to pull his shirt open without his realizing she had done it – and making little catlike mews of pleasure. He had looked down at her and felt her moving him inexorably backwards towards the sofa that was set crosswise on the stage for the drawing-room set, and he could not, did not want to, resist.

The noise of pulsing in his ears had become louder and the clamour in his groins more painful and urgent and he had taken a huge deep breath of excitement as she pushed him gently down on to the sofa, a breath that caught in his throat a little and made him cough. Just a small cough, to clear the tickle, to free him to listen to her exploring fingers on his body, but it grew in his throat, spread to his chest, reached his belly, his shoulders, every part of him and then he had been staring stupidly at her white wrapper. Not white any more but crimson-splashed, and then the splashes became a vast stain and she was shouting something, at the top of her voice, a shouting that had behaved very strangely, because it had steadily diminished in his ears the more loudly she had shrieked.

And then he had been alone, sprawled across the sofa on the stage at the Gaff quite, quite alone. The metallic taste in his mouth and the stickiness of his chin and hands had puzzled him at first, in a mildly academic sort of way. He had lain there on the sofa staring at his hands and his chest, seeing the stains there and wondering dreamily about them. And then, slowly, realization had come.

She had been there with him. Jessica. She had been there and now she wasn't. He had started to bleed again, had had another of those terrifying explosions of coughing and she had been there – and now she wasn't.

He could have died. He could have lain there alone and died in a welter of his own blood, drowning alone for want of care. And she had done nothing to find help. Had sent no one to him. Had just gone.

He had remained still for a while, trying to convince himself that he was wrong, that his unconsciousness had been only a short one, that she had only just gone to find someone to help. That soon the doors would rattle and Edwin and the others would come to find him, and pick him up and care for him and take him to Sir Frederick to be looked after and –

But he knew it wasn't so. Whatever interior clock it was that he had, it was an efficient one. A lot of time had passed since she had been there. The blood that had splattered his chest was dried and dun-coloured now, only the thicker patches of it retaining any stickiness. The taste in his mouth told him that at least an hour had gone by. She had left him ill and bleeding and done nothing to help him.

His anger at that had sustained him well over the next hour.

He moved carefully, feeling a dreamy sense of *déjà vu* that was curiously comforting. He could clean himself up and find a hansom and go to Nellie's and be all right. Hadn't he done so the last time this had happened? He was safe enough, even though this bleed had been much bigger, even though he had to take much longer over his cleaning process, was so much weaker and so much more languid.

He moved now in his bed, feeling the blankets rough against his back as the door to the balcony rattled and Nurse Wilmshurst came bustling out, a tray in her hands, and shook her head at him reprovingly.

'Mr O'Hare, I've told you and *told* you – no moving! All you may do is press the button on your bell to summon us if you have any need. Why do we provide all these splendid modern inventions if you won't use them? Is it there under your hand where I put it? Excellent! So you have no reason to budge – so budge you not! Now, I have your lunch here. It looks an excellent one, too, with plenty of things I'm sure you'll enjoy. Now, where's your napkin – ah here it is –'

She bustled about him, plumping pillows, arranging the napkin under his chin and settling the trayful of food at his side and he watched her gloomily, knowing there was no point in trying to tell her he was not hungry, that the beef tea she had pushed into him just an hour or so ago had left him feeling that he had taken enough nourishment for the next day and a half, for she would not allow him to talk, not allow him to do anything but open his mouth like a baby, and accept her determined spoon.

At least the hour or so spent over feeding him and then washing his face and dealing with the recurring indignity of bottles and bedpans before settling him to spend the long dead afternoon that lay ahead was something to do. It was the numbing tedium of his illness that was the worst part, he told himself as at last she disappeared back into the ward, bearing her bowls and pans with her, after drawing the long awnings round to keep the sun out of his eyes. And then, as the memories began to move in his head again, he corrected that; it was the time to think only of himself, of the past, of old loving and living and dead hopes and ambitions that was the worst. If he could just lie and stare at the ceiling and study the patterns of cracks it wasn't so bad. Oh, hell, it was all bad, every bit of it, and he felt the tears sting his eyelids and run down his cheeks and could not do anything to wipe them away, for he knew that any movement could bring that choking blood back into his lungs again, and anyway, why bother? There was no one there to see, nor would there be apart from Nurse Wilmshurst. And she, tactful girl, pretended not to notice the tears when they came, which they did with distressing frequency.

He slept a little that afternoon, and then woke and stared at the thickening clouds over towards the west as the sounds in the street below changed their nature, with fewer people bustling about, and fewer vans and carts, for as the Covent Garden day started early, it finished early too; and he tried to imagine how Edwin was behaving at this very moment. It must be close on six and he should be at the Gaff now, getting ready for the evening performance. Edwin working – and for the first time that day, his lips curved a little at the thought. It was a delicious notion that, Edwin being busy and anxious about something other than the number of lobster patties the cook had prepared for one of his eternal parties, or the temperature of the iced hock. Dear old Edwin. A real friend, one who cared and rallied round. Not like Jessica who had just –

But that was not to be thought of so he didn't, wrenching his mind back to his Gaff, and Edwin's care of it, and he tried to imagine the sort of show that would be appearing there tonight and could not. It ought to be *She Stoops to Conquer*, but with so many important members of the cast gone, what could Edwin do, after all, but what he had done? Music hall might not be anything very special, but at least it would be keeping his Gaff open. And that was all that mattered.

Because one day he would be well again. One day he would go back and try to make it all happen again. Good plays at reasonable prices, he murmured to himself sleepily, aware he was breaking Sir Frederick's no speaking rule, but needing to hear his own voice, however softly. 'Good plays at reasonable prices –'

The balcony door rattled again and this time it was Sir Frederick and he lifted his sandy brows at Luke, and said genially, 'Well, your nose looks well enough, m'boy! It's all I can see of you, with the blankets set so high, but it looks well enough –' And Nurse Wilmshurst, a little pink at the implied rebuke, came and helped Luke to lie higher in his bed and pulled the blankets down a little as Sir Frederick sat on the edge of the bed and took Luke's pulse.

'Eyes open and shut only, still! No speech. Right?' he said after he had tucked his turnip-watch back in his waistcoat pocket. 'Good man – I know it's dispiriting to have to be so silent, but it *is* important. The amount of effort needed to expel air through the larynx in speech is considerable, and may not be wasted in one as sick as you have been. You're improving, I believe, indeed you are. I think Patterson's regime is having some effect. I'm glad I'm able to give it you here even if I couldn't get you into his hospital at Frimley –'

Luke made a grimace, and Sir Frederick chuckled. 'Yes, my boy, I know. It hurts abominably. I don't enjoy such injections myself – and I've tried them to see what they feel like – but needs must when the devil drives. Are you ready, Nurse? Excellent – excellent –'

The trolley was pushed forwards by a solemn Nurse Wilmshurst, her cap-strings fluttering in the sharpening evening breeze, and she rearranged the awnings even more carefully so that no prying eye of a passing pigeon could observe the proceedings. Sir Frederick carefully filled his syringe with the straw-coloured fluid that was to be pumped into Luke's aching buttock.

'Fascinating technique, you know, m'boy,' Sir Frederick said. 'Quite fascinating. Doing it all m'self these days, you know, rather than letting Patterson. He's shown me the way, and it's not so hard. The blood I take from you each morning is separated and ready to be used by the next afternoon – and clearly the amount of plasma we derive varies, according to the speed with which the red corpuscles settle, but quite small samples seem to be providing us with enough serum at present. I shan't need any blood from you tomorrow in fact, since I have enough for the next dose from today's sample. That should cheer you –'

Still chattering busily to distract Luke's attention he went through the long ritual and Luke lay there, trying not to wince as the needle slid hot and hard into the flesh of his buttock, trying hard to convince himself that this auto-immunity regime would cure him, would close those hateful cavities in his lungs, would take him back, sound, to his Gaff and work, and perhaps to Letty –

He had to speak then and did, ignoring Sir Frederick's immediate frown.

'You told them. No one to know –' He whispered and Sir Frederick leaned forwards and put his hand over his mouth gently and said, 'Please, Luke! Don't risk it. We must use every effort we have to stop this consumption, and that means your effort too! But, yes I did tell them. I told them most carefully. Oliver, and your friend Zander. I gave them all your messages and instructions about your theatre, and about the work with cameras and so forth – I gave them it all most faithfully, I do assure you. And I was most particular, as you wished me to be, about not telling my young cousin Letty. So they're the only ones who know why. And they've both assured me that no one else will be told anything at all about you. And I must say, m'boy, you show an admirable good sense in this. I'm afraid that some young people are more blasé about phthisis than they have any right to be, and still persist in visiting sufferers, even at the risk of their own health. I always refuse to allow my tuberculous patients any visitors at all – and I'm glad I don't have to face too many of your friends demanding entry to persuade them of the importance of isolation in cases such as yours. You can rest assured, my boy, that no one shall know of you, or your disease, without your agreement. Now, let Nurse give you your supper and your tonics, and then sleep. It's going to be a long haul, but we can do it. Eventually.'

20

By the end of August, Letty felt she had been working at the Gaff for all her life. It became with great rapidity the core and heart of all her interests, and she threw herself into it with all her young energy. Donald Hyatt, his spirits lifted sky-high by her enthusiasm, responded by working even harder than before, if that were possible, and between them they revolutionized the Gaff.

Letty's first action was to study the way the place was victualled, for she had always had a gift for general organization and had learned much about feeding people from the years she had spent with old Bessie at home. All through Letty's growing years Bessie had fed not only the family but the vast numbers of visitors Sophie brought home, and had also cooked and brewed for the poor people who lived at Town End at Haworth and for whom Sophie had always been determined to provide. So, with such experience to draw on, Letty brought to the study of the Gaff's needs a considerable skill.

Much to Donald's relief she got Edwin to sack the barman who, she soon discovered, had been pocketing a sizeable share of the beer profits and replaced him with a middle-aged but still handsome and strong-willed barmaid, one Violet, who was transparently honest and also well capable of keeping her rowdy customers in control. Then Letty employed Violet's friend Grace, another woman of mature years, to look after the food, seeing no sense in doing as Edwin had done and buying ready-made food. She would equip a small kitchen at the back of the Gaff and there would be baked the pies and pasties the customers doted on, and also their own sausages and other comestibles.

Once she had set the commissariat to rights and shown Edwin that it could make even more profit than it had, she turned her consideration to the performance. That was a much harder nut to crack, for Seymour Spurgeon was a large and very stubborn man with whom Edwin had foolishly signed a contract which greatly favoured Spurgeon. He was a tolerable enough singer, but not, Letty felt, good enough to keep the Gaff busy in the winter to come when the customers would need extra tempting to come out of doors, so she decided that the answer to Mr Spurgeon's rather dull show was to wrap around it several other performers to make it seem more lively.

She said as much to Edwin who was perfectly happy for her to do this. He had returned to his indolent life at 47 Cheyne Walk with great relief, and was currently busily engaged in selecting the clothes he was to take on holiday, for, he told Letty solemnly, he was so exhausted he needed at least a month in Italy to recover, and was happy to leave all arrangements at the Gaff to her.

'Now you are running the place, my dear, you are in *complete* control. You wish to add other acts to the bill? Then by all means do so! I'm sure you'll discover how to find the people you want, and Donald will know how to see to it the bill runs smoothly, for he is an excellent stage-manager. I have arranged with the bank that you have charge of the Gaff's finances and that you will bank any profit yourself, so I can go off and recuperate with a clear conscience. Florence in September – it will be *bliss*. I only wish I could take you with me, my dearest Letty!'

So, she set about planning a bigger bill, and after long talks with Donald realized that she had far too little experience to handle this side of it. She decided to go and see someone who, she knew, had a great deal. He would help her, she was sure. And also, of course, there were other matters to discuss with him –

She went to see Oliver on a Monday night, always a quiet evening at the Gaff, leaving Donald ensconced in the small office to watch the customers, and took a hansom over to Kingly Street at about nine o'clock, when she was sure all was in good control at Luna Street. Oliver, to whom she had written to say she was coming, was sitting already waiting for her at his special table when she arrived and he greeted her with a wide smile and much agreeable fussing.

'Now, Uncle Oliver,' she said crisply, as she took off her gloves and folded them neatly. 'I am here on business matters, for you see, I am now emulating you, and running a theatre establishment!'

'And clearly doing it very well!' he said and smiled at her bright-faced eagerness, for she was looking very well indeed. 'I've heard what a success the place is and how irritated your opposition is and how the customers regard your Gaff as one of the best places at that side of town – no, don't look so surprised! I know everything that happens in this business, and virtually everyone in it. There's not much goes on in London theatres that I don't get the whisper of, sooner or later. Lilian Bayliss has been carrying on alarming about you, you know.'

Letty chuckled. 'She needn't. She's got all the custom she can handle, I'm sure, and has no need to grudge us ours. Now, Uncle Oliver, I have need of your advice and would be most grateful if you could put me in the way of finding some good performers. You see, the original plan for the Gaff, as you may remember, was to give plays, but I lack enough knowledge in that area just yet, and I shan't try a play again till the winter season starts. Right now I've got Seymour Spurgeon and –'

'Oh, a dreary performer!' Oliver said at once. 'Why on earth did you book him? Difficult man to deal with too, I'm told –'

'I know, but I didn't book him. But I thought if I put some decent acts round him he'd get the huff and go. I suspect he doesn't like sharing the bill with anyone he hasn't chosen himself –'

Now it was Oliver's turn to chuckle. 'You're learning fast, my girl, learning fast! And you want me to find you some acts he won't like and that you will, is that it? Nothing easier. Nothing easier, I do assure you. I'll send some people round tomorrow and you can take your pick. But now, I want to talk to you of something else.'

'Your cameras,' Letty said at once. 'Yes, I know. I saw the equipment in the store-cupboard and Donald told me about how the plans to use them had been made, and I'm most upset about it because of course I shall have to send them back to you. I really can't manage to –'

'Send them back?' Oliver said strongly. 'Not a bit of it! Never heard such a thing! What should I do with them, hey? No, my dear, they remain there at your Gaff and we shall use them the way it was intended they'd be used. It's all been planned out, as your Donald told you, and I've already talked to the performers I want filmed – Charles Coborn'll be the first, and he's just waiting the word from me, though he can't start till after the summer show he's in at Broadstairs closes, but that'll be over in another month or so. Then there's Lottie to talk to, and dear old Randolph and –'

Letty was staring at him with her mouth half-open, and now she shook her head firmly. 'Uncle Oliver, do stop! I can't do this film business for you, you must know that! I know you made an arrangement with –' She bent her head and smoothed her gloves on the table in front of her. 'I know you made this arrangement with Mr O'Hare but –'

He brushed that aside as though she were just an irritating child. 'Oh, my dear, don't worry about that! It's all arranged with Luke! He knows that –'

Her head snapped up and she stared at him with her eyes blazing.

'What was that?'

He looked discomfited then, and made a face. 'Oh dear, oh dear, but I really almost forgot. And I – well, the thing is, my dear, I did as it were talk to Luke about the matter of the films and it was agreed I should go ahead as best I could, but that was before your friend Zander had the good sense to set you there in charge. I was going to deal with him, you see, with Luke's approval, but now you say you will be handling it all, why it's as easy as kiss your hand! We shall make the films together and –'

'You know where Luke is,' she said it almost dully and he nodded.

'Yes, but I promised him –'

'That you wouldn't tell me where. Yes, I understand.'

He peered at her as behind her his little orchestra, returning from their mid-evening break, began to tune up their instruments.

'You sound a little miffed, my dear? No? Well, I'm sure you understand really – these things affect different people different ways, don't they? You should know that, with your hospital work, shouldn't you? Different people have different ways, yes – where was I? Oh yes, the films. Well, now I suggest that we settle down to draw up a list of the people we shall film and, then I shall arrange the bookings and together we'll set to work to make the films. I dare say I can manage well enough, for I have learned a lot from my good friend Mr Paul at Muswell Hill and I shall show you all I can, for my old eyes are not as good as they were, and I shall need your young ones to see the best way about things. Leave it all to me my dear, just leave it to me and we shall be well on our way, and no more than a little hiccup because of young Luke's – well, never mind.'

And with that she had to be satisfied. Not that she wanted to probe him further, for now her feelings had hardened into a very solid determination. Luke had chosen to run away from his Gaff in order to run away from her, and had chosen to take a red-headed idiot with him; he had chosen to tell some of his associates where he had gone with strict instructions that she, Letty was not to be told. Well enough. If that was how it was to be, so it was, but she would show him, she would show them all, how good she could be at the task she had set herself. She would run the Gaff, and the filming affair, so well that it would blossom into a vast enterprise which would make a large amount of money and would make everyone grateful to her.

Then, when she had done it, and Luke chose to return from wherever it was he and his hateful partner were now hiding, she would be lofty and noble and walk away from it all, expecting no personal recompense, making no demands at all, simply disappearing into the nowhere as thoroughly as Luke himself had done, and rejecting him as firmly, if not more firmly, than he had rejected her. That would fill him with the most painful remorse and would show him just how hateful Jessica was, for she, of course, would be spiteful and would soon show her true colours and be very unattractive as a result –

All of which was a very agreeable fantasy with which to soothe herself to sleep each night in the little room at the back of the Gaff (for it had been agreed she would take over the manager's accommodation) but which always shivered and died in the clear light of morning.

Her feelings about Luke and his hateful behaviour were the only sharp edges in her otherwise smooth life. Each and every day was filled with absorbing activity, but not so filled that she had no time for her own personal interests. She had conceived the notion of being herself one of the acts in the bill and, with Donald's aid as critic and adviser, she was practising the songs she had long ago learned to play on the piano and sing in her light contralto, building them into an agreeable little repertoire in which she was becoming more and more confident. She had decided she would try herself out on a dull Monday soon, when the house was reasonably receptive but not too boisterous, and if it was successful would use herself as filler for the present entertainment; and later, when they put on a play again, perhaps as an entr'acte item.

Oliver, true to his promise, helped her devise an agreeable bill which included a juggler and a magician as well as a singer and a comic, and the audience welcomed the change vociferously and showed how much they preferred the new acts to Mr Spurgeon to such good effect that he lost his temper one night in the wings when one or two tipplers gave him an unmistakeable boo, and tore up his contract. Which suited Letty very well, although of course she made the necessary regretful murmurings, and left her free to offer her customers only the sort of act they really enjoyed.

She was also free to work harder during the day at the film side of the enterprise. Oliver had come over to Chelsea Reach to show her how to use the cameras and, after much trial and error, and a sad waste of film, she had developed some considerable ability, learning how to assess the quality of the available light, how to dispose other lights about the place to augment the natural light, and how to arrange the performers (and she filmed her own current singers and jugglers for these practice sessions) so that she obtained the best view of their movements through her viewfinder.

She would stand there, bent over her polished wooden camera, her eyes fixed to the scene in the little viewfinder, cranking the handle at the steady regular rhythm that was necessary and calling her instructions and encouragement to her performer as she did so, while Oliver sat on one of the benches just behind her and watched, enthralled. He was clearly delighted with her and with all her doings, and she for her part found his company very agreeable and very reassuring. He never offered any advice on what she should do, unless she asked him; he never ventured any opinion of the workings of the Gaff other than approving ones, unless she requested criticism, and that helped her to ask him freely for all the aid she needed.

Over and over again it was a few shrewd words from Oliver that prevented her from agreeing to something for the Gaff that would not have been to its benefit. Over and over again it was his few murmured suggestions that helped her to get the best out of an uncertain act on the bill. And over and over again, it was his long friendships with the established music-hall stars they wanted to film which made them easier to deal with and better able to give of their best for her lens.

It was on one late September afternoon when they had filmed Charles Coborn singing his song, 'The Man Who Broke the Bank at Monte Carlo', that she found that her own ability to make her own decisions and make them well had developed to a stage at which she could trust herself to make her own judgements.

Coborn had arrived in rather a fussed state, though he was usually a most dignified little man – he was some four inches shorter than Letty – because he had just been given his first copy of a new recording of his famous song. It was a much clearer gramophone record, he told Letty with much excitement and drama, than the previous one, and he was most concerned to try to persuade the shops that sold these items to rid themselves of all their old stock and use only this new material.

'For you see, m'deah, Miss Lackland, I've made it sound so much better!' he told Letty as he watched his dresser unpack his familiar costume of evening suit and top hat and monocle ready for the filming. 'I seek always the best, only the best, and now I have something that *is* the best it worries me dreadfully to think that some may hear a lesser performance –'

'If we make this film so that it matches your new gramophone record, Mr Coborn, that may help,' Letty ventured and he cocked one of his bushy eyebrows at her. 'Hey, my deah? Don't foller you, doncher know.'

'Well, sir, I thought – if we play the record on a gramophone at the same time as we film you, and you sing along to it as though you were singing for the film, why the –'

A slow grin spread across the singer's long and usually rather lugubrious face. 'I like it, my deah, I like it! Have you a gramophone here?'

'Indeed yes, sir. We use it in the entr'acte sometimes, when the orchestra's having supper – Donald –'

After some bustle they were all ready, with the gramophone set with its great ribbed horn facing the stage, and the camera poised in the same direction. Donald had, with much grunting and pushing, opened the vast side-panels that gave to the westwards, for it was late in the afternoon now and the sun was low, and turned the stage on its great cup and ball so that it was set to make the best use of the golden evening light. Letty had also set some limelights in the corners so that the centre of the stage was a blazing core, and Coborn jumped up over the footlights and placed himself in the very middle of that central blaze with all the aplomb of the dyed-in-the-wool professional, but for all that shooting his cuffs a little nervously.

Letty, watching him, realized that the man was, for all his experience, a good deal more tense than he liked to be and she called to him in an offhand sort of way, 'Mr Coborn! Shall we just run through it to see how it will feel? Just a short rehearsal, you know? I shall crank the camera so that you become accustomed to it, but I won't use any film. Just so that you can relax and be comfortable, you know – and we'll play your record of course –'

'Yes – indeed, yes, my deah. Get the feel of it, hey? Capital notion. Capital. Let me know when you're ready, and we'll start.'

'I'll leave it to you, sir,' Letty said, as she took her place at her camera. 'I'll start when you do. It's just a rehearsal after all – Donald, perhaps you'd wind up the gramophone –'

The tinny sound began to move through the Gaff, as the horn amplified it and sent the song rolling out, and Coborn shot his cuffs with great style, and bent one knee and arranged one hand in a most *degagé* manner, holding a long cigarette in the other hand with a cultured droop of the wrist, and as the recorded words began, joined in so that he was singing in chorus with himself.

> As I stroll along the Bois Boulogne
> With an independent air,
> You can hear the girls declare,
> 'He must be a millionaire!'
> You can hear them sigh and wish to die,
> You can see them wink the other eye
> At the man who broke the bank at Monte Carlo –

He capered with all his usual aplomb, but with something else, a sort of offhand easiness that was very beguiling, and as Letty steadily turned her handle, never taking her gaze from her viewfinder, she knew her instinct had been right. Telling him that he was not being filmed at all had given Charles Coborn, that seasoned old performer, just that comforting reassurance he needed to give the performance of his lifetime. And her spirits expanded and filled her chest with such satisfaction that she could have shouted aloud.

'Well, sir,' she said as diplomatically as she could when he had finished to the small but very enthusiastic applause of Oliver, Donald and the stage-hands who were there to help for the afternoon, 'Do you think you'll do as well for another try?'

'Hmph!' Coborn said and watched Donald wind up the gramophone again. 'D'you know, m'deah, I found that went very well! Very well. Wish I'd done it for the film, that I do –'

'Well, that's all right then,' Letty said with satisfaction, and began to fold up her equipment. 'I thought that went well too. And of course I was taking it, for all I said I wasn't. I thought it was worth trying.'

Oliver laughed somewhere behind her, and after a moment

Coborn chuckled too. 'You're a cheeky gal, for one so young and new at this game!' he said. 'Not that everyone isn't new at it, of course. Mind you, it's a pity to see a bright gal waste efforts learning how to use something that can't last much longer. Only agreed to do this to please me old friend Lackland, doncher know –'

'Oh, don't you be so stuffy, Charles!' Oliver said, and came out of the darkness of the auditorium to the vivid light on the stage. 'This is the theatre of the future, this is! It'll be here long after we've turned into worm-feed, and don't you doubt it. Did well, my young cousin, didn't she? Proud of you, Letty, that I am. Got a real talent for handling these chaps,' and he slapped Coborn on the back, and the little man looked dubious for a moment and then grinned.

'Well, if you're right, Lackland, we'll have to be looking to the politics of it you know, that we will! These managements exploit us all badly enough as it is – no, not *you* old man. We all know you're one of the best guv'nors in the business – but the others. And if there's money to be made with these damned contraptions, heaven help us all! We'll be cows ready to be milked, and that's a fact. The way some of us already are – doncher know –'

'You'll get your payment for this, Charles, never fear,' Oliver said cheerfully, hurrying him on his way and leaving Letty to unload her camera under the dark cloth cover; but when Oliver came back he was looking thoughtful.

'Letty, m'dear, you showed a great deal of wisdom handling Charles like that! Difficult chap, you know – difficult. All that Scottish blood in him, I dare say. I was thinking – just thinking, you know, nothing more – how would it be if we tried to make some different sorts of films? My original plan was just to record all the great stars, and then perhaps to keep on building up the acts until they were fit to record, and then using them to make complete film music-hall bills. But now, well, I was thinking – maybe we could go further. Make a few stories, don't you know? What do'you think? Would you like to try?'

She stood there and stared at him, her lower lip caught between her teeth. 'Me? Make – do you mean do stories like those I've seen with babies being rescued and dogs chasing firemen and –'

He shook his head impatiently. 'No, not at all, not at all! Stories with people speaking lines, as they do in plays – we could show them with an actor off-stage saying the lines, the way Coborn there was singing to his own record. Or perhaps – look, when we get the film developed, shall we try to see how that works, play it and the record together, you know, and then see what we can do? We may even be able to get the actors on records too, so that we don't have to send people out to every hall that shows the films. I'm not sure how it'll all work, because I've really only just thought of it, but you see what I mean? Shall we have a try?'

21

October burned itself out in a blaze of golden leaves to become a wet and sometimes foggy November. Fortunately for the Gaff's business the fog was not severe enough to stop all traffic, as it had done four years earlier, but it was raw enough weather for people to want to stay at home in the evenings so the Gaff did not do the sell-out business they had become accustomed to. Not that Letty worried unduly about that, for the profits were healthy, she found, as she spent long hours poring over the ledgers – healthy enough for her to feel reasonably confident about the future.

Life had settled comfortably for her, and she was in many ways a contented person. She and Oliver were experimenting with great delight with their 'story' films, teaching actors to say their lines clearly and with plenty of lip movement so that they could be matched with a recording of the play. They had thought at first it would be easier for the actors to record the words first, and then to make the films, speaking aloud to their own recordings, but they found the reverse was true. Changes in inflexion, in mood and in emotion caused changes in speech, and such changes were more easily accommodated if the actors were filmed first and recorded afterwards, while they watched their film efforts on the screen. So she and Oliver, with Donald as ever hovering to assist, would spend the mornings filming when what little light the grey London skies afforded was at its best, and their afternoons recording, taking their heavy projectors and the developed film across London to the studios of a gramophone company in Victoria, in the new and very splendid motor-van that Oliver had purchased.

Letty had demurred at that expense, but Oliver had refused even to listen to her; he was now well-embarked on being the

216

Most Modern of Modern Theatre Impresarios in London and was even learning to drive the contraption, with the aid of the mechanic he had had to hire when he bought it, and was enormously happy. And seeing him so contented helped her to be happier too. And knowing that she had given him a whole new purpose and interest to his life in joining him in his film exploits was very warming to her spirits.

But she was not fully content, for all that. She would watch her music-hall bill go through its early doors performance and check that all was well with it before being free to leave the auditorium and stage for the evening – it having been decided that Donald could easily cope with the second house without aid – and then settle to checking the necessary paperwork, sitting tucked away in her little office at the back of the Gaff, hearing the distant sound of the music and the applause, and keeping her head bent over her work in the pool of light thrown by her desk-lamp. She had found that by concentration on such work she kept thoughts of her own feelings well under control; when she was counting up the cost of the sausages and computing the profit made on cooking and selling them, or totting up the price of perforating film, she couldn't think at the same time of Luke and his defection.

But there was nothing she could do to prevent such thoughts from creeping into her mind when she was not busy. She would have thought that by now the pain would have eased; that she would have been able to shrug him off as one of those experiences that come to people, but then are left behind. She would have expected that by now she would be as she had been almost nine months ago, when she had first met him – her own person, as far as her emotions went. But she was not, and busy and happy though her work made her – and there was not an atom of doubt in her mind that she had made the right decision about leaving Nellie's and a medical career – her free time was bleak and depressing.

It was not that she did not try. She would give in to Edwin's entreaties to come to his perpetual parties, walking along the dark and river-murmuring Chelsea Reach to the warm and bright house; would sit and listen to the ragtime music, even dance to it sometimes when Edwin insisted on dragging her to her feet; would join in the eager clatter of actors and painters and sculptors about the most exciting new exhibitions and books and plays; but somehow her heart was never really in it all. She felt like an outsider, like someone watching all these people from the far side of a great glass wall, and the sense of solitude that filled her was not agreeable.

One activity, however, that did help to thin the glass wall, if not precisely shatter it, was attending Suffragette meetings. Dora Montefiore was a most persistent lady and not one to let go easily of a promising recruit, and though at first Letty had resisted her attempts to get her to go to meetings, on the genuine grounds that it was difficult to get away from her work at the Gaff, she succumbed eventually when the activities of Christabel Pankhurst, up in Manchester, filled all the news-papers and every gossip's mouth. Her interruption of Sir Edward Grey's speech at the Manchester Trade Hall, and her subsequent incarceration as a common convict dressed in broad arrows had stirred many feelings, not least Letty's, and that, combined with Dora's persistence, rekindled all her old interest. It *was* unjust that women as intelligent, as thoughtful, as upright and worthy as these women should be treated as political upstarts. It *was* wrong that energetic people should be deprived of rights enjoyed by half the population simply on the grounds of their gender. And she would think of Edwin who was, she could not deny, a rather silly man, dearly as she loved him as a friend, and contemplate the fact that he could vote and thus affect the laws of the land, while she herself could not, and her anger flowed inside her. It was a comforting feeling, replacing the bitter hurt and sense of worthlessness that Luke's behaviour had set there, and she nurtured her anger and fed it regularly by making every effort to attend as many as possible of the meetings of which Dora Montefiore gave her notice.

It was in mid December that Dora returned to her attack on the matter of a play about women's suffrage. Ever since the day when Letty had been so unfortunately abused at her protest against paying rates, Dora had been full of remorse and therefore most particular in her dealings with her, clearly biting her tongue rather than haranguing her, as was her normal mode of behaviour, and Letty had appreciated that. But on this particular evening she had clearly felt she could wait no longer.

It had been a misty rainy Sunday afternoon, and she had bidden several of her WSPU friends to tea at her house at Upper Mall in Hammersmith, and Letty, with no work to do that afternoon to occupy her mind and keep Luke out of it, and no desire to spend the time listening to any more of the chatter at Edwin's tea-table, had accepted her invitation. And been glad that she had.

They had sat about, five women in a comfortable relaxed cluster, laughing a lot and talking only a little of politics, and Letty, tired because they were rehearsing a modest pantomime for the Christmas season at the Gaff, had been grateful for that. She had sat curled up on a heap of cushions near the brass fender in the cluttered red-papered cosy sitting-room staring dreamily at the flames leaping in the grate and enjoying the scent of the muffins Dora was toasting on a long fork, sipping her tea and just being comfortable.

'You look a little tired, Letty,' Dora said quietly.

'Hmm? Well, a little perhaps. We're doing a pantomime, you see. That's a very new thing for us. We usually put on music-hall in the evenings – I only do plays of any sort during the day for filming, and then Uncle Oliver usually does most of the production work for that. You met him, last time you came to visit the Gaff, do you remember? But I have to do most of this rehearsing myself, because he's so occupied with organizing his own Christmas Entertainment for the Celia Rooms, so –' She yawned suddenly. 'Yes, I'm tired.'

'But you're enjoying it?'

'Oh, greatly! It's very interesting to see patterned entertainment put together – not like a music-hall bill where each performer is responsible for his own work, plans his own moves and so forth. All you do to put on a music-hall bill is stage-manage really – make sure the musicians have the right music, play it in the right order, make sure the props are ready to hand and things like that. But this is different –'

'Would it – this pantomime – be the same as putting on an ordinary play?'

219

'Much the same, I imagine. I've only ever acted in such plays – I've never been fully responsible for the direction, you know? And though you learn a lot from being part of it, you never learn as much as you do from actually doing it. Uncle Oliver says he thinks I'm a good director for this pantomime. That's very encouraging, isn't it?'

'I wonder if you're good enough to do the thing I have to offer you?'

Letty was at once all caution. Gentle and protective though Dora had been towards her these past months, she had no illusions about the relentlessness of her ideas and ambitions. 'That all depends on what you mean,' she said carefully.

Dora laughed, and took the muffin she was toasting from her fork and tossed it to one of the others, before skewering another and toasting that.

'Don't sound so dubious, my dear! No one will force you – it's just that I have been writing something.' And to Letty's surprise she blushed slightly in the firelight and then looked sideways at her and laughed, somewhat shamefacedly.

'I dare say you're told that by all sorts of people, aren't you? Mrs Pankhurst once told me that the world is full of people who believe they are natural authors. She's always being bombarded with essays and pieces of polemical prose about the Suffrage movement which she says are totally dreadful and totally unpublishable in her newspaper *Votes for Women*. But I have not been writing prose. I have here a sort of play –'

'Oh,' Letty said, not sure what else she could say, for she too had been offered plays and entertainments which were really dreadful by some of Edwin's friends. She sincerely hoped Dora was not about to join their ranks.

'Well, not precisely a play,' Dora said, and gave the last muffin to Letty, dusting off her fingers before reaching over to the small table on the far side of the fireplace to pick up a small pile of paper, which Letty could now see was covered with close-written lines. 'It's more a mock melodrama really. It is about women's suffrage of course, but the villains are Sir Edward Grey and friends, and the heroines are Mrs Pankhurst and her friends, and there are many songs, and some dancing and – well, will you read it? And if it is of any interest to you as a piece for your theatre, will you put it on? I could hire my own theatre of course and sell tickets to people to come and see us do it in an amateur way but there'd be small point in that. It would be only those who agree with our opinions who would come to see it, anyway. A waste of time. It's *new* minds I want to convert to our cause – and the minds of ordinary people, too. The sort of people who come to your Gaff. If we could see this performed at your theatre it could be, I know, a great service to the cause.'

'Dora,' Letty started carefully, looking with some hopelessness at the pile of paper. 'Dora, I –'

'I know,' Dora said swiftly. 'You must make money for your employer. And if this is not a show that your customers will like then you cannot do it. I kept that in mind when I wrote it. I ask you only to read it and consider it as you would any other. After all, it might *just* possibly be quite good, mightn't it? You'll never know if you don't read it, will you?'

So, Letty had to agree to take it away with her, and she went back to the dark Gaff from Hammersmith, travelling on the top of a brightly-lit omnibus, for there were few hansoms about on so raw and bleak an evening, with her heart in her boots. Telling friends that a piece of work over which they had laboured long and mightily, and of which they were deeply proud, was useless was always painful. And she cared a great deal for her friend Dora and had no wish to hurt her feelings.

But to her delighted relief, she found there was no problem. She had taken a shower in the little room that had been specially built at the back of the stage for the actors (and as ever she had to push away the memory of the night Luke had told her of the accommodation that was to be provided, and how happy she had been with him then) and then, wrapped in her lacy cotton nightdress and with her thick woollen dressing-gown tied around her waist and her hair hanging loosely down her back, had curled up on her bed in the tiny room that was her sole domain, and in the light of the small bedside-lamp, begun to read.

It was when she heard herself laugh aloud before she turned the very first page that she knew she had no further cause to fret. Dora had produced a splendidly lusty piece of work. It was a full-blooded melodrama, with the cohorts of evil personified as horned devils, top-hatted moustachioed villains and masked burglars named Sir Edward Grey, Henry Campbell Bannerman and Winston Churchill, all politicians known to be anti women's suffrage; and with heroines who were to be dressed as fairies, angels, beleaguered virgins and noble matrons to represent the trio of Pankhurst women together with their friends Annie Kenney, Mrs Drummond and Mrs Pethwick-Lawrence. The action they were given to play included a great deal of knockabout farce along classic *commedia dell'arte* lines mixed up with parodies of familiar comic songs (including for example a cheeky version of Charles Coborn's song, now called 'The Girl Who Broke the Peace at Old Grey's Meeting') and vigorous choruses.

Even as she sat there in her tiny room in the lamplight Letty could see it all taking place on her small stage and found herself devising production ideas that would underline the message that Dora had built into her writing. It was amazing just how theatrical and successful a piece it was, Letty told herself, as she settled down to sleep that night. She would never have thought Dora had it in her.

Uncle Oliver too agreed that it was a good piece of work when she sought his opinion, and well worth doing in theatrical terms; but he was a shade worried about its political content, he told her.

'Hmph,' he said, as he put the script down after reading it while Letty had been preparing film for the next morning's work. 'I like it as a piece of entertainment, no question of that. Excellent entertainment. But I can see trouble if you do it.'

'What sort of trouble? You've always said yourself that as long as you give customers lots of value for their money and real entertainment, you can't be wrong. So if this is entertaining, how can it cause trouble?'

'People don't like to be lectured from a stage,' Oliver said. 'Not when they've paid good money down for their pleasure. No, don't like it one bit, they don't. There were a lot of those pro-Boer songs going around in the war, you know, and there were some ugly scenes, I remember, very ugly, over at Collins's when old Percy Blenkinsop tried to put them over, nearly mobbed the stage they did. People were feeling patriotic, you see, and didn't like anyone turning up and telling 'em they was wrong, that was the thing. Now, lots of people think all this women and votes stuff is a lot of nonsense, don't like it a bit. Think it'll get their wives going, make them uppity and all that –'

'I hope it does!' Letty said warmly. 'The way some men treat their wives –'

'That's as may be, my child, that's as may be. But while it's the men who buy the tickets then it's the men who call the tune. And this tune ain't one they'll like. Good stuff, I grant you. But I wouldn't do it if it was offered me for the Celia.'

Letty put away the last reel of film in its metal box and wrote the name on the label and then stood and stared at him with her lower lip thrust forwards, thoughtfully. 'Because there might be trouble?'

'That's right.'

'Not because it's not good enough?'

'Oh, it's good enough all right –'

'Then I'll do it,' she said after a moment and he looked at her and shrugged.

'On your own head be it,' he said, and then smiled. 'But I'll help you if you like. Not sure I like the message in it much m'self, but I know a good piece of fun when I see it. As long as you do it here, and it's not at my place, no reason for me to worry, hey? I'll see what I can do to sort out the casting, if you like. I dare say we can find ourselves a plump partridge somewhere to play young Winston, and as for the Pankhurst women – they tell me they're handsome fillies, yes, handsome fillies. Dare say we can match them for looks as well –'

Christmas went by in a flurry of activity at the Gaff for Letty, for which she was grateful, for her mother, in her regular weekly letter, had suggested that it would be agreeable if Letty could come to Haworth for the holiday. But she had been deeply unwilling to do that. It had been while she was at Haworth in the summer that she had suffered the most poignant part of her pain over Luke, and she feared returning to it, as a toothache sufferer fears biting on the tooth after it has been treated. What she had left to deal with now was a deep dull ache and she had taught herself to live with that. To return to Haworth, away from the soothing balm of daily work here at the Gaff could, she feared, bring back the pain in all its old severity. Even to see her mother and good old Samuel and Bessie would not be worth it. And of course she would also have to see Barty, and she could foresee nothing but squabbles and misery all round if *they* were together. So, she stayed at the Gaff, while Donald went to spend the holiday with his own family in Sheffield, and worked harder than she had ever done since coming to Chelsea Reach, for the pantomime was very successful and filled the house to capacity each night.

The New Year brought with it flurries of snow and a bitter frost, but the roads were passable and the mood of London was cheerful; people seemed to want to be entertained and the attendances at the Gaff in the evenings soared and the pantomime had to be extended due to the popularity of its cast – a splendid Joey Grimaldi sort of clown and a great many very beautiful ballet girls – and the fame of the place spread further afield. Now audiences came not only from Chelsea and over the river from Battersea but also from Lambeth and Stockwell and even as far as Brixton in the south, and from Fulham and Shepherd's Bush and Hammersmith in the north.

They could have filled the house twice over every night, they told each other jubilantly, she and Donald, and took on extra front-of-house staff and doubled the order for beer and sausages, and added a few bottles of good wine and better quality brandy too, for now they were attracting some members of the richer classes as well as their poorer customers. And if Letty wondered briefly how Luke would feel to see his original idea for his Gaff so diluted she did not tell anyone of it.

Dora's play went into rehearsal in the middle of January, when the snow had degenerated to heaps of grey sludge on the pavements outside and the weather had settled into that grey remorseless dullness that was so much a part of a London winter. The outside conditions seemed to inject the cast with greater energy, however, for they threw themselves into the piece with enormous gusto, and often improvized, adding bits of ridiculous business to make the characters even stronger. By the end of the first two weeks of rehearsal, the Villains were the most evil and laughable politicians that could ever have been seen anywhere and the Heroines the most spirited and noble creatures that ever set foot on a limelit stage. The whole thing grew and developed like a living creature.

Happily the actors were all in sympathy with the themes of the piece. Jenny Ryman, the girl who was playing Christabel Pankhurst, the most heroic of the heroines, was particularly fiercely partisan and added more and more power to her performance, until one of the other members of the cast told her in all seriousness that if she didn't watch out, the audience would think she really was the lady firebrand in person.

'And then heaven help you,' he said and grinned. 'I've heard there's plenty of men have turned out and thrown stones at her up in the North. Don't want any stones flying here when we open, do we?'

'Don't be absurd,' Letty had said sharply and frowned. 'This isn't meant to be any sort of goad to an audience, you know! We want it to show people that there are things that are wrong in the world and show them in a light-hearted way. We want them to join the WSPU after they've seen it – but don't go saying there's any risk of violence, for heaven's sake! You know how gossip of that sort gets about. The last thing we want is trouble-makers turning up to the show to stir up difficulties. Do keep quiet about it all, please.'

'Bit late for that, missus,' said Joe Macauley, who was playing Winston Churchill, a part for which his cherubic face well suited him. 'I was taking a jar in the old Kings Head and Eight Bells only yesterday, and they were talkin' about us there. It's well out that we're doing this show, *and* what it's all about. I reckon we're in for a really lively time when we open next week! I'm looking forward to it m'self. Like to see an audience get itself steamed up, I do. Bit of participation like this works like a bottle of pepper sauce on a barrel of oysters.'

'Not too peppery, for all that, I hope,' Letty said uneasily, and called them back to work, the break they had been sharing now over. 'I was planning to do some filming of the first performance. It's not been done before, with an audience in front, and it's something I wanted to try. If they jump around too much I won't get very good film, will I?'

But she did get film and very interesting film too.

22

It had been raining hard all day, sending sheets of water slanting across the grey satin road to splash against the walls of the Gaff and send runnels of water under the big main doors. The actors arrived wet and cursing, shaking out their umbrellas and stamping their wet feet and complaining about the effect the weather had had on hair and complexions, and gratefully drinking the hot cocoa that Donald had prudently prepared for them. The excitement was running high, even higher than it usually did for a first night, for it was clear to everyone that a great deal of public interest had been whipped up in their production. There had actually been a demand for booked seats, which had never happened before. Most of the Gaff's usual customers were prepared to take their chances on getting in on the night; but now people seemed determined to be there for the show and wanted to claim their places in advance.

Letty had, however, decided not to change the Gaff's usual system and refused to accept such bookings, never dreaming it might be a decision she would regret. It had to be as it always had been, she told all enquirers. First come, first served, when the doors opened. So, the well-dressed people of Chelsea and Kensington went away muttering about the inconvenience of having to come early to claim places, and the street urchins of Battersea and Lambeth made themselves farthings by offering to stand in the queue for the early doors for anyone from their own mean and miserable streets who wanted to be sure of a place.

All of which affected the actors considerably, honing them to a finer edge of nervousness and that had the effect of making the mid-afternoon run-through for technics a shambles. Jenny

Ryman, almost distraught with the tension of it all, suddenly announced she couldn't remember a word, not a single *word* of Christabel's dialogue, and Joe Macauley developed an eye inflammation when a cinder flew at him from the spluttering limelight and almost wept with the pain. At which point Edwin came into his own. He had been bustling about all day, getting in everyone's way, quite entranced by all the fun, as he put it, only too eager to be at the Gaff again now the hard work of rehearsal and preparation was over. And when the actors became so temperamental that Letty nearly flew into a rage – deeply involved as she was with organizing a suitable place for her camera, and special lighting, so that she could film the whole performance – he stepped in and took over. He soothed, he cajoled, he chattered, he tut-tutted and murmured, and slowly the actors calmed down, became sleekly sure of themselves again, and filled with just enough anticipation to make it possible for them to perform but not so much that they were useless.

Letty, her head spinning with all the fuss and worry of the preparation for the performance, also had to worry about the food and drink ('It'll be standing-room everywhere,' Donald announced. 'No doubt of it. And if the beer runs out they'll slaughter us. I've sent over to Whitbreads for another ten barrels and how about getting in some extra pies from the bakery over at World's End?') and the methods of film changing ('It's no use thinking you'll have time to reload between takes. You'll lose half the show that way,' Oliver said, fussing anxiously among the great cans of film and the viewfinders and the spare crank-handles. 'We'll be best off with two cameras. That's got to be the answer, that's what we'll have to do. I'll send over to Paul's right away – he'll get me one here in no time. And we'll need a platform, up here, just a couple of rostra'll do and then we can move each camera in between takes – oh, if only I could be here to help! Are you sure you can manage with just that little lad to reload for you? If only I could be here – but I've got to be at the Celia, old Will off ill and all – can you manage?') as well as Violet's and Grace's fussing about the security of their cash-takings ('An audience that size, stands to reason there'll be some right villains about, and I don't want no one picking up my cash-box in the fuss and running off with it. 'Ow about a chain-bag, like, the sort I could tie to me belt? Then they'd be stealin' me and all if they tried to pinch it –') and by the half when the actors had at last scattered to their dressing-rooms to make up, she was almost exhausted.

But not quite. She stood there in the middle of the auditorium and looked about as objectively as she could. The rows of benches with their brightly-coloured cushions stood mutely expectant of the eager rumps that would soon thump on to them. The bars at the back glittered with shining mirror and piles of tankards and glowed with polished wooden beer-barrels. The food bar at the side was piled high with pies and sausage-rolls and massive ham sandwiches which filled the air with a comforting scent of crustiness and savoury tastes that made her mouth water, for she had no time to eat anything since a snatched slice of toast for breakfast, over twelve hours ago. The great red tab-curtains looked as though they had been carved out of crimson rock, so steady and solid did the rich folds look in the gleam of the golden footlights, and at the back, tucked behind the last row of seats on a makeshift rostrum stood her two cameras, hooded now with sheets of black cloth. There were a few spotlights along the sides of the auditorium, trained on the stage, and they lit it to a stunning brightness.

And though she did not mean to think it, though she had promised herself she wouldn't, she could not help but wonder what Luke would say if he could see it all now. His Gaff, with an eager audience outside waiting to come in – and she could hear the muffled roar of their chatter and laughter from beyond the great doors as they stamped and shouted and pushed each other in the long queue that had formed over an hour earlier – and a splendid show waiting to be put on. It was just what he had wanted and planned, and she, Letty Lackland, had brought it to this state of poised expectancy.

But it was not, as she might have expected it to be, a gratifying thought. It should have filled her with pride, with a sense of having paid Luke back for his ill-treatment of her. She should have felt as children do when they have triumphed over a playground enemy and shout their jeering, 'Yah, yah, *yah*!' at the defeated one. But she did not. She was just filled with a great sadness, a regret that someone else should have the pleasure and the satisfaction that belonged to him. And she took a deep breath and closed her eyes for a moment, not wanting to admit the truth that lay behind the way she felt; that she still loved him as much as she ever had, and always would, however badly he had behaved. How hateful to be so much in love and to feel so ill about it!

'Miss Letty, do we take the door bars down?' Donald called and she looked up and then at the fob-watch pinned on her green merino bodice and grinned at him and raised both hands in the air with her fingers crossed.

'We take 'em down, Donald. Here's luck!' And she turned and waved at Violet in the bar and Grace at the food-counter before hurrying over to take her own place in the little box-office by the doors with Donald at her side. They had decided that tonight they needed to be as careful as they could about money; Violet and Grace weren't entirely wrong to be so concerned about casual thievery.

And in they came, in a flood, pushing, shoving, shouting, some of them greeting her by name – and she was glad to see her regulars – but others just thrusting their threepences at her and then plunging onwards to secure the best seats. She couldn't help but notice that the well-dressed Chelsea and Kensingtonites who had come seeking booked seats earlier that day were not among the crowd. These people all came from over the river, she was sure, as she made a conscious effort not to wrinkle her nose against the smell of the unwashed ones. These were the people for whom the Gaff had been founded, she reminded herself firmly as she swept the piles of coins into the iron cash-box before giving it to Donald to take and stow away in the office. 'I mustn't regret the fact that they're here in even larger numbers than usual. It's their theatre, after all –'

Not that all the audience was gutter-born. Dora Montefiore had arrived early with a cohort of her WSPU ladies and they were ensconced firmly in the front row, Dora positively pale with expectation; they waved and grinned and nodded at Letty

as she made her way through the hubbub to the camera rostrum at the back where her young helper, a young boy Donald
had recruited to act as camera-loader, was waiting for her.

The noise around her seemed to diminish in her ears as she
went through the order of tasks young Alf would have to
perform for her, and he, quick and sharp as only a London
guttersnipe could be, nodded, birdlike and eager, and
reassured her he'd 'do it right as bleedin' ninepence and no
error', in a hoarse and earnest little voice. And she took a deep
breath and turned to look at the crowd, now milling about the
bar and the food-counter and pushing their way back to their
seats while clutching tankards high over their heads and
cursing back at those who complained at being splashed as they
passed. It was a cheerful enough mob, but somehow she felt
uneasy. She could see several familiar faces, people who had
been coming to the Gaff for every show they had given since
she had been there running it, sometimes coming more than
once to the same show, but there were a great many strangers
too, and some of them looked unpleasantly large and dour.

She shook herself a little and, as much for something to do
while she waited the last ten minutes or so for the show to start,
decided to take some film of the audience. It would be an
agreeable way to start their show of the play, she thought, as
she lined up her viewfinder on the front rows, and Dora no
doubt would be pleased to see pictures of herself enjoying her
own special night; and she began the steady carefully-timed
cranking that would give the best finished result.

Watching them through the viewfinder in their miniaturized
state she became even more uneasy about her audience. There
were knots of men with their heads together, clearly whisper-
ing seriously; they were not like the cheerful chatterers in
other parts of the house, but looked more like thieves planning
a robbery than people out for a night of relaxation and fun –
and again she shook herself. This was nonsense, a notion born
of Joe Macauley's chatter, Violet and Grace's forebodings, and
Oliver's doubts. And she suddenly wished very much indeed
that he was here at her side. That bumbling old man, who
chattered on and on and was always so stubbornly set on doing
what he wanted the way he wanted to do it might exasperate

her sometimes, but he was a comforting person to have around for all that.

But he wasn't here and that was all about it, she told herself sturdily as the house-lights dimmed under the invisible guidance of Donald, now safely settled in the stage-manager's chair backstage, and the little orchestra broke into one of the first melodies of the show. And she took a deep breath and lifted her head to enjoy to its full that special and for her, favourite, moment, when the house slid into hushed and expectant silence, and the curtain stood poised to rise.

It went up to a great roar of delight, for the stage was filled with a line of pretty girls, dressed in attenuated and rather cheeky versions of a policeman's uniform. They were showing a great deal of plump thigh as well as considerable expanses of pink bosom and the men stamped and laughed as the girls began to sing with great gusto and tunefulness the parody song that set the tone of the show:

> Has anybody here seen Pankhurst, P-A-N-K-hurst?
> Has anybody here seen Pankhurst?
> Pankhurst from the Free Trade Hall –

The first half went like a firework explosion; act followed act, chorus followed chorus to an ever-increasing roar of joy from the audience and Letty, sweating under the lights and the effort of keeping her cranking arm steady, stood there with her back bent and her eyes glued to the viewfinder and gradually her fears subsided. She had been foolish to worry. The show was going well, amazingly well, the jokes were being greeted with great relish, the political jibes were getting precisely the reaction Dora wanted (and Letty could see her there in the front row, sweating and beaming with her hat askew on her wispy grey head in her excitement) and no one was going to do anything tonight but have fun.

It was towards the end of the second half that the ripples began. The interval had been a hectic one for all the front-of-house staff, every drop of beer and every last sausage disappearing into eager throats, and the show had started again with, 'It's a bit of a ruin that Winston's knocked abaht a bit –', when in the back row men started swaying from side to side, forcing others in the same row to do the same. That caused a certain amount of noisy complaining from those who didn't want to sway, but since Dora and her party had moved to the back of the auditorium to arrange the pile of leaflets about the WSPU that they planned to give out at the end of the evening, the complainers were able to move forwards to their empty seats and that little swell of ill-temper settled down.

But not completely. As the show went on there began a counterpoint of jeers weaving in among the laughter and the jokes. 'What's your 'usband 'avin' for 'is dinner tonight, lady? Dead pussy?' shouted one man at a scene in which Jenny Ryman as Christabel was being particularly impassioned in her pleading for justice for women, at which a roar of combined disapproval and encouragement went up from different parts of the house. And then another chanting, 'Put the women to bed, put the women to bed – they're better off in bed or dead, better off in bed or dead –' at which once more the audience took sides, some shouting him down and others egging him on and joining in.

There was just another ten minutes to go, with the whole cast on stage for the big finale, 'It's a great big shame, and if the law belonged to me –', with Joe, as Winston Churchill, pretending to be the great performer Gus Elan, when the whole thing violently erupted. From the very back, seven men stood up and, shouting hoarsely and largely incomprehensibly began throwing fruit. They were one of the groups which had made Letty uneasy when she had seen them earlier; she had noticed they were all wearing big overcoats, but thought nothing of that; in such cold and wet weather heavy coats made sense. But these had clearly been worn for the usefulness of their capacious pockets rather than for comfort and, as the shower of tomatoes and rotten oranges shot at the stage, she could have wept at her own foolishness for not realizing why these men had been dressed so.

The audience surged to its feet and some at the front picked up pieces of fruit that had missed the stage and began to throw them back as the cast, startled and unable to see clearly what was happening because the lights filled their eyes to a dazzle, let their song peter out in puzzlement, and one or two cried out as a tomato or hard little apple hit them.

After that Letty couldn't be quite sure what happened. She had just stood aghast, and then, aware at last that small Alf was pulling on her skirt, heard what he said and after one blank moment obeyed him.

' 'Ere, lidy, 'ere, take their bleedin' pictures – take their bleedin' pictures! I've pointed the bleedin' box at the buggers –take their bleedin' pictures –'

And she did. She cranked the handle of her camera like a thing possessed, changing from one to the other as young Alf feverishly reloaded them, moving the cameras, which was difficult for they were not designed to be so used, as much as she could to get in sections of the audience that seemed to be the most ferocious. Had anyone asked her at that moment why she was doing it, she wouldn't have known how to answer; she just knew it was important to keep cranking, and keep cranking she did.

Even when the noise became more ominous, when the creaking and crashing of broken furniture and smashed glass was added to the roar of human voices, even when women began to shriek in real pain and the set on the stage crashed down in a welter of torn lathes and canvas as some of the audience surged on to it; even when shrill whistles and bobbing blue helmets announced the arrival of the police, she went on cranking until her arm ached and her eyes, fixed to the viewfinder, ran with tears of concentration. She only stopped when young Alf pulled on her sleeve again and shouted, 'No more film, lidy. We used all the ten cans we 'ad – every bleedin' bit of it – but we caught the buggers, di'n't we? We'll show 'em 'oo did it, once you got your films to show 'em, eh? Won't the beak give 'em what for when 'e sees their ugly mugs doin' all of this? Cor – ain't it all an 'orrible bleedin' mess –' And Letty stared round and blinked and stared again, and was too amazed to say anything, to do anything but look, her eyes wide and her face rigid with shock.

The seats lay in heaps of splintered timber, the cushions were torn and ruined, the white walls were splattered with marks of rotten fruit that had landed to make great splashes of filth, the mirrors behind the bars had disappeared into heaps of glittery shards and there were broken tankards hurled everywhere. The great crimson tab-curtain of which she had been so proud lay in a useless torn heap on the front of the stage and the set was a complete shambles.

Suddenly the ground on which she was standing rocked violently and she stared down to see what had happened small Alf grappling with a big man – one of the original fruit-throwers – who had, it seemed, suddenly noticed for the first time the square wooden boxes on their rostrum and was determined to destroy these objects as well as those he had already pulled apart. She reached out towards him to help Alf push him away as another man came lunging towards her, and a piercing shriek filled her ears; and she realized, to her own amazement, that it came from her own throat. The rostrum rocked even harder and the cameras shook on their tripods and she reached for them and seized them just as a couple of policemen came pushing through the mob towards her. As she went down one of the cameras, toppling with her, landed on her ankle and the searing pain that went through her made her shriek again. But both cameras had collapsed on top of her, and even in this hubbub she could tell she had not heard the sound of shattering glass coming from their delicate interiors. Whatever had happened to her Gaff, at least Oliver's cameras were all right, she realized as the policemen hauled the two men away, and she looked at Alf and he, picking himself up from the dust of the broken rostrum, winked at her and said in his hoarsely cheerful voice, 'There, lidy! Got it all right and safe, 'aven't we? Been a bit of an evenin' 'asn't it, one way 'n' another?'

And all she could do was sit there on the floor, her arms clutching two heavy wooden cameras, her head against a pile of film cans and her foot hurting quite abominably, and laugh and laugh at his cheerful dirty face until the tears ran uncontrollably down her face.

23

'Oh dear, oh dear, oh dear –' Oliver said and blinked and then said again helplessly, 'Oh dear.'

'Well, it could have been worse,' Letty said as encouragingly as she could. 'I mean, no one was badly hurt – the cast got away to their dressing-rooms and no one followed them there, so that was all right, and from all accounts Violet gave as good as she got and knocked one man clean out after he'd broken the mirror – she loved that mirror, Violet did – and most of the damage can be put right fairly easily, Edwin thinks. It's not structural – apart from a few lights pulled off the wall. Dear old Edwin said we can put it all straight again in a week and he's willing to foot the bill, and he'll try to be better insured next time – and I *did* save the cameras!'

'Oh dear,' Oliver said and stared at the pile of cameras and cans of film that the cab-driver had obligingly carried into the Celia for her. 'I'm glad you did, of course, but I'm not sure – I mean – here, at the Celia! With Phoebe coming today and everything and she'll be sure to ask awkward questions if she sees them and – oh, dear!'

Letty stared at him and then pushed her hat further back on her head. She was sitting on a small chair beside one of the tables in the middle of the Celia, in a patch of the sunlight thrown in through the open front door – for at last the weather had changed and the cold January rain of the previous day had given way to a bright frosty morning – and had been feeling tolerably well pleased with herself under the circumstances. But confronted with Oliver's blank consternation in the face of her tale of last night's momentous doings and her rescue of his expensive possessions, was frankly amazed.

And not a little nettled, and she said tartly, 'Well, I'm sorry if I'm a trouble to you. I was merely concerned to protect your property, and that was why I made shift to load everything into the cab and bring it here to you when there is much work to be done at the Gaff, and that quickly! I'll call another cab now and take it all away again if that's what you want – but don't blame me if they break in and start more damage and get into the store-room where we keep them and you lose them altogether!' And she got painfully to her feet and hobbled across the big supper-room towards the front door.

At once Oliver was fussing after her, clucking hen-like in his agitation. 'Oh, my dear Letty, you mustn't be so – so – you really mustn't – it's just that m'sister – so tiresome about money and her children and grandchildren – and there's me not told her yet about – you see how it is, but I'm deeply grateful, of course I am, and now – what *have* you done to your foot?' For as he had reached her the toe of his boot had touched her shoe and her face had whitened with pain, and she had swayed against his restraining arm.

'Here, my dear child, come and sit down at once – oh dear, oh dear – what have I done? And you so good about my cameras and – now let me see – my dear child! That's a shocking injury, shocking! Can't have you walking about on that, now, what are you thinking of? You should be resting it, indeed you should – why, you might have broken it –'

'It's all right,' Letty said as the sick giddiness that had filled her at the impact began to clear and she peered down at her foot, which he had arranged on a stool, and stared at it. 'I say, it does look a bid odd, doesn't it?' she said doubtfully. 'It wasn't like that this morning when I left the Gaff. Though it's been hurting more and more all morning –'

The ankle above the edge of her black kid boot was swollen and tense and she touched the skin gingerly with her forefinger. Even under the brown of her lisle stockings she could see there was a deep purple bruise and as she touched it the pain surged up again, making her head swim once more.

'I'd better get that seen to at once, at once, now – Will, where's Will? Oh, drat the man, away ill, I'd forgotten – then Bert, you go and find a hansom and help me carry poor Miss Lackland out to it, and then we'll see what they say at the casualty department. And Bert, carry this film and these cameras – careful, mind, they're very valuable – carry them to the cellar store-room – between the vegetables and the game-larder – and lock the door and give me the key, and do it before my sister – before Lady Caspar gets here, but get the hansom first and hurry –'

She sat there dreamily and let them fuss around her, Oliver carefully easing off her boot – which exercise hurt dreadfully until it was at last free and then felt a little easier – and the waiter whistling in the street outside for a cab to take her away. She didn't care much what happened now, she discovered. She was just very tired, and it was agreeable to sit here and not to do anything much at all. It wouldn't have been so bad if she'd had any sleep, but what with all the mess at the Gaff to clear up, and worrying about the cameras and the cast and how they would manage that evening, she had done little more than snatch an hour or so's doze at around three this morning. She had intended to go back to the Gaff after this expedition to check with Donald about the possibility of putting on some sort of show – if only choruses round the mercifully-undamaged piano – just to show the regulars that the Gaff could be trusted to keep its doors open no matter what. But, she thought vaguely, just at the moment I don't really care what they do –

Bert the waiter carried her to the cab, grunting a little, for she was a well-built girl, and she was grateful for that, for now her boot was off for the first time since the injury – she had not undressed for that hour's doze – it had swollen to amazing proportions and it was quite impossible for her to put it to the ground.

The journey in the hansom was more disagreeable than she would have thought possible, for the loss of her boot meant loss of support for the injury. Every jerk of the horse's reins, every sway of the animal's back, made the cab rock and was transmitted to her ankle; by the time they reached their destination she was white and shaky again and almost in tears with it all.

Indeed she was in so much distress that it was not until a burly porter had been summoned with a wheeled bath-chair to lift her from the cab under the sympathetic and intensely curious eyes of a knot of passers-by who were enthralled by the whole performance, and had been lifted out and then trundled into the building, that she realized where she was.

'Uncle Oliver!' She almost wailed it as the chair was pushed across the terrazzo floor past the fascinated eyes of other patients on the benches in the waiting-hall. 'Uncle Oliver, why here? Why bring me to Nellie's? You must know it's the last place I'd willingly come as a patient after –'

'Oh, pooh, what does it matter where you are as long as you get help for that ankle? Shocking injury, shocking, got to see to it, and who better than m'brother-in-law Freddy, hey? Never mind your megrims, miss, get your foot mended, that's the ticket! Ah, you there, young lady – ah, nurse. Where's m'brother-in-law? Sir Frederick?'

The nurse who had been so hailed stopped and stared down at Letty with her forehead creased and then smiled in recognition. 'Why, Miss Lackland! How nice to see you again – good morning, sir. I'm afraid Sir Frederick isn't here at present. He's gone away, you know – there's an operation he had to perform for a special patient in Bradford in Yorkshire, I believe and –'

'Oh, tut tut! Oh dear, oh dear!' Oliver said, his face lugubrious in the extreme. 'What *shall* we do? Here we are with this shocking injury, and Freddy thoughtless enough to be away from home. Too bad of him, really it is, too bad! And when will he be back, hey? When will he be back, nurse, tell me that!'

'I don't know, sir, I'm afraid,' the nurse said. 'Shall I fetch Sister for you? I'm sure she'll –'

'She can't set a broken foot, now can she?' Oliver burst out irritably. 'It's Freddy we need and I think you should send him a message at once to come back to London immediately and –'

'Dear Uncle Oliver, there are other surgeons here, you know!' Letty managed to speak at last, for he had been burbling on at such a rate that she had not been able to stop him but now he peered down at her and blinked.

'Eh?'

'I'm sure it's nothing very terrible,' she said. 'And I'm sure

238

anyone here can arrange to deal with it. It needn't be Sir Frederick – indeed he wouldn't usually deal with this sort of injury anyway.Please, Nurse, whoever is on duty as casualty doctor will be able to help, I'm sure. If he's not too busy –'

The nurse smiled at her in understanding and went rustling away, her starched cap-ribbons flying, to fetch Sister and also the casualty doctor on duty, after leading Letty and her escort into a cubicle in the casualty department and pulling the curtains to give them privacy.

All the time Uncle Oliver fussed about her, trying to rearrange her foot comfortably and being solicitous with blankets which she didn't really need, she thought gratefully of the fact that Sir Frederick was not here. It had been bad enough to have been brought to Nellie's in the first place, to face people she had abandoned, to appear as some sort of failure in their eyes. To have been treated by Sir Frederick would have been to pile Pelion on Ossa; thank heaven he had been called out of London for one of his difficult cases. In her student days here she had been sorry when he had not been available to lecture and had muttered as much as her fellows about the tedious way provincial doctors made demands on him. But now she was grateful.

The doctor, when he came, proved to her great relief to be a total stranger. Clearly someone had left and new staff had been attached to the hospital, and it was her good fortune to be greeted by someone who knew nothing of her. That helped a lot, for it meant that Uncle Oliver was sent politely packing – something any of the doctors who knew him as Sir Frederick's brother-in-law would have found difficult to do – and she could be treated just like any other patient – competently but without any special privileges.

The drawback was however that there was a good deal of waiting about. Even Sister Casualty, who knew her and her old status as part of the hospital, could not countermand orders given by a doctor, and when Dr Steward decreed that this ankle should be visualized by the skiagraph before any attempt was made to treat it, and that there were already three patients in the department undergoing this complex and time-consuming care for whom she would have to wait, so it had to be. So Letty was sent in her bath-chair, her leg wrapped in a red woollen blanket, to wait outside the door of the Röntgen Ray department in the lower corridor until such time as the lordly experts within should be able to take a picture of her swollen blue ankle.

Not that she minded unduly. The chair was comfortable, and her ankle hurt less now, and she knew Uncle Oliver would keep his word, given as he was bustled away, to let them know at the Gaff what was happening, so she might as well go along with the situation. She might even be able to sleep a little while she waited, she thought drowsily, as the nurse arranged her chair outside the door to the Röntgen Ray department. Just for a little while –

'If this weather goes on improving like this, we'll be able to get you out on to the balcony again,' Nurse Wilmshurst said, and folded over his sheet with a practised flick of her wrist. 'You'll be getting too soft for words tucked up in here all the time!'

'Heaven forbid!' Luke said, and stretched a little, wriggling his toes against the blankets. It was still a luxury to be allowed to move freely and to talk, even though he had been given permission almost two weeks ago now. He would not have thought it possible that he could find any satisfaction in his present situation, but he did now. He looked across the room towards the mirror on the wall above the wash-basin and squinted at it, and then grinned. He did look better, undoubtedly he did. His face had lost that pallid translucent look it had had when he had first seen himself against his pillows, reflected in that little square of glass, and there was even some colour in his cheeks – not the hectic flush of fever that had been so much a part of him for so long, but a more normal pinkness that showed that his treatment was working.

Sir Frederick had told him that only the day before, when he'd examined him before going off for a couple of days to operate on a patient in Bradford. He had been chirpy and excited somehow, Luke had thought, as he had sat at the side of the bed, his eyes narrowed with concentration as he listed to the sounds of Luke's breathing through his stethoscope. As though he were going to meet a sweetheart rather than just do a piece of work, he'd thought, and at once had to shut out of his mind's eye the vision of Letty that rose in it. That happened more and more rather than less and less these days; visions of Letty triggered by any and every casual thought. As his health slowly improved and his strength came seeping back into him so had his manhood, and night after night he had lain in his solitary room wrapped in his blankets, trying not to be aware of the clamour in his body, the way his skin remembered the touch of Letty, the way his nose remembered the scent of Letty, the way his brain recalled the look of Letty. And now, listening to Sir Frederick talk of his forthcoming journey to Bradford and noticing his eager anticipation, he had had to work hard to stop his own errant thoughts.

'I wish I could be here when Patterson comes to see you,' Sir Frederick had said, folding his stethoscope before tucking it into his hat. 'I would have enjoyed seeing his pleasure in your excellent progress. By God, young man, but we thought we'd lost you, you know that? You were in a parlous state, very parlous state indeed when we got you in here. Knocking at St Peter's front door loud and clear you were. And now look at you! Put on a stone in weight, I swear, and the cavities in your apices shrinking under my very ears. I couldn't be more delighted with you, and that's a fact!'

'So when can I go back to work?' Luke had said eagerly and Sir Frederick laughed and made a grimace at Nurse Wilmshurst.

'Listen to him, Nurse! Trying to undo all our good work in one fell swoop. Not for a long time yet, m'boy. A long time. I'd like you to have a spell in Switzerland first. Maybe the summer months, hey?'

Luke had frowned sharply at that. 'Switzerland? My dear Sir Frederick, that would cost a fortune! I haven't money of that nature! Only responsibilities for others' money. I can't go travelling for my health, even if I wanted to –'

'Oh, as to wanting to, you'll get used to the idea! It's a beautiful country and consumptives get well there at a great rate – and you'll be delighted when you're there, and that's a promise. As for money – pooh to that! We here at Nellie's have our own arrangements for our own patients. We can in special circumstances send needy patients to the places their need calls for. And I am seeking to make such an arrangement for you. And if you argue at all I shall forbid you speech again, and see how you like that.'

Luke had subsided, frowning, but obedient because he knew he had to be. He had promised Sir Frederick that he would put himself in his hands to be well, and it was a promise he had to keep. If he was ever to go back to Letty and tell her –

'I hate the idea of being an object of charity,' he said fretfully. 'To be paid for, looked after –'

'Oh, as to that, don't be so arrogant,' Sir Frederick said calmly. 'Who are you to deprive good God-fearing people from exercising their duty to care for their fellow men? You will take as you are given and be glad of it. Now, this afternoon, you may sit out of bed for half an hour. In a chair. That should cheer you! Yes, I thought it would! And then, if you tolerate that effort well, we can arrange for your next skiagram to be done ready to show Mr Patterson when he comes to see you in a day or two. I have made all arrangements with Nurse Wilmshurst, and she has been told precisely how I expect you to behave in my absence. And if I hear when I arrive back that you have been misbehaving in any way, back on total bed- and voice-rest you go. Good afternoon, m'boy. I'm very pleased with you – and happy for you –'

And now, waiting for Nurse Wilmshurst to arrive with the bath-chair in which he would travel from his side ward in Men's Medical to the Röntgen Ray department for his skiagraph he smiled a little at the memory of his words. A good and caring man, old Sir Frederick; that he'd saved Luke's life he was in no doubt. Looking back now, he knew just how ill he had been, and it was not an agreeable vision to look upon. He had come as close to dying alone on that stage sofa at the Gaff as any man ever had, he told himself – and she had left him there, his so-called friend Jessica –

Another thought not to be entertained, and he cocked his head to listen for Nurse Wilmshurst, eager for his journey to the basement. It wasn't as though it would be anything special, he told himself as at last he heard the creak of wheels along the corridor outside. It was just that it would be an adventure, a marvellous change in the desperately dull routine of his illness to leave this little room with its green paint and its cracked ceiling. He wasn't going to do anything exciting or interesting in the Röntgen Ray department, but at least he would be going *out*. And he managed a breathy little whistle as at last, wrapped again in those tedious blankets, he began his slow stately journey, pushed by Nurse Wilmshurst, along the corridors towards the basement.

24

'As neat an excision of an ovarian cyst as any I've seen,' Sophie said approvingly, and nodded crisply at the nurse who bent over the patient's inert body to check her pulse. 'I do congratulate you, Freddy.'

He was washing his hands at the basin in the corner and smiled a little crookedly at her over his shoulder.

'Thank you. I can't deny it was tricky. The posterior uterine artery ran perilously close to the lower surface – big thing, isn't it? Must weigh close on a couple of pounds, I'd say.'

'More, I suspect,' Sophie said absently as together they left the patient's room and made their way down the richly-carpeted staircase to the dining-room below, where the patient's husband waited anxiously for them. 'Freddy, are you well? You look more than a little tired – how long since anyone checked on *your* health?'

'Oh, stuff,' he said easily and smiled at her, but she was not beguiled. There was a faint blueness about his lips and a drawn look on those thin cheeks that her long experience told her needed to be taken seriously.

'We'll talk about it later,' she said firmly and pushed open the dining-room door to nod reassuringly at the dumpy middle-aged man who was standing there waiting for them.

'She's well, Mr Exley. Sir Frederick removed the cyst without any undue loss of blood, and it clearly is not a malignant condition. She withstood the anaesthetic very well, and is already beginning to come out of it. A month or two of convalescence and you'll be able to take her to the Riviera for her full recovery. I'll see to it that the nurses are supervised, and I'll be visiting each day until I take the stitches out. Now – Sir Frederick must return to London and I must be off to my clinic –'

'I'm that grateful to you, Sir Frederick,' Exley said, coming fussily across the heavily-furnished room to pump his hand. 'I told Dr Lackland 'ere I wanted the best man for my Jenny, the very best, and she told me to send for you, and I'll not deny I thought at first it was family partiality, like, that made 'er recommend you; but my wife, she said as anything Dr Lackland said is law, so you it 'ad to be. And to 'ear as it's all gone so well – well, I can't tell you 'ow relieved I am! Name your fee, sir, name your fee. You'll not find George Exley backward in coming forward when there's real worth to be recognized. Just name your fee –'

Freddy smiled and quirked his lips as he caught sight of Sophie's expression. 'My dear sir, my fee is as I told you before I operated. Ten guineas – I ask no more –'

'But you can give a decent contribution to the clinic if you're so minded and you've the brass to spare,' Sophie said coolly. 'I've any number of patients with similar conditions to your wife's for whom we can't afford to bring London surgeons up here, and every penny we can get to aid them is welcome. Shall we say a hundred guineas, Mr Exley? For the anaesthetic and my care and for your gratitude to Sir Frederick?'

Exley's face lengthened for a moment and then he grinned and nodded. 'You're a hard lass, Dr Lackland, always was! But a fair one. You'll 'ave your hundred, so you shall. No one can say George Exley's mean, not when it's 'is Jenny as needed the care. Now, there's good brandy 'ere and my, people'll bring you any comestibles as you've a fancy for, if you touch the bell there, and I'll be away to see the lass before going off to the mill. Lost a full half-day already over this business and that's no way to make the guineas to pay out, eh Sir Frederick? No! Well now – thanks again, Sir Frederick, thanks again. The cheque for your fee'll be ready in my book-room before you go –'

They sat and ate sandwiches and drank coffee, rather than brandy, in a companionable silence after he'd gone bustling away, and then Sophie said abruptly, 'Have you seen my Letty, Freddy?'

He put down his cup and leaned back in his chair, not

looking at her.

'No,' he said. 'But I hear what she's doing. Just as you do, I imagine.'

'Oh, she writes letters regularly enough,' Sophie said and got up and went over to the big mullioned window to stare out over the moor towards the smoky chimneys of Bradford. Exley, as one of the richest mill-owners in the West Riding, lived in one of the most desirable houses in the whole town. 'She tells me what she is doing at this theatre of hers, and about her films and so forth – but not about how she *is*. If she were on happier terms with Barty – well, there it is. They're not, so he won't visit her and report back to me, and I can't ask it of him. But I need more than just letters –'

'From all I hear she is really happy. Though –' He stopped and she turned and looked at him sharply.

'Though what?'

He sat and stared at her broodingly and she came back to sit on the armchair next to him, her face anxious; he smiled, and again she was very aware of the pallid blueness of his complexion. 'Oh, it's an indirect thing – it's just that I have a patient. He's a sort of cousin – on Phoebe and Oliver's side. Has Letty spoken to you of him?'

Sophie looked at him, her face puzzled.

'Luke O'Hare,' Freddy said.

'Luke O'Hare,' she said quietly and then nodded. 'Yes, she spoke of him. Not as a patient of yours but as a young man at this theatre –'

'He's a patient now,' Freddy said, 'and one I have been most concerned about. Pulmonary tuberculosis with severe cavitation at the apices –'

There was a little silence between them then and after a moment Sophie said, 'She's visiting him?'

'I forbade all visits.'

'Thank you. I'm grateful for that. He's infectious then, and –'

'Oh yes. We've got positive cultures from his sputum. He was admitted after a couple of very nasty haemoptyses –'

Sophie took a sharp little breath. 'And they were together a great deal before that?'

'I don't know. They might have been. I did consider sending for Letty and asking her to let me check her, but I'd hoist myself with my own petard there. I'd promised the boy I'd tell no one where he was, you see. And most particularly Letty. He'd been worrying about that – he's a good lad, you see – so I had to promise. And I thought – well, she sees a good deal of Oliver, and you know what a fussy old woman *he* is. If she were ill, he'd soon see to it I knew of the matter. He's a good soul, my brother-in-law.'

Sophie nodded again, her face relaxing a little. 'So she's all right at present? And she hasn't seen him for – how long?'

'We admitted him – oh, around six months ago now. Under Patterson's treatment –'

'Auto-immune therapy –'

'That's it. I've been making daily preparations of his own serum and injecting it. He's done very well, very well indeed. The apical cavities seem to be diminishing, going by his breath sounds – I'll have new skiagraphs to see by the time I return. I expect good pictures and he really has progressed on complete rest and a high diet. Saw him yesterday and was most pleased with him. But that's the trouble, you see –'

'You can't keep visitors away from him for much longer.'

'Precisely. If the new skiagraph in fact shows he's progressing as well as I think he is and his next sputum sample grows clean, then I've got to start a more normal regime. And that worries me. Letty –'

'She'll want to visit him,' Sophie said softly. 'And though they had their disagreements, as far as I understand the matter, the fact that he is ill –'

'And the fact that it's phthisis, and you know as well as I do what effect that has on a young man's – ahem – emotions –'

'Oh, damn it all to hell and back!' Sophie said explosively. 'I don't want her marrying a consumptive! What sort of life would that be for her? Bad enough she's chosen to racket around in this business she's in – it took all the courage and –and – love I had to bite my tongue over that. But how can I bite my tongue if she chooses to marry a consumptive?'

'I may be wrong, Sophie,' Freddy said, and looked wretched. 'Perhaps I shouldn't have said anything about it, but

247

it's been worrying me. I saw the boy just before I left Nellie's to come here – but I could be being foolish. It may be that he'll remain anxious not to see her? I did feel he asked me to keep my counsel for her sake – it wasn't that he did not wish to see her. It was that he wished to protect her –'

'And once he knows he is no longer infectious, that his laboratory tests give a negative answer, he'll see her. And then, if the disease flares again –'

'You know as well as I do, Sophie, that there's nothing more unpredictable than a case of phthisis. One patient curls up and dies when his care is of the best, and another thrives and throws it off when he lives a dreadful neglected life. Who of us can ever put our hands on our hearts and swear to a prognosis? But I'll do what I can to hold them apart. If his report from Patterson is all I hope it will be, I'll be sending him to Switzerland.'

She frowned at that. 'Expensive.'

'So it will have to be. I can do it through the hospital. As long as Phoebe doesn't know –' He reddened then. 'Damn it. I shouldn't have said that.'

'I'm sorry,' Sophie said and leaned forwards and touched his hand. 'Is she being difficult?'

He looked at her, his face very still, and for a moment she saw him the way he had been one night long ago at Gatti's restaurant, under the arches in Villiers Street – an eager-faced man, past his first flush of youth even then, but vigorous and wiry, and looking at her with a message of need for her and desire for her on his face that was unmistakeable. And now, all these years later in Bradford, a respectable middle-aged matron with white hair, talking to an elderly man with sparse hair and a lined and tired face, she felt herself redden and become breathless at the memory. And she leaned back in her chair so that her face was shadowed by the wing pieces on the back.

He seemed to share her discomfiture for he too leaned back and after a moment said in a rather tight voice, 'No, not precisely difficult. Just – just being Phoebe. She worries too much about money, I fear. About who has what, and how it is spent. For my part, I don't think we are short of any vital needs. But she feels that – well, when the drugs manufactory and the chemists' shops went to my half-brother Daniel and his family after my step-father died, she took it very ill – thought we should have had it – and now old Oliver's baulking at making a will in favour of the family – well, you can imagine how it is. We do well enough, you understand, and I don't think we need fret over the family – they're all warm enough, even Ambrose in Canada –' He shook his head then and rubbed his face wearily with one hand. 'I'm talking too much, I'm afraid. It was just that I wanted you to know about Letty. Thought you ought to –'

There was a little silence and they sat there in the darkening room as the January afternoon dwindled away over the cold moors outside and then she stirred and said, almost shyly, 'I could add to the fund for sending him to Switzerland if you feel –'

'No!' he said vigorously, 'it won't be necessary. I'm sorry that aspect of it slipped out. I am perhaps more tired than I thought or I wouldn't have mentioned it. I assure you that the costs will be found and found easily. He'll be sent there as soon as I can arrange it. And if I can keep them apart till then, I shall. Will you speak to Letty on the matter?'

She laughed a little at that, a small and rather sad sound. 'How can I? She's a woman grown, not a child to be led any more. I pushed her too hard as it was. That's why she's living this absurd life she is. You spoke of being hoist with your own petard – how do you think I feel? I can't speak to her of her private life unless she asks me to because everything I've ever believed in, everything I've tried to rear my children to be, forbids such meddling on my part. I ache to meddle – and I can't. It's hell –'

'Children,' said Freddy softly. 'Our children. Such a hurt to us, always such a hurt. Even when you love them. Indeed, particularly when you love them. You remember my son Ambrose? Whenever I see Lewis with his Miriam at family parties and meetings I think of Ambrose and the pain is as great now as it was fifteen years ago when it all happened – greater, perhaps. And I too have no right to meddle.'

'I remember,' she said, gently and leaned forward in the

shadows to touch his hand, 'and I am sad for you. I have no right to complain of my three. They have grown well enough –'

'And so have my other two,' he said and then more strongly, 'and I am selfish and greedy to fuss so, Sophie. I must return to London. There is so much work to do, so many matters to sort out – the hospital and home. And –' He shook his head. 'It all seems so effortful sometimes, and rather pointless.'

The edge of anxiety that had been in her sharpened and she said quickly, 'Freddy – I said before that you should see someone – shall I check you? Would you trust me?'

He laughed at that. 'Of course I'd trust you – you're a fine clinician. But I don't need any sort of check and refuse flatly to consider it! I am well enough. Just tired. And perhaps –' And now he reached out and took her hand. '– And perhaps I allowed myself to become a little over-excited because I was going to see you. That's why I accepted this case, you know, Sophie. To see you. I do little provincial surgery these days, but to see you – you've always been very special to me, my dear. You always will be.'

She looked at him there in the dusk, at the way his eyes gleamed a little in the poor light and felt his hand, warm yet papery and light-boned on hers and after a moment leaned forwards and kissed him gently on his dry straight mouth and felt his lips relax under hers after one startled moment.

'And I feel the same affection for you, Freddy,' she said gently. 'I always have cared deeply for you. Not perhaps as you wanted me to – there was Gil you see, and dear Wilfred and – well, it's all ancient history now. But never forget that you hold a special place in my esteem, will you?'

'Thank you,' he said after a moment. 'Thank you, Sophie. It's been a good world these past lonely years, knowing you were in it. A good world. And I shall look after your girl as best I can because of you. Don't worry, Sophie. I'll keep them apart. Somehow.'

25

She had fallen fast asleep, for all that the chair was rather less comfortable than she had first thought it, pressing into her spine unpleasantly when she leaned back; but her fatigue had overcome all that, and she had slept, deeply and dreamlessly.

And had woken so abruptly that it had made her gasp as the chair lurched and she tried to sit upright, quite forgetting about her leg, and her own movement shifted her ankle and made her yelp with the pain.

'Oh, I'm so sorry,' a voice behind her said. 'So sorry – I didn't mean to move your chair, but it was difficult to get this one past yours! Hold still, my dear, and I'll be very careful –'

So Letty held still, as the nurse behind her manouvered first Letty's own chair, and then the one she was pushing, and her heart slowed down from the way it had raced when she had been woken, and she leaned back against the wickerwork as the other chair came alongside her.

She turned her head to look, not because the other chair was a matter of any interest to her or because she wanted to see who occupied it, but simply because it was there, and saw a bundled figure with a red blanket pulled over the ears and a tangle of thick dark hair showing above it, and she thought suddenly of Luke and was angry with herself. Trying to keep her guard up against intruding thoughts was difficult enough at the best of times, but so much harder when she had been fast asleep, and when her foot was hurting so, and when someone with hair like his went by.

The chair made its passage without mishap and the nurse turned it as she reached the other side of the door and set it alongside in the opposite place to her own and fussed over the occupant, showing her back view of print dress and starched apron to Letty's languid gaze; the fuss of the collision over, she was ready to doze off again.

'There!' the nurse said in her high rather hectoring voice. 'Now you just keep that blanket up like that to keep the draughts off, while I go and check how long they'll be. They sent up for you to come down so it can't be long –' And she straightened her back and with a brief and brilliantly-professional smile at Letty pushed open the Röntgen Ray department door and disappeared.

Leaving Letty staring across the narrow space that divided the two bath-chairs at Luke.

It was as though nothing at all odd had happened at first. She stared and blinked and stared again and then said in a perfectly ordinary voice, 'Oh. Hello, Luke.'

And he stared back, incongruous in his bundle of blankets and said in an equally ordinary voice, 'Hello, Letty.'

And then they sat and contemplated each other in blank silence as around them the hospital buzzed and hummed and clattered with its own existence. For the rest of her life Letty would remember those sounds; the distant clash of metal gates as the lift that served the upper stories was opened and closed; the rumble of wheels as trolleys bearing patients went busily along the interminable corridors; the clack of hurrying footsteps as nurses and doctors rushed about their business and the more friendly clatter of dishes and spoons as food trays bearing the patients' midday meals were carried from the kitchens to the wards.

'I'm not sure I believe this,' he said then, and his voice seemed to her to be a little husky as though he had not been in the habit of speaking much lately. 'It is you, isn't it Letty? I'm not imagining it? Why are you here?'

'I might have broken my leg,' she said, and was surprised at how hoarse her own voice sounded in her ears. 'There was a – something happened at the Gaff. I'm to have a skiagraph done, to see what the damage is. Why –' But the question stuck in her throat. He looked pale and ill and much thinner than he had been when she had last seen him, or seemed to be in the face certainly, for she could see little of the rest of him in the tangle of blankets that were wrapped round him, and she was suddenly frightened of the answer she might receive.

'I didn't want you to know,' he said after a moment, and his voice sounded more normal now, more like the voice she remembered and had ached for all these months. 'I didn't want you to know. I told everyone not to tell you, so that you'd not come near me, so that I couldn't harm you, and now you're here. It's – I don't think I believe it –'

'Told them not to –' and she tried to sit up more straightly and again had to wince and subside. 'Tell me what? I thought you'd just – that you and – you'd gone away and –'

And even now she couldn't say it, couldn't put into words her sick misery at the thought that he and Jessica had gone off together and abandoned her and the Gaff and Edwin and everyone else.

'It's impossible, isn't it? You try to do what you think is right, and it all goes wrong. Or maybe it goes the way it was meant to in the first place. Maybe I wasn't meant to do as I did, and this is fate or providence or something stepping in and –'

'Mr O'Hare, I know Sir Frederick said you can talk now, but that doesn't mean you can go chattering and carrying on in this fashion!' The nurse's voice was scandalized and she stood in the doorway with her hands on her hips so that her elbows were akimbo, looking at Luke very severely. 'Now just be quiet, and wait a few moments, and they'll do your skiagraph then. And you, Miss Lackland. They asked me to tell you that you'll have yours done immediately after and they're sorry to keep you waiting. Miss Lackland – now, would you be a relation of our Sir Frederick? He's a wonderful doctor, isn't he, Mr O'Hare? He looks after us, doesn't he? Yes. And very annoyed he'd be if I let you chatter on and get yourself excited, so if you please, Miss Lackland, while he waits you'll have the goodness not to talk to my patient!' And she threw an upwards glance of mock despair at male foolishness at Letty before disappearing into the Röntgen Ray department again.

'Why are you having one of these things done?' she said and stared at him hard, trying to see what was wrong with him, as if that were possible, and he leaned back in his cocoon of blankets as though he were trying to increase the distance between them, and said in a muffled voice, 'It's not important.

253

She said I was to be quiet. So I'd better.'

'You're doing it again,' she said furiously, unable to control her reactions. 'You're doing it again! Being hateful and cold and – why? What did I ever do to deserve it? I thought we were friends, you and I. You don't treat friends in this way, surely. If you wanted to go off with your wretched Jessica you were free to do so! You don't have to treat me so cruelly, nor do you have to be so hateful now! I asked only what –'

'Jessica!' He was sitting upright again now, staring at her and the vigour of his movement had sent the blankets down to his shoulders so that she could see him more clearly, and her chest contracted with tenderness at the sight of him. His hair was sadly overgrown and he was ill-shaven and he looked thin-cheeked and sad, though not as ill as she had first thought, for there was a good colour in his face. 'Jessica!' he said again. 'That one, who left me coughing my life away and left me to die there and didn't get help or –'

He stopped as suddenly as he had begun and leaned back in his chair again, trying awkwardly to pull the blanket up over his ears and face once more but failing, and she stared at him, trying to understand and suddenly, she did.

She saw herself at her mother's side, in the old two-horse carriage, on a round of visits in Haworth. She was about twelve or thirteen, no more, and home from school for the holidays, and had so much wanted to go to all the invalids' houses with her mother, finding them fascinating and fun to be with, for there was always someone to fuss over the doctor's little daughter and perhaps give her a piece of parkin or chocolate cake. But at this house her mother had said firmly, 'No. Not here, Letty. She's a case of open consumption, and you might get the contagion. Not here –'

And she had looked at the window and seen a child not much older than herself peering out, a thin-faced child with her hair in a tangle and her eyes wide, and had shivered, knowing how dreadful consumption was, and not wanting to go into the house at all.

'Oh, no,' she said now. 'Oh, Luke, no. Please say it isn't.'

'Isn't what?' he said and he muttered it, like a child caught out in a minor sin.

'Have you consumption? Is that what you meant? Is that why you're here? Because of consumption?'

He took a deep breath and she saw his shoulders slump.

'Of course it is, you foolish creature. Of course it is. Can you think of anything else that would have kept me away from you when I love you so much?'

The door clattered open again and Nurse Wilmshurst came bustling out, all officious busyness and chattering brightly, and seized Luke's bath-chair and pushed him into the department, nodding back at Letty over her shoulder as she closed the door, saying cheerfully, 'Not long now, Miss Lackland. Not long now!'

Leaving Letty sitting there blank with astonishment and an enormous fear for Luke, but also a vast and totally unreasonable joy as she stared at the closed door and listened to the hospital and its noises and tried to set her upside-down world back on its heels again.

'Well, I had to do as he asked, didn't I?' Oliver said reasonably. 'You can understand that, surely? Would you have done any differently in my shoes?'

'I suppose not,' Letty said, and smiled at him, a great dazzling happy smile that lifted her face and narrowed her green eyes almost into oblivion and Oliver smiled back, feeling an even greater warmth for her than he usually did, if that were possible, for she looked so beautiful somehow, so very much more delightful than she had, and she had always been good to look at, heaven knew.

'But now I know where he is, nothing in the world will stop me seeing him – not even Sir Frederick,' and she looked very fierce and Oliver smiled again.

'I wouldn't be too sure of that,' he said and laughed. 'Not too sure at all, knowing m'brother-in-law. Strong-willed chappie, our Freddy. Not easily put about by anyone. Except perhaps m'sister –' And he looked gloomy for a moment.

'Well,' Letty said. 'We'll set that aside at present. No point in fussing till Sir Frederick can talk to me about Luke tomorrow, and then we'll see. Right now I have to talk to you about what I can do about this film. What do you think?'

'It's splendid stuff, splendid! I couldn't be more delighted with it, indeed I couldn't. I can see just where we ought to edit it, the bits we should get rid of you know, for they're too blurred, and then we'll have as good a piece of actuality film as any old Paul ever made.' And he rubbed his hands together like a child faced with a tray full of lollipops and looked very gleeful indeed.

'Oh, as to that, there's no doubt plenty of people will want the film!' Letty said impatiently. 'I've told Dora Montefiore and she's very excited. She wants it to be made into a special "Votes for Women" show and to send it all over the country for WSPU meetings. It's not that I'm concerned about. The thing is, you can see quite clearly, can't you, the people who did it all? Look, I'll run it again and you'll see what I mean –'

And hobbling a little awkwardly on her crutches but with great energy, she took the film from its canister and set it on its sprockets in the projector and waved at Bert, the waiter, to come and let down the screen over the little stage and to put out the lights in the supper-rooms. Which he did, sighing a little, for it was only an hour or so to opening time and lots still to be done to get ready for the evening's business at the Celia.

She settled herself as comfortably as she could behind the projector, setting her plaster of Paris splinted leg out at an awkward angle so that she could sit down, and began to turn the handle at the exact speed so that the shadows began to dance on the little white screen and they both watched eagerly as Bert stood and hovered behind them, as fascinated by it all as they were.

It was eerie watching it all happen again, but in a silence that was only broken by the buzzing of the machine as the film turned on its sprockets and rewound on the other side. The faces of the people eating and drinking and laughing ('I like those close-up shots you got, Letty,' Oliver said enthusiastically, 'indeed I do. You've got a lot of real character there –lovely –') and then the stage as the curtain rose ('Lovely, lovely, Letty! Look at that, will you. Bert, did you ever see as clear a shot? Oh, well done, Letty!'). And then suddenly the change in the audience, the pushing figures, the raised fists, the open mouths ('Damn me, you can almost hear the wretches, almost hear 'em. It's like being there, it really is. Oh, but I wish I had been! I'd have shown them where they got off, that I would!' fumed Uncle Oliver), and then a great lurching as the fighting grew more and more intense and the camera shifted its angle. Uncle Oliver was silent now, and Letty glanced sideways at him in the flickering lights thrown by the projector and saw his round face tighten and his jaw harden and she said urgently, 'Watch their faces, Uncle Oliver, watch their faces!' And he nodded silently, never taking his eyes from the screen until the film spluttered out into a wild flapping as the last couple of feet ran through.

'You see what I mean?' Letty said, as Bert hurried to put on the lights again and set about finishing his table-laying, and Letty put away her film. 'Did you see? They were clearly recognizable, weren't they?'

'Oh, yes. Know those horrible men anywhere, I would, if I saw 'em again,' Uncle Oliver said and then shot a sideways glance at her. 'You're not suggesting we go after 'em and confront 'em, are you, m'dear? They looked ugly customers to me and –'

'No, of course not!' she said and shook her head at him, irritated a little by his inability to understand. 'Of course not! I told Edwin the same thing when I showed the film to him as soon as I got it back this afternoon. It's been three days now since it all happened, and the police haven't been able to catch one of the wretches – and with being cooped up in Nellie's as I was with this tiresome cast on my leg, there was no way I could help. But as soon as they said I could come out and walk about on crutches, why, I went straight away to collect the film and show it to Edwin, and now you've seen it I want to show the police! So that they can recognize the people who were there and not only catch the men who did all the damage and find out why they did it, but also get some of the other people who were there to be witnesses. Because you see you can't take a film to court if you catch them, can you? You need people to tell what they saw. That's the law, I know that. Well, now I'm asking you if you don't agree it's a good idea to show the police so that they can find their witnesses. I've got to ask your permission you see, because it's your film.'

He blinked up at her and shook his head. 'It's not *my* film, precisely,' he said uncertainly. 'It's yours. I mean, you took it and suffered a good deal in the getting of it. It's yours, my dear, not mine. I make no claim –'

'Dear Uncle Oliver,' she said firmly, 'I must insist. The cameras are yours for you paid for them, and you paid for the film too and for the developing, so of course it's yours. As for my part in it – why, I was employed by the Gaff at the time, so my time is the property of my employer – and that's Edwin. And he thinks I should show the police the film to help them catch the men who did it. He thought perhaps we might even get some work done by them to repair the Gaff properly – though when I saw the place this afternoon I was amazed at how much of the cleaning-up darling Donald has managed!'

He smiled again at her eagerness and the brilliance of her smile and marvelled once more at how very lovely she was looking for all the awkwardness of the white cast that held her leg imprisoned and the way the crutches pushed her shoulders up so painfully.

'My dear, I cannot see it in such – well – such cut-and-dried terms, indeed I cannot. As far as I am concerned the film is yours, and you may do as you wish with it, including giving it to your suffragettes rather than selling it to Mr Paul if that is what you prefer. But –'

'Oh, the wspu will buy it!' Letty said at once. 'They will pay as much as Mr Paul would and make better use of it. So we make a proper profit and still do some good to a worthwhile cause!'

He laughed aloud at that, and patted her shoulder. 'My dear, you promise to be a very fine business woman indeed if you go on thinking in that manner! Well, we shall see – I must clearly set my affairs in order one way or another soon and that means – well, never mind. You'll know soon enough! Meanwhile, child, by all means show your film to the police. It's a splendid notion, and if it helps them catch the villains who did all that damage and tells us why it happened, why, so much the better! You say they've got the Gaff tidied up a bit now?'

'Oh, yes indeed! You should see how splendidly Donald has set it to rights. Edwin bought a new mirror for the bar, and that's put back so Violet's happy, and the cast spent half their time this past few days repairing the seats and sewing the ripped cushions and they've built the set again, and they're performing tonight. Will you come and see the show, Uncle Oliver? The second house? We're doing seven o'clock and ten o'clock every night to the end of January, to get some of our money back – and the takings are good, because the word's gone round and everyone wants to see the show that caused a riot! Did you see the *Morning Telegraph* yesterday? That had a great account of it all and Dora is delighted for, as she says, it's all marvellous publicity for the cause – so will you come to the ten o'clock performance? We've always got a couple of house-seats held back and it's such a splendid show, really it is –'

'Well –' he began and then laughed at the sight of her face. 'Well, all right my dear, I shall. Glad to. It's such a delight to see you on your feet again and so lively in spite of your broken ankle. It must be very painful –'

'Not any more,' she said. 'Not any more.' And she looked down at her cast and grinned at him. 'Indeed I'm glad it happened, for without it I'd not have gone to Nellie's and I'd never have known Luke was there and – well, now I know that Luke is there, and that he's all right and that he didn't – everything is – well, my ankle just doesn't matter. Dear Uncle Oliver, I've even forgiven you for not telling me where he was! You know that – you do understand how much I love him, don't you?'

'Yes,' he said. 'Yes, I think I do.' And he looked at her a little mournfully and thought confusedly of the pretty girls he had known in his life, of Amy most particularly, but also of others who had danced and laughed and capered through his Celia Supper Rooms and then danced away, telling him over their shoulders of their love for someone else – and then shook himself a little, for he was old now, old enough to be this particular girl's grandfather, let alone father, and to think of her in any way but a fatherly one would be highly improper. And he got to his feet, feeling his joints creaking a little and grimacing at it and said as cheerfully as he could, 'Well, I must set about getting my own first house tonight on its way, if I'm to come to your second one! So, you be on your way, my dear, when Bert's fetched a hansom for you and –'

'Oh, sir!' It was Bert who interrupted them, hurrying across the supper-rooms from the little office at the back, where he had been answering the telephone. 'Oh, sir, I got a urgent message for you, sir, from your sister, Lady Caspar. Sir – she says as 'ow you're to come and see 'er at once on account 'er 'usband's bin took bad. Shall I call you a cab, sir, so's you can go?'

26

'Of course I shall come with you,' Letty had said firmly, swinging across the pavement towards the cab on her crutches. 'I wouldn't dream of letting you go alone. If I'm in the way when we get there, then I shall sit and wait for you to see you home again. Don't argue, Uncle Oliver. Just get in the cab, do. I'll get in afterwards so that you can help me up.'

And he had been glad that she had so insisted, for sitting there as the cabbie pushed his sweating horse through the heavy evening traffic that filled Covent Garden, and then through the equally heavy press in Oxford Street as he made his way northwards to Bloomsbury, he felt surprisingly shaky and her presence beside him was a comfort. It was absurd, he told himself as he polished his glasses on the end of his scarf, a trick he always used when he was agitated in any way, absurd to be so anxious. There could be a dozen reasons why Phoebe had sent for him – Freddy could have no more than a severe cold or a migraine headache. Phoebe could be very dramatic when it suited her, and who should know that better than he, her brother? She had sent him plenty of imperious messages over the years, expecting him to drop everything of his own to come to deal with her affairs; this was just another such time, so he kept telling himself as the cab at last wheeled into Tavistock Square and stopped outside the big house.

But the look on Jeffcoate's face as he opened the door to them dashed that fragile hope. He looked almost ludicrously anxious as he peered out into the winter darkness and then his face lifted as he saw it was Oliver.

'Oh, sir, I'm that glad to see you! Sir Freddy's been asking for you this past hour, that he has. You're to go straight up, if you please sir – oh, miss, I didn't see you there –' for Letty had taken rather longer to climb the flight of steps from the street to the front door. 'I'm not sure as they'll let you go to Sir Freddy, miss, though I could ask Mr Lackland – it's Mr Lewis Lackland as is looking after him you see –'

'Please don't worry,' she said, and leaning a little awkwardly on one crutch to release her hand reached out and touched Uncle Oliver's cheek. 'You go and see him, Uncle Oliver,' she said gently. 'I'll wait here for you –'

'Yes, yes, go up at once,' Oliver said a little distractedly and then peered at Jeffcoate again. 'M'sister, Jeffcoate, where's she?'

'In her boudoir, sir, with Mrs Cicely and Mr and Mrs James, and there's all of the family on their way, they said and –'

Oliver whitened. 'Oh no, Jeffcoate! Is it that bad? What's happened?'

'I don't know rightly, sir,' the old man said, and his eyes were filled with tears now. 'All I know is he come back from Yorkshire that tired, and him and madam had a few words and then – I just heard the bell ring like a mad thing and there he was as grey as a man's face can be, and all breathless and madam that upset – so I sent for Mr Lewis right away, and he come and put Sir Freddy to bed, and oh, sir, Mr Oliver, I'm that afraid, I am!'

'Go on, Uncle Oliver,' Letty said softly. 'I'll stay with Jeffcoate,' and she gave him a little push and after a moment he went, climbing the stairs heavily and slowly, like a child on his way to a disagreeable experience, and Letty stood beside the old butler and watched him go, her own throat as tight with anxiety as she had ever known it to be.

'Please, Jeffcoate,' she said after a moment, 'could I have a cup of tea, do you think?'

The old man looked at her, and blinked and then sniffed and rubbed the back of his hand across his nose and nodded, all at the same time.

'Yes, miss, glad to, miss, right away –' and he went away, limping a little, but clearly grateful to have something to do, and she watched him go and sighed and then made her awkward way to the side of the hall where a chair was set in the shadows of the library door. She didn't want tea, but she knew that Jeffcoate undoubtedly needed to make it, so drink tea she would.

She sat and listened to the silence of the house, feeling the weight of anxiety in it, and trying to see with her ears what was going on. Somewhere in this network of luxurious rooms Lady Caspar was sitting with her son and daughter and daughter-in-law. Somewhere, Cousin Frederick was lying in bed looking grey and ill with Oliver beside him, and probably Lewis Lackland too, and she tried to imagine what they were saying and what was going on, and suddenly unbidden thoughts of Luke came into her mind. What will happen to Luke if Cousin Freddy dies? Who will look after him, who will decide what will happen to him, who will give or withhold permission for me to visit him? And she hated herself for the selfishness of the thought and moved restlessly in her chair, so that her crutches, which she had rested against the side, clattered to the floor.

She bent to pick them up just as the door behind her opened and someone came out and came to help her pick up the crutches and she looked at him over her shoulder.

'Cousin Lewis!' she said, after a moment. 'I thought you'd be upstairs with Cousin Freddy –'

'He's got a nurse there at the moment,' Lewis said, and gave her her crutches. 'What are you doing here?'

'I was with Uncle Oliver when the message came. What's happening, Cousin Lewis? How ill is he? What's the matter?'

He was silent for a moment, staring at her thoughtfully, and then said abruptly. 'I don't know how ill he is, if by that question you mean to ask what his prognosis might be. He had a violent attack of angina, with a temporary loss of consciousness, which is never a good sign, and when I got here, his pulse was fluttering and there's still pain in the upper left chest and left arm. As one who was a Nellie's student for a while, the significance of that should be clear to you.'

'Yes,' she said uncertainly. 'An – he's had an infarction?'

'Yes. An infarction. If he's fortunate, he will not have another. If he isn't so fortunate –'

'Yes,' she said and took a deep breath. 'Yes. I understand. Is there anything I can do to help?'

He smiled briefly at that. 'No, my dear. I've just telephoned to Nellie's to have the best nurses sent here. Sister Spruce will come herself. That woman knows more about the care of heart cases than any doctor in the place apart from Freddy himself.' He shook his head then. 'That's the major problem, of course. Freddy knows perfectly well what has happened and has a lively awareness of all the possibilities. That can hardly be conducive to the sort of peace of mind he needs to protect him from another occlusion of one of his coronary arteries. As you will recall from Freddy's own lecture, anxiety in these cases is to be avoided –'

He was talking almost to himself now and she said a little timidly, 'I – I suppose I may not see him? I have a great fondness and a – a debt of gratitude to him that –'

'I'll see,' he said. 'There's the family gathering of course, and they'll want to see him. I can't have him overtired – wait here, I'll see.' And he went away, striding across the big hall and taking the wide staircase two treads at a time.

Jeffcoate came with the tea after a while and then went away to see if Lady Caspar and her family wanted any and she sat there as the big grandfather-clock in the corner ticked its sonorous way through the next hour. The first house at both the Celia and the Gaff were well under way, she thought, and again castigated herself for being so heartless as to care about such things when Cousin Freddy was lying there upstairs with his heart poised on the edge of destruction. How could she be so selfish and so wicked?

But for all her animadversions against herself, she could not help thinking of her own affairs. How much would she be able to see of Luke now? Would whoever succeeded Freddy in his care (and even if Freddy got over this attack, clearly he would be an invalid for some time, and others would have to deal with his patients) – would that doctor allow Luke to take part in talking and planning the work of the Gaff, even though he couldn't actually be there, so that he could feel part of his own venture again? Would there be a recurrence of the violence that had hit them, or was it, as Dora Montefiore had insisted it was when she had come to Nellie's to visit her while she was having her leg set in plaster, a direct attack on the WSPU rather than on the Gaff itself? Above all, when would Luke be free of his disease – for she refused to even consider the possibility that he would not fully recover – and return to normal life? When would he marry her?

For that was something upon which she had completely made up her mind. Luke was her man, the only man she could ever want or need, and she was never going to allow him to be taken from her again. Marriage was the obvious and only possibility – and even though he had not mentioned such an arrangement she knew her own determination would see it through. She was quite serene on that point. 'A New Woman,' she whispered to herself. 'A New Woman. I know what I want and I go and get it. And I want Luke –'

There was a sound above her then and she lifted her head to stare up the staircase and saw Oliver standing there leaning over and beckoning, and she swung to her feet, manipulating her crutches with all the speed she could, and made the difficult ascent of the staircase.

'I – you are to go and talk to Freddy, Letty. He wants you,' Oliver said quietly, and she peered at him, trying to see some expression on his face, but up here the lighting was dimmer and more diffused and all she could see was shadows.

'How is he?' she asked equally quietly and his voice came back sharply out of the dimness.

'Dreadful. He's dreadful. I never thought to see my good old Freddy look like that. We were children together, you know. We played in the snow in Aunt Abby's garden and he made a slide and m'father was there and – he looks dreadful.' And now she could see he was in tears and did not know what to do, could only stand abashed in the face of his simple and uncomplicated grief.

Along the corridor a door opened and a shaft of light sprang across the heavy carpet, lifting its blackness to a rich crimson and Lewis appeared in the doorway and called softly, 'Letty?'

'I'm coming,' she said, and leaned across and kissed Uncle Oliver's wet cheek and then swung away towards the lighted doorway.

'He's anxious to see you,' Lewis said. 'It seems that he's been rather involved in your affairs – be careful, Letty. He's very ill indeed. I suspect he's had another small attack since the first one. His pulse is bad. I've managed to get his wife to understand she mustn't agitate him – be a good example to her, please –' And he stood back to let her enter the room.

She was very frightened as she stood there leaning on her crutches. The room seemed to stretch in front of her for miles, for it was high and the corners were shadowed, only the centre where the big bed stood being at all well illuminated. She could see beside the bed on one side an armchair, and in it the figure of Lady Caspar, her head down and her shoulders slumped, a very strange posture for that usually very erect lady, and hovering behind her her two children, James and Cecily. Behind them was Bella, James' wife, and Letty was suddenly very aware of being an outsider here. The real family was just those four people, Freddy himself and his wife and children. No one else. She shouldn't be here, she shouldn't be disturbing him, and she almost turned to say as much to Lewis, to try to escape the need to walk into that big terrifying space.

But she did not, for Freddy moved his head on his pillow and she heard his voice, thin and breathless but clear for all that.

'Letty?' he said. 'Is that Letty?'

'Yes, Cousin Freddy,' she said and moved then, crossing the room silently on the thick carpet, and came to stand beside the bed.

'Sit down,' he said. 'It's easier than looking up at you,' and obediently she lowered herself on to the counterpane, and Lewis, who had followed her, took her crutches from her, and she arranged her stiff leg as best she could, fussing over it a little to delay the moment when she would have to look at him.

But she could not delay it for long, and at last she lifted her chin and stared at the face on the pillow.

He seemed to have shrunk, to have fallen in on himself. His temples looked hollow, they were so shadowed, and his nose seemed to have been carved out of cold yellow wood, it was so sharp and jutting. His cheeks had small high patches of colour on them, almost as though they had been painted there, Dutch doll fashion, and his eyes glittered hotly as he stared at her.

But then his lips moved, curled into a smile and suddenly he was Cousin Freddy again, not the frightening stranger he had seemed and she smiled back, relieved and comfortable for a moment and said softly, 'Hello, Cousin Freddy.'

'Foolish child, breaking your foot. Pott's fracture, they tell me.'

'Yes. But it's fine. I'm in plaster. They made a lovely cast for me.'

'Young bones. You'll heal fast.' He closed his eyes a little wearily and across the room there was a soft sound as Lady Caspar gulped and whispered something and he opened his eyes again and said in an even softer voice, 'Must talk to you, Letty.'

She leaned forwards, touching his hand. 'Please, Cousin Freddy – don't tire yourself –'

'Promised your mother –'

There was a little hiss of sound from across the room as Lady Caspar straightened her back and took a deep breath and Letty felt rather than saw James lean forward and set a warning hand on her shoulder.

'Promised your mother –' Freddy coughed, a hateful bubbling sound and Lewis leaned forwards and slipped a hand behind his head so that he could lift it at the same moment that a nurse, wearing the familiar print dress and beribboned cap and starched apron of a Nellie's sister came to do the same and there was a little bustle as they settled him again. When he spoke again his voice was stronger.

'Luke – they told me you've seen him. That you know.'

'Yes,' Letty said, puzzled now, and more alarmed than ever. 'Please, Cousin Freddy, don't exert yourself so – whatever this is it doesn't matter and –'

'I promised your mother,' he said fiercely and with a sudden loudness and this time Lady Caspar actually made a sound, a sort of cross between a bark of anger and a moan and Letty looked at her and shook her head to show how mystified she was and then back at Freddy.

'He's consumptive. She's worried. Doesn't want you to wed a consumptive. I promised her I wouldn't let you. You can't – I –' He seemed breathless then and stopped and closed his eyes and Letty again leaned forwards to touch his hand.

He seemed to recover then and opened his eyes once more

and managed that small smile again and said in a half whisper, 'I meant to be so diplomatic. Takes time, diplomacy –'

She sat there and waited, trying to clear her mind, to understand the situation and failing, and knowing it was because she didn't want to understand.

'My mother –' she said after a moment.

'Saw her. Yesterday. Day before – can't remember. She's worried because of Luke. I told her, he's improving. He is, Letty. Improving. Could be well again. In time, well again –' He smiled at her then, turning his head on his pillow. 'Not like me. Silly, really. Never thought it'd be like this – it's not so bad, dying. Easy really – just tiring –'

She felt the tears on her cheeks then but didn't remember shedding them and took a deep breath through her nose and swallowed and said more loudly than she had meant to, 'You're not dying –'

'Silly child. I know. Been round death all my life – listen, Letty, be patient, please? He'll get better. Going to Switzerland. It's all arranged, going to Switzerland, year or so, he'll be better. Marry him then. Not now. Please? Your mother –'

He closed his eyes and the room slid into silence and she sat there and stared at his face, at the faint movement of his flaccid lips as he took his shallow uneven breaths and tried to fit it all tidily into her mind. He had promised her mother she would not marry a consumptive. He had promised her mother – and he was telling her Luke would get better. In a year or so. A *year* or so.

She tried to see herself spending a year without him now she had found him again and she couldn't; how could anyone look down the vista of so many long months and days of aloneness? How could anyone expect them to be apart when they loved each other so much? It was none of her mother's business, and she had no right to meddle – and the old familiar anger rose in her and filled her with warmth and strength again and she lifted her chin and said softly, 'Cousin Freddy –'

He opened his eyes after a moment and stared at her blankly as though he didn't know who she was and then his gaze cleared, sharpened, and he said, 'Letty. Sophie's girl –'

'I can't promise, Cousin Freddy. I love him and I can't

promise.'

'Better for him if you do,' Freddy said, and now his breath was a whisper. 'Give him something to get well for. Make Switzerland easier –'

'We could go together –'

'No – not the same. Better if he needs to get well, better to have a goal. Do it for him, Letty. Give him a goal. Not for me or your mother. Do it for him –'

'You'll have to go soon, Letty.' It was Lewis's voice that brought her back, as he leaned forwards and put a hand on her arm and she looked up at him and nodded and then looked back at Freddy. He was lying just as he had been all the time but now there was an expectancy in his eyes, somehow, an alertness that hadn't been there before and she smiled at him crookedly and said, 'And you said you had no time to be diplomatic!'

He smiled and it was almost as though he'd laughed aloud. 'Yes. Diplomatic. But you understand? You'll wait?'

'What else can I do?' she said, and as Lewis's hand on her elbow urged her to her feet, said it again. 'What else can I do? I'll have to wait. A year or so, did you say? I'll have to wait.'

27

The station was awash with noise and steam and people and voices and smells. Smells of coal and soot and hot coffee and cold lemonade from the stalls and sweating porters and perfumed parasol-bearing lace-trimmed fashionable women and shag-smoking unwashed very unfashionable men and chocolate-smeared children and the horses that stood waiting patiently in the line of hansom cabs, and above all of excitement. The whole place seemed poised on the edge of emotional explosion and she stood beside the bookstall waiting for the parcel of *Blackwood's* and the *Strand* and *Punch* and *Illustrated London News* and *National Geographical* magazines she had bought and tried to relax her shoulders, to prevent herself from catching the contagion of it and exploding inside. She had to be calm and sensible, and behave as a New Woman should. Under control. It wasn't easy when all she wanted to do was cry and shout and stamp her feet in anger and tell them all she'd do as she wished, exactly as she wished and not as other people told her to –

'I got chocolates and apples and a few oranges and then I saw some splendid bonbons and I thought he might like those, and how about some shortbread? D'you think he'd be able to carry it all if I got it? And –'

'Uncle Oliver, you must have bought the entire shop!' she said, and he looked down at his armful of parcels and laughed, rather shamefacedly.

'Well, I dare say I was a bit extravagant, but it's a long journey to Switzerland and you never know what he might need and –' The bookstall assistant leaned forwards and gave her the parcel of magazines and he laughed then. 'And look at you! My purchases at least will be consumed and become less of a burden. Yours'll be there to be carried all the way – all the way to Switzerland and getting heavier all the time! Are you all right, my dear?'

She smiled at him, trying to keep her lips firm and to look insouciant and relaxed and knew he was not fooled.

'I'm fine,' she said. 'Fine. Just leave me be. Will – will they be long, do you think?'

'Not long,' he said. 'Perhaps we could go to the buffet, have a glass of something sustaining? Hmm? What d'you say to that? Not for me of course – gives me the most terrible indigestion, o'course, but a little brandy'll do you the world of good – come along, m'dear, brandy we shall get you –'

They pushed their way across the milling concourse, past the excited children and dogs in travelling baskets barking miserably and porters swearing and sweating over piles of luggage, for it was a busy day at Victoria at a busy time of the year – June, and the summer holidays beginning and family parties from Twickenham and Kilburn, Holloway and Camberwell were converging on the railway to start their glorious sand- and sun-filled days at Bognor and Hastings and Margate sands and she looked at them as they passed and wished most fervently that she were one of the matriarchal figures fussing over nursemaids and shrieking little boys and grizzling little girls and weary husbands. If only she and Luke –

Not to be thought of, and she allowed Uncle Oliver to lead her into the buffet and settle her at a table and fetch her a small glass of brandy, glad to be away from the happy families, glad to be freed from hating them because they were so happy and she was not.

They drank their brandy in silence – Oliver apparently having absent-mindedly forgotten his anxiety about indigestion – and she let the thoughts pleat themselves into a pattern in her head, making no effort to prevent or guide them. It was all she could do as the clock on the wall crept round to three o'clock. That was when they had said he would arrive from Nellie's. Three o'clock –

Tonight at the Gaff they should take a good house, plenty in the box-office cash-box. The new show was going very well.

They seemed to like *The School for Scandal* especially since she had incorporated the new stage business Luke had devised to make it more modern, much more midsummer 1906 than summer 1778. Luke had been so right about that. You could give ordinary uneducated people classical theatre, even if it was well over a hundred years old, if you treated it as though it were modern, rather than some sort of treasure that had to be handled like glass.

'That's how I produced *She Stoops* you'll remember,' he had written in the long letter of instruction he had sent before she started rehearsals. 'Do it in the same irreverent nowadays sort of manner and they'll pack the house, I promise you –'

And he'd been right, of course. If only he could have been there to see the success of the opening night! Yes, she'd directed it, yes, it had been her voice which had instructed the cast, her orders they had carried out, but it had been undoubtedly *his* production, stitched together through the reams of letters they exchanged between Covent Garden and Chelsea Reach. Night after night she had sat there in her small room at the back of the Gaff, curled up on her bed and writing, reading, writing more and then reading again, poring over his precious letters as though they were his own living breathing body there in her hands. It had been all she could do. What else was possible when the embargo on visiting him was maintained so steadily by Lewis Lackland? She had promised to abide by his decisions, and she had to do it.

Even though he was improving steadily. Even though Edwin and Uncle Oliver were both allowed to visit him. The fact that she alone had been barred had angered her bitterly, had made her fit to break her promise to Freddy before he had died, that cold January night almost six months ago. But Lewis had made her understand at last, and she had bitten down her hurt and her misery and obeyed.

'You must understand, Letty, that tuberculosis has a powerful effect on the emotions. And they in their turn have an equally powerful effect on the body. If a consumptive patient becomes excited, his fever increases, his disease spreads. That is why we take babies away from newly-delivered consumptive mothers – it isn't just to protect the babies from infection! It is to protect the patient herself from over-emotional attachment. It's the same with your Luke. I know how he feels about you. I'm his physician now and he talks to me, and I encourage him to do so, for dammed-up feelings are as damaging as over-excited ones. I have to tell you that if you two were together at all it would be too much for both of you. His control, I fear, would not be equal to the situation. He needs as well as loves you, Letty, for which reason you must stay away from him. I am sorry to speak so of – of such physical matters to you, but you must be made to understand. He cannot risk being with you.'

He had leaned forwards then and taken both her hands in his. 'I know how it feels to be in such a situation, Letty. I have suffered it myself. My wife – Miriam, you have met her, I know – Miriam and I were apart for three years, even though we loved each other as dearly as you and Luke do. We had to be separated for different reasons, I grant you, but it was just as painful. For you it needn't be longer than another year – if you stay away now and let him recover at his own rate.'

So it had to be, though he had agreed to allow this meeting today. Just a fleeting five minutes, he'd told her firmly, as the stretcher was carried from the ambulance across the concourse to the waiting train that would carry him to Switzerland and convalescence.

'I can't forbid that,' he had said smiling a little. 'The journey itself is going to upset him and he'll need a few weeks there in Interlaken to regain his equilibrium before he begins to make the progress we confidently expect. So you're being there won't hurt too much.'

With which grudging permission she had to be content, and now she sat here in the Victoria station buffet watching the clock creep round – surely the wretched thing had stopped? – to three o'clock.

'– At the seaside, perhaps. Studio's all very well, but a bit of open air could be most exciting,' Oliver was saying.

'Hmm?' She put down her brandy glass, not enjoying the sharpness of the spirit on her tongue and looked at him with a small frown between her brows.

'Tch! I knew you weren't listening. Wretched girl!' But he

273

said it fondly. 'I was saying, when you close the Gaff in August for the month, if you're still determined not to take a holiday yourself, we could use the time to make some story-films outside the studio. We could go to Margate and set up some outdoor adventures. Boats and rescues and so forth. Now, that could be a very successful line, and if we ask your clever friend Dora to write one of her funny stories to use, it could all be very jolly and –'

His voice dwindled away in her ears, as he chattered on and she sat and looked at him affectionately. Dear Uncle Oliver. So loving and so generous and so very proud of the way he had had his own way over it all. She had demurred furiously at first, not wanting the burden of what he wished to give her, but Luke, in his long letters, had helped her see she had been wrong about that.

'Dearest, if he wants to make us his co-heirs, that surely is his business! I know he has had a bad time at his sister's hands – she is most furious that he refused to allow her children to have it all, and I understand is nagging him most cruelly about it. But for all that I've never seen him happier, more pleased with life, or for that matter, so well. He is not young any more, but since he has made this decision, he certainly does not seem so old! So I have told him he must do as he sees fit *and you should do the same.* And if he sees fit to endow the Gaff, and the film studios – which, let us be honest, look set fair to make more money than they cost if you go on doing so well with the ventures, you clever wretch – that, surely, can't be bad! I don't relax into comfortable laziness, thinking I need not work in future, simply because Uncle Oliver has, in the good old Dickensian sense, provided us with great expectations. Quite the contrary. It gives me something else towards which to aim my efforts to be healthy again. And I will, my darling, I will, I promise you, be rid of this hateful disease, and will return to you and to our work, and then won't Uncle Oliver be pleased. Meanwhile, my own darling, take care of him, and let him love you and give to you. It takes a generous spirit to accept the gift of the munificent. I believe you have such a spirit –'

'Three o'clock,' Oliver's voice cut into her reverie, as with enormous relief he surged to his feet, collecting parcels and dropping them and fussing round her so that she dropped hers too, but then at last they were together and on their way.

Across the concourse again. Past the family groups again. Past the entrances to the platforms with their great panting trains waiting to swallow up the hordes of people who milled so eagerly about them like worshippers at a shrine. Past the lines of hansom cabs to the end of the road where the ambulances were arriving for the hospital train that was to leave platform seven for Dover, Calais and on across Europe to Interlaken.

And all the way she felt as though she were dreaming. This was not really Letty Lackland, the mistress of the Chelsea Reach Gaff, the busy administrator and camerawoman of the newly-incorporated Gaff Film Studios, the independent friend of artists and sculptors and businessmen, the New Woman who owned her own life and ran it firmly in her own way. She was instead a child wanting her comfort and security, a child needing love and reassurance, and for a moment she thought of her mother, so far away there in Yorkshire who had, as part of her caring and loving, so deprived her daughter of what she most desperately wanted; and, instead of being angry with her as she had been all this past six months, she wanted her to be there, to hold her safe and warm and content, to make the coming meeting and parting easier.

But as they reached the ambulance that had Queen Eleanor's Hospital emblazoned on its sides she took a deep breath and refused to allow herself to think such foolish thoughts any more. She was to see Luke for the first time in six months. She was to talk to him directly instead of just through letters. She might even be able to touch his hand, feel the warmth of his skin on hers for one fleeting moment. That was all that mattered, that was all she needed to think about.

She stood there on the edge of the pavement, watching them open the back doors of the big ambulance, watching as the stretcher was carefully removed and set on its wheels to become a trolley and then, as the nurses fussed over the figure lying bundled on it, at last tipped up her chin and stepped forwards.

He was staring round, looking for her as eagerly as she had

been looking for him and when he saw her it was as though his whole face lifted with relief.

'They said they'd let you be here,' he said, his voice muffled in his blankets. 'I wouldn't let myself believe it.'

'I'm here,' she said, and bent and slipped her hand beneath the blankets, reaching for him and then he was there, his hot rather damp fingers clutching hers so tightly that they hurt; and it was a pain she gloried in.

The ambulance-driver took the foot of the trolley and the nurse the head and Oliver fell into step on the other side as she walked beside on Luke's left hand, holding it tightly all the time, and the little procession moved off as people scattered to make way in front of it, some backing away fearfully, well aware of the disease that was suffered by people who travelled to Switzerland on special trains.

'So much to say, Luke, my darling,' she murmured after a moment, and she was aware suddenly of Oliver being studiously unconcerned with their conversation, staring about him brightly and whistling casually between his teeth and she wanted to giggle. 'So much to say, and I can't think of a single word.'

'Me too. Darling, you'll write to me? Every day?'

'Twice a day,' she promised. 'You too –'

'Of course – try Shakespeare to close the season. *Midsummer Night's Dream* – do it like panto, a bit – lots of knock-about and frilly fairies, you know. Not too serious. Open the stage up as though for a film, on hot nights – let the air and the sky in. That'll give it a lot more reality – darling Letty, I do love you – say you love me.'

They were reaching the barrier now, the point at which they would have to part and she said urgently, 'I love you, I love you, I love you. Yes, I'll do it that way. Open the stage doors, as though it were a film. Maybe film it too. Dearest Luke, I want to come with you – no, I don't. I mustn't say that. Forget I said it. I want you to be well and to come back soon.'

'He said it'll take a year. I'll do it in six months. You watch – six months, Letty. I'll be home for Christmas. We'll do the pantomime together –'

They were making them part, the ambulance driver and the

nurse, never breaking step, pushing onwards, past the barrier and then through it and his hand slipped out of hers as she had to stop and watch him go, saw his head turning on the pillow as he tried to look back and she lifted her hand to wave to him, even though she knew he couldn't see her and then, as the curve of the platform took him out of sight, went on watching long after he had disappeared.

'I'll take you to Gunters for tea,' Oliver said after a long pause and she laughed a little shakily, and wiped the back of her hand across her nose.

'Darling Uncle Oliver. Your cure for everything is food and drink.'

'It's not such a bad idea at that,' he said practically. 'Not at all a bad idea. Doesn't let you down, you know, a good cup of tea and a cream cake. Makes you feel a bit better. And it can't argue back –'

And he linked his arm in hers as she laughed again, more strongly now, and went out to the cab-rank with him and he hailed a hansom as the whistle behind them blew and the green flag waved and the Dover boat train began to chug its grey panting way out of the sidings and steam of a hot June afternoon in London on the way to the clean cold air of Switzerland. Her entire heart and soul were going with it, but she'd live without them somehow till she got them back. Somehow. And meanwhile there was Uncle Oliver and the studios and Edwin and the Gaff and Donald and Violet and Alf and *Midsummer Night's Dream* to plan and *The School for Scandal* to see off and work, work, and more work.

'That's really the cure, you know,' she said as the cabbie whipped up his horse and they started the journey through the dusty streets to Piccadilly and Gunters. 'Work. That never lets you down, does it? Though it might argue back. Sometimes –'

'Speaking of which, you didn't say anything about my Margate plan, did you? Now, what I suggest is this – we take a boarding-house for the whole month, and take Donald and young Alf and the actors down with us and –'

And their cab was swallowed up in the haze of the traffic and the noise and the dust as they talked and planned all the way to Piccadilly.